W9-AMQ-587

"Mr. Darling, meet your shop assistant."

Words failed him. Rational thought failed him.

Those magnificent violet eyes speared him as the sheriff helped her stand so that he could free her wrists.

"*You* are Nicole O'Malley?"

"In the flesh." The perfect lips thinned with displeasure, then winced as she gingerly rubbed the skin where the rope had chafed.

Quinn winced along with her. He pinched the bridge of his nose. *Way to make a great first impression, Darling.* Then he recalled her culpability in the situation.

"Why did you attack me?" he demanded.

"I thought you were an intruder. Why did you sneak in here after hours?"

"I didn't sneak. This is my store. Besides, the door was unlocked."

The sheriff snapped his knife closed and slid it into his pocket. "I think I'll leave you two to get better acquainted." His smile was rueful as he passed Quinn. "Welcome to Gatlinburg."

Karen Kirst
and
Keli Gwyn

From Boss to Bridegroom
&
Family of Her Dreams

LOVE INSPIRED
INSPIRATIONAL ROMANCE

If you purchased this book without a cover you should be aware that this book is stolen property. It was reported as "unsold and destroyed" to the publisher, and neither the author nor the publisher has received any payment for this "stripped book."

LOVE INSPIRED®

INSPIRATIONAL ROMANCE

Recycling programs for this product may not exist in your area.

ISBN-13: 978-1-335-45673-1

From Boss to Bridegroom and Family of Her Dreams

Copyright © 2021 by Harlequin Books S.A.

From Boss to Bridegroom
First published in 2015. This edition published in 2021.
Copyright © 2015 by Karen Vyskocil

Family of Her Dreams
First published in 2015. This edition published in 2021.
Copyright © 2015 by Keli Gwyn

All rights reserved. No part of this book may be used or reproduced in any manner whatsoever without written permission except in the case of brief quotations embodied in critical articles and reviews.

This is a work of fiction. Names, characters, places and incidents are either the product of the author's imagination or are used fictitiously. Any resemblance to actual persons, living or dead, businesses, companies, events or locales is entirely coincidental.

This edition published by arrangement with Harlequin Books S.A.

For questions and comments about the quality of this book, please contact us at CustomerService@Harlequin.com.

Love Inspired
22 Adelaide St. West, 40th Floor
Toronto, Ontario M5H 4E3, Canada
www.Harlequin.com

Printed in U.S.A.

CONTENTS

Karen Kirst was born and raised in East Tennessee near the Great Smoky Mountains. She's a lifelong lover of books, but it wasn't until after college that she had the grand idea to write one herself. Now she divides her time between being a wife, homeschooling mom and romance writer. Her favorite pastimes are reading, visiting tearooms and watching romantic comedies.

Books by Karen Kirst

Love Inspired Suspense

Explosive Reunion
Intensive Care Crisis
Danger in the Deep
Forgotten Secrets
Targeted for Revenge

Visit the Author Profile page
at Harlequin.com for more titles.

FROM BOSS TO BRIDEGROOM

Karen Kirst

I will praise thee; for I am fearfully
and wonderfully made: marvellous are thy works;
and that my soul knoweth right well.
—*Psalm* 139:14

To Meredith Black—
many thanks for your encouragement
and sound advice. I'm so grateful the Lord
brought you into our lives. Love you, dear friend!

Chapter One

June 1882
Gatlinburg, Tennessee

There was an intruder in the mercantile.

In her haste, Nicole O'Malley had forgotten to lock the rear entrance, and now she was alone.

While not common in this area, robberies weren't unheard of. In fact, this very store had been targeted two years ago, and her oldest sister, Juliana, kidnapped by outlaws.

A shudder ripped through her as stealthy, faltering steps echoed down the long hallway that led past the private quarters, storeroom and office to where she'd been dusting shelves in the front area of the store. Whoever had dared enter after hours was up to no good.

Alarm pooling in her belly, Nicole seized a large enamel pot from the nearest shelf and wedged herself into the narrow space between the high shelving unit and door frame. She lifted it high over her head.

Her sister had been fortunate. She'd escaped unharmed.

Would Nicole face a worse fate?

What if he had a gun? What if he shot her on sight?

That's why I have to be faster than him. Seize the element of surprise.

The footsteps neared. Paused somewhere in the vicinity of the office immediately on the other side of the doorway. Her hands curved around the pot handles until they bit into her palms. Heartbeat roaring in her ears, her arms began to tremble from the strain. The safe containing the money was in the office. If he went in there, she could try and sneak out the front entrance.

But he didn't enter the office. Instead, he stalked through the doorway. Halted inches away, hands on lean hips as he surveyed the interior. By now things like his scent—peppermint of all things—and impressive height were registering.

The intruder seemed to be cataloging the goods. What was his plan? Steal the valuables and sell them for profit?

He started to pivot in her direction, and she caught a glimpse of sleek jawline above a starched white collar. Nicole's throat closed up. She would *not* be taken hostage like Juliana. If he had time to draw his weapon, she was done for. *It's now or never.*

She swung with all her might. The impact of the heavy cookware against his head knocked him forward. He grunted, hands going up as if to defend himself from another blow.

Go. Now. The pot hit the just-swept floorboards with a dull thud. She dashed into the shadowed hallway, desperation powering her rubbery legs. A low growl cracked the air. He scrambled into the hallway after her. Without warning, strong arms stole around her waist, halting her forward movement and digging into her stomach. She was shoved face-first against the wall. His large body followed, heaving chest pinning her.

"Who? Why?" he panted against her ear, hot breath fogging her neck.

"Let me go, you ill-bred ruffian!" Raising her foot, she slammed her heel down, grinding it into his boot.

He gasped, jerked, and Nicole slipped sideways out of his grasp.

"Oh, no, you don't."

He captured her before she could put any sort of distance between them, this time seizing her arms in a painful grip. Ignoring her struggles and seething threats of retribution, the intruder propelled her into the store, snatched a silk tie from the rack on the counter and tied her wrists behind her back. Anger pulsed at her temples. "You won't get away with this," she said.

He spun her to face him, pushed her into the lone chair and, shoving aside her skirts, bound her calves to the chair legs. Insides quivering with indignation, she did everything she could to make things difficult for him. She wiggled. Strained against the ties.

When she delivered another threat, he straightened to his full height, folded his arms and glared down at her, his honey-colored eyes glittering with ill humor. "If you don't want me to gag that pretty little mouth of yours, I suggest you shut it."

A lock of jet-black hair flopped over his left eyebrow, and he shoved it back, wincing when he came into contact with what was probably a good-size knot on his head.

"I don't know what your story is, lady, but you had

better hope it's a good one. You'll be telling it to the sheriff here shortly."

Her frazzled mind belatedly homed in on his accent. It wasn't the slow, easy drawl typical of East Tennessee. His words were clipped. Fast. Northern?

Dread clawed upward into her throat, nearly choking her. *Please don't let this be who I think it is.* Nicole did a quick inventory of his appearance—quality brown leather boots peeked from beneath perfectly creased blue trousers. His navy vest and white shirt had been crafted from sturdy material. He didn't dress like a ruffian. Didn't look like one, either, with the clean shave, neat haircut and carved features. Power and authority cloaked him.

"Did you say sheriff?"

"Sure did." He jabbed a finger in the air above her nose and quirked a mocking brow. "Stay put."

Outrage flamed in her cheeks. "Wait. I can explain—"

But he was already undoing the knob lock. "Save it."

The door clicked shut behind him.

Nicole listened helplessly to the retreating footsteps of Clawson's new owner—and her new boss. She hung her head in defeat. She was never, ever going to live this down.

Quinn Darling made his way down the boardwalk, head throbbing with each step. That was a fine welcome to his brand-new life. He'd wanted change, a simpler existence than he'd led among Boston's elite. Nothing simple about being assaulted by a madwoman the second he arrived.

Gatlinburg had the appearance of a peaceful place.

Majestic mountains cradled the town, green slopes cast in waning golden-orange sunlight. Businesses lined either side of Main Street, and a white church boasting stained-glass windows sat at the far end, surrounded by rolling fields and scattered tree groves.

Spotting the lone horse outside a building marked Jail, Quinn picked up his pace. His muscles ached from days of travel; his belly was protesting the long hours since lunch and his headache—compliments of *her*—had quadrupled in size. He wanted the female out of his possession so that he could unload his personal belongings and explore the store that belonged to him.

"Excuse me," he addressed the rugged, fair-headed man behind the desk. "Are you the sheriff?"

Eying Quinn, the man stood, hands perching on his gun belt. "Shane Timmons. How can I help you?"

"The name's Quinn Darling. I purchased the mercantile from Emmett Moore."

The caution in the lawman's eyes receded a little. "We've been expecting you, Mr. Darling."

"Yes, well, I've only just arrived. You can imagine my surprise when I discovered a trespasser in my store. I'd appreciate it if you'd come and fetch her."

"Her?" His lips twitched. "What does this trespasser look like?"

"Deadly." His fingers once again prodded the tender knot at the base of his skull. She knew how to put up a fight, all right. When the sheriff, who looked to be in his mid-to-late thirties, appeared to be fighting an expression of amusement, Quinn continued, "Beautiful, but in a fatal, black-widow sort of way."

"Huh." Unhooking his Stetson from the chair back, Timmons nodded to the door. "Let's go take a look."

They crossed the nearly deserted street. The few remaining stragglers openly stared. "Do you have a lot of crime here?"

The lawman shot him an enigmatic look. "Depends."

"On what exactly?"

"On what you'd describe as a lot."

Hardly a helpful answer. Emmett Moore had assured him Gatlinburg was an ideal place to set down roots, find a God-fearing wife and pursue a new and different lifestyle—one where friendships weren't based on business connections or social standing or amount of accumulated wealth. He hadn't said a word about crime being an issue.

Too late now. Quinn kept his silence as they approached the entrance.

When they entered the darkened area, his captive jerked her head up, expressive eyes wide and accusing. Sheriff Timmons took one look at her, shook his head and strode to the nearest window, yanking the thick curtain open with a snap. Soft evening light spilled into the space, giving Quinn a much clearer view of the woman in the chair.

He sucked in a breath. If he hadn't just tussled with the little wildcat, he might've been duped into thinking her a complete innocent. Maybe it was the bride-white dress. Or the youthful perfection of her skin, like finest alabaster, in direct contrast to the thick mane of glossy raven curls spilling from their pins and framing her delicate face. Her eyes were an unusual color a man wouldn't soon forget—lavender ringed with deep violet—accentuated by a fringe of thick, inky lashes and topped with sweeping, elegant brows. Her dainty, bow-shaped mouth added to the illusion of innocence.

Timmons somberly bent to unknot the silk ties at her legs. Her lashes swept down and hot color surged in her cheeks. Quinn studiously avoided looking at the layers of snowy-white petticoats. In the heat of the struggle, his focus had been on restraining his assailant, not whether or not his actions were that of a gentleman.

"You might want to interrogate her before you release her. This one's unpredictable." In addition to the knot on his head, his toes would likely sport a nasty bruise, thanks to her.

"No need. This here isn't a petty thief." Shane paused, amusement twinkling in his blue eyes. "Mr. Darling, meet your shop assistant."

Words failed him. Rational thought failed him.

Those magnificent violet eyes speared him as the sheriff helped her stand so that he could free her wrists.

"*You* are Nicole O'Malley?"

"In the flesh." The perfect lips thinned with displeasure, then winced as she gingerly rubbed the skin where the ties had chafed.

Quinn winced along with her. He pinched the bridge of his nose. *Way to make a great first impression, Darling.* Then he recalled her culpability in the situation.

"Why did you attack me?" he demanded.

"I thought you were an intruder. Why did you sneak in here after hours?"

"I didn't sneak. This is my store. Besides, the door was unlocked."

"I think I'll leave you two to get better acquainted." The sheriff's smile was rueful as he passed Quinn. "Welcome to Gatlinburg."

Placing the ties atop a wooden counter worn smooth from years of transactions, she attempted to divest the material of the wrinkles with the press of her hands. He attempted to ignore the contrast of jet curls against milky skin.

"You're three days late," she said.

"An unavoidable delay." Irritation sharpened his words. None of his previous employees had dared question him. But after this regrettable first meeting, he supposed he owed her an explanation. "My wagon suffered a broken axle. I assume Emmett and his wife have already left?"

"You assume correctly."

"That is unfortunate. For both our sakes."

She finally gifted him with her attention. "How so?"

"Because that leaves you to give me the grand tour."

Her hands stilled atop the lengths of silk. "I have no say in the matter, do I?"

"You *are* in my employ." He did nothing to mask the challenge in his tone. Had Nicole O'Malley spoken to Emmett Moore this way? Or was it just him and the fact he'd tied her up invoking this attitude?

Her stiff spine stiffened a fraction more. Her glare could've frozen the rain-swollen river out back. "You manhandled me."

Now would be a good time to point out he'd merely been reacting to the threat he'd perceived in her. His mother had reared him to be a gentleman, however, and so he refrained. "I apologize."

She considered him for a long moment, dipping her head as if she were a duchess and he a lowly estate servant. "I suppose I owe you an apology, as well."

Quinn bit the inside of his cheek to keep from retorting. He wasn't at his best right this minute…travel weary, hungry and hurting. Tomorrow would mark a new beginning between them. For now, he merely wanted to see his store.

Abandoning the ties, Miss O'Malley gestured to the long counter topped with glass display cases. "As you can see, we keep the more expensive items under lock and key. Silver, crystal, jewelry." Pivoting neatly, she gestured to the shelving units running the length of the walls on either side of the hallway door. The bottom half consisted of closed cabinets and drawers, while the top half was all open shelves. "And here we have a vast assortment of goods."

Quinn walked slowly past her, his attention on the haphazard collection of canned foods, boxes of wafers and cookies, tableware and linens. Mantel clocks and kerosene lamps perched on the top ledge. When he reached the end, he opened the nearest drawer and frowned at the mess of paper scraps and writing instruments. "Why isn't the merchandise more organized?"

"Order and neatness weren't among Emmett's strengths."

Posture proud and regal-like, she folded her hands amongst her lace-scalloped skirts. While she'd spoken without censure and her expression revealed not a hint of disdain, he sensed Miss O'Malley didn't approve of the former owner's management.

"It's been this way for as long as I can remember," she added. "The arrangement may not make sense, but the customers know where to find everything."

Quinn approached, stopping closer than necessary simply to gauge her reaction. She didn't retreat. Her lips tightened in disapproval or dislike, he couldn't tell which.

"Show me more."

Again, the royal-like dip of her head. Adjectives scrolled through his mind and, as was his custom upon meeting new people, he began a mental list of attributes. *Reserved. Prickly. Beautiful.* Too bad that last one didn't appear to extend beyond the surface.

Moving between the two counters, she led him down three side-by-side aisles crammed with a variety of goods—tools, animal traps, ready-made clothing, toys, books and paper products, barrels packed with pickles, flour, sugar and crackers and more. A woodstove occupied the far back corner, surrounded by several chairs and a spittoon. A checker set perched atop an upturned barrel.

"What is this?"

"This is where our male customers gather."

Dark tobacco stains marred the floorboards, indicating not everyone had good aim. The upscale Boston establishments his family had frequented would never have allowed such a thing. "How often?"

"Whenever we're open."

Quinn blinked, searched her face for a sign she was merely jesting. There was none. "Do you mean they gather here every day?"

"Every single one."

"Are we talking an hour or two in the afternoons?"

"No, they pretty much hang around from dawn to dusk."

"Let me get this straight—these men sit here for countless hours, disrupting the flow of foot traffic and taking up valuable space that could be used to house more items? And that was acceptable to the Moores?"

"It's the way things have always been done. Besides, they're harmless."

She refolded a calico shirt on a display table piled with neat stacks of ready-made clothing that likely didn't bear the Darling name. While his family's garment factories currently supplied the Northern states, his father had plans to expand in the future. There was no question of the venture failing. Anything Edward Darling put his hand to succeeded.

Clawson's Mercantile in the Tennessee mountains was far removed from Boston and the Darling empire, however. His father had nothing to do with it. Whether it failed or flourished was entirely up to Quinn. For the first time in his adult life, he had something entirely his own. This store was his chance to prove to himself that he was capable.

"Not everyone lives close by. Some customers travel an entire day to get here. This is where they catch up on local happenings and reconnect with old friends."

If Quinn had arrived before Emmett's departure, he could've discussed this and much more with him. The delay had cost him. He ran a finger along the cold metal stove that wouldn't be lit for many months.

"Simply because something has gone on for a long time doesn't mean it can't be changed." *Never be afraid of change, son. Be bold but prudent.* Quinn may have earned a business degree from Harvard, but his practical knowledge he'd gleaned from working side by side with his father. He gestured to the chairs. "These are going away."

She looked at him as though he'd suggested they set

up a piano in the corner and hire saloon girls to sing for the customers. "Where will the men meet together?"

"I saw a café across the street. Let the owner of that establishment deal with them."

"You can't do this."

"The last I checked, my name was on the deed. I can and I will."

"Have you ever managed a store before?"

Not accustomed to having his competence called into question, he retorted, "Until recent weeks, I was second in command of the Darling empire—a garment production business that supplies much of the Northeast. I believe I can manage to operate a small country store."

Her smirk poked holes in his calm demeanor, allowing tendrils of irritation to curl into his chest. He inhaled deeply, the odd mixture of scents around him—leather, the vinegar-laced smell of pickled fish, the fruity tang of plug tobacco—reminding him of why he was here. For change. A simpler life. A chance to carve his own way in the world, to prove to himself he could succeed apart from everything his father had built.

One prickly shop assistant would not mar this experience for him.

She brushed past him, snowy skirts whispering as she rounded the last aisle and pointed to the low cushioned benches beneath the windows flanking the front door. "This is where the ladies socialize. I suppose you want to be rid of these, too."

Wonderful. More people gossiping instead of shopping. "I don't object to customers resting for a few moments. The benches stay. For now."

Her displeasure was written across her features.

"How long have you worked here, Miss O'Malley?"

"Since January."

Six months. Enough time for her to become accustomed to conducting business in accordance with Emmett Moore's policies. No doubt she wouldn't welcome his views. She would simply have to accept that he was in charge. If she couldn't adapt to his approach to the business, she could always quit.

Spinning on her heel, she led the way as they retraced their steps. When they reached the row of candy-filled glass containers, he lifted one of the lids and snagged two peppermint sticks. After popping one in his mouth, he offered the other to her.

Her serious gaze shifted between the candy and his face. "No, thank you."

"Free of charge, of course." He waved it beneath her nose, interested to see if she'd accept.

"Sugar is bad for your teeth."

He removed the minty stick from his mouth and grinned. "I've been partial to sweets since boyhood. Does it look like my teeth have suffered?"

Startled by the question, she gave them a cursory glance. "Uh, they appear to be in fine condition."

"See? No harm in indulging yourself every now and then." He extended the candy once more.

She was loath to take it, that much was clear. She did, though, in order to appease him. The graze of her fingertips across his palm arrowed into his chest, and the urge to capture her hand in his caught him unawares.

"Thank you," she murmured.

Deliberately stepping away, he didn't draw attention

to the fact she didn't immediately sample the treat and, instead, held it awkwardly at her side. Turning back to survey the store that was nothing like he'd imagined, he said, "I suggest you prepare yourself, Miss O'Malley. There will be changes ahead."

"You should prepare yourself, as well, Mr. Darling." Retrieving a bead-encrusted reticule from a drawer, she deposited the peppermint inside. "The response to your changes may not be what you expect or desire."

Chapter Two

The moment she spotted her new boss conversing with her cousin Caleb, Nicole's already nervous stomach squeezed into a hard knot beneath her sternum. Pace slowing, she toyed with the idea of feigning illness. Humiliation surged. She'd replayed last evening's events a thousand times and it never got any better.

"Mornin', Miss Nicole," old Martin Walton called from the rear door of the barbershop. "You're lookin' as fresh as a flower today. When are you gonna find a man and settle down?"

"When I find one as worthy as you, which we both know is highly unlikely."

He grinned, revealing crooked teeth, and went back to sweeping. "You might be surprised."

With a wave, she continued on her way. It was a familiar conversation. He was kind, harmless, his teasing lacking bite. The sight of his stooped frame in the barbershop never failed to strike her as out of place, though. In her mind, the shop would always belong to Tom Leighton, a close friend of their family. Tom had abruptly left Gatlinburg back in April, and her younger sister, Jane, had yet to recover.

Nicole envied Tom. He'd escaped this town, something she yearned to do, had been set to do when a shortcut through the woods six months ago altered her life. Her plan of opening her own dress shop in Knoxville had had to be postponed, at least until she figured things out. *If* she ever figured them out.

As she made her way along the riverbank, a gentle, honeysuckle-scented breeze caressed her cheeks. Down below, the greenish water gurgled lazily along, a family of brown-tufted ducks skimming the opaque surface. The mercantile's springhouse sprawled at the water's edge. Constructed of river rock and kept cool by the rushing water, it was the perfect place to store perishable items such as the milk and cheese supplied by her Uncle Sam's dairy. Caleb made deliveries several times a week.

"Nicki."

Her cousin knew perfectly well she despised the shortened version of her name and yet insisted on using it. "Morning, Caleb."

Briefly greeting his horses, Midnight and Chance, she used the wagon bed as a barrier between her and the two men. They were surprisingly similar in coloring…inky-black hair, brown eyes and sun-kissed skin. But where Caleb was scruffy, his hair slightly mussed, Quinn Darling was as neat as a pin. His clothing bore the mark of wealth, his bearing that of privilege. He looked rested this morning, hair slicked off his face and lean cheeks freshly shaved.

She wondered if his head was paining him. Not that

she planned on putting voice to a question that would call forth the embarrassing incident.

Arms folded, wearing a grin that stretched from ear to ear, Caleb hooked a thumb at the man beside him. "Quinn told me about your meeting last night."

Her heart sank. Quinn's eyes—a shade lighter than Caleb's—crinkled with mischief. How dare he smile at her after deliberately relating embarrassing details?

"Nicole was a knowledgeable tour guide."

What all had he told him? Quinn's intent regard smacked of smug arrogance. Her palms itched to slap it right off. The man knew absolutely nothing about her!

"Nicki is nothing if not professional," Caleb said.

Ha! If he could only read her thoughts right this moment…

Pushing off the wagon bed, Caleb held his hand out to Quinn. "It's a pleasure doing business with you. I've got to get home and check on my wife."

"Oh, is she ill?" Concern pulled his brows together.

"Not in the normal sense of the word." A proud grin flashed. "She's expecting our first child this fall. She tends to overdo it."

"Rebecca's aware of her limitations," Nicole pointed out. "You're being overprotective."

"One day you'll have a husband who dotes on you, Nicki. I guarantee you'll relish every minute of it."

Nicole squeezed the reticule in her hands until the beading bit into her palms. Acutely aware of Quinn's scrutiny, she tipped her chin up. "You're speaking fairy tales, cousin."

"I don't think so. Remember what I said about making plans for your life?" He winked, the scarred flesh around his eye stretching.

How could she forget? The recent conversation plagued her in the oddest moments. Their extensive family had been gathered at his parents' home. When she'd expressed her firm intentions to wait for marriage and children until she'd achieved success with her seamstress shop, a venture that could take years, he'd loudly announced his expectation that her plans would fall apart. *In their hearts humans plan their course, but the Lord establishes their steps.* The verse he'd quoted refused to leave her, raising questions she wasn't brave enough to face.

"Goodbye, Caleb."

He tipped his hat and grinned. "I'll tell Becca you said hello." Swinging up onto the seat, he released the brake and set the wagon in motion.

All too soon, she and Quinn were left to stare at each other. He did a slow inspection. Confidence in sadly low amounts that morning, she'd dressed in one of her favorite outfits, a lavender dress adorned with deep purple ribbons.

"You look to have suffered no ill effects from our confrontation," he said.

His features portrayed nothing of his thoughts, not appreciation or distaste. Nothing, which left her feeling unbalanced. Hefting a round of paper-wrapped cheese beneath one arm, he held out the other for her. "Shall we go inside?"

Loath to touch him, Nicole adopted a similarly bland expression and forced her bare fingers to his forearm. The heat and strength of corded muscle bled through his shirt's fine material. Shock shimmered through her as the totally inappropriate urge to explore his physique surged. Close contact with men was limited to her uncle and cousins, and much of the time she succeeded in keeping them at arm's length. This touch, though impersonal, ricocheted through her defenses and opened up a yawning cavern of inconvenient awareness.

I don't need anyone. She'd been telling herself that since the moment she realized she was different and no matter how hard she tried, she would never measure up to her sisters.

She focused on the narrow steps. "What exactly did you tell Caleb?"

"You have no cause to worry, Miss O'Malley. Despite what you might think, I am a man of discretion. It would not be in either of our best interests if the details of our…misunderstanding were to be revealed. Especially in my case, considering I'm a newcomer and in need of earning the locals' trust and respect if I am to be successful in this venture."

The tension she'd experienced since first spotting her cousin eased somewhat. Neither she nor Quinn planned to speak of the incident. And Shane Timmons was not what one would call a gossip. Like herself, the sheriff was a loner, a private man not given to conversation. No one would learn of the incident from him. And perhaps, given enough time, she'd manage to look her boss in the eye and not remember their initial encounter

"Will I be meeting any more O'Malley family members?"

"I come from a large family, so it's unavoidable."

She felt his appraising side glance. "How large?"

"Caleb is the youngest of three. Josh is the eldest, and Nathan is the middle son. All three are married.

Their parents, my uncle Sam and aunt Mary, have a farm close to town."

"What about you? Any brothers or sisters?"

"Four sisters. Two older, two younger." Might as well prepare him. "All possessed of beauty, grace, generosity of spirit and keen intelligence. My sisters are not only admired by the locals, they are upheld as the epitome of what a female should be."

At the top of the stairs, she snatched her hand free and waited for him to open the door. Hand resting on the knob, he studied her. "You excluded yourself in the description. Are you not upheld as the epitome of female desirability?"

Nicole swallowed the familiar bitterness, aware it was unbecoming and futile. She'd stopped questioning God a long time ago. "You will come to discover that I am nothing like my sisters, Mr. Darling."

He opened his mouth to speak again, thought better of it and wordlessly opened the door, allowing her to enter first. Glancing into the private quarters on her left, she noticed Ruthanne had left the cheerful red-checked curtains behind, no doubt for Quinn Darling's benefit.

For what must be the umpteenth time since learning of their plans to move east, Nicole wished Emmett and Ruthanne could've remained here. While absentminded and a bit disorganized, Emmett had been a kind and understanding boss. The practical knowledge she'd gained in her employment here would benefit her in the running of her own shop. In a different town, where no one knew her or her family.

He must've noticed the direction of her gaze, for he gestured to the pile of trunks shoved beneath the window. "The space is hardly large enough to accommodate one person. Not sure how the Moores were able to make it work as long as they did. Are you aware of any land parcels or homes for sale? I would like to pursue a permanent residence as soon as possible."

Continuing into the long, windowless office, she slipped her reticule from her wrist and stored it in the top left desk drawer. "Maybe you should hold off until you're sure you want to stay. Gatlinburg can't possibly compare to Boston."

"That's the reason I chose it."

"Why Tennessee? Why this store? You aren't related to Emmett or Ruthanne."

"Not family, but they are friends of my father." Setting the cheese atop the paper-littered desk, he folded his arms and leaned forward at the waist. "Can you keep a secret, Miss O'Malley?"

His lithe, powerful body blocked the exit, and, despite not being claustrophobic, she felt his nearness suck the air from the tight space and render her lightheaded. She now knew what a cornered animal felt like.

"I'm not a gossip, Mr. Darling."

"Somehow I sensed that about you." He edged even closer, lowered his voice to a confidential whisper. "The reason I came here was to avoid the authorities. You see, I—I killed a man. Shot him point-blank. It was self-defense, but I don't have evidence to back my claim. You won't tell anyone, will you? I hear prison food is deplorable. And I doubt the beds are comfortable."

"I—" Completely breathless now, Nicole pressed a trembling hand to her throat. For a couple of seconds, she actually believed him. Then she noticed the upward tug at the corner of his sculpted mouth, the muted sparkle at the back of his eyes.

He was making fun of her, the suave, worldly-wise Northerner toying with the naive mountain girl. Well, she received enough mockery from the local thick-headed males. She wasn't about to put up with it from Quinn Darling, boss or no boss.

Chin up, she stepped forward. "Let me pass."

His brows shot to his hairline. Turning sideways, he did as she asked. She turned in the direction of the rear exit.

"Where are you going?"

At his curious, bordering-on-nervous tone, Nicole smiled to herself as she strode down the hallway. "To pay Sheriff Timmons a visit. I'm afraid I can't keep your secret, Mr. Darling. I refuse to work for a cold-blooded murderer."

Catching up to her, he snagged her arm. "Wait."

Memories of what had occurred in this hallway less than twenty-four hours ago overtook her—him impris-oning her against the wall, her pitiful efforts to fight back. She shook them off with effort. *What's wrong with me? Why am I allowing him to get to me?*

"It was a joke, Miss O'Malley." His smile begged forgiveness, the look in his eyes expectant, confident of her reaction. "You will find being outrageous is one of my many faults. I blame it on having a gullible younger sister."

The man's charm and good looks might've proved a lethal combination were she not dead set on a course free of romantic entanglements. "Since I only just met you yesterday, and that meeting left much to be desired, you'll understand my need to consult with Shane on this, see if there are any wanted posters bearing your likeness."

His smile remained, but unease flickered in his expression. "You can't be serious."

"What would you do in my position?" she asked innocently, enjoying seeing him squirm.

"I cannot have a rumor such as that running rampant in this community."

"It's no fun being made to feel a fool, is it, Mr. Darling?"

His gaze scoured her face, searching intently, the tension ebbing from his stance.

"Life is short, Miss O'Malley," he murmured silkily, tapping her lightly on the nose. "You should learn to take it less seriously. And the next time you are tempted to lay the blame of our unfortunate first meeting at my feet, keep in mind that it was *you* who ambushed *me*."

Nicole floundered for an appropriate response. He baited her, and yet *she* was the one who needed to loosen up? She wanted nothing more than to ram that arrogant condescension down his throat.

Pounding on the front door startled them both. Fishing a polished pocket watch from his navy vest, he frowned. "We don't open for another half hour. Is this a usual occurrence?"

"No. Suppliers making deliveries use the rear entrance."

"I had better go see what our early visitor wants."

Curious, Nicole trailed behind him. She didn't at first recognize the hulking form through the glass. His long strides eating up the space, Quinn flipped the lock to admit the older man.

"Good morning, sir. Please, come in. How can I be of assistance?"

"Who are you?" he snapped from the other side of the door. "Where's Mr. Moore?"

That voice. She knew it from somewhere.

"The Moores have moved to Virginia, and I am the new proprietor of this mercantile. The name's Quinn Darling. It is a pleasure to welcome you, Mr.—"

The man entered. Snatching the battered hat off his head and mopping his unruly silver hair out of his eyes, he shot her a dismissive glance. "Carl Simmerly."

The face combined with the name weakened her knees, and she braced her hands against the counter for support. He had come back.

Out of the corner of his eye, Quinn noticed his assistant's brittle armor had shattered. Hunched over the counter, she watched the stranger with wide, flustered eyes, the swirl of violet stark against moon-white skin. Interesting.

"I wanna post this notice." Mr. Simmerly thrust a wrinkled paper into Quinn's hands.

Quickly scanning the scrawled writing, his concern grew. This man was searching for his missing children, a fifteen-year-old girl and seventeen-year-old boy. "Your children have been missing a long time."

The bulky man's lined jaw worked. "Going on six months now. I'm desperate to find them."

A quiet gasp came from Miss O'Malley's direction. Averting her face, she fiddled with the roll of brown paper used to wrap purchases.

Quinn motioned to the board where news postings were hung. "Of course. I'll post this right away."

"My place is on the outskirts of the next town, Pigeon Forge, so I can't get here as often as I'd like. I plan to return next Saturday to see if anyone has come forward with information."

"You have my prayers, Mr. Simmerly."

His mouth tightened in a way that made Quinn think he didn't appreciate the sentiment. As a fairly new Christian and filled with enthusiasm concerning his relationship with his Creator, he couldn't fathom anyone not wanting divine assistance.

With a curt nod, Carl Simmerly stuffed his hat on his head and bustled out the door, the bell's ring loud in the wake of his departure.

"Can I see that?"

Pivoting, Quinn handed her the posting, observing her features as she read the descriptions. Her glossy curls had been tamed into submission, and the lavender confection she was wearing the perfect foil for her skin. Dressed as she was, his assistant could've easily fit on the streets of Boston or the upscale mansions his family and friends' families owned. She certainly wasn't what he'd expected a simple mountain girl to be like.

Miss O'Malley's lower lip trembled. She bit down hard on it. The action momentarily paralyzed him.

There was no denying she was an exquisite creature, her loveliness without rival, and as the eldest heir in the prominent Darling family, he'd known his share of beauties. But she was not the uncomplicated, sweet-natured woman he craved in a wife. He'd had enough of difficult women.

"I'll put this with the others," she said at last, moving to an area on the wall where different notices had been nailed.

Leaving her to scan the notices, Quinn tugged open the scratchy wool curtains. Beyond the glass, several horses and riders traveled down sun-washed Main Street. Excitement peppered with trepidation balled in his gut. How would his first day go? He may have held the second in command position at Darling Industries, but he had no firsthand experience with patrons. *Lord, please give me guidance and wisdom.*

"Have you seen Mr. Simmerly before?"

Heading for the counter, she paused to straighten a stack of catalogs. "A couple of times around town. Why do you ask?"

"His presence seemed to distress you."

Without looking at him, she continued between the counters and, stopping before a row of aprons, chose a black one and slipped it over her head. She deftly tied the strings behind her waist. "You're imagining things. That knock on the head must've hindered your senses, Mr. Darling."

He didn't believe that for one moment, but as they were set to open shortly, he let the matter drop. Snatching a lemon drop from the glass containers, he leaned a hip against the shelving unit and sucked on the sugary treat. "Mr. and Miss are too formal for my taste. Do you have any objections to the use of given names?"

"You want me to call you Quinn—" her lips parted "—in front of the customers?"

"Or Darling, if you'd prefer."

At her incredulous expression, a chuckle slipped between his lips. The woman had absolutely no sense of humor. Teasing her was going to make this venture that much more enjoyable.

Chapter Three

"Such a pretty fabric." Nicole folded the yards of green paisley within the confines of the paper length and tied it up with string. "You've chosen well, Mrs. Kirkpatrick. Will you be making a dress for yourself?"

The elderly lady nodded, gray eyes optimistic behind thick spectacles. "I'm not as gifted with a needle as you are," she said, eyeing Nicole's lavender shirtwaist enhanced with delicate black stitching and buttons. "But hopefully the dress will look decent once I'm finished."

Making note of her purchase in the ledger, Nicole slid the package across the counter and smiled. The sweet widow was one of her favorite customers. "I can't wait to see the finished product, Mrs. Kirkpatrick. And thank you for your patience."

Hugging her purchase to her chest, Mrs. Kirkpatrick slid a dubious glance at the other length of the counter, to where Quinn was supposedly helping James Canton. Judging by James's disgusted expression and the way Quinn pinched the bridge of his nose in frustration, he wasn't helping much.

"Maybe you should lend him a hand."

Nicole considered this. He'd made it clear managing a country store was well within his capabilities, hadn't he?

When the group of elderly gentlemen in the far corner erupted into laughter, and her boss winced as if in physical pain, she gave in to the pulse of compassion. He'd obviously changed his mind about evicting the checker players. She could afford to help him out.

"I suppose you're right. Have a good evening."

"See you in church tomorrow morning." She bustled toward the exit.

Quinn was glaring at the cages on the counter and the squawking chickens inside. "Need some assistance?"

Despite a long and trying first day, he looked decidedly unruffled save for the hint of uncertainty in his aristocratic features. He was good under pressure, she'd give him that.

"I would appreciate it."

To James, she said, "Are you buying these chickens or selling?"

"Selling." He looked relieved to be dealing with someone who knew what they were doing.

Hefting the oversize ledger onto the counter beside the cages, she flipped through the pages until she found his name. Quinn watched as she inserted the value of his chickens into the first column.

"Will you be purchasing anything today?"

"A pound of sugar is all."

"I'll get that for you." To Quinn, she said, "Normally we'd put these chickens outside on the boardwalk for customers to see, but since we're closing in thirty minutes, we'll store them in the barn out back. Would you mind taking them out there while I finish up this transaction?"

"Not at all." He reached for the cages. His smile had a grim turn to it. "I apologize for your wait, Mr. Canton. Please tell your boy to help himself to a bag of penny candy free of charge."

James's brows went up at that. At his young son's hopeful grin, he nodded his acquiescence. "Much obliged, Mr. Darling."

Quinn walked out, cages held away from his body as if the chickens were diseased. Fighting the urge to roll her eyes, Nicole readied the sugar and waited patiently for the little boy to decide which candy he wanted. After father and son left, she assisted two other customers, then went to flip the sign over. The trio in the corner shuffled out. Quickly sliding the lock into place, she retrieved her basket from beneath the office desk and rushed to fill it. A wedge of cheese, a tin of peaches, a sack of dried pinto beans. She frowned at the nearly empty produce bins. It was too early in the year for most fruits and vegetables. A delicious-looking batch of asparagus had come in that morning but was too expensive for her budget.

The rear door opened. Nicole dashed into the office and returned her basket to its spot. Pulling the palmsize ledger from the desk drawer, she was inserting the items she'd just taken and the cost of each when her boss stepped into the doorway.

Half sitting on the desk so that his muscled thigh nearly brushed her arm, he smiled ruefully down at her. "You were amazing today, Nicole. In his letters, Emmett indicated how valuable you were to this business. Now that I've watched you in action, I can see he was right."

She stared at him. His masculine appeal, his succinct accent pronouncing her name, rendered her mute. Quinn was sophistication personified, yet there was a rugged strength beneath the fine appearance and expensive clothing.

"You were efficient," he went on. "Civil to the customers, in some cases anticipating their needs." His lower leg swung back and forth, stirring her skirts. "That is something you won't find in Boston's finer establishments."

Irritated that he affected her at all, she laid her pencil down and arched a single brow. "I'm surprised you'd find anything to impress you in our crude little backwoods store."

His leg ceased its motion. "I'm curious. Do you find it difficult to accept compliments in general or is it me that is the problem?"

Nicole's jaw sagged a little at his bluntness. "Do you always speak exactly what's on your mind, Mr. Darling?"

"It's Quinn, remember? And I asked you first."

Replacing the ledger, she pushed to her feet. "I don't have time for witty banter, Quinn." She winced at the informality. "I have floors to sweep, merchandise to straighten and work awaiting me when I get home." Once her errand had been completed, of course.

When she made to move past him, his fingers closed over her wrist. "What sort of work?"

"If you must know, I'm a seamstress. I have dress orders to fill. Trousers that need adjusting."

A line appeared between his brows. "Go home. I will tend to the cleaning."

Heat spread outward from his touch, delaying her response. "Y-you don't have to do that."

"I know, but you did the lion's share of the work today because I hadn't a clue what I was doing. I was sorely out of my element. Which brings me to my request."

He was readily admitting his shortcomings? "What sort of request?"

Laughing, he said, "Do not look at me as if I am about to suggest something improper."

Smoothing her features, Nicole extracted her arm from his hold. "What then?"

"You obviously know what you're doing around here. I had planned to arrive in time for Emmett to show me the ropes, but since I wasn't able to, I wonder if you would be willing to tutor me."

The prospect of spending even a minute more than necessary in Quinn's company did not appeal to her in the slightest. Despite the humble nature of his request, his self-important air remained intact—no doubt a result of living a privileged, entitled life typical of the wealthy. Worse than that, he seemed to gain a great deal of pleasure from provoking her. Something she could do without.

But how was she to refuse him? If he didn't learn to run the store, hectic, chaotic days like today would become the norm.

"Fine. I'll do it."

"Wonderful. Do you have time tomorrow after church?"

Nicole thought of the sewing projects she really

needed to complete. "I will give you two hours. No more."

His blinding grin served to enhance his good looks, if that were even possible. "You are a jewel."

Quinn couldn't stop staring at the jarring sight of his prickly, reserved assistant cradling a slumbering infant in her arms. The church service had drawn to a close, and folks were gathering their things and making their way along the aisles to the exit, stopping to exchange pleasantries here and there. Nicole was standing against the right wall near the piano. Sunlight streamed through the stained-glass window behind her, bathing her in an ethereal glow. That wasn't what had arrested his attention, however. It was the way she was looking at that baby.

Gone was the cool detachment, the wariness that typically marked her delicate features, and in its place was a vulnerability, a tenderness that made Quinn feel as if he were intruding on a private moment. He'd only just met her, but he knew instinctively she would not be pleased to know her inner emotions were on display.

A heavy hand clapped onto his shoulder, and he turned to see Shane Timmons. He looked slightly less dangerous this morning, blond hair brushed off his forehead and hard cheeks free of scruff.

"Afternoon, Sheriff."

Memories of their last interaction pushed to the forefront of his mind. He imagined the sheriff had had a good, long laugh over his and Nicole's misunderstanding.

"Call me Shane." He removed his hand. "How are

you settling in? Did you get things cleared up with Nicole?" Subtle humor lit his assessing blue gaze.

"I suspect it will take some time to settle in. And for her to forgive me for trussing her up like a common thief."

Nodding, Shane's attention swiveled to the object of their conversation. She was still standing apart from the people he assumed were her family members. A lone buoy in a swirling sea of humanity. Was that her doing or theirs? *Why do I care?*

"Nicole is…" Shane trailed off, rubbed his chin in thought.

"Prickly? Difficult? Completely lacking a sense of humor?"

His brow quirked. "I was gonna say hard to get to know. She strikes me as one of those women who'd be worth the effort, though."

Quinn ran his fingers along the spine of his brand-new Bible. He wasn't sure he agreed with the other man's assessment. "Sometimes a man gets burned for his trouble."

Before Shane could respond, the reverend joined them and welcomed Quinn to town. When there was a break in the conversation, Quinn made his excuses and worked his way through the pews to Nicole's side.

As if sensing his approach, she lifted her head, shoulders tensing when she spotted him. Her countenance transformed into something statue-like. Emotionless. Her eyes were a deep, bruised purple in her pale face, perhaps an effect of the jet-black material of the formfitting, cap-sleeved blouse she'd paired with full purple-and-black-striped skirts. A small black hat perched atop her upswept curls.

Quinn considered tweaking the single rogue tendril caressing her cheek simply to see her reaction. "I didn't figure you for the maternal type," he said in the way of greeting.

He instantly regretted the comment, could see in her pained expression that his observation stung. Before he could backtrack, she leveled a frosty glare at him. "I'm not. That doesn't mean I can't enjoy other people's children, however."

He turned his attention to the light-haired infant resting comfortably in her arms. "What is his name?"

"*Her* name is Victoria," she responded in a softer tone. "She's my cousin Josh's daughter."

Reaching out, Quinn lightly skimmed the downy soft hair. "She's family, then."

Subtly returning his attention to Nicole, he watched her watch the baby, intrigued when her guard slipped again and she went soft before his eyes. If she ever were to look at a man like that…

A tall man with a goatee, accompanied by a sophisticated young woman with hair the color of chocolate and intelligent green eyes, rounded the pew.

"We should get this little princess home before she wakes up and demands to be fed."

Nicole carefully transferred the infant to her father's arms, tucking the blanket about her small body. "Josh, have you met Quinn Darling?"

Measuring blue eyes slid to his. He nodded a greeting. "Pleased to meet you. This is my wife, Kate."

"A pleasure to meet you," Quinn shook her proffered hand. "That is one beautiful baby."

"Thank you. We think so, too." The smile Kate directed at her husband was at once peaceful and adoring.

At the look passing between husband and wife, Quinn experienced a twinge of jealousy. Thoughts of settling down and starting a family of his own had been plaguing him of late. Since accepting Christ six months ago, he'd begun to pray for a wife of God's choosing. He wanted what his parents had—a loving partnership based on trust and true companionship—a rare occurrence in his high-society world where many marriages resembled business transactions.

"You're the owner of the furniture store?" He addressed Josh.

"That's right. Kate runs her photography business out of the same space if you're ever in need of a photo."

"No plans to hang one of myself on the wall, but I'll keep it in mind for when my family visits. I peeked at your inventory through the window. Impressive selection."

Nicole's expression challenged him. "He's crafted every single item in that shop by hand. The locals prefer his furniture to those available through mail-order catalogs."

Hugging his daughter to his chest, Josh shifted uncomfortably. "Obviously, I can't supply every item those large companies offer."

Quinn aimed a wide grin at his assistant, letting her know the dig didn't sting. "In business, competition is unavoidable. It isn't always a bad thing."

Her gaze slid away from his, but not before he caught the flare of displeasure.

Kate tugged on Josh's sleeve. "We should go."

"I'm sure I'll see you around," the other man said to Quinn.

As soon as the couple headed for the exit, a pair of

flame-haired, green-eyed twins flanked Nicole. "Aren't you going to introduce us?" This from the one in green.

With a resigned sigh, Nicole said, "Quinn Darling, meet my younger sisters, Jane and Jessica."

"I'm Jessica." The one who had spoken grinned cheekily, jammed a finger in the other twin's direction. "She's Jane."

"How do you do." Jane, dressed in head-to-toe blue, spoke in a more demure fashion.

"Pleased to meet you both," he said, unsure if he'd ever be able to tell them apart.

"Don't forget me." A petite young woman with a mass of white-blond ringlets crowded in beside the blue twin. She thrust out her hand. "Hi, I'm Megan. I'm the second oldest. That's my husband over there, Lucian Beaumont."

Quinn followed her gaze to a tall, distinguished man with olive skin and dark, wavy hair. Nicole hadn't been kidding when she'd said the O'Malley family was extensive.

"We have another sister, Juliana, who lives in Cades Cove with her husband and young son."

Shaking her hand, Quinn studied their faces. While Megan and the twins did not share the same coloring, they had the same cheekbones, nose and chin. Nicole looked nothing like them.

"Do you and Juliana look alike?" He posed the question to her.

Indefinable emotion darkened her eyes. "No."

Megan shook her head, setting her curls to bouncing. "Juliana and the twins look very much alike. Nicole and I are the odd ones."

The look Nicole shot her bordered on accusing. "You

are not the odd one. You all have the same facial structure. I don't look like any of you." To Quinn, she said, "My mother assures me I wasn't found in the vegetable patch. I have my doubts, however."

The twin in green… Jessica, he thought it was, chuckled. "We like to joke that Nicole is a long-lost princess."

"Jessica," her twin warned with a frown.

"What? She certainly acts like it sometimes."

Megan sighed as if she'd heard it all before. "You take after Grandma O'Malley. You have her hair and eyes."

"Too bad she's not alive to validate the fact O'Malley blood runs through my veins."

The sisters fell silent, and Quinn realized he'd stumbled upon a touchy subject.

"Do you have lunch plans, Mr. Darling?" Jane asked.

"No plans." He adjusted the Bible in his hands. "I had thought to dine at Plum's Café, not realizing the establishment was closed on Sundays."

"You must have lunch with us," Jessica piped up.

"Yes, please do." Jane's smile was genuine.

He studied Nicole's expression, frustrated when he couldn't read it. "I'm not sure your sister would approve considering she's now consigned to endure my presence on a daily basis. She's already promised to help me this afternoon."

"We have to eat first. You should sample Jane's cooking," Nicole said soberly. "And Jessica made pie for dessert."

"I have a weakness for sweets."

A single raven brow arched. "I've noticed."

"Then it's settled." Jane clapped her hands together. "You're coming home with us."

Chapter Four

Quinn soaked in the serene beauty of their surroundings, the endless green forests on either side of the lane alive with birds and squirrels and other wildlife. Gardenia blossoms sweetened the humid air.

"I'm glad we chose to walk." The twins had needed time to put the finishing touches on their meal. He looked over at Nicole strolling quietly beside him. He added *content with silence* to the list of her attributes. "Too much inactivity and I get surly."

"We wouldn't want that, would we?"

He laughed outright at her sarcastic tone. "How could I have forgotten you got a taste of my surliness? Although, that was mostly your fault."

"My fault?" she gaped.

"If you hadn't given me the worst headache in history, I wouldn't have had cause to be."

Stopping short, she crossed her arms and glowered. "You weren't the only one with good reason to be upset. Never in my life have I been handled in such a degrading manner."

Memories surged…the roughness with which he'd bound her wrists. His mother would be appalled.

Guilt pricking his conscience, he sobered. "For that, I am truly sorry. My only defense is that I was acting on faulty assumptions. Will you forgive me?"

Some of the starch went out of her. Her lowered eyes tracking the grass-smattered lane beneath her black boots, she nodded. "Maybe you could get someone to take you hiking in the mountains."

He blinked at the sudden change of topic. "Are you volunteering?"

"Me? No. I don't have that kind of free time. Caleb knows the high country like the back of his hand. I'm sure he'd be willing to take you."

From what he'd observed of the couple that morning during church, the man would not willingly leave his expectant wife, not even for a day's outing. Nevertheless, he said, "Maybe I'll speak to him about it."

"What did you do in Boston to stave off the surliness?"

"Are you familiar with the sport of fencing?"

"I have heard of it," she said drily.

He smiled, silently reminding himself not to assume the locals were cut off from the world. They had access to books and newspapers. And he wasn't the only out-of-towner to move here. People from all walks of life had passed through the town, carrying with them stories of other places.

"I took up fencing a few years ago. My good friend Oliver and I practiced several times a week, and we entered competitions on a regular basis. That and swimming helped channel my energy. I enjoy people-watching, too, so I often strolled the city streets."

Not only did he miss the competitions, he missed his outgoing, boisterous friend. As soon as he was settled, he'd extend an invitation. Always up for an adventure, Oliver was one of a handful of people who'd approved of Quinn's plans. Since he wasn't engaged or married, an extended trip to Tennessee wasn't out of the question.

Nicole batted away a fly, nose wrinkling adorably. One look at the raven-haired beauty, and his friend would be instantly smitten. He wondered what his assistant would think of Oliver.

An uncomfortable feeling slid into his chest. The heat was suddenly too much. Shrugging out of his coat, he slung it over his shoulder.

"You never told me why you left a city full of unlimited opportunities to start over in our unremarkable town."

"It's not easy to explain." He began walking again, and she fell into step beside him. "My family has been blessed. My great-grandfather Edward Darling founded Darling Industries, and it's grown into a prosperous empire, for lack of a better word. We provide solid employment for a vast number of people. We're in the position to fund many charitable works. That part of our life I am proud of. However, one doesn't hold that particular position in society without having certain social responsibilities, ones I have grown exceedingly tired of in recent years."

"You were required to entertain them?"

"According to my father, we have to coddle our current business partners and woo new ones in order to maintain our current level of success."

Her gaze abandoned a bird's nest in a nearby tree

and fastened onto him. "What do you have against parties?"

He kicked up a shoulder. "I enjoy music and dancing and excellent food. I guess what bothers me is the shallow nature of it all. We weren't vacationing with these people because they were family or close friends. It was for the sole purpose of insuring their continued support. I began to crave genuine relationships."

Quinn thought of his last disappointment—Helene and the conversation he'd overheard between her and her friends—and how it had confirmed that a life of social climbing, the relentless pursuit of increased wealth, was not for him. "More than that, I needed to prove to myself that I could make it on my own. That I could accomplish something worthwhile apart from Darling Industries."

"How did your parents take the news?"

Kneading the back of his neck, he winced. "I didn't exactly prepare them. I waited until after I had already purchased the store."

Dark brows lifted until hidden beneath the side sweep of her hair. "So it would be too late for them to try and talk you out of it?"

Perceptive went onto the list. "Partly, yes. I also acted quickly in order not to lose the opportunity. My father, especially, was blown away by my decision. Unlike my mother, he hadn't seen the signs of my dissatisfaction. I suspect he thinks I will tire of small-town life and return within six months' time."

Her brow creased, and she would've spoken if a bundle of reddish-brown fur hadn't ambushed her ankles.

He put a hand out. "Careful—"

"It's all right. He's a friend of mine." Humor laced her voice as she bent and scooped up the wriggling dog.

Quinn watched, fascinated, as Nicole's reserve melted away. Unmindful of her outfit, she snuggled the animal close to her chest, laughter as light as tinkling glass hovering in the still air as the dog attempted to lick her face. Without the armor in place, her radiance shone like rays piercing the clouds, her loveliness making his heart thump and his stomach twist uncomfortably.

Who was the real Nicole O'Malley? The lethal attacker with the killer aim? The distant duchess capable of giving a man frostbite with a single glare? Or the warm, alluring woman with soft eyes and a smile that promised dreams-come-true?

Quinn drew closer and, after letting the dog sniff his fingers, buried them in the thick fur. His scrutiny wasn't on the dog, however. It was on Nicole's face, waiting for—and dreading?—the inevitable change.

"What's his name?"

"Cinnamon."

He'd noticed her extra attention to Caleb's horses yesterday morning. "You have a soft spot for animals and babies."

"That's because they don't judge." Twisting slightly, she glanced at the wide clearing that had opened up on their left and extended as far as the eye could see. "He belongs to my aunt and uncle." In the distance, blue-toned mountains were framed against cerulean sky. A two-story cabin sat right in the center, surrounded by a large barn and outbuildings. Another, smaller cabin was tucked against the far left tree line. "Caleb and Rebecca live in the small one, and Uncle Sam and Aunt

Mary have the large house. Rebecca's younger sister, Amy, stays there with them. Josh and his wife, Kate, have a cabin behind the main house. Their property adjoins ours."

"Family members that are also neighbors. That's convenient."

The guardedness rushed back, and he wondered at it.

"It can be." With a brief kiss to Cinnamon's head, she set him on the ground and watched pensively as he raced across the grass, diverted by a flitting butterfly.

At the decided lack of enthusiasm, he made to question her, but she headed him off. "We shouldn't linger. Jane will worry the food might get cold."

Quinn fell into step beside her, glad of the interruption. Her personal life was none of his business. In fact, he should probably limit spending time with her outside of the store. Maintaining a civil working relationship was paramount to success. Failure was not an outcome he was willing to explore.

Nicole watched as Quinn effortlessly charmed her mother and sisters. Seated diagonally from her at the head of the table, he answered their incessant questions with practiced ease, completely at home in their humble cabin in spite of the air of old-money clinging to him.

The black pin-striped suit coat, which he'd slipped into once again before entering their home, molded to the wide span of his shoulders like a second skin. *He must have a personal tailor.* He'd slipped the buttons free before easing his lean body into the scuffed wooden chair, giving her a glimpse of the silver-filigreed vest and crisp white shirt underneath hugging his torso.

Had he been born a charmer? Or had his skills been honed by his high-society life? Either way, he annoyed her.

She skewered a potato with more force than necessary, and it disintegrated into mush. Quinn's vigilant liquid eyes focused on her. One brow lifted in silent question. Nicole mimicked his expression. The slow, impertinent smile that followed made her insides jittery. Not familiar with this particular reaction, she frowned at him, which only served to widen his smile.

Lowering her gaze, she concentrated on sipping the fragrant tea without spilling it.

"Won't you miss living in Boston?" Across from Nicole, Jessica eyed their guest with open admiration.

Laying down his fork, he fiddled with the teacup's handle. "I will miss my family. And my favorite Czech bakery. They sell the most delicious *kolaches*, pastries filled with cheese or fruit." His expression turned wistful. "I'm at peace with my decision, however. I look forward to experiencing life in a rural, close-knit community."

Nicole hid a smirk with her napkin. He'd soon learn small-town life wasn't all lemon drops and roses.

Jessica looked at Nicole. "Our sister has talked about leaving Gatlinburg behind and starting fresh in the big city for years."

Nicole restrained herself from kicking her under the table. It wasn't that her dream was private—everyone in town was aware of her plans. But Quinn was her boss. Now that he knew she intended to leave town, he could possibly decide to find an early replacement.

A tremor of unease wound its way through her. She desperately needed the income.

Quinn was looking at her with a strange mix of surprise and disappointment. "Is this true, Nicole?"

Before she could formulate an answer, Jane leaned forward in her chair, auburn hair brilliant in the afternoon light streaming through the windows. "Tell him your plans."

"I told you I was a seamstress."

"Yes… I recall the conversation."

"My goal is to open a boutique of my own in Knoxville."

"When?" He sat motionless, good humor draining away.

"She was supposed to go in March," Jessica piped up. "She refuses to tell us why she had to postpone."

"I—"

Their mother aimed a reprimanding glance at her youngest daughter. "That is Nicole's business, young lady. Don't pester her."

"Yes, ma'am."

Nicole attempted to gather her wits. No one could discover the true reason for the delay. "I—I will have the necessary funds eventually."

Still unsmiling, Quinn sighed. "Emmett did not mention your plans. Your expertise will be missed."

"I promise to give you ample notice of my departure."

As if sensing her turmoil, he said, "I want you for as many days as I can have you."

Nicole's lips parted. Jessica giggled.

Red slashed his cheekbones as it sank in how his

words had sounded, and he looked uncharacteristically uncertain. "I meant—"

"I know what you meant." Dropping her napkin on the table, she stood abruptly and gathered her plate and silverware. "If we're going to have time to look over the ledgers today I suggest we go. I have alterations to do later."

"But you haven't eaten dessert," Jane protested.

Their mother rose, as well, smiling broadly at their guest. "I'll send some with you. I'm sure you will want to take a break at some point."

Nicole stumbled, nearly dumping her dish. Sure, she'd seen that speculative gleam in her mother's eyes before, but in regards to her sisters. Not *her*. Surely she didn't think she and Quinn would make a good match!

Setting her dishes in the dry sink, she pitched her voice low. "Please tell me you aren't entertaining romantic notions about me and my boss."

Alice patted Nicole's arm. "Would that be so bad? He seems like a fine young man."

Remembering his arrogance as he'd loftily informed her of impending changes, she swallowed a retort. Fine young man? Huh. "I'm not interested in him or anyone else. I have plans, remember?"

"Have you consulted God about those plans?" It wasn't a harsh question. Concern and understanding were reflected in her lined face.

"I know you'd rather I stay here and, like Megan, settle down and maybe start a family. That's not me. And, since God made me, He knows I wouldn't be happy living a conventional life."

Nicole wasn't about to admit that lately she'd been experiencing rogue thoughts...like what it might be like to have a man adore her the way Lucian did Megan. Or what it would feel like to hold her very own baby in her arms. Josh and Kate's little girl, Victoria, had worked her way into her heart with zero effort. Simply holding her, absorbing her innocence and sweetness, had altered her view of parenthood.

"Well, it can't hurt to have a friend, can it?" Her mother sliced up two generous portions of pear pie.

Nicole didn't want Quinn Darling for a friend. The debonair Northerner wasn't exactly comfortable to be around. On top of that, he was the last person she'd feel inclined to share confidences with.

When the dessert was carefully placed in a small basket, Nicole endured a motherly hug. "I'm not sure what time I'll be home. Don't expect me before supper, okay?"

Hopefully she could hurry along this session with Quinn. There was an errand she couldn't put off.

Nicole pressed against the lichen-coated tree trunk, listening, waiting, heartbeat loud in her ears as she stared at the run-down shack tucked between three trees of varying size. In the lush canopy far above her head, birds were constantly in motion, the flap of their wings competing with rustling leaves and swaying limbs. A tickle on her pinkie caught her attention. Brushing off a tiny black ant, she checked the dense woods behind her. No one. Good.

Gripping the basket she'd snuck out of the mercantile following her blessedly brief tutoring session with Quinn, she picked her way over exposed roots and the damp, mossy forest floor. The midsummer sun rarely breached the leafy banner, and last autumn's fallen leaves had yet to fully decompose. The air was dense, fragrant and slightly moist. Trickling stream water pulsed beneath all other forest sounds.

At the shack door, she rapped her knuckles against the brittle wood in a distinct pattern. A few seconds passed before the door scraped open and a young man with pleasant features, albeit strained and pale, stared back at her. His dishwater-blond hair hung limp across his forehead.

"Nicole."

Shuffling a step back with the aid of his cane, he admitted her.

"How are you, Patrick?"

"Nothing has changed since the last time you asked. That was what? Two days ago?" His attempt at a smile failed, pain clouding his gray eyes.

She wished for the hundredth time he'd gotten proper care for his injured leg, wished he'd agreed to let her summon the doctor. It hadn't healed properly, hence the ongoing pain.

Patrick's younger sister, Lillian, greeted her with her customary hug. Nicole returned the embrace without a trace of awkwardness. She'd grown accustomed to the sweet-natured girl's affection.

Lillian released her. "You look especially pretty today. How was the church service?"

"I'll tell you all about it in a moment." She lifted the basket. "First, I brought you some things."

"You always do." Patrick had lowered himself onto the ladder-back chair in the dim corner. Her ongoing charity bothered him a great deal. He was aware, as they all were, that he and his sister couldn't survive without it.

"She knows we'll pay her back someday." Lillian carried it to the tiny, lopsided table shoved against the wall beside the door and eagerly lifted the checkered material. Her wavy flaxen hair, caught in a neat ponytail and tied with a strip of leather, hung to her waist and shone in the lamplight. Several hours remained before dusk fell, but the single window let in precious little natural light.

Moving to sit on one of two narrow beds, Nicole pondered their reaction to her news. The ancient bed frame creaked under her weight, and the mattress was pathetically thin. The ticking would need to be replaced soon. How was she supposed to accomplish that without arousing suspicion? Sometimes, the weight of this secret was almost too much to bear.

Lillian exclaimed over the paper and pencils. The fifteen-year-old was too thin, as was her brother, her skin as pale as the paper in her hands due to spending most daylight hours in this ruin they called home. Neither could detract from her fair beauty, however. Big, cornflower-blue eyes shone in a face that seemed perpetually filled with hope.

Patrick didn't share his sister's optimistic outlook. His worries, his deep-seated concern for his sister, cloaked him in perpetual strain. Bouncing the cane between his fingers, he stared hard at Nicole. "You look more pensive than usual. What's bothering you?"

After six months of almost daily visits, they treated her as an older sibling. She considered them friends of the dearest kind, friends she'd never dreamed she'd find in her hometown. Patrick and Lillian didn't care what her last name was. They didn't know her family or that she paled in comparison to her sisters—Juliana, beautiful and courageous; Megan, the romantic dreamer who brought joy to children's lives; sweet-tempered Jane, whose generosity of spirit bordered on legendary; and high-spirited Jessica, the twin who could bake her way out of any fix.

No, they liked her for her. A heady experience, it was the reason she'd do anything to protect them.

"Something happened yesterday before we opened the store."

While she'd told them about her new boss, she'd left out the details of their first meeting. Patrick scowled. "It was him, wasn't it? Our stand-in father was in town again."

"I didn't recognize him at first, but he introduced himself to Quinn." Clasping her hands tightly on her lap, Nicole suppressed a shudder. "He had a sign with your names and descriptions, and he asked Quinn to post it on the board."

White lines bracketed Patrick's mouth as he gripped the cane. "Did he?"

"No. I asked to see it and, when he wasn't looking, I slipped it in my pocket."

Lillian sank onto the mattress beside Nicole, fingers worrying a tear in the coarse blanket. "You could get in trouble if he finds out."

"I don't like this," Patrick said.

Nicole couldn't feel bad about what she'd done, not knowing how risky hanging that sign would've been.

"Don't worry. Quinn's so busy plotting modifications to the store, he won't even notice."

"Even if you did post it," Lillian said, "I don't think we'd have anything to worry about. It's not like we go anywhere where people would see us or ask our names."

Their forced solitude, their bleak existence, was like a gaping wound that refused to heal. No matter where she was or what she was doing, she couldn't *not* think about them here with no one but each other to talk to. Nicole *hated* that they were being punished when they were innocent of any wrongdoing. "I was hoping he'd have given up by now," she admitted.

"Carl won't do that," Patrick said, defeat weighing him down. "He wants the necklace."

She'd seen the ruby-and-diamond necklace that once belonged to their late mother. While she wasn't an expert on jewelry, it appeared to be of great value. And because Carl had been married to their mother, he surely thought of it as his property.

"He will also go to any lengths to punish us for disappearing with it."

She stared at his injured leg. Carl had done that to him. If he got his hands on Patrick a second time, there was no telling what he'd do.

"Let me involve Shane Timmons," Nicole entreated, not for the first time. "He's a fair man. He'll help you. And you'll finally be able to resume a normal life."

Patrick dropped the hand he'd placed over his face and jutted his chin in that stubborn way of his. "As a sheriff, he's duty-bound to follow the law. We're still minors. He'd be forced to reunite us with Carl."

"He's not our father," Lillian piped up.

"Doesn't matter. He's our legal guardian."

Knowing where the argument was headed, Nicole stood and sighed. "I have to get home."

"We'll see you tomorrow?" Lillian pushed to her feet, her countenance resigned.

"Of course." Pausing with her hand on the door latch, she looked at Patrick. "Please think on what I said."

"It's no use, Nicole. Your way will lead to trouble. If Carl finds us, he will finish the job he started. I won't be able to protect Lillian. You don't want that on your conscience, do you?"

Soundlessly letting herself out, Nicole sagged against the door and closed her eyes. Without her, there would be no one to help them. No one to keep their secret. As long as Patrick and Lillian needed her, she was stuck in Gatlinburg.

Chapter Five

The siblings' predicament still weighing heavily on her mind the next morning, Nicole wasn't prepared for the sight of her boss hefting chairs along the back hallway. He was dressed as impeccably as usual, black hair neatly combed, and beneath the rolled-up sleeves thick forearms lightly sprinkled with dark hair were visible. Sturdy shoulders bore the weight effortlessly.

"Duchess. You came." A brash grin curving his lips, he stopped in front of her, his tall frame blocking her way. Beneath the scent of peppermint wafted soap and spice and man. "I thought after yesterday's session you might've given up on me."

Nicole pursed her lips together to stop the forming compliment. Quinn was in possession of a keen mind. It hadn't taken him long to catch on to the trade credit system. She wasn't about to boost his already healthy self-confidence, however.

"Why did you call me that?"

"Duchess?" His honey eyes twinkled. "It fits you." Was he implying she acted like a snob? That she thought others were beneath her? Because that was so far off the mark—

"As much as I'd like to stand here and chat with you," he said, adjusting his grip on the chairs, "we've a mountain-size job ahead of us. I need for you to make up a sign letting customers know we'll close today at noon and reopen tomorrow at the same time."

"Why would we do that?"

"After you left, I spent several hours examining the current arrangement and deciding how best to rearrange the merchandise. I've hired a couple of men to help us implement my plan."

Flustered, the significance of the chairs finally sank in. "Are you going to put those back once we've finished?"

"No. I told you my store will not be a gathering place." His brows shot up. "Do you know how difficult it's going to be to get those tobacco stains off the floor?"

Nicole was on the verge of warning him of the consequences when she stopped herself. Quinn Darling had overseen a vast clothing conglomerate. He thought running a country store was small potatoes, so why would he heed her advice?

"I'll go make that sign."

Pressing against the wall to avoid brushing against him, she waited for him to pass. Instead, he set the chairs down and folded his arms across his chest. The movement brought him too close in the narrow hallway. The fact they were completely alone in the building wasn't lost on her.

Not that she feared him. Despite Quinn's singular ability to get under her skin and lodge there like a stubborn splinter, she felt completely safe in his company. Safe was not the same as relaxed, though. Whenever he was nearby, her skin felt too tight. Her pulse raced. Her entire being came alive, senses soaking up every detail—everything from the heat blazing off his skin to his short, clean nails to the throb of his heartbeat in the hollow of his throat. Talk about disturbing.

"Something on your mind, Duchess?"

She lifted her chin. "Don't call me that."

"I can see the disapproving light in your eyes. Tell me what's on your mind."

Somewhere outside, a horse whinnied and male voices could be heard.

"Most people don't appreciate change. Evicting the checker players isn't going to go over well. The same goes for rearranging the goods. While I can see the wisdom of such a plan, I'm not sure the customers will respond positively."

"Hmm." His probing gaze roamed her face, making her feel exposed. "I understand your point of view. However, I'm of the opinion that, while change may not be welcome in the beginning, it doesn't take long for people to adjust."

The rear bell rang, signaling a delivery. With another of his devastating grins, he moved out of her space and retrieved the chairs. "I'll get that."

As he strode away from her, Nicole found that she could breathe easier. Think more clearly.

"Can't say I didn't warn you," she muttered, heading to the office to do his bidding.

If she was a duchess, what did that make him? King?

She spent the bulk of the morning answering the same questions over and over. Why were they closing? Why wasn't the checker game set out? And her personal favorite, for which she had no answer—what was that pesky Northerner thinking?

About five minutes before noon, as the last customer was leaving, Quinn waved three young men through the entrance.

"You're right on time." Shaking their hands in turn, he glanced over at Nicole. "You're already acquainted with Miss O'Malley."

Clamping down on the familiar dread fixing her boots to the floorboards, Nicole forced her gaze to Kenneth Jones. Blond, blue-eyed and as solid as an elk, he'd been a thorn in her side ever since she'd turned down his invitation to the harvest dance last year. Kenneth did not take rejection well.

"Yes, sir. We grew up together." Kenneth adopted a respectful air, but his eyes gleamed with anticipation. No doubt he saw this as the perfect opportunity to harass her—no O'Malley family members in sight.

His friends, red-haired, freckled Timothy Wallington and lanky Pete Ryan wore matching predatory smiles. In this trio, Kenneth was the leader. They behaved in accordance with his whims.

Reminding herself she wasn't in any real danger, she wiped her damp palms against her apron and squared her shoulders. Hateful words couldn't inflict lasting pain. Not from someone who wasn't important to her.

Quinn beckoned the men to the counter where his sketches were lined up and explained exactly how he wanted things to proceed. His directions were clear and concise.

She listened with reluctant admiration. Here was a man who knew what he wanted and how to get it.

A force to be reckoned with. With his wealth and influence, he'd be used to people obeying him without question.

"Kenneth, I'd like for you to remove the tools from that middle shelf." He pointed to the long interior wall. "Once you've done that, Nicole can clean them and then organize the ready-made clothing there so that it is alongside the fabric bolts."

Quinn looked at her, brows raised. "All right with you?"

Aware of Kenneth's leer, she jerked a nod. So they'd be working side by side. She could handle whatever he dished out.

With Pete and Timothy assigned to the middle aisles, Quinn retreated behind the counter to address the shelving units and drawers there.

"I'll go and get the water," she told him, retrieving the pail from a hook near the aprons.

Already comparing the shelves to his sketch, Quinn nodded absentmindedly.

A beefy hand snatched the handle from hers. "I'll help you." Propelling her along the hall, Kenneth said in a voice that carried, "The stairs are steep. Wouldn't want you to trip and break something."

"I don't need your help," she said through gritted teeth.

At the door, the pretense fell away. "You've always been a snob, you know that? Thinking you're better than everybody else. Too good for our humble town. One day you'll regret looking down your nose at me, little witch."

She inwardly grimaced at the taunt that had originated on the school grounds. "It was a silly harvest dance, Kenneth. Forget about it."

His nostrils flared, lips flattening into a sneer. "I will as soon as you've learned your lesson." Turning on his heel, he tossed over his shoulder, "Get your own water."

Hurrying out into the searing midday heat, Nicole descended the stairs on unsteady legs, angry at herself for letting a bully like Kenneth intimidate her. One word to any of her cousins was all it would take to be rid of him. But whining to them felt wrong. She was no longer a child. If she planned to make it on her own in the city, she'd have to deal with problems herself. There'd be no well-meaning protectors to the rescue.

Scooping water out of the rain barrel, she went back inside and, studiously avoiding all four males in the room, gathered soap and rags while waiting for Kenneth to unload the shelves. He ignored her for the most part, but his dislike was made plain in the dark looks cast her way. Working in the aisle behind them, Pete and Timothy's low conversation was interspersed with laughter that sounded mischievous to her ears. Were they laughing at her? Plotting something?

On edge the entire afternoon, she trained her attention on the tasks Quinn gave her. It wasn't until she and Kenneth had moved to the china display that things went awry.

She was carefully removing a stack of dinner plates when Kenneth's hand shot out and, seizing her wrist, yanked so that she tipped the lot of them. The crash reverberated in the silent store. Stunned disbelief held her frozen.

An expression of false concern settled across his

features. "Uh-oh. That's going to be expensive to re-place. Mr. Darling, I'm afraid your assistant got care-less with the merchandise."

Straightening from his crouch at the opposite end of the room, Quinn's frown carved deep grooves on either side of his mouth. He came and surveyed the shards littering the floorboards. Beyond his shoulder, Pete and Timothy elbowed each other.

A resigned sigh escaped him as his gaze prodded Nicole's. "Clean up this mess. And from now on, ask for help with the heavy stuff. Kenneth will be happy to help, I'm sure."

"Anytime." Kenneth's smile held a hint of cruelty. Quinn couldn't see it, because he was looking at her with something akin to disappointment.

Indignation seared her, burned into her cheeks. If she confessed the truth, Kenneth would only deny it. Her trustworthiness would be called into question.

Subduing the urge to stomp her feet, she croaked, "It won't happen again."

"Will she have to pay for the damage, Mr. Darling?"

Quinn's brow furrowed. "That won't be necessary this time."

This time. An unspoken warning to not make the same mistake again.

When he'd returned to his work, she shot her nem-esis a scorching glare. "How could you do that?" she demanded.

"I didn't." His upper lip curled. "You did."

Leaving her to clean up alone, Kenneth went and pretended to help his friends. Nicole took out her frus-tration on the broom. Being blamed for something that wasn't her fault left a bad taste in her mouth. Anger and humiliation warred for supremacy.

She could hardly bear to look at Quinn. Irrationally, she blamed him for not seeing through Kenneth's act.

The remainder of the afternoon and early evening crawled by. Just as escape looked likely, Quinn waylaid her in the office. The trio had left ten minutes ago, and she was eager to get away from her boss's assessing glances.

"It's late, Quinn. I'm exhausted and hungry." *I need time to recover before doing it all again tomorrow morning. No telling what my enemy has planned for me.*

"This won't take but a minute." He leaned against the door frame, hands in his pockets and ankles crossed.

"If this is about the dishes, I—"

"No." His expression turned thoughtful. "I detected something…off between you and Kenneth. Do you two have a history? Because if you're uncomfortable working with him, I can send him on his way in the morning."

"If you're asking if we've ever courted, the answer is no," she spluttered. "Absolutely not."

"Then what's the problem?"

Here was her chance to explain everything. To absolve herself and be rid of Kenneth and his buddies. But she was, above all, a private person. Exposing her problems to her boss didn't hold an ounce of appeal.

"No problem." Pushing an errant curl behind her ear, she rubbed a sore spot in her lower back. "If there are no more questions, I really do have to go."

Quinn didn't appear convinced. Still, he moved sideways to let her pass. As she was edging through the doorway and he was centimeters away, he said softly, "Good night, Duchess."

Nicole stiffened at the brush of his minty breath across her cheek.

She didn't like nicknames on principle. Caleb did it to tease her—good-natured, brotherly ribbing that nevertheless irked her. Kenneth's intent was to demean her. What was Quinn Darling's motive? And why did a little thrill zip up her spine?

Risking a glance at this close range, she didn't detect a trace of cruelty in those light brown eyes, merely lazy curiosity.

She was an enigma to him, was she? Well, he was wasting his time trying to figure her out. She wasn't about to divulge her secrets to the likes of him.

The locals weren't adjusting to Quinn's implemented changes as quickly as he'd hoped. Ever since they'd reopened three days ago, the customers had doggedly avoided him. Some went so far as to denounce his decisions to his face, unsatisfied with his explanations.

No amount of pleasantness or willingness to help had put a dent in their wariness.

Leaning against the shelving unit, he eyed the five-deep line of customers waiting for Nicole's assistance.

He caught the familiar elderly lady's eye and thanked the Lord he had a memory for names. His smile didn't come as easily as it had that morning. "I can help you over here, Mrs. Kirkpatrick."

Crinkling her nose, she shook her head, gaze skittering away.

The rejection stung. He, Quinn Darling, heir to the Darling fortune and a man whose very presence deemed a social gathering a success, could not convince the lady to let him wait on her. Weariness pressed behind his forehead, turning the slight headache he'd nursed since Nicole whopped him with that pot into a full-blown hammering against his skull.

He pinched the bridge of his nose. Shoving off the counter, he strode to his assistant's side. "I'll fill orders for you. What have you got?"

Her face a polite mask, Nicole's pencil hovered above the ledger and pointed at the row of red metal spice bins on the bottom shelf. "I need one ounce of cinnamon, four ounces of cream of tartar and one container of vanilla extract."

"Throw in a pack of chewing gum," the needle-thin man on the opposite side of the counter added.

"Coming right up, sir."

Grinding his teeth, Quinn quickly gathered the items. Up until this moment, he hadn't considered himself a proud man too good for lowly work. He hadn't started out at the top. Edward Darling had thought it important his son experience all facets of the industry. He'd done everything from sweeping factory floors to operating ten looms at once.

Why, then, was being reduced to Nicole O'Malley's go-to boy so difficult to swallow?

Because this is my store. I bought it with my own money, gave up everything I've worked for—upsetting a lot of people in the process—to start over in an unfamiliar place where I know no one.

Neatly folding the paper sacks, he slid them across the counter. "Will there be anything else?"

Lord Jesus, help me not to be prideful. Help me to win these people's trust.

The man squinted at his list. "Nope. That will be all."

Nicole informed him how much credit he had left and moved on to the next customer. Together, they worked through the line until the last person had been served. The clock chiming three o'clock split the weighted silence.

Without a word, Quinn pivoted on his heel and stalked down the hall to the cramped, low-ceilinged quarters. He needed an outlet for his pent-up frustration. Since he couldn't drop everything and go for a swim, going through the motions of making coffee would have to do. He was filling the kettle with water when Nicole peered around the door frame.

"Is it safe to come in?" she said, cringing when he thumped the kettle down with more force than necessary.

"Enter at your own risk." Snatching the tin of coffee grounds from the shelf, he slammed it down.

"Even if I come bearing gifts?" Emerald green skirts skimming the polished floorboards, she approached and slowly lifted her hand. Two peppermint sticks lay on her open palm.

He looked deep into her luminous eyes. "Are you trying to tame my surliness with sweets?"

"I am."

He glimpsed a flicker of compassion, almost imperceptible but there nonetheless, and the loneliness inside him receded a little. Two more attributes went onto the growing list. *Unpredictable. Kindhearted.* The second one was just a hunch and would need to be confirmed.

Quinn accepted the offering only to hold one up to

her lips, pressing gently. "I cannot be the only one to indulge."

Startled eyes stared back at him, confirming she wasn't used to his brand of teasing. *You didn't treat the women in Boston like this, though, did you?* a voice prodded. *Something in her manner provokes you to outrageousness.*

When she reached to take hold of the stick, her cool fingers closed over his, the contact unexpectedly comforting. Lowering his hand, he popped the sweet in his mouth and resumed the motions of making coffee.

"They do not trust me," he said, pulling down two blue enamel mugs from the shelf. "They lack confidence in me." He hoped she didn't recognize his underlying hurt.

"I don't think Gatlinburg has seen anyone quite like you."

Pausing in scooping the grounds, he cast her a sidelong look, smiling a little at her attempts to eat the peppermint without becoming a sticky mess. "What do you mean?"

"Have you looked in a mirror lately?" She waved her hand up and down. "You exude power and privilege, wealth most people around here can't even begin to imagine. Your slick ways and your funny accent sets you apart. It's painfully obvious you are out of your element."

"Don't hold back, Duchess," he said drily, "Tell me what you really think."

His ego sure was taking a bruising lately. His father would say it built character.

"That doesn't mean they won't come to trust you eventually. Are you a patient man, Quinn Darling?"

Irrationally, his conversation with Shane Timmons came to mind. The sheriff was of the opinion that, while hard to get to know, Nicole would be worth the effort. He wasn't sure he agreed. Nicole O'Malley was not even close to what he required in a wife.

She awaited his answer, calm and regal in her high-collared green confection of a dress, raven curls confined in a loose chignon at the base of her swanlike neck. How would she react if he were to sink his fingers in the beguiling mass?

"That all depends," he said on a sigh.

"On what?"

"On what it is I'm waiting for."

She didn't have a response, merely watched him with that stoic expression.

"I have a question for you." He imagined he could see her pulling her armor in close.

"Yes?"

He took his time pouring coffee into the cups. "Why aren't you gloating?"

"Excuse me?"

"You warned me. I didn't listen, and now—" he replaced the kettle on the stove "—they see me as the bad guy. I've been waiting for you to rub it in."

"You'll be waiting a long time."

He held out the mug. She studiously avoided his fingers. Quinn had noticed she took pains not to accidentally touch him. Why was that?

She wasn't shy. What, then? Did he make her uncomfortable? He frowned at the notion.

"You're not the type to point out a man's errors in judgment?"

"I clearly don't need to. It hasn't even been a week and you've already seen the effects of your decisions."

"You think I should open my store to loiterers."

"Folks will eventually get over you moving the merchandise around. The organization makes sense." Against the blue mug, her fingers were long and slender, piano-playing hands, his mother would say. "Prohibiting folks from gathering for harmless fun and conversation, on the other hand, strikes them as callous and unfeeling. They won't forgive you for that."

"It was purely a business decision," he defended.

"The wrong one."

The ringing of the bell echoed through the store, and Nicole left his quarters to go and greet the new arrival. He refused to be disappointed at her departure, even if, for a couple of minutes in her presence, the magnitude of his problems seemed to have receded.

Chapter Six

For the remainder of the afternoon, Quinn didn't attempt to wait on anyone. Instead, he focused on assisting Nicole and interacting with the customers in a nonthreatening way. He mulled over their conversation. She was right—in order to gain their favor, he was going to have to think less like a businessman and more like a member of this community. He was going to have to invite the checker-playing, tobacco-spitting gossip-sharers back.

Around five o'clock, an hour before closing, Kenneth and Timothy swaggered in and headed straight for the counter. Neither man observed him in front of the notice board. Remaining where he was, Quinn switched his attention to Nicole, curious to see if her behavior altered. He didn't buy her denial that no issues existed between her and the cocky blond.

What was she hiding? And why?

In the middle of helping a young mother with a fussy toddler clinging to her hip, Nicole's smile wavered the moment she became aware of the young men's presence. Her shoulders went rigid. When her gaze sought out Quinn across the store, widening when she encountered his steady perusal, his feet carried him straight to her side. Somehow, he sensed she needed him.

"Kenneth. Timothy. What can I do for you?"

"Afternoon, Mr. Darling." With smooth cordiality, Kenneth tapped a battered hat against his leg. "Came in for shaving soap. But Nicole knows what I like. I'll wait for her."

Nicole didn't react, didn't acknowledge their conversation in any way.

"I wouldn't want you to wait needlessly." Quinn moved to the case holding shaving supplies and opened the rear panel. "What brand?"

The flaring of his nostrils was the only sign of his displeasure. "Colgate."

Quinn wrapped up his purchase and took the payment. "Thank you, gentlemen. Have a good afternoon."

"If you have any other jobs around the store, we'd be happy to help out."

"I'll keep that in mind."

Glancing surreptitiously at Nicole, Kenneth tucked his purchase beneath his arm and left with his friend.

Quinn approached, lightly touched her wrist. "Do you mind watching the store for a couple of minutes? I've an errand to see to."

"Of course not."

Out on the boardwalk, the intense midsummer heat immediately closed in. Boston hadn't been nearly this humid. Wouldn't be long before his skin was slick with perspiration and he wished he didn't have to wear so many clothes.

There was no sign of Kenneth. Striding in the direction of the jail, Quinn was relieved to find Shane behind his desk, seemingly free to talk.

The man's features lit with mild surprise and the paper he'd been perusing hit the desk. "Trouble at the mercantile?"

"No." He gestured to the empty chair. "Do you have a moment? I'd like to ask you a few questions."

"Have a seat. What's on your mind?"

Dropping onto the unforgiving chair, he rested his ankle on his knee. "What can you tell me about Kenneth Jones?"

He thought a moment. "Not much to tell. Like most folks in these mountains, his family farms the land. Decent, hardworking people. Regular churchgoers." He tapped the desk surface. "Why do you ask?"

Quinn explained about the job he'd hired Kenneth to do. The tension he'd picked up on.

"You aren't aware of any romantic links or friendship between him and Nicole?"

Shane huffed a laugh. "Afraid I can't help you there. Keeping up with who courts who in this town is not in the job description."

Pushing to his feet, Quinn stalked to the barred window overlooking the street. While he recognized some of the passersby, he didn't know their names, reputations or their histories. "I'm at a disadvantage here. It's like trying to piece together a puzzle without first seeing the whole picture."

"All I can tell you is Nicole isn't one to frequent festivities. I can't recall her name being linked with anyone. If she attends a church social or dance, it's with her family."

Shoving aside the intense curiosity and twisted pleasure those statements evoked, Quinn turned. "To be clear, my motives for coming here are strictly professional."

The look Shane directed at him silently challenged that statement.

"I'm concerned because she's my assistant," he persisted. "If she has a problem with a customer, I need to know about it."

The tapping on Shane's desk increased. "Have you broached the matter with her?"

"I did. She wasn't forthcoming."

"Meaning, she denied there being a problem, and you don't believe her."

"Yes."

Shane slouched against the chair back. "Your only option then is to keep your eyes and ears open. You can't force her to confide in you."

If only he could. He stuck out his hand. "Appreciate the help."

Standing to his feet, the sheriff shook his hand. "I know how it feels to be the new man in town. Takes time, but eventually folks will open up to you."

Thanking the other man and feeling as if he'd made a trustworthy friend, he returned to the store in time to lock up and flip the sign to closed. When he spotted Nicole hunched over a small book and scribbling furiously, Quinn's gut tightened. He knew exactly what he'd see at her feet.

Acting as if nothing were amiss, he strolled past and headed into the office, suspicion burning his mouth like acid. For several days, he'd watched her surreptitiously place items in a large basket that she endeavored to keep hidden from him. It appeared his assistant was keeping more than one secret.

Was it possible she had been stealing from Emmett? The notion sickened him.

There was no other choice but to confront her.

Quinn stalked around the corner, scowling when she jolted in surprise and trepidation rippled across her features. He clasped his hands tightly behind his back. "May I ask what you are doing?"

"I—" Thick lashes sweeping down, she pointed to the book. "I—I'm entering my purchases. Emmett detracted the cost from my wages."

"I would like to see that." He held out his hand.

Her dark brows collided. "You don't trust me."

"You are my employee, Nicole. I need to be able to trust you. That's why I need to see it."

Her reluctance was plain as she handed him the book. Antagonism radiated from her stiff form. Quinn flipped through the pages, saw what appeared to be lists of ordinary supplies and entries by both Nicole and Emmett.

"New policy. When you make a purchase, I will enter it into this ledger, not you."

Nicole snatched it from his fingers, holding it to her chest like a shield. Deep purple sparks shimmered in her eyes. "Emmett didn't feel the need to supervise me in this."

"I am not Emmett," he snapped, angry at her for inspiring this distrust in the first place. "If you do not feel you can meet my standards, you can cease your employment here."

Again, he sensed fear in her.

"Fine." Hauling the basket up to the counter, she

opened the ledger and held it up to his face. "You're the boss. Go ahead. Inspect it."

Despising the position she'd put him in, he checked that the items she'd gathered matched her entries. "You may leave," he murmured, not looking at her. "I will see to the cleanup."

He noticed her hands shaking when they folded over the handle. She didn't speak, just whirled away from him and marched down the hallway, slamming the door behind her.

"What exactly are you hiding, Nicole? And what has you so afraid?"

"We have a problem."

Humiliation humming through her veins, Nicole plunked the supplies one by one on the tabletop. Candles. Soap. Tea.

"What is it?" Features pinched, Patrick leaned heavily on his cane.

"Not it. Who. Quinn Darling is the problem." Insufferable man. "He practically accused me of stealing."

Lillian, whose neat blue-and-brown paisley blouse and nut-brown skirt Nicole had fashioned herself, clapped a hand over her mouth. "How horrible."

Studying the growing collection of things she'd brought, Patrick's shoulders sagged. "It's because of your frequent purchases, isn't it?" He nodded to the table. "I'm not surprised he's suspicious."

Noting his growing displeasure, Nicole worked to calm herself. "I haven't done anything wrong. He knows that. However, I may have to stagger my visits for a while."

"Of course," Lillian placed a hand on Nicole's arm.

"We appreciate everything you do for us. We would never want you to put your job in jeopardy. Because of Patrick's traps, we have sufficient meat. And there's all the fish and crawfish, too."

The pair waited until dusk to do their fishing and bathing. While not ideal, it was the best way to avoid detection.

Patrick retreated to his corner chair, resting the cane across his knees. "Maybe we should move on to a different town. Somewhere farther away from Carl. We've taken advantage of Nicole's generosity long enough."

Both females gasped. Lillian rushed to crouch in front of him. "Patrick, no! I don't want to leave Nicole. She's our family now. Besides, there'd be no one to help us. No place to stay."

The younger girl's impassioned plea squeezed Nicole's heart. The fact that Lillian valued their friendship as much as she did filled her with an unfamiliar sense of connection, of being valued for who she was, not who her family was. Over the past six months, a bond had developed between her and these down-on-their-luck siblings. She was loath to sever it. But what did that mean for her dream? Did she dare attempt to take them with her?

She'd been supporting them here. There was no reason she couldn't support them in the city once she'd replenished her savings.

Would they want to join her? Out of respect for their feelings, Nicole hadn't shared her plans with them. Patrick, especially, would've refused her assistance if he'd known what she was sacrificing.

"I could find work." At his sister's protest, he said,

"Desk work. Something that doesn't require me to stand for long periods."

"Who would take us to this new town? Where would we live?" Launching upward, she paced in the tight space, golden hair bouncing between her shoulder blades. "People would ask questions. What if they guessed our identity? You said yourself that Carl is tenacious. Who knows how many towns he's visited." Seizing Nicole's hands, she exclaimed, "Talk some sense into him, please."

Briefly hugging her friend, Nicole moved to sit on the bed closest to him. "Let's not be hasty. Quinn has absolutely no notion about any of this. He didn't question my reasons for my purchases. It was my behavior that tipped him off. If I hadn't acted like I had something to hide, he wouldn't have suspected anything amiss. I'll be smarter from here on out."

Patrick was quiet for a long stretch. "Lillian, will you bring my satchel to me?"

When she'd done as he asked, he dug in the side pocket and, extracting a brooch, held it out to Nicole. "This belonged to our grandmother. Carl doesn't know of its existence. I'm not sure how much it's worth, but I want you to take it as partial payment for what we owe you."

The brooch was exquisite, a blue-and-white cameo outlined in silver and with a cluster of diamonds on the top. "I can't possibly—"

When his jaw went taut and his gray eyes grew stormy, she was reminded of her cousins and the lessons they'd taught her about male pride.

She gingerly plucked the brooch from his fingers. "It's beautiful, Patrick. Thank you."

Tucking it in her reticule, she determined to hold on to it for them.

Lillian pointed to the stew bubbling on the ancient stove. "Would you like to have supper with us?"

"I wish I could, but I have chores to tend to at home."

"Maybe another time. Oh, I finished some of the books you lent me." She pressed the volumes into her hand. "I liked *Wuthering Heights* but didn't care for the volume of poetry."

"Neither did I," Patrick groaned. "She's forced me to listen to it every morning the past week."

A smile broke through Nicole's reserve. "Got it. No more poetry. I'll bring replacements soon, Lillian."

Her blue eyes gleamed with interest. "I'm looking forward to it."

Nicole was grateful her friend enjoyed reading as it helped pass the days spent indoors. During her walk home, she found herself unexpectedly turning to God in prayer.

"Father God, I don't come to You often for assistance." Aloud, her voice sounded stilted. Casting about the forest to make sure she was alone, she lowered it to a whisper. "I'm in way over my head. I thought I could handle this one on my own, but I can't. Patrick and Lillian deserve better. They deserve a normal life, a chance at happiness. They are dear friends of mine, and it would mean a lot to me if You would fix this."

A squirrel circled the tree directly in her path, and she froze, keen to observe the animal.

"One more thing," she murmured. "Please help Quinn Darling mind his own business."

Chapter Seven

Friday evening, Nicole arrived at Megan and Lucian's too late to hear her sister entertain the local children with a story. Weaving her way through the sea of parents and children juggling glasses of lemonade and platter-size cookies, she reached Megan's side only to stop short.

"What is *he* doing here?"

Megan, who tended to dress like the characters in the books she was reading, resembled a shepherd girl tonight. Leaning on her curved staff, she searched the room until she'd located the source of Nicole's ire. Quinn stood in front of the parlor fireplace conversing with Cole and Rachel Prescott. "Lucian invited him."

"Why?"

Wasn't putting up with his superior presence all day at the mercantile enough? Must she be forced to watch him attempt to charm his way into folks' good graces during her off hours, too?

Things had been strained between them since the confrontation. She couldn't dismiss the accusation in his eyes, the humiliation she'd endured while he'd checked the contents of her basket against the ledger input.

"Lucian thought it might be nice for people to get to know Quinn in a casual setting."

"How thoughtful."

At the sarcasm rolling off her tongue, Megan turned to study her. "Why does his presence bother you?"

"Haven't you heard the phrase familiarity breeds contempt? I'm with the man way too much as it is."

"Hmm." Speculation swirled in her sea-blue eyes. "I don't think I've seen you this flustered over a man before. You've always maintained your composure, no matter how handsome the guy and with no thought to the courage it took for him to approach you."

She thought of Kenneth's invitation to the harvest dance. Caught off guard by his sudden appearance in her barn, she'd refused his request without hesitation. Had she been too harsh? Would he still be angry and revengeful if she'd taken pains to let him down gently?

Nicole schooled her countenance. If she didn't squelch the matchmaking light in her sister's eyes, there'd be trouble of the most embarrassing kind. "I am not flustered. *Irritated* would be a better word. Quinn Darling irritates me. But I didn't come here to discuss my boss." Holding up the slim volumes she'd borrowed for Lillian, she nodded toward the wide entrance. "I'm finished with these. Mind if I borrow more?"

"I told you already, you may take as many as you'd like." Megan's cheeks flushed with peach-hued pleasure. "I can't get over your newfound love of books. We finally have something in common."

Nicole grimaced as guilt washed over her.

Megan saw it and, smile fading, clasped her hand.

"Nicole, is something besides Quinn bothering you? I've had the sense something has been troubling you for a while. You can confide in me, you know. I won't judge."

"Like you confide in me?" she retorted.

The only reason she knew about Megan's struggle to have a baby was because Rebecca had let it slip. Her own sister had confided in Caleb's wife rather than her. While the knowledge hurt, it didn't surprise her. Nicole wasn't close to any of her sisters.

Freeing her hand, she continued, "We don't have that kind of relationship. Never have. I'm the piece of the O'Malley puzzle that doesn't quite fit."

Megan's sigh was audible above the chatter in the well-appointed room. "You do fit, Nicole. In your own way, you do. You just refuse to see it. And for whatever reason, you refuse to let anyone close. You're the one who throws up obstacles in order to keep the rest of us at arm's length."

Her words sliced deep. Megan was right. She had intentionally created space between herself and her sisters. And even though Nicole acknowledged the truth, recognized her role in the current state of their sisterhood, lifetime habits weren't easily broken. "I'm exhausted. I'm going to return the books and head home."

"Nicole, wait—"

Ignoring the soft protest, she hastened to reach the hallway. The sooner she left Gatlinburg, the sooner she could start fresh in Knoxville. Cultivate better relationships in her new surroundings.

At the far end of the hall across from the stately dining room, the softly lit library was blessedly empty. Scents of leather and paper masked the room's musty hint. Bold maroon wallpaper contrasted nicely with the dark wood furniture and gleaming floors. While she wouldn't choose to read in here, it would be a nice place to curl up with her needles and fabrics.

Thoughts in turmoil, she traversed the narrow space between the red-striped camelback sofa and floor-to-ceiling shelves on the wall behind it, absently skimming her fingers over the spines. Hitting upon the empty slots where her latest picks belonged, she slid them in and began hunting for stories that would please both siblings.

She was perched near the top of the rolling ladder, scanning the upper shelves, when an accented voice from the doorway startled her.

"I did not figure you for a reader."

Upper body swaying dangerously, Nicole dropped the book in order to seize the ladder with both hands. She scowled at the dapper figure striding toward her. "How did you figure that? Was it something in my eyes? The way I speak, perhaps? Do I not sound intelligent to your Northern ears?"

Quinn scooped up the book and, stretching his left arm behind her legs, gripped the opposite ladder edge. His face was upturned, brown eyes fastened onto her face and a slight pucker in his brow. "I observe people. Call it a hobby, if you will." He lifted the book to her. "I guess I was wrong this time."

The press of his muscular arm against the back of her knees rendered them practically useless. Oh, why must physical contact with him cause these strange bodily reactions?

"Are you attempting to trap me up here?"

Sparks of mischief kindled in his eyes. "I was preventing you from falling. Wouldn't want you to break something and be unable to perform your assistant duties."

"I wouldn't be in danger of falling if you would keep your distance."

One black eyebrow arching at her, he removed his hand but remained where he stood. Nicole carefully made her way to the bottom and retreated to the single window on the opposite side of the room, occupying herself with the view of the sweeping side yard bathed in the pastel orange and pink swirls of sunset. *Go away, Quinn.*

He didn't take the hint. Following her, his lean body boxed her in, not invading her space but close enough for her to sense the heat coming off him, smell his spicy—and no doubt expensive—cologne. A cushiony chair blocked her escape.

"What do you want?" Sighing, she turned to face him, realizing too late her mistake. Inches separated them. She found herself fascinated by the ripple of hard muscle beneath the fine white cotton shirt, the strong, golden column of his throat above the charcoal coat collar, his carved chin that was at once charming and obnoxious.

He was wearing a serious my-dog-just-died expression. "You want the truth?"

Not really. "Um—"

"I followed you because I wanted to apologize for the way I acted the other evening. I overreacted, and I'm sorry. You've given me no reason not to trust you."

"Oh."

"I couldn't help but notice, too, that you seemed

upset while talking to your sister. I came to make sure you were all right."

Nicole found herself tongue-tied. Quinn was worried about her? The knowledge didn't irritate her as it should. In fact, his concern caused a sticky-sweet warmth to build up inside.

"I'm fine."

"Why don't I believe that?" He cocked his head to one side, his astute gaze laying bare her inner secrets. "I've had plenty of time to observe you in the company of your sisters, and there exists a barrier between you. I've noticed you tend to keep everyone at a distance. I wonder—"

"Stop." The warmth dried up, leaving her empty and wanting. Angry, too. "Stop acting as if you know everything there is to know about me, Quinn Darling. You've twice accused me of being a thief, and now you're analyzing my family relationships?" She poked his chest, and he blinked in surprise. "You think you're so high and mighty because you're a member of the prestigious Darling family, heir to a vast fortune and lifelong resident of the great city of Boston. You think that because we talk slower and live in log cabins and wear calico and overalls that we're dull, illiterate provincials. Let me tell you something—your Harvard diploma doesn't give you the right to come here and judge us when it's clear you know nothing."

Pushing past him, she left the house without saying goodbye to Megan and without the books she'd promised Lillian. If she didn't get far away, she would be tempted to strangle her boss. The foreign notion evoked a bubble of hysterical laughter.

Admit it, a voice prodded, *you're angry because*

he echoed Megan's assertions. You're upset that he can see the truth about you. You're worried that, like everyone else in this town, he'll look too closely and find you lacking.

Quinn hadn't been able to get their exchange—and Nicole's obvious distress—out of his head. He'd tossed and turned all night, plagued not only by worries about how to secure the townspeople's confidence, but about her, as well.

Despite her air of competency, Quinn's perceptive nature had homed in on the vulnerability she worked valiantly to mask. His standoffish assistant had stirred his protective instincts to life, and he couldn't think of anyone who'd welcome his protection less.

A few feet below where Quinn stood on the river-bank, Caleb locked the springhouse door and maneuvered the steep incline with ease. Whipping off his worn Stetson to run a gloved hand through his black hair, he rested against the wagon bed. "That's the last of it. I'll have another delivery early next week."

Quinn pocketed the key Caleb held out to him. "We may need more cheese. It's popular with my customers, and Mrs. Greene has need of it for her café menu."

"We can provide whatever you need." Glancing in the direction of the bridge spanning the river, Caleb straightened. "Here comes my cousin."

Quinn squinted in the early-morning sunshine streaming through the leaves overhead. From this distance, he couldn't make out her expression. Her bright apricot skirts swished with each long stride, the nipped-in bodice and capped sleeves showing off her lithe figure. As she came nearer, he noticed her hair had been wrestled into a more severe hairstyle than usual, a tight, long twist nestled between her shoulder blades, not one lock out of place. What she couldn't know was the style showcased her most impressive feature—those unusual-hued eyes that appeared to glow with lavender light.

"Morning, Nicki," Caleb drawled with a wicked grin.

"Caleb." She flicked her cousin a narrowed glance before addressing Quinn. "May I have a word with you?"

Her resigned expression filled him with unease. Was she about to quit her position? His insincere challenge the other evening had slipped out, fueled by annoyance. He valued her work and would miss her competence and dedication when she left. "Certainly."

Placing a hand at the small of her back, he guided her farther down the grassy bank. A groundhog scuttled away, seeking refuge near the deep green water's edge, but he gave it only a cursory glance. "What's on your mind?"

Fingers plucking at the pleats on her skirt, she shifted away from his touch to stand facing him. Her chin went up. "It's my turn to apologize. You're my boss, and I shouldn't have spoken to you the way I did last night."

The tension left his shoulders. "It is true that I'm your boss part of the time. However, when we aren't at the mercantile, we are…" He rummaged through his brain for an appropriate label.

"Acquaintances."

Quinn frowned. That wasn't quite what he'd been going for. "Whatever we agree to call our relationship, you and I are on equal footing. It won't be easy at first, but we will find a way to navigate our interactions."

While her violet gaze was unflinching, he caught a flicker of something akin to trepidation. "I still have a job, then?"

"Yes, of course." He huffed a light laugh. "Nicole, I value honesty. I want you to be frank with me. I can handle whatever you feel the need to say."

Her thick lashes swept down to skim her cheeks. Boot toeing a cluster of dandelions, she nodded.

Behind him, Quinn heard the restless shuffling of Caleb's team. He half turned. "I think your cousin is ready to leave."

"I'll go on in and open up."

Sweeping past him, her sweet-as-a-rose scent enveloped him, and he watched her nimbly ascend the stairs, spine straight and shoulders set, posture fit for a queen. He never would've expected her to apologize, especially to him. One thing was certain—she prized this job and the income that would allow her to one day leave Gatlinburg.

He strode over to Caleb, ignoring his obvious amusement. "Help me out, O'Malley. Share your insight on how to best navigate daily interactions with your cousin."

He tilted his head back and laughed outright. "Not a chance, my friend. No one gave me a clue how to handle Becca, yet we managed to figure each other out just fine."

"You misunderstand." He held up his palms, "I'm not asking in a romantic capacity. Not at all. My interest is strictly professional."

Better watch it, Darling—wouldn't want to get struck by lightning.

"Whatever you say." Still chuckling, Caleb hauled himself onto the wagon seat and looped the reins in one hand. "I could give you some pointers, but I wouldn't wanna rob you of the fun of figuring her out on your own. If you can. Truth is, I haven't had that much luck."

With a final wave, he released the brake and set the wagon in motion.

"Fun?" he muttered to himself. "You and I have different ideas of fun, my friend."

Climbing the staircase, he left the cheerful birdsong and increasingly familiar hum and splash of the river behind in favor of the cooler, fragrant interior. Heading down the hallway and going straight for the jars of penny candy, his steps slowed as he attempted to make sense of the sight before him. Along the lengthy interior wall, where the ready-made clothing was displayed, Kenneth, Timothy and Pete surrounded Nicole.

Were they deliberately boxing her in?

One hand resting on the first jar's lid, he studied her face. While her eyes were defiant, her lower lip trembled. And her back was pressed against the shelving unit behind her.

Not acceptable.

Reminding himself to keep calm and not jump to conclusions, Quinn skirted the counter.

"Where's your broom, little witch?" Kenneth, whose back was to Quinn, taunted. The other two snickered.

"Was that your black cat I saw on the street?" Still unaware of Quinn's presence, Timothy elbowed his cohort.

Nicole's jaw went taut. "If you aren't here to do business, I suggest you leave. I have more important things to do than entertain you."

"I can think of a few ways you could entertain me."

When Quinn heard the silky innuendo in Kenneth's voice, his blood began to simmer. "May I assist you, gentlemen?"

The two who could see him stiffened, shrugging and shuffling their feet. Kenneth pivoted. "We're just perusing the goods, Mr. Darling. Seeing what might be of interest to us."

Tempted to wipe that smirk off his face, Quinn's fingers closed into fists. "Well, Mr. Jones, you and your friends are preventing my assistant from doing her job."

Placing his hat over his heart, Kenneth dipped his head in a mock bow. "My apologies, sir."

"Let's go, Kenny."

While the other two made for the exit, Kenneth nodded and turned as if to leave, at the last second shoving his face close to Nicole's and whispering something in her ear. Quinn was on the verge of physically removing him when he skirted away, deliberately toppling a stack of shirts onto the floor once he reached the end of the aisle.

"Oops," he said, and grinned over his shoulder.

Face averted, Nicole moved to straighten the mess. Quinn stopped her with a hand on her forearm. "Leave it. I'll take care of it."

Striding after the trio, he heard her call out. "Quinn, wait. What are you going to do?"

Out on the boardwalk, he closed the door firmly behind him, calling out for them to stop. They hadn't gotten far. Across the street, passersby looked their way.

"I will not allow my employee to be mistreated in

any way. If you bother Miss O'Malley again, you and your family members will be barred from this establishment." He met each man's eyes squarely. "It would be awfully inconvenient for you to have to travel to Pigeon Forge for your supplies."

"We understand, Mr. Darling." Timothy looked properly chastised, as did Pete. Kenneth, however, wasn't cowed in the slightest. Hooking a hand on Timothy's arm, he towed him away, Pete trailing behind.

Quinn rejoined Nicole inside, hurrying to help her shake out and refold the shirts. "I told you to wait."

She shot him a heated glance. "I can take care of myself, you know."

"I am well aware," he said drily, recalling her full-on assault that first night. Their fingers collided as they both situated a shirt on the stack. "This is my store, however, and I will not stand by and watch you or any of my patrons be treated in that manner."

"While I appreciate your efforts, I doubt it will have any effect."

Covering her hand with his, Quinn stalled her movements. "What did he say to you, Nicole?"

"Something stupid and not worth repeating."

He couldn't help but think about Tilly, his fifteen-year-old sister, and what he'd do if she was in Nicole's position. *Throttle the culprits, that's what.*

Her skin was like ice. Taking her hand in both of his, he tried to transfer his warmth to her. Her head was bent, so he couldn't tell if the contact bothered her.

"You denied there being a problem. Why?"

"He's angry, that's all." She shrugged as if it was no big deal. "I should've just gone to the stupid dance."

Light glinted in her confined locks. "Let me get this

straight. Kenneth is acting like a beast because you didn't agree to attend a dance with him?"

"I'm afraid I've dented his pride."

Beneath the unblemished skin, the bones of her hand were fragile. He released it in order to warm the other. He liked being connected to her, liked that she hadn't pulled away. Perhaps his nearness didn't bother her as much as he'd thought.

"That's not an excuse. He has no right to treat you like that…" The image of shattered china shoved to the forefront of his mind. Gently, he slid his fingers beneath her chin and lifted her face. "He caused you to drop the dishes, didn't he?"

Swallowing hard, she moved her head a fraction of an inch.

"I'm an idiot." Releasing her before he did something rash, like kissing that dainty mouth of hers, he helped her to her feet. "I'm sorry, Duchess. I should've suspected."

"You couldn't have known."

"You're not clumsy or careless. I know that."

She touched his sleeve. "Thank you."

"For what?"

"Sticking up for me."

"Even though you didn't require my help?"

She smiled at him, a genuine smile that transformed her face into something so beautiful and hopeful he didn't dare blink for fear he'd miss it. "I'll let it pass this time."

He knew then that, no matter how loudly and frequently she protested, he'd always rush to lend her aid.

Chapter Eight

Nicole withheld a sigh as Mr. Craig perused the newest selection of hair tonics beneath the glass. He wasn't one to rush the decision. While he hadn't yet found a cure for his baldness, he continued to test the latest concoctions.

Her gaze strayed once more to her boss, whose sinewy, suit-clad body was propped against the counter, arms folded across his chest as he conversed with Reverend Monroe. Late-afternoon light glinted off his dark hair, slicked away from his face in a dashing style. How he managed to appear neat and unruffled no matter how many customers came in or how stuffy the place got she couldn't fathom.

Snatches of their conversation drifted over. When the reverend asked how Quinn was settling in, she was surprised to hear him admit he wasn't having much luck with the locals and that he felt like an outsider. Considering his status in Boston, his troubles here must be particularly difficult to cope with.

"Give it some time," the reverend urged, craggy features sympathetic. "They miss Emmett. He was their confidant, advisor and friend."

Quinn nodded. His attention slipped to her and, embarrassed to be caught staring, she ripped her gaze from his worried one.

"I believe I've made up my mind." Mr. Craig smiled, revealing stained teeth. "I'll take the Imperial Hair Tonic." He pointed to the tall bottle in the middle.

"I'll wrap it up for you."

Ripping off a square of brown paper, she unlocked the case and lifted out the bottle. Quinn strolled up as she was handing the parcel across the counter.

"Appreciate your business, Mr. Craig." Quinn's smile was forced.

Closing the case, she said, "What was the notice Reverend Monroe dropped off?"

He pinched the bridge of his nose, leading her to wonder if he had a headache. "A reminder about the Independence Day picnic."

The calendar displayed on the wall showed the July Fourth holiday fell on a Tuesday. "Are you going?"

The foursome playing cards in the corner burst out laughing at some private joke. Quinn glanced over his shoulder at them, shaking his head as if he couldn't figure out why he was allowing them to waste space in his store. He wasn't thrilled to have them back, but Nicole thought he'd done the right thing. Pushing off from the counter, he came around and, passing her, retrieved a horehound candy from a jar.

She couldn't stop thinking about how his hands had warmed hers.

"I suppose I will."

At his marked lack of enthusiasm, she tried to see

things from his perspective. He'd left his home and family, with whom he'd apparently shared a close bond, and he was completely alone in an unfamiliar place where not everyone was happy he'd come. She recalled how, without the slightest hesitation, he'd defended her against Kenneth last weekend.

Dropping the case key in her apron pocket, she said, "Why don't you come with me? There will be food. Games. Music. It's a nice change from the routine."

He hesitated before popping the treat in his mouth, brow creasing as he considered. "I'd like that…if you're certain you wouldn't mind spending your day off with me."

An image of prior town-wide celebrations popped into her head, of enamored couples sharing picnics beneath the shade trees and strolling arm in arm. She shook off the unsettling image of her and Quinn engaging in such behavior. They shared a professional relationship. Nothing more.

Unlike other girls her age, she didn't pine for a clinging beau, didn't dream about marriage proposals. Romance was the furthest thing from her mind. So the fact that she'd contemplated—even for a second—such behavior with her boss bothered her no small amount.

"I'm certain."

He followed her into the office, bracing an arm on the door frame. Nicole didn't particularly like sharing this confined space with him because his presence made her twitchy. She became acutely aware of commonplace events—the pull of air into his lungs and subsequent exhale, the way his throat worked with each swallow, the movement of his lips as he spoke.

"Will your sisters be there?"

"You're a bit too old for them, don't you think? Jessica and Jane are only sixteen."

His brows shot up. Dropping his arm, he edged closer and propped his hip on the desk. A baffled smile mocked her. "While the twins are loveliness personified, I had not planned on offering for either of them. It was an innocent question."

Cheeks burning, she feigned interest in one of the many ledgers laid out on the desk, absently skimming the nearest one. He thought they were lovely, did he? Of course he did. *Please tell me you're not jealous,* an inner voice pleaded. *Quinn Darling can woo whomever he pleases.*

"I know I'm risking getting raked over the coals again for putting my nose where it doesn't belong," he said quietly, "but it's obvious there is tension between you and your sisters. I cannot help but wonder why."

If there had been any hint of lightheartedness in his manner, she would've refused to answer. But he was serious…even concerned. "How would you like it if you were constantly compared to your siblings? If your entire life, you'd been judged and pegged as the odd one in your family?"

A frown cut a groove in his cheek. "Why would you think that about yourself?"

Worrying the edge of her sleeve, Nicole hesitated. Baring her soul to him was a bad idea. The worst. "You wouldn't understand."

"You think I haven't had my share of problems?" he said softly.

"You're the Darling heir. Don't tell me Boston's elite didn't worship the ground you walked on."

A dry half laugh escaped him. "Solely because of

the fortune attached to my last name. My winning personality and natural charm wouldn't have gotten me
very far if my last name had been Smith or Jones and
I'd worked on the docks."

The glimpse of uncertainty in him stunned Nicole.
Where was her suave, confident, infuriatingly-sure-
of-himself boss? "I imagine it would be difficult to
wonder if every person in my life was there because
of me or because of the benefits of being my friend."

"You have no idea."

Shadows passed across his face, shadows she felt
certain not many people were allowed to see. She'd
misjudged him, had taken one look at his well-tai-
lored clothes, slick appearance and cool confidence
and assumed he'd led a privileged, problem-free life.
But money and status didn't solve the world's problems, did they?

She took a steadying breath. "When I was a kid,
my cousins and sisters were my only friends. I didn't
think it strange until around age eight. I noticed Juliana, Megan and the twins had friends who weren't
family members, boys and girls who *chose* to spend
time with them. I wondered why I didn't. Then Kenneth and his buddies started a wild rumor that I was
a witch's offspring and had been left on my parents'
porch as a baby." Grimacing, she fingered a rogue curl,
stretching the strand and releasing it to spring back
into place. "Since I didn't look anything like my other
sisters, the school kids latched on to it."

"That's ridiculous." He seemed transfixed by her
hair, as if he really wanted to test its texture.

Mouth dry, she moistened her lips. "I tried to be
more like my sisters but eventually concluded it was a

waste of time. I would never measure up. So I stopped trying to please others. Told myself their opinions didn't matter." At his sad expression, she hastened to add, "I don't mind being alone. I have plenty to keep me busy."

Liar, she told herself. *You want what Megan and Juliana have, what the twins share. You crave connection. Closeness. A sense of belonging.*

"Those people don't know what they're missing." Quinn's expression turned thoughtful. "You have a lot to offer, Nicole. I'm positive that if you were to let down your guard, people would respond to you. You're bright and creative. Considerate. Hardworking and driven. You are as worthy of friendship as your sisters."

Nicole floundered for an appropriate response. His gentle praise inspired pleasure and embarrassment in equal amounts. "Sounds like you had those qualities memorized."

"It's a quirk of mine," he said, and smiled sheepishly. "When I meet new people, I make lists about them in my head."

"Lists."

"Strengths and faults."

"I don't want to know the faults you've observed in me during our brief acquaintance."

"Attacking unsuspecting men tops the list."

Refusing to let him see her mortification, she smirked. "You can't place the blame for that entirely at my feet."

The rear entrance bell sounded, cutting off his response. He fished out his pocket watch. "Five thirty.

Awfully late for a delivery." He paused in the doorway. "We will continue this conversation later."

She nodded, grateful for the interruption. Now that Quinn was privy to her private struggles, she felt exposed and vulnerable. It was not a comfortable feeling.

The delivery was a large one. The driver had left the larger town of Maryville later than expected. Even with his help, unloading and sorting everything would take several hours. Quinn immediately cleared out the card players, closing the store several minutes early and paid a young boy to take a message to Nicole's mother letting her know she'd be late and he would see her home. He'd promised to treat her to supper at Plum's when they'd finished. Nicole wasn't sure she wished to dine alone with him, however. He couldn't know how an outing like that could be misconstrued. At least at the Independence Day picnic, they'd be surrounded by her family.

It was nearing eight o'clock when she and Quinn put the last of the perishables in the springhouse. Her arms and upper back muscles ached, as did her feet, and hunger gnawed at her. The ham, bread and palm-size portion of strawberries she'd had for lunch seemed very long ago.

Unable to stand to his full height in the small, squat building, Quinn hung a slab of dried beef from the low-slung rafters. "That's the last of it. Are you ready to head over to the café?"

Nicole shoved the last crock into the corner. Hunger drove her answer. "More than ready."

"I hope chicken and dumplings is on the menu," he said, and grinned.

She'd never stopped to think what he did for meals.

No doubt in Boston, he'd had all his meals served to him. "You don't know how to cook, do you?"

"I can manage decent coffee."

Careful not to bump into the ham hanging nearby, she straightened. "Did your family employ a French chef to prepare extravagant meals?"

His low chuckle rippled over her skin, raising goose bumps that had nothing to do with the river-water-cooled air. "Justin is from South Carolina, actually. But yes, he and his assistants do prepare mouthwatering meals for us."

"I suppose you lived in a grand mansion."

"Exceedingly grand." He didn't bother denying it. "Spacious, tastefully appointed rooms, priceless art, vast gardens with pathways and fountains." Cocking his head, he brought his brows together. "You would have no trouble fitting in there."

"Because I don't fit here?"

"You don't seem to *want* to fit here."

"You're right. I don't…hence the plans to leave." Done with the conversation, Nicole gestured to the door. Outside, the sun had dipped beneath the mountain peaks and the gathering shadows made it difficult to see. "I'm going to faint soon if I don't get something to eat."

"Let's get you fed, then."

As he maneuvered a turn in the cramped space overflowing with crocks of milk and sausages, jarred vegetables and fruits and dried meat, the door slammed shut with a bang, enclosing them in darkness. Shocked, neither reacted as the sound of the lock clicking into place and muted male laughter drifted to them.

"Nicole—" Quinn sounded strange "—what just happened?"

"I think…" Battling growing alarm, she blinked to adjust her vision. "Someone's played a dirty trick on us."

Desperation fired through her. She tried to shove past him, forgetting about the narrow opening running smack-dab in the middle of the puncheon floor, rigged to allow the constantly flowing river beneath to cool the interior. Gasping, she threw out her arms to try to regain her balance as icy-cold water seeped into her boots and drenched the bottom of her skirts and undergarments.

Quinn's hands closed over her waist, steadying her. He helped her up. In the darkness, she watched his shadowed outline crouch down, and suddenly his fingers were probing her ankles through the leather boots before skimming up to her calves.

"Are you hurt?"

"No." The gentle touch heated her chilled, wet skin, and the thread of concern lacing his husky voice warmed her insides. "You can stop now, Quinn. I'm fine."

Sighing, he slowly stood.

"We're stuck in here, aren't we?"

"Until someone misses us, yes."

Quinn went and pushed against the door. It didn't budge. The walls were made of river rock, which meant yelling for help wasn't likely to do them much good. "Your mother will worry when you don't return home. She'll send someone to search for us."

How long would it take for someone to find them? What if it took until morning?

Another shudder rippled through her. She refused to consider the potential for disaster.

"Are pranks such as these commonplace?"

"Commonplace, no. But they aren't unheard-of. Sometimes boys get bored."

His eyes gleamed in the darkness. "Is that who you believe the culprits are? Kids looking for a thrill?"

She bent to wring the excess water from her skirts. "I think there's a good chance it was Kenneth. He doesn't take confrontation lightly. Whatever you said to them might've set him on the idea of retaliation."

"Caleb and his brothers strike me as overprotective types. They haven't defended you against them?"

A dry laugh escaped. "Kenneth knows better than to bother me when my cousins are around."

Pushing off the door, Quinn edged nearer. "Why did you not tell them?"

"Like I said, I can handle whatever he dishes out."

While he didn't answer, she sensed he wasn't thrilled with her response. He slowly surveyed their surroundings. "I remember seeing a lamp over here." She heard glass clinking as he gingerly explored the springhouse's single shelf. He rummaged around until he found a match. The flame cast his face in eerie shadow. When the lamp was lit, he began to search the space.

"What are you looking for?"

"Supper."

Nicole couldn't summon the energy to help him. Weakness had invaded her body, her wet clothing sticking to her skin and making the temperature feel colder than it actually was. Of course, the ice blocks packed in straw lining the rear wall kept the air cool. Quinn whipped out his pocketknife and, kneeling at the floor opening, rinsed it in the river water. Then he located several cheese wheels and carved out wedges for them both. Next, he attacked a ham in the far corner.

Coming over to her, his lips compressed as he studied her face. "You should sit down."

All too happy to do as he suggested, she grimaced as the rock wall she leaned against leached more coldness into her back. While Nicole ate, Quinn dipped out milk into a tin cup he'd discovered on the shelf.

Lowering himself onto the space beside her, he held the cup out and nodded at the humble snack in her lap. "I know it doesn't compare to the café food, but it will hold us until we're rescued."

She took a generous sip of milk. "It's fine. My cooking skills leave much to be desired," she admitted. "When I'm on my own for meals, this is similar to what I'd fix for myself. Needlework is the only thing I excel at."

She tried not to fidget as he studied her outfit with a critical eye. Since free floor space was limited, he sat close enough that their shoulders pressed together.

"You are an excellent seamstress. Tilly would be thrilled to wear your creations."

She found that difficult to believe. His sister had access to the finest clothing money could buy. Unable to contain her curiosity, she said, "What is she like? And your brother. What's his name?"

Balancing his forearms on his bent knees, he rested his head against the wall and smiled fondly. "Tilly is a spirited, good-natured princess. She's a whiz at the piano and harp, and she loves horses. Oh, and she has my father wrapped around her little finger. Trevor is eighteen. Athletic. Popular. And keen on proving himself to the world...my father most of all."

"So he's like you."

Swallowing a bite of ham, he chuckled. "Yes, I suppose he is."

"It must be hard on him," she mused, thinking of her own older sisters, "to live in your shadow."

"Trevor and I have a good relationship. He's his own person."

Nicole wondered if that was truly the case or if, like her, his brother kept his true feelings hidden. "You must miss them."

"More than I could've imagined." He sighed. "As soon as I purchase some land and have a house built, I'll invite them for an extended visit. The banker told me about some available property behind the church. I'm going to look at it tomorrow."

"Are you absolutely certain this is where you want to settle? Once the novelty wears off, you might regret leaving Boston."

"This is my dream, Nicole. Like you have a dream, remember?" He nudged her shoulder with his own. "Like me, you'll leave your family behind to start fresh somewhere else. You'll be in a new place, surrounded by strangers and confronted with obstacles you didn't anticipate and aren't prepared for, but because it's your dream, you won't allow those things to distract you from your goal."

"You're right. I won't." Taking a final sip, she handed him the cup. "I have another theory about who could be behind this prank."

"Tell me."

"Not everyone is happy with the new ownership. It could be someone trying to send you a message."

He slowly nodded. "And, unfortunately, you got caught in the cross fire."

Chapter Nine

"Would you smack me if I put my arm around you?"

Nicole looked at him aghast. "Why would you want to do that?"

Quinn had held off asking as long as he could. "Because you haven't stopped shivering since your dunking. I can practically hear your teeth clicking together."

To him, the springhouse was cool, the constant flow of water pulsing moist air through the space. Because of her wet stockings and skirts, the temperature had to feel lower to her.

When she didn't respond for long moments, he tacked on, "If I hadn't left my suit jacket inside, I would offer you that."

"I, uh, suppose it couldn't hurt."

He couldn't help laughing. "Duchess, you do wonders for a man's self-esteem."

Lifting his arm, he settled it around her slender shoulders and tucked her against his side. A wave of protectiveness washed over him, catching him unawares.

"Let's not forget I am your employee." She remained

stiff, unyielding, as if his nearness was distasteful. "Pet names are not appropriate."

"I am not likely to forget," he intoned. "Just for fun, what pet name would you give me? Honey? Sugar? Lemon drop?"

"You are impossible."

"So I've been told."

Below her short sleeve, her exposed arm had become chilled. Bringing up his free hand, he lightly rubbed the skin. With a deep shudder, Nicole finally relaxed into him, seeking out and taking advantage of his heat. It felt an awful lot like a victory of some sort...her trusting him.

Now that she was completely within the circle of his arms, Quinn fought a sensation of light-headedness. To ground himself, he focused on the way her silken curls tickled his cheek. Her refreshing floral scent. The contrast of her soft curves to his hard strength. Nicole may exude a frosty exterior, but she didn't feel invincible or untouchable. Maybe it was the memory of her stilted revelation, the childhood pain that had pursued her into adulthood endowing him with this insight.

The longer he held her, the longer he wanted to hold her. His hand growing tired, he settled it atop hers on her lap.

She stiffened. Quinn immediately removed his hand. "Sorry. I didn't mean to make you uncomfortable."

"If they try and force us to marry—"

"Whoa. What?" Pulling away from her, he squinted in the dim light. "Enlighten me as to what you are referring."

"I guess you haven't heard about Caleb and Rebecca's reasons for marrying," she huffed. "Didn't I warn you small-town life isn't rosy-hued perfection?"

"Caleb and Rebecca adore each other."

"It wasn't always that way. They would never have married if she hadn't spent a week nursing him to health with no one but her thirteen-year-old sister for company. Because they were unchaperoned, the town leaders pressured them to marry. To restore their reputations."

Quinn heard the disgust in her voice. "Why would anyone try and force us?"

"If we're stuck here the entire night alone, people will assume the worst."

Reaching up, he massaged his throbbing temples. Questions about his moral character was the last thing he needed. "Unfortunately, this sort of thing doesn't only happen in small towns. I've heard about a couple of instances back home where determined debutantes tricked eligible bachelors into similar situations."

With a shiver, she crossed her arms over her middle. "I don't care what anyone says, I'm not marrying you or anyone else. Nothing is going to stop me from achieving my dream."

Given her sister's intimation that she'd delayed the move to Knoxville, the vehemence of her words surprised him. "If that's the case, why didn't you leave months ago?"

She sucked in a startled breath.

"Are you sure this desperation to leave isn't a simple case of you running from your family?" he prompted. "Your reputation?"

Expression turning frigid, she scooted as far away from him as possible. "My reasons are really none of your business, Quinn. You forget that we're boss and employee. Nothing more."

Shifting around so that he was presented with her back, she hugged her knees to her chest and rested her head atop them.

Quinn buried his fingers in his hair, aware that his assistant was one of the few people on earth with the ability to upset his natural equanimity. The woman was not only unpredictable but as prickly as a porcupine. Any man fool enough to pursue her would wind up with scars to show for his efforts.

I won't have to put up with her insolent attitude forever. It's not that Nicole isn't replaceable. I'll find a suitable candidate to take her spot. Preferably male. Less drama.

As the minutes ticked by, the silence became increasingly awkward. Nicole hadn't made a peep, and he wondered if she was dozing.

When his stomach growled an hour later, he got up to stretch his legs and pound on the door again. The paltry snack hadn't appeased his appetite, and he couldn't stop daydreaming about Mrs. Greene's dumplings. The cold was starting to become bothersome, too. Fortunately for them, it wasn't wintertime. They really would've had a problem on their hands then.

His fist began to sting from the constant pounding.

"You're wasting your time." Nicole's somber voice reached him over the sound of rushing water. "No one can hear you."

Quinn rested his forehead against the door, defeat a sour taste in his mouth. May as well accept they'd be spending the night here. If word got out, his hopes of ever gaining the townspeople's trust and respect would be dashed. Especially if they didn't fulfill expectations and marry.

Even with his back to her, he heard her shivering. A sigh built in his chest.

He pivoted to address the huddled form. "Look, I know you detest me, but I think for both our sakes you should let me hold you again."

Half twisting, Nicole contemplated him with a shocked expression. She visibly swallowed. Reluctantly nodded. Moved to lean against the wall.

Tamping down rogue anticipation, he eased down beside her and gingerly looped his arm around her shoulders once again. She was colder than before. Would this prank end with her falling prey to illness?

When she wrapped both arms about his waist and snuggled into his side, Quinn's heart thumped out a dire warning. *Sure, I'm lonely, but I can't let her touch go to my head.*

She lifted her face to lock gazes with him, and he fought the impulse to toy with her curls.

"You're wrong, you know."

Quinn's brows lifted. "About?"

"I don't detest you."

Laughter erupted. She never failed to surprise him. "Glad to hear it, Duchess. Glad to hear it."

Nicole sighed contentedly and snuggled closer to the warm chest cradling her. What a delicious dream she was having. Self-indulgent and lovely, too lovely to be real. Subconsciously she recognized she shouldn't be enjoying her boss's embrace.

Quinn. The springhouse.

Struggling to lift her heavy, gritty lids, the sensation of floating through the air startled her. She flailed out an arm. When she didn't encounter the stone wall, she panicked.

Quinn's hold tightened. "It's all right. I've got you."

At last her vision cleared, and she blinked up at twinkling, diamond-bright stars in the black sky above. "How did we get out? Wh-why are you carrying me?"

He flicked her a glance, long strides evening out as they topped the riverbank. "You might want to keep your voice down," he murmured. "Unless you want someone to discover we spent half the night together."

"I won't let that happen," a second male voice inserted.

Despite the fog of sleep yet lingering, she knew the owner without having to see his face.

"Caleb? What are you doing here?"

He kept pace with Quinn, and even from this angle she could see the controlled anger in his features.

"When you didn't show, Aunt Alice sent the twins to our place. I came searching for you."

"How did you know where to find us?"

"I've been looking for several hours. The springhouse was my last resort."

Caleb's team entered her line of sight. Without a word, Quinn placed her gently on the wagon bed. The instant he released her, she missed the reassurance of his all-encompassing heat, and it was on the tip of her tongue to call him back.

Her cousin must've handed Quinn a blanket, because he was wrapping it around her, his manner attentive and concerned as if she were a child in need of coddling. She didn't challenge him, however. She was limp with fatigue and cold. And very, very self-conscious.

Caleb left them to take his place on the wagon seat.

When Quinn had finished, he surveyed his work, lines of worry about his eyes. "Are you warm enough?"

"How long was I asleep?" *Did I drool on your shirt? Snore?*

"Several hours."

She shuddered. It must've been torture for him, required to hold her for that length of time. "I didn't realize…"

"Hey." Carefully, he brushed the curls from her temple. "It wasn't a hardship, okay? No reason to fret. I nodded off a time or two myself."

Nicole stared up at him. There were no words to express her emotions. While she was grateful for his attentiveness, this was the first time she'd been that close to a man. Not only in the physical sense. She'd revealed private things, things she hadn't shared with anyone else. Ever. The experience was so far removed from her reality she was having trouble processing it.

"Time to go," Caleb said over his shoulder. "We can hash this out tomorrow."

Quinn lightly tapped her chin, a trace of a smile gracing his drawn features. "Get some rest, Duchess."

As Caleb guided the team in the opposite direction, she couldn't tear her gaze from Quinn's unmoving form there in the middle of the lane. Something foreign was taking root in her heart, something an awful lot like affection.

She could not allow it to grow, to flourish. When she left Gatlinburg, she would be taking her whole heart with her.

Chapter Ten

Three cups of coffee and his eyes still burned from fatigue. Quinn hadn't slept once he'd climbed wearily to his quarters. He'd lain in his lumpy bed, listening as raindrops pattered against the shingles, his mind full of the night's events.

He wouldn't soon forget how it had felt to cradle a sleeping Nicole in his arms. While he'd told her the truth—he had dozed off and on—much of the time he'd simply reveled in her warmth and softness, fascinated by the serene arrangement of her features. She'd looked younger…untouched by life's troubles.

It had taken all of his self-control and quite a bit of prayer to rein in the drive to kiss her awake. Maintaining his honor had been difficult. Nicole's storybook beauty impacted him. Didn't matter if she was asleep or wide-awake and on the verge of strangling him. But she wasn't interested in romance, or in staying, and giving in to shallow attraction would only complicate matters.

It's not all about her outward appearance, though,

is it? I like her sharp mind, her dedication and commitment, her strength.

So she had admirable qualities. That didn't make pursuing her a wise choice. Besides, he couldn't shake the feeling she was hiding something.

"Quinn?" A hand passed in front of his face. "Anyone home?"

"Caleb." Straightening from the notched-log wall beside the mercantile entrance, he grimaced. "A little lost sleep didn't used to bother me."

Black Stetson pulled low over his eyes, the other man surveyed the handful of people hurrying up and down the boardwalk. "Josh warned me to get as much as I can before the baby's born."

Quinn noted the trace of anxiety underlining the wry humor in his voice. "How many more months?"

"Four. Doc thinks the baby will make an appearance in October or early November."

He started in the direction of the jail, and Quinn fell into step beside him. "You must be over the moon."

"I am. Can't help being apprehensive, though. Any number of things could go wrong." Dodging a low-flying wasp, Caleb shot him a sharp glance. "Don't tell Becca I said that."

He held up his hands. "I wouldn't dream of it. She's probably anxious, too, this being her first."

"I'm trying to leave it in the Lord's hands. Trust Him to keep them safe."

"But it's not easy," Quinn supplied, knowing how hard it was not to worry about the store and whether or not he might fail.

Looking out for approaching wagons, Caleb nodded before stepping into the street. "Exactly."

He asked something he'd forgotten to last night. "How did you know to look in the springhouse? The lock was on the door."

"My aunt mentioned there'd been a delivery." His mouth flattened. "That and the fact I couldn't find you anywhere else. Nicki isn't one to explore the forest or hike the side of a mountain, so I suspected you were close by."

At the door to the jail, Quinn stopped him with a lifted hand. "I want you to know I respect Nicole. I didn't do anything that would cast doubt upon her virtue."

"Let's hope this stays out of the gossip mill. While I thank God Becca and I wound up together, I wouldn't wish a forced marriage on anyone." Gripping the door handle, Caleb waved a greeting at a passing rider. "Especially you two. My cousin is dead set on life in the big city. She'd be miserable and make you miserable in the process."

Entering the jail, Quinn digested the words, glad he'd come to the right conclusion. He could work with Nicole, be her friend, but nothing else.

Shane was at his desk, as usual, gold star winking where it was pinned to his vest. A large mug of coffee occupied his hands atop a stack of wanted signs.

"Morning, gentlemen."

Quinn sat in the lone chair while Caleb dragged another from the corner.

"I heard you had an interesting night," Shane said.

Quinn scowled. "Interesting doesn't really begin to cover it."

One corner of his mouth lifted. "You have a theory about who was behind it?"

"I do."

Sprawling in the chair, Caleb rested his hat on his chest. "Let's hear it."

Quinn hadn't wanted to share in front of Nicole last night. Her cousin was going to be irate when he found out she'd kept Kenneth's behavior from him, and she hadn't been up to a verbal barrage after what she'd been through.

"Did she mention Kenneth Jones invited her to a harvest social last fall?"

Caleb's eyes narrowed dangerously. "No. Why?"

"Apparently he hasn't yet gotten past the fact she spurned his request."

"Talk, Darling."

Quinn outlined Kenneth's behavior, including the incident with the plates. He ended with the warning he'd issued to all three young men.

Caleb got up to pace, fury hovering about his prowling form. "Nicki should've told me. I would've put a stop to it."

"She's an independent woman," Quinn said.

"Too independent, if you ask me," he retorted.

The sheriff scraped his fingertips across the bristles on his jaws, expression thoughtful. "That's quite a warning, Quinn. Are you sure you're willing to follow through?"

"While I understand how such actions might impact my position here, I refuse to stand by and let them harass her."

Caleb slammed his hat on his head and strode for the door.

Shane shot to his feet. "Where are you going?"

"To confront that idiot—where else?"

Quinn stood, as well, gaze bouncing between the two men. "To tell the truth, I wouldn't mind riding along."

"Not a good idea," Shane said, skirting the desk and joining Caleb at the door. "If you go over there itching for a fight, he's only going to deny having anything to do with last night. Give me time to gather evidence."

"He's bullying Nicki," Caleb gritted out, muscle ticking in his cheek.

"I know. I don't like it, either. But we have to keep this thing quiet. I haven't forgotten that awful visit to Rebecca's cabin and you laid up with a bullet hole in your leg."

Caleb's dark gaze locked with Quinn's, even though he was addressing the lawman. "It wasn't you pressuring us to marry. It was the reverend and Doc."

Bullet wound? He made a mental note to ask Caleb for details later.

"You don't want that for Quinn and Nicole," Shane said. "And that means getting a handle on your anger. Allow me to do my job."

A sigh gusted out of Caleb. "Do it fast."

Snagging his hat from the coatrack, Shane reached around him to grab the door handle. "I'm going over there right now. Join me." Over his shoulder, he said, "You too, Quinn. The more eyes, the better."

"Mornin', Miss Nicole. You look as fresh as a summer flower."

Passing the rear entrance to the barbershop, she mustered up what she hoped was a convincing smile. "Good morning, Martin. Looks like it's going to be a hot one."

He eyed the blue expanse above, the tree branches that hung unmoving in the sweltering air. "I think you're right."

Waving, she continued on her way, curls bobbing against her shoulders. She didn't feel fresh or beautiful. She'd overslept and, without the time to properly arrange her hair, she'd settled for brushing out the tangles and leaving it loose.

Her steps faltered when three figures came into view near the springhouse. Crouched on the bank, Shane combed the grass with outstretched fingers. Caleb stood a few feet away, his hat's brim shadowing his face as he scanned the water's edge. Near the top of the bank, Quinn's head came up at her approach. Murmuring something to the others, he strode quickly to meet her beneath the towering oak tree.

"Nicole." He came near, seemingly distracted by her hair. Heat flared in his expression, turning his honey-colored eyes to liquid gold. "I like this look."

The feeling of weightlessness she'd experienced in his arms came rushing back. "Mama didn't wake me at the usual time."

He blinked and schooled his expression to professional courtesy. "I forgot to tell you to take the morning off. You could've stayed home and rested."

"The last thing I want is for the culprits to think their prank impacted us."

His brows drew together. "Are you all right? No sniffles? No chills or tight feelings in your chest?"

He was serious. "I'm not going to come down with pneumonia, Quinn. It wasn't that cold."

After a quick glance over his shoulder, he lowered

his voice. "Listen, you should know your cousin is not in the greatest of moods."

"Well, he did spend half the night searching for us."

"It's not that. I told him about Kenneth."

"What? Why?" Irritation sharpened her voice. "That wasn't your decision to make."

He set his jaw. "I disagree. When his actions affect your ability to do your job, I get involved. It wasn't just you stuck in that springhouse." He moved his face closer. "And if word gets out, it won't be just you stuck in a sham marriage."

Nicole sucked in a ragged breath. The prospect of becoming Quinn's wife had her tummy doing somersaults. "We are not getting married. I'll skip town first."

"And leave me to deal with the consequences alone? Is the idea of marriage to me that distasteful to you, Duchess?"

The nickname sounded more like an endearment each time he used it. "Marriage to anyone right now is out of the question."

Caleb's voice intruded. "I want to talk to you, Nicki."

Uh-oh. That stony expression did not bode well.

Quinn wrapped his hand around hers, warm and heavy, earning him a startled glance. What was he doing?

"Actually, that chat will have to be postponed," he said. "I need to go over a few things with my assistant before we open. Business-related things."

Caleb noticed their joined hands and arched a questioning brow. "Is that so?"

Almost instantly, Quinn untangled his fingers to

slide them up to the spot above her elbow. "And since I haven't had breakfast, we'll be having our discussion at the café."

He didn't give Caleb a chance to respond. With a brief wave, Quinn guided her around the corner and onto Main, his touch insistent. She shook him off as they walked beneath the café's awning.

Waiting until another couple disappeared inside, she scowled at him. "I don't recall agreeing to have breakfast with you."

"Would you rather I'd left you to be raked over the coals?" A baffled smile lent him a boyish air.

"I can deal with Caleb. I've been doing it my whole life."

"Resistant to help."

"Excuse me?"

"Is it due to standard stubbornness or pride?" He stroked his chin, mischief twinkling in the brown depths. "Or perhaps a need to prove to yourself that you're capable?"

Understanding dawned. "Here's one for your list—insufferable."

Spinning, she yanked open the door and would've entered the café ahead of him were it not for his fingers snaking around her arm. Large body crowding her, he dipped his head down and murmured against her hair, "I have a theory about why you speak freely with me. It's our proximity in age. If I were say, ten years your senior, you would allow me the proper respect."

Tingles of anticipation feathered across her neck, at odds with the urge to punch him. "The same way you treat me with professional courtesy?"

Pulling away, she flounced to an unoccupied table

in the far corner, folding her hands tightly beneath the table to keep from snatching up the butter knife.

Quinn followed at a more leisurely pace, smiling at those he passed before easing into the chair opposite her. After they'd ordered—milk, a boiled egg and biscuit for her, coffee and a full breakfast plate for him—he leaned back and rested his hands in his lap.

"I suppose our relationship was doomed from the first moment."

"Relationship?"

"We do have one, Duchess. It's called an employer-employee relationship. And it's gone awry. Certainly nothing like what exists in my father's offices."

Nicole had no trouble picturing Quinn in that environment. His workers must've responded to his charisma and confidence with absolute devotion.

"You sort of inherited me with the purchase," she conceded. "Fortunately, you will get to choose your next one."

Sooner rather than later, she hoped. After their enforced closeness last night, her awareness of him, her sensitivity to his voice and touch, had increased tenfold. She found herself foolishly wishing for that closeness again, no matter that he was her boss. He infuriated her and intentionally provoked her without remorse.

Quinn was right—their interactions were far too personal, and, since she didn't know how to reclaim the proper distance, she was going to have to find a way to survive until she moved away.

Chapter Eleven

Humming a favorite tune, Quinn turned down Nicole's lane feeling more like himself than he had since his arrival three weeks ago. He'd awoken shortly after dawn and, fencing gear in hand, found his way to a remote spot in the woods not far from town and practiced his parrying for several hours. Muscles burning and sweat pouring off him, he'd returned to his quarters for a bath and a shave, after which he'd attended a brief service at the church, where several town leaders spoke and those in attendance sang patriotic songs.

Independence Day was turning out to be one of those perfect summer days, the temperature warm not sizzling and the humidity low, chubby white clouds floating in a sky so blue it hurt to look at it. Bees buzzed and frogs chirruped. The furious flapping of birds' wings rustled tree limbs overhead. The moss-and-magnolia-scented air provided a sweet perfume to rival anything on his store shelves.

Along with every other business in town, the mercantile was closed, and he fully intended to enjoy this rare time of leisure. That he was attending the holiday celebration with the O'Malleys merely enhanced his mood. Alice and the twins put him at ease, welcoming him as if he were part of the family. He was also looking forward to getting to know Nicole's cousins and their wives better.

Neither the failure to discover evidence linking Kenneth to the springhouse ordeal nor the fact he wasn't making much headway with the locals could pierce his good humor.

Passing the enormous barn and a vegetable garden with tidy, orderly rows, he touched a finger to the golden asters flanking the steps before bounding onto the porch of their two-story cabin and rapping lightly on the door.

Jane—or was it Jessica?—greeted him. "Mr. Darling, won't you come in?"

The faint blush and shy smile clued him in. "Thank you, Jane." He entered, his smile widening at her obvious surprise. He made note of her petal-pink blouse for later.

"Nicole will be down in a moment." She indicated the steep, almost ladder-style steps disappearing into the ceiling. "Would you like to join us in the kitchen? Mama is packing our basket."

He followed her through the crowded, narrow dining space and into the homey kitchen. Alice and Jessica—clad in watered-down green—looked up from the counter with sunny smiles. "Quinn—" Alice appeared pleased to see him "—I'm glad you could join us. Nicole overslept this morning, and I'm afraid she's running a bit late."

Concern flared in his chest. He'd been on edge the first day or so after their ordeal, watching for signs of encroaching illness. He couldn't get the shock of her icy skin out of his head, her piteous shudders. *That's not the only thing I can't forget.*

Even now, he recalled with ease how perfectly Nicole had fit in his arms, the wondrous awe of cradling her while she slept, vulnerable and all her usual guards discarded. The silkiness of her hair… *Enough, Darling.*

He cleared his throat. "I hope she isn't coming down with anything."

Alice smiled at his consideration. "I think this is more a case of getting to bed later than usual. My middle daughter tends to become engrossed in her sewing projects and lose track of time."

Quinn would dearly like to see her in such a state. Would she be as impeccably neat as usual, not a hair out of place, or would she be rumpled, raven locks haphazardly tumbling about her shoulders as she lost sense of time and place?

Encouraging himself to keep his thoughts on the right track, his gaze fell on a familiar blue box of chocolate-cream drops perched on the pie safe ledge.

"Nicole favors those, doesn't she? I didn't think she had much of a sweet tooth, but I've noticed she can't get enough of the cream drops."

Jessica and Jane exchanged a doubtful look. Alice's brow screwed up as she placed a bread loaf in the basket. "Nicole doesn't often indulge in sweets."

Jessica went to examine the box, pulling it down from the shelf. "I didn't notice this was even here."

Confused, Quinn said, "Could she have brought them home for you?"

Even as he said it, the feeling in his gut said something wasn't right. Nicole had purchased no less than four boxes in the past two weeks. They weren't expensive, but they weren't cheap, either. She wouldn't have gotten them for the sole purpose of forgetting them on a shelf.

Jane shrugged. "If she did, she didn't say anything."

Alice patted Jessica's shoulder. "Would you be a dear and carry this out to the wagon?"

Jessica hefted the basket, turning down Quinn's offer to help. Untying the faded apron about her ample waist, Alice hung it on a hook beside the back door. "Would you mind if the girls and I went on ahead? I'd like to pick out a prime spot before the crowds descend. There are only so many shade trees to go around."

"We'll catch up to you."

She patted his shoulder in a motherly gesture that had loneliness arching through him. He was surprised by how much he missed his mother's hovering, as he'd called it, the questions that should never be put to a fully grown, adult male. *Did you eat all of your breakfast? Are you getting enough sleep? Are you honestly planning on wearing that particular coat with that shirt?*

Soon, he comforted himself. Soon he would make a decision about the land parcels he'd surveyed last week and get started on a permanent home.

After Alice and the girls left, Quinn wandered around the living area, a space overflowing with couches and furniture. They could do with a little more elbow room, he thought, touching a finger to the painting propped on the mantel.

"That was a gift from Rebecca," Nicole informed him as she reached the bottom of the stairs. "It's my favorite flower."

Turning his back to the cold fireplace, he skimmed her neat-as-a-pin image and was hit with the strange desire to muss her restrained curls. "You look impeccable, as always."

Taking in her lilac ensemble, he never would've guessed she'd been in a rush to get ready. She was as cool and composed as ever. In that moment, he made it his mission to upset that composure at some point today. Nicole O'Malley needed to learn to take life a bit less seriously.

"Thank you." Double-checking the pearl buttons on her bodice, she craned her neck to see past the dining room. Silver earbobs winked at her earlobes. "Are they waiting outside for us?"

"Actually, your mother asked if we'd mind meeting them there. I believe she was anxious to claim a spot."

"Oh."

"Are you regretting volunteering to accompany me?"

"No," she replied too quickly, jerking up her chin. "Are you regretting accepting? Our arrival won't go unnoticed, I assure you. Hazard of small-town life."

Striding forward, he took hold of her elbow and turned her toward the door. "I'm no stranger to gossip, Duchess." Opening the door, he ushered her onto the porch. "Gossip is quite common in my social circles. Today I will be the envy of every man in attendance, young and old, because I have the loveliest lady in Gatlinburg on my arm."

Nicole disengaged her arm and glared at him. "Were you born this way or is it an acquired affliction?"

"To what are you referring, my dear?" Quinn bit back a smile as her color heightened.

"The charm oozing from your pores." She flicked a hand up and down the length of him. "Do they teach that course at Harvard? How to spout ridiculous flattery at will?"

He lost the smile. "Why is it so difficult for you to accept a compliment?"

This aloof, don't-come-near-me attitude masked low self-esteem. Amazing that an accomplished young woman like Nicole could doubt herself.

His serious tone must've unnerved her, for she stormed down the steps ahead of him. "The church is a good twenty-minute walk from here. We should get going."

Sensing her need for space, Quinn purposefully didn't offer his arm as they walked along the serene, country lane leading to town. The silence between them was companionable, despite her irritation with him. He liked that they could be in the empty mercantile together and not feel the compunction to fill the silence with unnecessary conversation.

By the time they'd reached Main Street and he popped into the store for the lunch basket he'd ordered from Plum's, she no longer looked as if she wanted to strangle him.

She did appear nervous, however.

Locking the front door and pocketing the key, he fell into step beside her. The church property was teeming with people. Food tables had been set up along the side of the clapboard building, the wide, grassy area dotted with blankets and clusters of people setting out picnic baskets. Fiddle music drifted down the street.

Another sigh reached him as they passed the post office, and Quinn cast her a sidelong glance. "You are wishing you hadn't asked me, aren't you? It's all right if you'd rather go and join your family. I'm sure the reverend and his wife would allow me to join them."

Nicole's steps faltered. "It's not that." Thick, black lashes lowered to brush her cheeks. "I, uh, I've never had an escort before."

"To the Independence Day celebration?"

"To *anything*."

Quinn was hard put not to let his surprise show. The familiar drive to protect her arrowed through him even as an unwise sense of satisfaction took hold.

Passing beneath the branches of the outermost tree in the churchyard, he trained his gaze on the kaleidoscope of smartly dressed people. "Then I am indeed a fortunate man. I will warn you that I am not accustomed to sitting on the sidelines while others have all the fun. As you are my date, I expect you to join me."

Nicole followed his gaze to the lively two-legged race being set up beneath the trees edging the property.

Panic rippled across her features. "Quinn, no."

"Oh, yes." He caught her hand as she made to escape, weaving his fingers through hers and starting in that direction.

She dug in her heels. "I don't participate in silly games."

"I didn't peg you for someone who allowed others' opinions to dictate her actions."

"What's that supposed to mean?"

"Do you honestly care what these people think about you?"

Nicole chewed on her lip, troubled violet gaze sweeping the crowds.

"Come on," he cajoled, tugging on her hand, "you never know. You just might enjoy yourself."

To his surprise and pleasure, she gave in. At the starting line, Quinn got the rope from the man in charge and, binding his ankle to hers, tried not to think about their first meeting and his ungentlemanly actions. The other contestants' competitive smiles held unspoken questions. They were clearly intrigued by his and Nicole's participation, although whether due to her involvement or the nature of their relationship he hadn't a clue.

Quinn counted himself fortunate no one had learned of their time in the springhouse. While he liked Nicole and was certainly aware of her as a woman, he wasn't keen on marrying her. She was prickly and complicated. He preferred sweet and biddable. She was set on becoming a successful businesswoman. His heart's desire was a traditional family.

Of course, searching for a suitable wife among Gatlinburg's residents would have to wait until his house was built and his position in the community more settled. Occasionally spending time with Nicole—as friendly business associates—was perfectly acceptable.

As they hobbled to the starting line, he curled an arm about her petite waist and pressed his mouth to her ear. "Relax, Duchess. Put your arm around me."

She grimaced but did as he suggested. "You think I don't know you're trying to annoy me with the nickname?"

He barked out a laugh. "You make it too easy."

"And what is this exactly?" She waved a hand between them. "Trying to make me miserable?"

"On the contrary. I'm trying to get you to enjoy yourself."

"This isn't my idea of enjoyment."

The pistol shot rang out. Nicole's gasp was whipped away the moment he jolted them forward. Their progress was awkward, stilted, and they nearly landed in a tangled heap half-a-dozen times. Onlookers' cheers spurred them on. Quinn didn't mind that they didn't win. Not when her cheeks were flushed and her eyes sparkled like precious jewels.

Untying the rope, he pointed at her. "Is that a smile attempting to break through?"

"Not quite." She gave him an arch look.

"Guess that means my work isn't finished."

Taking her hand again, he pulled her through the crowd to the rear of the church, where ladies were competing in a skillet toss.

"I'm not doing that."

"What if I offered you a dollar's worth of fabric?"

Her arms, folded across her chest, fell away, and she stared at him with parted lips. "You're serious?"

"I am."

"Make it store credit, and you have a deal."

"Fine."

"Fine."

With a bracing breath, she tugged off her reticule and tossed it at his chest. He fumbled to catch it before it fell to the ground. "Minx."

Watching her march up to the organizer, Quinn couldn't swipe the goofy grin from his face. It remained for the next hour as he persuaded her to take part in musical chairs—which he won—a cakewalk and a sawing contest. They both worked up a sweat on that last one, and by the end he'd accomplished his goal—Nicole laughing freely, inky curls escaping their pins to caress her nape and excitement animating her features.

"I need a drink," she panted, sagging against the solid oak trunk.

Quinn propped an arm on the nearest limb and leaned in, gingerly wrapping one of her curls about his finger. "I will procure you a drink just as soon as you admit you had fun."

A light breeze rustled the green leaves overhead and skimmed their heated skin. Although people milled about the grounds, laughter and children's shrieks and music filling their ears, here beneath this outlying oak it felt as if they were the only ones in attendance. Nicole had gone still. Watchful. Puzzling emotions swirled in her luminous eyes as he explored the texture of her hair.

The air between them thickened, weighted with awareness. He hadn't realized how close their faces were. Her bow-shaped mouth, pink and soft, parted on a sigh. Quinn swallowed hard.

That wasn't an invitation. *Was it?*

His heart picked up speed, pumping hard like it did in the midst of a fencing match.

She's your employee, Darling. Hands off.

It wasn't easy heeding the voice of reason. Not when she was warm and close, her expression open to him like never before.

"I, ah—" he awkwardly disengaged his finger "—suppose we should probably join your family. I've monopolized your time."

She blinked. Color flooded her face. "Yes, that's a good plan."

As they traversed the dandelion-dotted field in silence, careful not to accidentally brush against each other, he wondered how much experience Nicole had had with interested suitors. Probably little to none, if he was her first date.

Quinn wondered if she'd meet someone special in the city, if she'd ever make room in her life for anything other than her sewing. It'd be a pity if she spent the whole of her life alone. Nicole had a lot to offer, even if she wasn't aware of it.

He had never been in love. He'd thought he had something special with Helene Michelson. The daughter of millionaire Donald Michelson, she'd arrived in Boston with her parents eighteen months ago and had made an instant impression on him. Petite, blonde and outgoing, she'd shared his passion for athletic pursuits, eagerly joining him on horseback riding and boating excursions. After months of courting her in earnest, Quinn had begun to consider marriage.

That was before he overheard her talking with her friends. He'd learned she wasn't as interested in being his wife so much as being a Darling. His name—and the status attached to it—had been her desired prize.

The revelation and subsequent breakup had spurred the beginnings of his shift in priorities. He didn't want a superficial life. He craved something substantial. Something real. Lasting. Precious.

Luring Nicole out of her shell was fun, even fascinating at times, but it was a temporary distraction. She didn't meet his requirements. And he certainly didn't meet hers.

Chapter Twelve

What almost happened back there?

Thick grass snagging on her hem as they neared her family's picnic spot, Nicole felt strangely let down, which in turn left her cranky and resentful. Inviting Quinn to join her had been a dumb idea. He took pleasure in pushing her out of her realm of comfort, teasing her all the while, prodding at her defenses until she was open and exposed and then...nothing.

She was a game to him. A shiny, new toy to explore and then discard.

Why am I letting him get to me, anyway? I'm not interested in romance.

Beneath all this pulsed an undercurrent of guilt. Here she was, freely attending a holiday celebration, while Patrick and Lillian were stuck in their meager shack, trapped there until the sun went down. Lillian would take such delight in the music. And Patrick would relish the food. He, especially, needed encouragement. Friends his own age.

This isn't fair, God. I hate what they're having to endure.

When they reached the soaring, wide-limbed sugar maple where her sisters and cousins and extended family members had gathered, Nathan's wife, Sophie, took one look at Nicole and gaped. She elbowed Nathan, who was seated beside her. As a speculative smile creased his face, Nicole fiddled with her earbobs. Was her appearance causing this reaction? Her hair was a mess and she was *perspiring*. In public.

Or was it Quinn's presence beside her?

Hopping up, Sophie made eye contact with Rebecca, who was relaxing against Caleb's shoulder, and Megan.

Sophie reached her first. "Can I talk to you?"

"Um, I guess so."

"If you're ready for lunch, there's a spot beside the twins." Sophie flashed a smile at Quinn. "I won't keep her long, I promise."

Linking arms, the shorter girl led Nicole a short distance away, using a cluster of dogwood trees to block them from view.

Nicole spoke first, attempting to head off the coming inquisition. "That's a new dress. Did you make it?"

Skimming her palms over the paisley skirts, Sophie blushed prettily. "I've been practicing what you taught me. Does it look all right?"

Nicole circled her, tugging here and there to test the stitches, satisfied with the way the cotton draped her form. Before Sophie married Nathan, she'd been a tomboy, content in men's clothing and her honey-blond hair in a haphazard braid. Nicole had gladly aided in her transformation to stylish young lady.

"Your skills have improved. It's beautiful. Your hair looks nice, too."

Sophie beamed, fingers skittering over the sophisticated twist. "Nathan doesn't mind whether I wear it up or down." A dimple flashed. "Actually, that's not true. He prefers it hanging loose so he can run his fingers through it."

Nicole squelched the burst of envy. She absolutely was not jealous. "That would hardly be appropriate for an event such as this."

Megan and Rebecca rounded the dogwoods, and Nicole found herself the center of attention. "What?"

Megan seemed to be bursting with curiosity. "You came with Quinn."

"So?"

"I thought you didn't like him."

Sophie rolled her eyes. "What's not to like? He's handsome, a true gentleman and the way he looks at you…"

"He's my *boss*," Nicole muttered, instinctively clamming up. "I only asked him because he hasn't made many friends here."

Rebecca gasped, jade-colored eyes going wide. "*You* asked *him*?"

"I can't recall a time you ever gave a man the time of day." Megan's white-blond curls shone in the bright sunshine, her porcelain skin enhanced by the aquamarine hue of her formfitting dress. "Come on, sis. Tell us the truth. You fancy him, don't you?"

Nicole could feel the emotion leaching from her face, could feel the ingrained response kicking in. *Stay cool and deny everything*, her mind was insisting.

Her and Quinn's conversation that night in the springhouse came back to her. He'd been adamant in his opinion that others would like to get close to her. Sophie, Megan and Rebecca were family. How many times had they reached out to her, only to be rebuffed? *It's my fault I feel left out, isn't it, God? Not theirs.*

Please help. Sharing my innermost thoughts doesn't come naturally. Of course, I don't have to tell You that.

"To be honest…" She pushed the words past her dry throat, clasping her hands tightly at her waist. "I can't explain how I feel about Quinn."

The three females surrounding her exchanged glances.

"Try," Megan insisted.

"He is good-looking." At Sophie's nod, Nicole held up a finger. "But he knows it. He's bossy. Smug." She recalled how he'd defended her against Kenneth and his buddies. "He's also protective. Brave. He values honesty. Family."

Rebecca smoothed her rich, copper-streaked brown hair away from her brow. "That's a good start. How does he make you feel?"

"Oh, that's easy. Angry. Frustrated—" she ticked off her fingers "—confused."

"Confused?"

"When he puts his arms around me, I kind of melt into him and I feel safe and warm and yet—" She broke off, not about to admit this unnameable longing he evoked in her.

"Wait. He put his arms around you?" Megan's brows shot to her hairline. "Did he *kiss* you?"

Oops. She wasn't supposed to mention the spring-house.

"*Ew.* No, my boss did not kiss me." Although, hadn't that been on both their minds mere minutes ago? His perfect, slightly arrogant mouth had hovered inches from hers, brown eyes glittering. Her palms went damp.

"Why was he holding you?" Rebecca said.

"I—I was cold. Look, I'm starving. I didn't eat breakfast."

Her sister stopped her exit with a gentle, staying hand. A trembling smile lit up her face. "It means a lot that you shared what's in your heart, sis."

Nicole found herself returning the smile. "It wasn't as horrid as I thought it'd be."

Megan hugged her. "Don't worry, we won't repeat a word."

Thankfully Quinn didn't ask about their conversation. Nor did he try to goad her into taking part in any more contests. They passed the remainder of the afternoon in the company of her family, her uncle and cousins engaging him in a variety of topics.

It was midafternoon when they began to pack up their things. Nicole assumed she'd accompany her mother and sisters home while Quinn returned to his quarters in the mercantile, but he insisted on walking with her.

"It's the gentlemanly thing to do. It's my duty to see you home."

"It that a Boston rule?"

"It's a Darling rule." He waited patiently for her to take his arm, challenge lurking in his eyes.

The afternoon had been a trying one on many levels. She yearned to be alone with her thoughts, needle and thread in hand and a creation taking shape beneath her stitches. But he was adamant.

Sighing, she took it, keenly aware of the hard muscle beneath her fingertips and the occasional brush of their shoulders as they walked. Strolling along the darkened store fronts, she glanced surreptitiously at his profile.

Had Quinn ever been in love? He'd intimated people admired him solely for his wealth and status, but there was more to him than that. In addition to his good looks, he had a quick wit and dynamic personality. He could be kind and thoughtful when he put his mind to it.

Not that she'd ever tell him that.

"What's brewing in that mysterious mind of yours?" Angling his head, he met her gaze head-on without missing a step.

"I'm wondering how you managed to escape the parson's trap."

"Ah. I thought you didn't consider me suitable husband material."

"I never said that, you know."

"You didn't have to," he said, and chuckled softly.

Her heart skipped a beat, wondering what it would be like to be Quinn's wife. His high-handed attitude would make her crazy within a week…and they'd argue in spectacular fashion…but she'd heard about makeup kisses. And she imagined Quinn was an expert in that area.

"In the eyes of Boston's impressionable young socialites, I'm certain you were considered quite the catch."

They crossed the wooden bridge suspended above the bustling river, their boots thudding against the worn slats. Something in his expression turned pensive, and she wondered at the cause.

"As a matter of fact, I came very close to binding myself to one particular young lady. I suppose I'm fortunate to have discovered her true motives before it was too late."

The hurt in his voice troubled her, and she unconsciously squeezed his arm.

"I'm sorry, Quinn."

"I was sorry for a long time, too."

Nicole strove to comprehend this revelation. So much of the time, he projected a carefree attitude. To know that his heart was as capable of injury as the next person's altered her view of him.

Against her better judgment, she gave in to the burning desire to question him. "What happened?"

He averted his face toward the lush forest on his side of the quiet lane, steps steady and slow and matched to hers.

"You don't have to tell me," she murmured. "I shouldn't have prodded."

"I had begun to suspect I was in love with Helene," he started quietly.

Envy snaked its way around her throat, surprising in its intensity, threatening to choke off her air supply. It was wrong, so wrong to envy this unknown woman who'd ensnared Quinn's affections. *Good thing you don't covet his admiration*, she comforted herself. *That would be unreasonable. And foolhardy.*

"We had a lot in common. I assumed we could have a good life together." His lips flattened. "Turns out I misjudged her. Helene wasn't with me because she cared about me, about the man I am when the superficial is stripped away."

"She was after your fortune?"

"And the prestige that comes from marrying into the Darling family," he said matter-of-factly.

"So Helene wasn't from an affluent family?"

His lip curled. "As a matter of fact, her father was a business associate of ours. Socially speaking, we were on equal footing."

"I don't understand."

"The thing is, Duchess, having money sometimes generates intense greed. People become obsessed with having more. Always more."

They passed beneath a low-hanging branch, startling a pair of mourning doves. She tracked their upward flight.

He'd said he'd come here for a simpler, more meaningful life. Nicole finally understood what drove him.

"I'm sorry," she said again, wishing he hadn't had to endure such treatment.

Her heart fluttered at the appearance of his soft smile. "Don't be. If it weren't for her, I wouldn't have recognized what my life was missing. I certainly wouldn't have wound up in this tiny mountain town."

"Most of Gatlinburg's marriage-minded young ladies come from humble homes. Aren't you worried history will repeat itself? Even if you weren't rich, the fact that you own the mercantile makes you a desirable candidate."

His gaze probed hers for long, unsettling moments—surely the yearning sliding through the honeyed depths wasn't directed at *her*—before shifting to the lane winding through the trees. His shrug offset his serious demeanor. "I'm trusting God to lead me to the right woman. That's all I can do."

Ignoring the pinpricks of discomfort his words inspired, she drawled, "Well, if the numerous longing looks cast your way today are anything to go by, you won't lack for options."

"I'm sure I don't know to what you're referring."

At his mock innocence, she rolled her eyes. "You mean you didn't see Harriet Nichols nearly tripping and falling face-first into her potato salad when she passed by you?"

"It would've been impossible not to." He chuckled, shaking his head wryly.

They fell into a companionable silence, with Nicole mentally cataloguing every simpering whisper she'd intercepted while with Quinn. Not one unattached young lady hadn't noted his presence. As soon as the locals figured out that he was all right for a Northerner, he'd be fielding supper invitations left and right.

When her lane came into view, she slipped her hand free and stepped away. Here in the pleasant shade, his hair was a richer hue of black, his skin a shade paler and an undergrowth of bristle visible along his jaws.

Why must she notice these things? And why did he have to be tantalizingly handsome?

"I can make it the rest of the way without incident."

Slipping his hands in his pockets, he smiled, teeth flashing. "Thank you for today."

"In spite of my high-handed escort, I had fun." She smiled. "See you in the morning."

She'd half turned to leave when his words stopped her. "Oh, I meant to ask you. I saw a box of cream drops in your kitchen earlier. Your mother and sisters didn't have a clue who they were for."

The burning intensity in his eyes belied his casual tone.

"Why do you care?"

"I noticed how you favor them." He shrugged. "Just wondering who liked them so much."

Lillian adored the dainty chocolates. Couldn't get enough.

A panicky feeling skittered through her, white-hot anger on its heels. "You have no right to interrogate me about my purchases. You don't treat your other customers this way. Don't do it to me."

This anger inflicted pain. She didn't want to be angry at him, not after his revelation and the sense of connectedness it had given her.

Quinn's cool fingers closed over her wrist. He bent close, concern warring with suspicion. "You're overreacting, don't you think? It was a simple question."

Lifting her chin, she glared at him. "Not so simple. Once again, I get the feeling you're accusing me of something underhanded."

"I admit your behavior has led me to wonder if you're hiding something. Are you?"

Ripping free of his grip, she gritted, "Goodbye, Quinn."

He didn't say a word as she stalked away. In fact, it was his utter silence that had her glancing over her shoulder at him. Spying him shoving up his sleeves and examining his arms, she stumbled to a halt.

"What on earth are you doing?"

"Checking for scars." A fierce scowl creased his features. "You, Nicole O'Malley, are the prickliest, most frustrating—" He rammed his fingers through his hair. "I had better stop before I say something I'll later wish unsaid." With a stiff, formal bow, he said, "Until tomorrow, Duchess."

Shocked into silence, Nicole watched him stride

away, despising the awful way he'd uttered the endearment and wishing—absurdly—that things could be different between them.

Chapter Thirteen

Quinn was going to be sick.

Standing on the riverbank the next morning, he surveyed the destruction of property. The springhouse door stood ajar. Crocks had been dragged out and smashed to bits, the earth beneath them soaked with milk. Broken jars shone in the early light, jewel-hued vegetables lying discarded in the grass. Half-submerged cheese wheels littered the water's edge.

What a complete and utter waste.

He didn't hear Nicole's approach until she was right beside him. "Quinn, what happened?"

Having recovered from his irritation with her—he wasn't one to hold a grudge—he flicked her a quick glance, absorbing her serene, ice-blue-bedecked elegance. The shock and disgust swirling in his gut was reflected on her face.

"Someone is trying to send a message. What that might be, I have no inkling."

She clasped her throat. "This is horrible. Can anything be saved?"

"The springhouse is empty. The perpetrator did a thorough job."

The anger humming through his veins was understandable. The defeat riding along with it, on the other hand, wasn't something Quinn was used to handling.

"I have the funds to replace everything, of course." He toed a shard of broken glass. "What bothers me is the malice behind the act. A waste like this is hard to take when there are people in the nation who don't have enough to eat."

"When did you discover it?"

"Just a few minutes ago. Doesn't look like animals have disturbed anything which tells me it's a recent job."

Her hand on his shoulder startled him. Glancing down into her jewel-bright eyes swimming with compassion, he wondered how one woman could evoke such opposing emotions. There were times he didn't know if he wanted to shake her or hug her. Or kiss—

Quinn crushed the thought before it could fully take hold. *Focus on the issue at hand, Darling.*

Frustration broke through his reserve. "I don't understand why someone would do this. I've done everything I can to befriend the townspeople, to garner their trust. And now this…"

"It could be someone who doesn't like the fact you've taken Emmett's place." She removed her hand, a dark frown forming. "Or it could be Kenneth and his friends."

Quinn had seen the trio at the celebration and prayed they would keep their distance, for both their sakes. A public confrontation would've only served to embarrass Nicole and worsen general opinion of him.

"You've worked here for six months. Has anything like this happened during that time?"

"No, but you're forgetting you stood up for me. No one has ever done that."

"I will always stand up for you, Nicole."

His vow had obviously flustered her. When there was no snappy comeback, he sent her inside to put up a sign letting customers know there wouldn't be any dairy today. While she manned the store, he fetched Shane, who was equally disturbed by the senseless crime.

Shane helped him clean up. Quinn thanked the man, then went inside to find the store packed with customers. Nicole, who was dipping out flour for an impatient woman at the counter surrounded by four whining kids, cast him a *help me* look. Six people stood behind the woman. Sending up a prayer, he plastered on a pleasant smile and offered to help the next person in line. Their eagerness to conduct business and be on their way overruled their wariness of him, for he found himself with his own line for the first time since his arrival.

Fighting off a sudden attack of nerves, Quinn disbursed their orders without complication. Not only did he know the location of every item in his store, he was able to calculate trade credit. Being Nicole's helper all these weeks had paid off. When the last person in line smiled her genuine thanks and left satisfied with the service, he briefly closed his eyes. At last. Progress. *Thank you, God.*

The small triumph eased somewhat his upset over the springhouse.

But then Kenneth, Timothy and Pete waltzed in, elbowing each other and laughing, and his mood soured again.

Nicole looked up from her ledger and paled. Quinn immediately went to stand next to her, resting a reassuring hand against the small of her back. "I will not let them hassle you."

"No need to worry about me." Edging sideways, she put distance between them, forcing him to drop his hand. He intercepted a customer's curious stare and understood her reaction.

"Right."

Speculation about their relationship running rampant through town wasn't what either of them needed. Still, he stuck close to her, determined to prevent a repeat of last time. His assistant was a strong, independent woman, but going up against three oversize idiot males wasn't likely to have a good outcome.

Kenneth made eye contact across the store, his arrogant smirk making Quinn's blood boil. The young man was the only one with obvious motive for revenge. A bully like him wouldn't take kindly to being chastised in the midst of Main Street for all to see. As Nicole had suggested, he had reason to retaliate.

There was no way to prove his theory. Shane had promised to return that evening to conduct a second search, but he'd warned Quinn not to get his hopes up.

The men's laughter grated on his nerves. Nicole's composure became increasingly strained as she measured out fabric for a young lady. He could see the tightening about her mouth, the slight trembling in her hands.

Anger spiking, he was about to order them to leave when Megan and Lucian entered. The trio sobered at the sight of Nicole's sister and brother-in-law. While Lucian Beaumont was not related by blood, he was an imposing man both in physical stature and manner, his confidence a product of an upbringing and family situation that mirrored Quinn's.

As the couple approached the counter, Kenneth led his friends out the door.

Quinn was satisfied to see Nicole's stance soften with relief. The knowledge that he'd willingly shelter her from any and all trouble should've bothered him more than it did. He felt the same way toward his sister. Made sense that he'd feel this way about someone in his employ.

He greeted Lucian with genuine warmth.

The dark-haired man pointed at the sign in the window. "What happened to your dairy supply? Caleb been shorting you?"

"Not exactly."

When he'd informed them both, Lucian's countenance grew troubled. "Do you have any suspects?"

"I have my suspicions, but no way of proving them. Yet."

Glancing around at the handful of customers still browsing the aisles, the other man said quietly, "Why don't you join us for supper tonight? We've been meaning to invite you, anyway. It would give us a chance to discuss matters in private."

"I'd like that."

Tucking her hand in her husband's, Megan leaned across the counter. "Come with him, Nicole."

She hesitated in tying up the fabric with a string. "Can't. I have too much to do after work."

Quinn refused to be disappointed. He was in her company all day every day.

"Are you sure?" Megan persisted. "Can't your chores wait an hour or two?"

"No, I'm sorry they can't." Noting her sister's crestfallen expression, she tacked on, "Maybe another time."

The couple stuck around for ten more minutes before taking their leave. The rest of the day passed in a blur and, before he knew it, Shane was back for another search. Quinn left Nicole inside to lock up.

Fifteen minutes into their search, she descended the stairs and walked over to where he was crouched in the grass. She dangled her basket in front of his nose.

"Would you like to examine the contents? I have the ledger listing my purchases in my reticule."

The sheriff gave her a brief, considering glance before returning his attention to the grassy expanse beneath his boots.

"Not this time."

Sighing, she inclined her head in that regal way of hers. "Good evening, then."

Watching her stride away, Quinn gave in to the needling sense that she was hiding something. He stood up and brushed off his pants. "I forgot I have some urgent business to tend to. Would you mind if I left you to it?"

The sheriff nudged the brim of his Stetson farther up his forehead, sharp blue gaze assessing. No doubt he saw right through Quinn's lame excuse.

"Go ahead. I'm almost finished here."

Feeling foolish but intent on discovering Nicole's secrets, he followed her at a distance, praying she wouldn't turn around and spy him. What reason could he possibly give for following her?

When she ducked onto a barely discernible path leading into the heart of the forest, Quinn's gut clenched with dread.

Where was she going? And what would he find at the end of this path?

He wasn't sure he wanted to find out.

Nicole accepted the steaming bowl of fish stew, wondering how she could explain away—again—her lack of appetite once she returned home. Her mother was starting to become suspicious. Like Quinn. Suppressing a wave of irritation, she turned her attention to her friends.

"This is delicious, Lillian."

Cheeks pink, and damp tendrils adhering to her forehead, Lillian perched on the other bed with her bowl. "Tell me about the picnic. Did they have fried chicken?"

Nicole felt perspiration forming on her nape. The interior was stuffy and uncomfortable. It would only get worse as the summer progressed.

"I didn't see any, but I'm sure there was."

Savoring another bite of the surprisingly fragrant stew, she hoped she'd remember to ask the twins to prepare some fried chicken so that she could sneak a few pieces to the girl. In the corner, a quieter-than-usual Patrick trained his attention on his meal.

She lowered her spoon. "I wish you could've been there. There were games and music."

Patrick scowled into his bowl. At Lillian's wistful sigh, Nicole's appetite vanished. Forcing the rest of the contents down, she placed the dish in the bucket.

"I'll take these to the stream and wash them for you."

"No." His head shot up, pale eyes narrowing. "What would someone think if they saw you? We've already had one close call."

Lillian stuck her tongue out at him.

"What happened?" Dismayed, Nicole looked from one to the other.

Patrick dragged his glowering gaze from his sister to answer her. "Lillian was doing her nightly washing in the stream when a couple of elderly hunters came waltzing through the woods. The only thing that saved her is the fact there was a full moon and she didn't have need of a lamp."

"They didn't see me, though, did they?" Lillian didn't appear the least bothered.

But the near miss bothered Nicole. Gaze roaming the cramped shack, the pitiful state of their so-called home, she felt sick inside.

"We have to tell Shane," she blurted. "This nightmare has to end."

Lillian's light brows crumpling, she lowered her bowl to her lap and stared glumly at her brother. While the younger girl would never complain aloud, Nicole sensed she would willingly go to the sheriff if only Patrick would agree.

As expected, he shook his head. "Can't risk it."

"This has nothing to do with me." Nicole threw her hands up and paced the tiny space. "I have no problem helping you. Believe me, I wouldn't be doing this if I didn't want to help. But it's killing me to see you living like this! You're my only true friends in this town." Tears welled up in her eyes, taking her by surprise. "It's not fair."

Lillian hurried over to wrap her in a hug. "I'm so thankful you found us. You were our answer to prayer."

Astonished by the notion that God would willingly choose to use her to accomplish His ends, Nicole couldn't form a coherent response. She awkwardly patted Lillian's back and blinked away the tears.

Patrick watched them warily. "Crying isn't going to change my mind, you know," he said, setting his bowl aside and using the cane to gain his footing.

"I'm tired of this half life." Lillian pulled out of the hug to face him. "We have to consider bringing someone else in besides Nicole."

"We don't know if we can trust this Sheriff Timmons."

"Nicole trusts him. That's good enough for me." Lillian put up a hand to stall his response. "Promise me you'll think about it."

He heaved a sigh. "Fine."

Somewhat mollified, the blonde's smile returned.

Nicole had her doubts he'd ever agree to her suggestion. "I have to go. Thank you for the meal."

Outside, dusk had fallen. Patrick followed her through the door, his manner uncharacteristically self-conscious. Then he stunned her by giving her a one-armed hug.

Stepping back, he cleared his throat, the tips of his ears pink. "Thank you for all you've sacrificed for us. I'll never forget it."

"I would do it all again," she admitted. "You and your sister mean the world to me."

Throat working, he gave a half wave and, shuffling inside, gently shut the door.

Bemused, she swung the empty basket to and fro as she traveled the familiar path. The waning light struggled to penetrate the trees. Shadows thickened, spurring her to walk faster.

She hadn't made it very far when, out of the bushes, flashed a tall male form. A firm hand clamped down on her arm. Nicole jumped and would've screamed had she not instantly recognized the distinctive hint of peppermint in the air.

"Quinn!" She was going to throttle him! "What do you think you're doing?"

Quinn towered over her, his hair mussed and tie askew, nostrils flaring. "Who was that young man?"

Fear temporarily eclipsed her ire. He'd seen Patrick. What if he told?

Tempted to retreat, Nicole ordered her feet to stay put. Gone was laid-back Quinn. This was intimidating Quinn, the one she'd glimpsed in the mercantile when Kenneth and his friends had come in. Anger poured off him in tangible waves, every inch of his muscled body primed for battle. He was one enemy she did not want to make.

He invaded her space. "I saw you hug him. Does he live there? Please. *Please* tell me you haven't been so foolish as to carry on a secret assignation with him."

Just like that, her fear disintegrated. Spluttering, she shoved at his solid—and immovable—chest.

"You don't know me *at all* if you can suggest such a despicable thing." Chin angled upward, she glared at him nose to nose. "Get out of my way, Darling."

Something akin to astonishment flared in the amber depths of his eyes, but he didn't move a muscle.

"That was Darling with a capital *D*, you big oaf."

When she sidestepped to go around him, he smoothly moved to block her exit. "You're not going anywhere until you tell me what's going on."

"Then I guess I'd better get comfortable," she quipped.

"Do not push me, Nicole." His eyes narrowed. "I will have your secrets one way or another."

Chapter Fourteen

The hint of relief on Nicole's features confirmed his decision to follow her. The weight of her secret—he shuddered to think what it might be—had to be a considerable burden. Quinn wondered just how long she'd been hiding this part of her life. And to what end? Forbidden romance?

He couldn't deny the jealousy and inexplicable sense of loss he'd experienced upon seeing her and the stranger embracing. Shoving those useless emotions aside, he held tight to his concern for her well-being.

"Is he who you've been purchasing the supplies for?" He managed a semi-calm tone of voice.

"What I do during my off time is none of your business."

"It's been going on for a while, hasn't it? Since before Emmett left." Her sister's words came back to him. "Have you been supporting him since the beginning? Was that why you took this job?"

She'd gone still, watchful. On alert for a way of escape from his presence and this conversation. In the muted light that reached them here in this remote spot, her violet eyes were deep pools of wariness, her shiny pink lips pressed together in a straight line, and he noted the odd trembling in her slender frame.

His irritation ebbing, he settled his hands on her shoulders, thumbs rubbing a reassuring pattern across the soft blue fabric of her sleeves.

"You can trust me, Nicole."

She gulped. "I'm not so sure about that."

That hurt. "I have never given you reason to doubt my intention to protect you." *Even from yourself.*

Her shoulders slumped as the fight left her. "You aren't going to let this go, are you?"

"I'm afraid not."

"Then I suppose a meeting is in order."

Stepping aside, he followed in her wake. The run-down shack looked worse up close. Surely this was merely a meeting place and not a permanent residence.

She rapped out a series of knocks. A secret code between her and her love interest?

Quinn's chest constricted as they waited. Finally, the door scraped open.

"Back so soon…" The young male voice trailed off as light gray eyes landed on Quinn. He recoiled. "Who's he?"

"May we come inside?" Nicole's manner was resigned.

Her companion lingered in the doorway, weight supported by a cane. He was younger than Quinn had first thought and sickly in appearance, mouth tight with pain and skin nearly translucent.

Reluctantly, the boy admitted them. Quinn worked to keep his features schooled as he entered the tiny space that, from the looks of things, was indeed a home. A pitiful one. Movement in the corner caught his eye. A fine-boned girl latched on to Nicole's arm, eyes wide and hunted as she stared at him.

"Nicole?" she squeaked.

Similar in coloring and appearance to the lad, she was most likely his sister. Perhaps he'd jumped to the wrong conclusion.

"Patrick. Lillian. This is my boss, Quinn Darling," she announced darkly. "He followed me."

Quinn inclined his head in greeting. "Which one of you would like to explain what's going on here?"

Patrick sank heavily onto a chair in the corner, hands hanging on to the cane between his legs. Chin jutted at a stubborn angle, he said, "That depends on what you're planning on doing with the information."

"I can't say until I know what it is you're hiding. And you *are* hiding something, or else you wouldn't be living here." He flicked a hand about him. "My assistant wouldn't be doing your shopping for you and making clandestine deliveries."

"We haven't done anything wrong!" Lillian burst out.

Nicole's glare shooting daggers at Quinn, she addressed Patrick. "Just tell him the truth. He won't let this matter rest until you do. He's stubborn and hardheaded."

He was stubborn? What about her?

"These past six months, Nicole has been instrumental in keeping my sister and I alive and safe."

"Safe?" Quinn repeated. "From who?"

"The man who married our mother and later murdered her."

Nicole clapped a hand over her mouth. "Patrick!

Why didn't you tell me?" Rushing over, she knelt before him, fingers gripping his knee. "How did it happen?"

Quinn's gaze narrowed at her open concern for the lad. She very clearly cared for him. How deep did her feelings go?

Patrick ducked his head, hair sliding forward. "They were arguing. He pushed her. Hard. She struck her head."

"She never woke up." Lillian hung back, her legs pressed against the bed opposite, keeping her distance from Quinn.

Scooting out a chair he hoped would bear his weight, Quinn sat down and crossed his arms. "How about we start at the beginning?"

As he listened to the entire story, bits and pieces supplied by all three, his concern for the siblings' welfare deepened and his admiration for his assistant blossomed. He couldn't have imagined her capable of such a noble act. He'd pegged her wrong from the start.

"What are you going to do with this information?" Patrick's knuckles were white on the cane.

"I need to give the matter some thought. One thing's for sure—you cannot remain here. We'll need to find you more appropriate lodgings."

Trepidation tightened the lad's mouth. "If people find out about us—"

"Please don't worry." Quinn stood, noting the darkness and lack of moonlight beyond the window. "I'll do everything in my power to keep you safe." Extending his hand to Nicole, he said, "Your family will be wondering where you are. I'll escort you home."

She hugged both siblings. He couldn't detect anything other than sisterly affection on her part. Nor did Patrick look at Nicole like a man infatuated.

Borrowing a lamp, they entered the woodland path, crickets' chirrups and frogs' chorus echoing through the night. "I have to ask," he said when the suspense became too much to bear. "About you and Patrick… are you…a couple?"

She stumbled over a root. When he steadied her, she shook off his hand. "Of course not. He's younger than me! Besides, I think of him as a brother."

Relief spiraled through him.

"Wait. Do you think *he* thinks—"

"No. I saw no evidence of that."

"I take it you saw something in my behavior that made you jump to that conclusion?"

Quinn chose his words carefully. "Not exactly. You are, however, more open, more demonstrative with them than anyone else."

"They're my friends."

He didn't respond. Didn't disrupt the silence that fell awkwardly between them during the remainder of the long walk to her cabin. His head was too full of discovery.

At the entrance to her lane, Nicole stopped. "You're angry."

He lowered the lamp to the ground. "You're right. I am."

"Well, that's too bad—"

Quinn silenced her with a finger against her lips. "I'm angry because Patrick and Lillian have had to live like fugitives when they've done nothing wrong. I'm angry that you've had to shoulder this burden for so long. They're the reason you've had to postpone the move to Knoxville, aren't they?"

Curling her fingers about his, she pulled them away from her mouth and down to her side but didn't release his hand. "I care about them."

"I know you do." He drank in her upturned features, gaze touching on each point of beauty. Mysterious and alluring like a fine painting, she possessed a hitherto unknown depth he yearned to explore. "I have never admired a person more than I do you in this moment."

Her lips parted. "Quinn."

Ignoring the inner voice yelling at him to stop, to remember who he was and who she was and cease this nonsense *at once*, he cupped the side of her neck. The soft mass of her hair felt like rich mink fur against his skin.

Weaving a little to the side, she braced her hands against his biceps. "I—I feel dizzy."

With his heart thundering in his chest, his fingers closed around her waist and he lowered his head until their breaths mingled and the tips of their noses bumped.

"That's good," he murmured, "because I do, too."

Quinn drew her steadily closer, her voluminous skirts tangling with his pant legs and their boots colliding. When he had her as near as he dared, he fastened his attention on her dainty mouth, aware this wasn't his best idea. Aware but too far gone to heed the voice of caution, which in his case wasn't very loud or insistent.

Besides, he'd given her plenty of opportunity to slap him. Or shove him away. She hadn't, which meant her common sense had gone the way of his.

He carefully brushed his lips against hers. No pressure. Easy. Gentle.

Nicole tightened her hold in response and, with a rush of sweet breath fanning over his mouth, went up on tiptoe to return his kiss.

The world around them ceased to exist. There was only Nicole anchoring him to the earth, her scent enveloping him, her softness a balm for his loneliness, her breath sustaining him.

He deepened the kiss, lips tangling with hers. She followed his lead with endearing eagerness. *Devastating* moved to the top of the list of her traits.

She's innocent, Darling. The reminder had his mind reeling with the implications. *She's leaving. You're staying.*

Nothing could come of this. Nothing but hurt feelings.

This was the best moment in her life.

She had never felt so alive, so *in tune* with another human being.

Quinn saw her as no one else did—she'd hidden nothing about her personality from him—and still he was kissing her, clinging to her the same desperate way she clung to him. He was holding himself back for her sake. Quinn may be many things—cocky, nosy, too handsome for his own good—but for him, her well-being took precedence over everything else. He was her overzealous, self-appointed protector. Who could've guessed the one man who could take her from mildly annoyed to spitting mad in mere seconds could also lavish her with tenderness and make her feel wanted, even cherished, when no one else had?

Please let this continue forever.

Forever?

Forever meant staying in Gatlinburg. Giving up her dream.

She wasn't prepared to give up her dream for anyone. Postpone, yes. Give up completely? For a man who hadn't even asked her to?

Even knowing this, her heart squeezed into a tight ball of regret when Quinn abruptly jerked his mouth from hers. His breathing off-kilter, he stepped out of the embrace and sank his hands deep in his pockets, eyes dark and turbulent.

The hot imprint of where his hands had been on her skin began to cool, and she struggled with the need to resume that contact. Because now that there was air and space between them, the loneliness rushed back in, along with the feeling of *apartness* that had dogged her since childhood, and she hated that feeling even more now that she'd experienced connection. And not with just anyone.

With Quinn.

"I shouldn't have done that." His voice was a throaty rasp.

Clenching her fingers into fists, she pressed them against her sternum in a vain effort to numb the pain blossoming there. He would not be kissing her again. She wouldn't experience the wonder of his embrace again. It was for the best, but that didn't mean she didn't mourn the loss.

"I shouldn't have taken advantage," he continued with a frown. "I'm your boss."

Sucking in a ragged breath, she did what she had to do to salvage their working relationship. "We're both adults. Why can't we simply put this behind us? Forget it ever happened?"

"I can't say I'll be able to forget—" his gaze went nearly black in the darkness "—but I can be professional from here on out. That is, if you're willing to continue working with me."

"I still need this job."

A door slammed in the distance, followed by Megan's voice. "Nicole? Is that you?"

What was her sister doing here so late? "I'll be right there," she called over her shoulder. Not looking at Quinn, she said, "I have to go."

He bent to pick up the lamp, his face sharp angles and shadows. "Will I see you in the morning?"

"Of course." Did that breezy voice really belong to her? She possessed serious acting skills.

He hesitated as if there was more he wished to say. "Good night, then."

"Good night."

It wasn't easy walking away from him as if he hadn't just irrevocably altered her life.

"Oh, Nicole?"

You can do this. A few seconds more and you can escape.

Pivoting on the dark path, she waited for him to speak.

"Don't worry about your friends. We'll think of a solution to their predicament. Together."

Together. As they'd be hour after hour, day after day. And she was supposed to keep up this pretense—that he was just her boss and she was merely his assistant and nothing whatsoever had changed between them?

That Quinn hadn't awakened crazy, wonderful, downright terrifying emotions in her?

She'd been pretending all her life that being the odd sister didn't bother her. She had feigning apathy down to an art. This would be no different.

Chapter Fifteen

Megan was descending the porch steps when Nicole reached the cabin. "Was that Quinn?"

"Yes."

"It's awfully late to be working, isn't it?" Ringlets gleaming in the darkness, she squinted at the distant lane leading to town.

With a noncommittal sound, Nicole changed the subject. "Is there a particular reason you're here?"

"Mama mentioned Jane's been feeling down lately, so I came to try and cheer her up."

"Considering her reason for being sad, do you think you're the right person to do that?"

Nicole wasn't trying to be mean, but the truth was the truth. Jane had been infatuated with Tom Leighton for years. He, however, loved Megan. He'd even proposed to her and had been so devastated over her rejection that he'd eventually left town.

"Jane doesn't blame me for his leaving," she said stiffly. "Personally, I'm not sure if he'll return."

"And even if he did, I don't think the two of them would end up together. Tom sees her as a little sister. "

Sinking on the top step, Megan patted the space beside her. "Is that what you and Quinn are? Just friends?"

Nicole didn't wish to speak of him. Still, if she was to ever enjoy deeper relationships with her sisters, she was going to have to reveal a bit of herself.

Sitting beside Megan, Nicole adjusted her skirts and folded her hands in her lap. Somewhere in the woods behind the barn, an owl hooted.

"He kissed me tonight."

Megan squealed and clapped her hands together.

"He apologized afterward."

That dampened her excitement. "Why? What did he say?"

Nicole found herself pouring out the details. It was nice to share her burden, even if she wasn't seeking answers. There was no future for her and Quinn. Perhaps there'd be someone in the city who'd make her feel this way. Better, even.

"What are you going to do?" Megan said at last.

"Nothing. We're going to put this behind us and focus on maintaining our professional relationship."

"Will that make you happy?" She pivoted, leaned forward at the waist to peer directly at her. "Because I have to say, Quinn strikes me as sort of perfect for you."

"He's not part of my plan. Marriage is something I'll have to wait for until many years down the road. I've worked too hard and too long to make my dream into a reality to simply let it go."

"Plans can change," Megan suggested lightly. "Have you prayed about whether or not your dream lines up with what God wants for your life?"

No, I haven't, she thought guiltily. "God knows my desire. He created me, after all, and blessed me with this ability. Mama's always quoting that verse from Psalms…'Delight yourself also in the Lord, and He shall give you the desires of your heart.'"

"Have you ever considered He might fulfill your desires in a different way than you've imagined?"

She couldn't fathom any other way of accomplishing her dream. Besides, what possible objection could God have to her moving to Knoxville? He was aware of her discontent.

"Enough about me. Tell me about your trip to New Orleans. When do you leave?"

Each summer, she and Lucian traveled there to visit Lucian's father.

"August fifth." Dipping her head, she concentrated on her clasped hands. "We're planning to visit an orphanage there."

Surprise skittered through Nicole. "Oh? I hadn't realized you were considering adoption."

"Lucian and I have been praying for God to bless our union with children, whether that be through natural means or adoption."

"Well." Unused to private confessions, she scrambled for an appropriate response. This was the first time Megan had revealed her longing for children to her. Watching her fidget with the ruffles on her skirt, Nicole was struck with a surprising thought. Could her big sister find it as difficult to confide in her as Nicole did? After all, this was foreign territory for them both.

"I think it's wonderful," she said, meaning it. "You've always wanted a big family, and you have plenty of space in that monster of a house."

Lifting her head, Megan smiled tremulously, moisture shining in her eyes. "I don't care how I become a mother, I just want a house full of children to love and nurture."

Warmth and a strange but not unwelcome sense of closeness spread through Nicole. "I hope you get what you want," she said shyly. "And I'm glad you told me."

"Me, too." Then Megan surprised her with a hug. Easing away, she tugged playfully on one of Nicole's loose curls. "We should talk like this more often."

Throat thick with emotion, Nicole nodded. She had Quinn to thank for this step forward. He was the one who'd encouraged her to reach out.

If she was smart, she'd take what she learned from him into her new life.

Quinn was watching Shane exit the mercantile early the following morning when Nicole seized his hand and yanked him into the office, where she all but accosted him.

"What happened to keeping my friends' secret?" she demanded, red splotches on her neck and cheeks and eyes spitting violet-hued fire. "I thought you'd agreed to consult them before involving the sheriff or anyone else."

His instinctive reaction—to glibly comment on how her irritation with him merely served to enhance her beauty—would not achieve the professional atmosphere he'd promised himself he'd provide for her.

"There's no need to get upset. Shane dropped by to tell me he doesn't have any leads regarding the springhouse crime. I stand by my oath to you and your friends. I will not breathe a word to anyone until we figure out the next step together."

"Oh." She turned away from him to sift needlessly through the papers on the desk.

Quinn assessed her neat, stylish appearance, lingering on her upswept hair and the curve of her ear. He was sorely tempted to close the distance between them, wrap his arms around her and plant a kiss against her nape. Soothe her worries with soft whispers.

His pulse picking up speed, he'd taken a half step in her direction before he even realized it. He grimaced. Keeping things strictly platonic was going to be a daily battle.

Trapping his hands in his pockets, he forced himself to remember she was in his employ. As her boss, he had a duty to insure the workplace was safe for her. The last thing he wanted was for her to worry about possible advances from him. He needed for her to focus on her job.

"What are you thinking?" he asked, leaning against the doorpost.

"I have my doubts Patrick will agree to involve Shane." She stacked papers that didn't need straightening. "My numerous attempts have proved futile."

He sensed her frustration. Understandable, considering the effort and sacrifice she'd sunk into their situation. "He hasn't had a dose of the famous Darling charm, though, has he?"

When her lips compressed and she shrugged, he said in a more serious tone, "Patrick knows this is no kind of life for his sister. I'll appeal to his honor as her protector. He'll see reason."

"I hope you're right."

"Don't worry. After work, I'll stop by Plum's and pick up supper for the four of us. We'll figure out a solution tonight."

Her luminous eyes lifting to his—and the faith she was putting in him—was like a gift.

"I'm sorry I jumped to the wrong conclusion. I shouldn't have questioned you."

He had to get out of there before he did something stupid.

Nodding, he backed out the door and into the hallway, gesturing to the storeroom. "Can you check on the front? I've got to see about…something."

Her confused expression stayed with him as he took refuge amongst the shelves. *Better confusion than revulsion, Darling.* Twenty minutes of him pacing and praying passed before he felt ready to rejoin her. The banker, Claude Jenkins, entered just as Quinn reached the counter.

"Quinn." He smiled and waved papers in the air. "Good news. The land purchase contract is ready to sign. Soon you'll be an official Gatlinburg resident."

Several customers glanced up from their shopping to watch the exchange. How would this news affect those locals who hadn't yet accepted him? Would they be more inclined to trust him?

Opening the silver-and-crystal case on the other counter, Nicole shot him an indecipherable look. He didn't have to ask her opinion on the subject. Although she knew what had precipitated his desire for a simpler life, she couldn't understand why he'd want to tie himself to her quaint mountain town.

The thought came to him then that he had the means to replenish her savings. She'd unselfishly used it to help two people who were of no relation to her. Strangers who'd desperately needed someone to care for them and who had no way of repaying her. While he dreaded the thought of her leaving, after last night's embrace and his current battle to keep his distance, perhaps it would be best if she left sooner rather than later.

The banker stood before him, expectant.

"That's wonderful news," Quinn said. "Nicole, will you be all right by yourself for a few minutes?"

"Of course."

He waved the big man through. "Come on back to the office."

When Quinn shut the door, Claude continued to smile his encouragement. "Buying this property is going to go a long way toward cementing your position in our town. Already, I've heard positive comments about you from several patrons who were hesitant at first."

Laying out the paperwork, he pointed to where his signature was needed.

"Progress is a good thing." Sinking into the chair, Quinn took several minutes to peruse the document. Satisfied, he located a pen and added his signature, a little thrill of excitement offsetting the on-edge feeling he'd had since Nicole arrived.

He'd allowed this unwise attraction to distract him from his goals. First and foremost, he had to tend his store and its ongoing success. Secondly, he had to get a permanent home built. The living quarters, though cramped, were adequate, but they weren't home. And his residing in them didn't communicate serious intentions to the townspeople. In their minds, he had the wherewithal to jump ship any moment he pleased.

His thoughts straying to Nicole once again, he reminded himself that once his home was finished, he'd be free to turn his focus to finding a suitable wife.

With the chicken and dumplings consumed, followed by generous helpings of chess pie, Nicole sat back and watched Quinn. He appealed to Patrick's sense of duty to Lillian, calmly and systematically knocking down argument after argument.

She could see that he wasn't simply doing this for her. He genuinely cared for the siblings' future. Their safety. That his privileged upbringing and his vast circle of influential friends hadn't made him into a snobbish boor impressed her.

Face it, Nicole, she told herself, *a lot of things about Quinn Darling impress you.*

Sipping her watered-down lemonade, she pushed memories of his lips molded against hers out of her mind. The memories had crept in hundreds—no, thousands—of times today as they'd dodged and sidestepped each other, extra vigilant to avoid physical contact. More than once, she'd caught him staring at her mouth.

If only this was a surface-deep attraction.

No question Quinn was a striking individual, with his sleek hair and chiseled features, generous lips that could so easily slip into a lazy, confident smile. His stylish clothing, usually made up of safe, business-like colors like navy and black and charcoal, hugged his body, showcasing his lean, powerful physique. He moved with grace and purpose. No hesitation for the heir to the Darling empire.

Nicole's problem was that, irksome qualities aside,

she genuinely liked Quinn. The way his mind worked. His caring nature. His determination and drive, which mirrored her own. He could've complained about his struggles. Instead, he'd admitted he needed her assistance and set about learning how to run the mercantile. And, despite his frustration with the locals' resistance, he'd done everything in his power to win them over, humbling himself in the process.

Liking her boss in this way could not only lead to a very uncomfortable working relationship, it could have her questioning her decision to leave Gatlinburg. That was something she couldn't allow to happen. She had to focus on her dream. Later, once her boutique was open and her reputation established, she could think about marriage.

The acceptance in Patrick's voice caught her attention. "And if I agree to go along with your plan? Where would we stay while the sheriff investigates our situation?"

Quinn turned in his seat to look at her, unaware she hadn't been following their interaction. "You're more familiar with the options than I am. Do you have any suggestions?"

Lillian and Patrick waited, tense and apprehensive.

"As a matter of fact, I do. My sister and her husband, Megan and Lucian Beaumont, live in a spacious, two-story Victorian near town. They have ample rooms available. I'm certain they'd be happy to have you stay with them."

While Lillian's eyes sparked with interest, Patrick looked unsure. More charity, he must be thinking.

"They don't have any children," Nicole added, "and

my sister is desperate for someone besides Lucian to lavish her attention on."

Quinn's approving smile made her feel ridiculously giddy. "Would you mind stopping there on your way home? I can accompany you if you'd like."

More time in his company, trying to remain cool and unaffected? No, thanks. She needed a reprieve before her test of endurance started all over again tomorrow morning.

"I thought you were going to pay Shane a visit."

Retrieving his pocket watch, he frowned at the time. "It is getting late. I'll go to the jail first and speak with him, then swing by your cabin so that we can update each other."

"All right." Standing to her feet, she spontaneously hugged Lillian and Patrick, anticipation singing in her veins. Soon, very soon, they'd leave this nightmare behind.

Chapter Sixteen

Muttering under her breath, Nicole glared at the uneven stitch—her tenth in as many minutes—and snipped the thread so that she could start again. It didn't usually take long for a project to dominate her attention and push her worries aside, but she couldn't help reviewing today's events. Plus, she was on edge waiting for Quinn's footsteps on the porch.

The mantel clock chimed eight o'clock. A quick glance out the living room window revealed a typical summer evening, waning light turning the distant mountain sides a deep, purplish blue. A pair of blue jays swooped past.

Where was he?

A sniffle snagged her attention. Curled in the cushioned chair opposite Nicole's spot on the sofa, Jane lowered her book to her lap and swiped at her wet cheeks. Straight auburn hair collected at her nape with a navy blue ribbon, skin dewy and eyes large and shadowed, she looked young and innocent. Not that Nicole would voice such a thought. Jane and Jessica were both eagerly anticipating their seventeenth birthday in September.

"Sad story?" Nicole said.

"He doesn't love her." Her lower lip trembled. "He doesn't care that she loves him. Has *always* loved him."

Uh-oh. She wasn't talking about a fictional hero and heroine, was she? This was about Tom Leighton.

Jessica, whose habit was to bake in the evenings, must've sensed her twin's angst, for she materialized in the doorway. Flour dusted her nose.

"He's been gone awhile, Jane," she said softly. "He didn't tell anyone where he was going or when he was coming back."

Jane jutted her chin. "I know him. He won't leave his homestead to fall to ruin."

"He's a barber, not a farmer," Jessica pointed out. "For all we know, he could've written to Mr. Jenkins to put it up for sale."

Another fat tear dripped to her chin.

Nicole wished she could think of something comforting to say. She secretly agreed with Jessica—it wasn't likely Tom would return. Megan's rejection had hit him hard. He'd sold his business. He hadn't even returned for his mother's funeral. There wasn't anything left to draw him back.

"I thought he'd at least write and let me know he's okay." Jane looked miserable.

"He should have known you'd worry," Nicole agreed.

Jessica frowned, twisted the towel in her hands. "Do you want to help me finish up the cake for Mrs. Taggart?"

Jane sighed. Snapping the book closed, she laid it on the coffee table. "Sure, why not?"

When the girls had left, Nicole stared at the dress she was making for Rachel Prescott and offered up a prayer for her sister's broken heart. In time, Jane would realize a future with Tom was out of the question. The wound would heal, and she'd find a new love.

Just as Jane would forget about Tom's charms, so would Nicole forget about Quinn's. A new city, combined with all that was required in building a business from scratch, would do the trick.

Ten minutes later, his heavy tread on the steps alerted her to his presence. The twins were still working in the kitchen, and their mother had retired early.

Heart pounding, she set aside the material, careful not to unravel the thread from the needle, and went to admit him.

"Hi," she said.

Holding on to the door, she adopted a nonchalant air and tried not to ogle his slightly disheveled appearance. His suit coat and vest were nowhere to be seen, and the top buttons of his white shirt were undone, revealing smooth, tanned skin. His dark hair was mussed, and a hint of stubble darkened his jaw.

"Hi." He smiled faintly. "Sorry I'm late. Shane had company when I arrived."

"Would you like to come inside?"

He gestured to the rocking chairs on the porch. "It's nice out tonight. Mind if we talk out here?"

She closed the door with a soft click. Quinn waited for her to choose her chair before taking the other one. Gazing at the mountains rising above the treetops, he said, "I hope I never take these views for granted."

"Does your land have a similar one?"

"My land." Turning his head to regard her, he smiled broadly. "I like the sound of that. The house in Boston, the offices and the factories all belong to my father."

"Here the mercantile is solely yours, as is the property."

"Exactly. And to answer your question, yes, it does have a favorable view. I can hardly wait to draw up plans for the house."

"House or mansion?"

His lips twitched. "I will keep it tasteful, never you fear."

Nicole likely wouldn't see the finished project before she left. The thought saddened her. Lucian and Megan had insisted on assuming financial support for Patrick and Lillian, which meant she could pour every cent of her income into savings.

"How did the meeting with Shane go?"

"As I'd suspected. Shane's a fair man. He's promised to look into the matter."

"As soon as my sister and Lucian heard about their plight, they offered to take them in. I didn't even have to ask."

"Were they upset with you for keeping this secret for so long?"

Recalling the heated lecture she could've done without, she put her foot down to stop the rocking motion and gazed at the shadows gathering in the forest beyond the barn.

He followed suit, his expression going somber. "Nicole, you do realize that in hiding Patrick and Lillian, you put your own safety at risk."

Her mouth tightened. "I've already had one set down

today, thank you very much. I don't require another. Besides, I was careful."

"You mistake my intention." His voice came out as a caress. "I'm not chastising you. I simply wish that you'd felt free to enlist help. A family member or a friend to help shoulder the burden."

The depth of his concern robbed her of speech. Reaching into her pocket, her fingers closed over the siblings' brooch. Quinn's brow wrinkled when she held it out to him.

"What's this?"

"It belonged to Patrick and Lillian's grandmother. He gave it to me as a form of payment. I couldn't tell him I had no intention of cashing it in. Will you keep it in the store safe for them until their stepfather is dealt with?"

Their palms skimmed together, and warmth pooled in her middle the same instant his gaze went dark and searching. The air sizzled as if humming with mini-lightning strikes. Then he broke the connection, sucking in a stuttering breath, head bent to study the piece of jewelry.

"I'll keep it safe for them," he said, without looking at her.

"Thank you."

Minutes passed without either of them speaking. Lightning bugs flashed in the gathering darkness, weaving patterns above the rows of vegetables.

When he finally lifted his head, his features were unreadable but his eyes burned with searing intensity.

"You're an amazing woman, Nicole O'Malley. You deserve to be happy. To realize your dream."

Amazing? No one had ever uttered such words of praise to her before.

You haven't allowed anyone close enough, a small voice reminded. *Haven't given anyone a chance to know you.*

What did it mean that she'd dropped her defenses with Quinn?

"You've proven yourself to be a valuable asset," he continued, "and I believe a pay raise is in order."

She blinked, confused at the subject change. "A pay raise?"

Emmett hadn't seen fit to increase her wages in the time she'd worked for him. Where was this coming from?

"You're worth it. Besides, you need to replenish the funds for your boutique. This way, you can make the move to Knoxville sooner."

Her insides twisted into painful knots. He sounded almost eager to be rid of her. He certainly didn't seem to care that they'd be residing in different cities and would probably see each other only once or twice a year.

That house or mansion or whatever of his wouldn't stay empty for long. He'd find a nice, sweet girl to settle down with and start a family.

A bereft sensation lodged in her chest, the stark loss of it freezing the breath in her lungs.

She thought of Jane's heartbreak and assured herself this wasn't the same. At all. How could it be? She didn't love him. Sometimes, she didn't even like him!

It was just that Quinn was the only man who'd seen her for herself, the person she truly was inside when the O'Malley name, along with her reputation and the cloak of apathy she used as a shield, was stripped away.

He'd *seen* her and deemed her worthy.

How was she supposed to forget that?

Nicole's sister could hardly contain her excitement as she led Patrick and Lillian on a tour of the ground floor. Lucian's gaze trailed his wife, his smile affectionate. The couple's genuine warmth would go a long way in making the siblings feel comfortable in their temporary home.

Quinn glanced at Nicole, who'd linked arms with Lillian the moment they'd ascended the grand house's sweeping front porch and refused to leave the frail girl's side. While Lillian gaped in unconcealed wonder at the soaring library shelves stuffed with books, Nicole frowned at Patrick's pained, pale countenance.

The boy would have to be seen by the doctor. His leg wound clearly hadn't healed properly.

As if sensing the direction of his thoughts, Lucian motioned to the plush sofa and chairs situated before the fireplace. "Why don't we have a seat for a moment? Mrs. Calhoun, our cook, has prepared a special treat in preparation for your arrival." He moved to the wide, arched doorway. "Megan, care to lend me a hand?"

Megan took his outstretched hand and accompanied him down the hall.

Patrick sank into the nearest cushioned chair, white lines bracketing his mouth. Quinn prayed the brave young man would be able to find relief. He'd be sure to discuss the matter with Lucian.

Sensing Nicole's worried gaze, Quinn intercepted it and offered what he hoped was a smile of encouragement. That was the extent of what he could offer her. Touching her, even briefly, carried immense risk. Those tense moments on her porch last night proved it.

Thankfully he'd reined in his foolish longings.

Going to stand at the window, he propped a shoulder against the frame and watched as she and Lillian whispered together on the sofa.

"Mr. Darling?"

"Yes, Lillian?"

Toying with the ends of her long, wavy blond ponytail, cheeks bright pink, she said, "Thank you again for the clothing and supplies."

"It was very generous of you," Nicole said. Hands folded primly in her lap, she made a striking picture. Clad completely in black—anti-summer and in opposition of the happy events of this day—the look should've been severe. It wasn't. The hue, which matched her carefully styled curls, added luster to her pearl-like skin.

"Glad I could help."

Patrick stuck out his chin. "We'll pay you back someday."

Quinn's first instinct was to insist it was a gift. But he recognized the boy's need to contribute, to repay perceived debts, when he'd been the recipient of charity for so long.

"Perhaps you could help me in the store after Nicole leaves."

Brow furrowing, he snapped his attention to Nicole. "You're leaving?"

Lillian looked stricken. "Where are you going? You're coming back, right?"

Uh-oh. Mouthing *I'm sorry* to a flustered Nicole, he

wished he'd kept his mouth shut. He'd assumed she'd told them.

Sadness stealing over her face, she took the other girl's hands in hers. "I've tried to think of an easy way to tell you both."

When she'd revealed her plans, the siblings sat there looking stunned. And guilty, which was exactly why she hadn't told them, Quinn realized.

"I promise to come and visit you as often as I can. And once I'm settled, you can come and visit me."

Patrick kneaded his forehead. "I wish you'd told us in the beginning. We could've moved on—"

"No. The truth is, I needed you as much as you needed me."

"I don't understand."

"Before you came along, I had never experienced true friendship. Trusting others isn't something that comes naturally to me. But with you and Lillian, I felt free to be myself."

Again, Nicole looked at him, and he got the feeling he was included in the handful of people who'd seen the real woman beneath the icy facade.

Lillian clung to her. "I'm going to miss you so much!"

From this angle, he could see Nicole's battle to keep her emotions at bay. Leaving Gatlinburg wasn't going to be without cost.

Quinn wouldn't allow himself to imagine what daily life would be like without her, how strange the mercantile would feel. Why imagine when he'd experience the reality soon enough?

"We don't know what's going to happen to us or

where we'll end up," Patrick said gruffly. "We can't take advantage of your family's kindness indefinitely."

"What if Sheriff Timmons believes Carl's account of what happened?" Lillian pulled back, worry pulling at her mouth. "What if he makes us go with him?"

"Shane's not going to do that." Pushing away from the wall, Quinn went to sit on her other side. "He and his deputy are going to your stepfather's homestead today. They won't reveal your whereabouts just yet."

Lucian and Megan walked in bearing trays of lemonade and an assortment of sweets. While Megan played hostess, Quinn caught Nicole's attention and motioned to the door.

"Please excuse us for a few moments," she announced to the room in general, rising and smoothing her full skirts.

In the hallway, he gestured to the rear of the house. "Care to take a quick stroll about the gardens? Lucian insisted I see them before I go. Seems to think I'll be impressed."

"This is hardly the time." Her dark brows collided.

"I will not keep you long," he promised.

"Fine."

She preceded him out the door and onto the wide porch. The heat hit them like a wave, and Quinn immediately removed his coat jacket and looped it over the railing. Nicole removed a fan from her reticule and lazily fanned herself.

They strolled along stone pathways beside lush flower beds lined with meticulously pruned bushes. Bright yellow golden asters mixed with delicate purple Southern harebells and Turk's Cap lilies. Azaleas in varying shades formed the outer row.

"I owe you an apology." He stopped to face her. "It wasn't my intention to put you in a tight spot."

"I should've told them." Perching on a stone bench, fan discarded on her lap, she observed a pair of butterflies. "I'm worried what will happen to them, Quinn. Their stepfather strikes me as a determined, ruthless man."

Unable to resist comforting her, he sat and took her hand in his. "I care about their well-being, too, and you have my word I'll do whatever necessary to protect them."

"You're a kind man."

He laughed outright. "You don't have to act so surprised."

"Well, I couldn't fathom making such an observation the first night we met."

Their intertwined hands resting on the cool, gritty stone between them, his chuckles rumbled in his chest.

"Seriously, Quinn, you've been a huge help in this situation. It means a lot to them. And to me."

Suddenly her soft-as-velvet lips were grazing his cheek, shocking him into silence.

He could so easily turn this into a real kiss. All he had to do was twist his head to the right a few inches. They were alone in this romantic, orderly maze of flowers and trees, shielded from the house. No one would see them.

Quinn squeezed his eyes tight, battling this yearning for her that, should he give in to it, would confuse their friendship.

He dropped her hand and shot to his feet.

"We should rejoin the others."

"It appears I'm not the only one who finds it difficult to accept compliments."

Nicole brushed past him. Flouncing down the pathway, her hem swiped at the fragile stems edging it. Quinn sighed. She was irritated with him again. Or had his reaction to her unexpected overture embarrassed her?

Either emotion was better than hurt feelings.

At least he could face her at work Monday morning with a clear conscience. She didn't have to know his heart was a little bruised.

Chapter Seventeen

"It was kind of Quinn to give you the day off. Saturdays must be the busiest shopping day of all."

Lounging on the quilt beside her mother and making a clover chain, Nicole observed the twins wading calf-deep in the river.

"He can be nice when he puts his mind to it."

He'd delayed opening in order to help with Patrick and Lillian's move. After their walk in the flower gardens, he'd told her to take the rest of the day off. She hadn't argued. Not after her silly kiss and his abrupt reaction.

She needed space from him and all the turmoil he was stirring to life inside her.

"I wish you would've felt comfortable confiding in me. I would've helped you, you know. And those poor kids."

At the underlying hurt in her mother's voice, Nicole shifted her gaze. Butter-yellow sunshine highlighted the age spots on her cheeks and glinted off her spectacles.

"I'm sorry. It's just that…if I'd told you, I would've been breaking my promise."

Her mother cupped her cheek. "I love you, sweet daughter. I wish your father could see you now. He'd be incredibly proud."

Nicole blinked against an onslaught of emotion. Her mother wasn't normally a demonstrative person. And she rarely spoke of her deceased husband.

"You think so?"

"You're a lot like him, you know. Quiet. Private. He wasn't one to share his thoughts."

Bittersweet pleasure spread through her chest, and she dashed away rogue tears. She *hated* crying in front of others, no matter who it was.

Nicole had been small when he'd died suddenly of heart failure. As her mother's observations sank in, she couldn't help but wonder if things might've been different had he lived.

"Will you tell me more about him?"

Her smile wistful and full of sadness, Alice shared tidbits and stories Nicole couldn't recall hearing. All too soon, Jessica and Jane interrupted, laughing and dripping on the quilt, bits of grass dirtying their feet.

Eager for time alone to process the revelations about her father, Nicole decided to stay behind and soak up another hour of sunshine.

"Don't linger too long," Alice advised, hefting the basket containing their leftover food. "It's nearing four o'clock, and we'll be having supper in a couple of hours."

"All right, Mama."

Alice and the twins left, but she was hardly alone. Other families were enjoying this mid-July Saturday, blankets spread out in the rolling, clover-dotted fields and fishing or swimming in the river. Untying her bonnet, she lay back and tilted it so that her face was shielded from the light. The scent of grass and baked earth filled her nostrils. The longer she lay there, the more the tension she'd been carrying around these past months melted away.

Patrick and Lillian's well-being wasn't solely her responsibility anymore. Shane, Quinn, Lucian and Megan were all willing and able to do their part. She hadn't realized until this moment what a toll their predicament, and her part in caring for them, had taken.

If not for her confusing feelings for Quinn, she could be almost content.

She drifted to sleep replaying their earlier conversation and the feel of his smooth, firm jaw beneath her sensitive lips.

Masculine laughter startled her awake.

Struggling to clear the fog from her mind, she blinked, frowned at the unfamiliar plaid shirt filling her vision. Where was she? The hard ground beneath her clued her in. She'd fallen asleep, but for how long?

A sharp yank on her hair had her gasping.

"Hurry up."

Timothy? What was he—

The glint of a knife blade flashed near her nose, and fear cascaded into her bloodstream. She shoved at the broad chest hovering over her. "Get off me!"

The chest didn't budge. "Hold her down. And make sure she doesn't scream."

That was Kenneth's voice. Was Pete with them? Where was everyone? Why wasn't anyone helping her?

"Hel—"

A rough, sweat-dampened hand smashed her lips to-gether, stifling her plea. Kenneth's face appeared above her. His callous sneer filled her throat with bile. Some-one pulled on her hair again until her eyes smarted with the pain.

When large hands clapped onto her legs to still her squirming, Nicole knew true terror. Obviously she'd slept longer than she'd realized and the other folks had already left. Otherwise, someone would've intervened.

She was alone with a man whose wounded pride had obliterated common decency and his cohorts, who didn't think to question him. Up until this moment, she hadn't believed them capable of violence.

Please, God. Thoughts failed her. Passing seconds stretched into an eternity as the men's raucous laugh-ter assaulted her ears.

Kenneth was making a sawing motion with the knife. She braced herself for pain that didn't come.

Suddenly, he leaped off her, a victory whoop fill-ing the air. He was waving something above his head. Her legs were abruptly released. The hand imprison-ing her mouth fell away.

Heart shuddering like a frightened rabbit beneath her rib cage, she couldn't seem to force her muscles to move. She lay there on the quilt, frozen. Confused. Dread coated her mouth.

"I cut off the witch's hair," Kenneth chortled. Be-side him, Pete and Timothy laughed so hard they bent over, hands on their bellies.

Arms like jelly, she pushed herself into a sitting po-sition. Kenneth noticed. Lunged at her.

"You always did think you were better than everyone else, you little witch," he spit, tossing the black thing on her lap.

She yelped, batted at the thing until she recognized the ribbon attached. The ribbon she'd tied her hair back with that morning.

"My hair!" Hands flying up, she whimpered when she encountered the short, uneven ends. "What have you done?"

Kenneth roughly seized her jaw in his hand, bringing his face near. "You're lucky we didn't scalp you," he growled. "If you breathe our names to another soul, you won't be so lucky next time."

Pete grabbed his arm. "Let's go."

They left her then.

Sick to her stomach, tears streaming down her cheeks, Nicole curled in on herself, comforted by one fact—soon she would leave this town, and she was never coming back.

Emerging onto the boardwalk, Quinn locked the front door with a weary but satisfied sigh. The afternoon had passed in a blur. Without Nicole there to help, the customers had had no option but to deal with him. For the most part, they'd been patient and civil. Perhaps the news of his land purchase had already traveled the town's grapevine and they'd accepted he wasn't going anywhere.

Offering up a silent prayer of gratitude, he set his feet toward Plum's, mouth watering at the thought of Mrs. Greene's yeast rolls slick with melted butter. He was ravenous.

Traversing the dusty street, a bark of laughter from the vicinity of the post office caught his attention. Kenneth and his buddies stood in a circle of about half-a-dozen young men, talking and gesturing wildly. Whatever they were saying evoked a mixture of disbelief and reluctant amusement.

Appetite forgotten, Quinn had the overwhelming urge to see Nicole.

Pivoting sharply, he dodged a horse and rider and strode in the opposite direction, regretting his decision to delay purchasing a horse of his own. He was out of breath by the time he reached her cabin.

It's probably nothing. Better prepare a sound reason for your unannounced visit, he told himself.

Alice opened the door, and the smell of roasted beef and fried onions hit him, reawakening his hunger. Maybe he could finagle a dinner invitation out of this. Enjoying a meal with his assistant and her family was preferable to a meal alone in the café.

"Mrs. O'Malley." He tipped his head in greeting. "I apologize for dropping by unannounced, but would it be possible to speak with Nicole?"

Behind the spectacles, her eyes crinkled with concern and she eyed the whitewashed sky beyond his shoulder. "She hasn't yet returned from our picnic. I was expecting her an hour ago."

Lassoing his imagination, he forced a calm he didn't feel. "If you point me in the right direction, I'll go and check on her."

"Oh, would you? I was going to send one of the girls once we'd finished in the kitchen."

"Can I borrow one of your horses?"

"Certainly. And once you've brought her home, I'd love for you to have supper with us."

"Thank you."

But satiating his hunger no longer dominated his thoughts. All he could think about was her tormentors, gleefully gloating on the boardwalk.

After fifteen minutes of slow progress through the woodland trail, he reached the clearing. With the faint sound of trickling water riding the gentle breeze, he scanned the verdant landscape. The green fields stood empty. Portions of the riverbank were dotted with willow trees. Drawing closer to investigate, he spotted a hunched, black-clad figure seated at the water's edge.

He breathed a sigh of relief. *See? All that worrying for nothing. She's fine.*

Dismounting, he led his borrowed mount through the high grass, calling out to her when he drew near. She didn't respond, however, and the bonnet's brim hid her face.

"Nicole?" He stopped directly beside her, unease slithering through him. Surely she wasn't still irritated with him?

He dropped onto the grass, and she shifted slightly away from him.

"What's the matter? Are you upset with me?"

He'd never known her to completely ignore him. Annoyance sharpened his voice.

"Your mother is worried about you."

A small sniffle caught him off guard. She was crying.

Sad…not angry. Trying to hide her tears from him.

"Hey." He settled a hand on her shoulder, and she jerked as if prodded with a branding iron. "Okay, you're starting to scare me," he exclaimed. "Why won't you speak to me?"

Gently taking her chin, he urged her head around

and received a shock. Her face was ravaged with tears, skin red and splotchy, lips trembling, violet eyes awash in misery.

His heart stopped. "What happened?"

Throat working, Nicole untied her bonnet ribbons with trembling fingers. Then she slowly lifted it from her unbound curls. Curls that had been shorn off to about an inch below her ears.

Without thinking, Quinn reached out and fingered a lock of hair. This hadn't been done using scissors, but with a blunt instrument.

"Kenneth was here." A shudder racked her shoulders. "I fell asleep, and when I woke up he and his friends were holding me down. For a minute, I—I thought they were going to—" She pressed her lips tightly together as more tears seeped out.

Rage, searing and white-hot, seeped into his gut as he pictured the ugly scene.

"Tell me exactly what they did," he managed, fingers shaky as they trailed her cheek.

The account came tumbling out, her terror at finding herself at their mercy tormenting him. He would make sure they paid for their crime. He may not be the law in this town, but he had a different sort of power at his disposal.

Justice was going to have to wait, though. Right now, Nicole needed comforting. And Quinn desperately needed to be the one to give it to her.

With effort, he bottled the burning drive for retribution and worked to gentle his words and touch.

He fished out his handkerchief and wiped the moisture from her cheeks. Her luminous gaze clung to his as he worked, her hitched breaths settling into a more natural rhythm, the trusting nature of her regard nearly felling him. Her trust didn't come easily. That he'd somehow won it humbled him.

When he'd dried her tears, he gingerly fluffed her shiny locks. He gave in to the temptation to explore the silky texture. She watched him with wide, barely blinking eyes.

"This length suits you, you know," he murmured. "It draws attention to your eyes, not to mention the elegant line of your jaw."

A line appeared between her brows. "You're just saying that to make me feel better."

"I have always been honest with you, Duchess. And right now, I can honestly say you take my breath away."

She sucked in air, pink lips parting. "Quinn."

Fingers grazing her cool cheek, he leaned in close and brushed his lips against hers in a light, barely there kiss. Her warm breath mingled with his. A bruising, sweet ache built in his chest. Instead of deepening the kiss as he yearned to do, he wrapped his arms about her, tucking her head beneath his chin, holding her as he'd done in the springhouse. Warming her. Cradling her. Protecting her from his own foolish wishes.

This woman had plans. Plans that had nothing to do with marriage and family. Plans for a new life far from Gatlinburg. And him.

They remained locked in each other's arms until pink streaked the sky and lightning bugs blinked on and off on the opposite side of the river.

She pulled away first. Grabbing her bonnet, she said, "I shouldn't put off going home any longer."

Quinn hurried to his feet, dusting off his pants before extending a hand to her. "I'll take you home, seeing as I have your horse in my possession."

Avoiding his gaze, she nodded, springy ringlets caressing her jaw. He hadn't lied. While short hair wasn't the fashion, it did suit her.

They rode together in silence. Quinn took guilty pleasure in holding her close, his arms looped about her waist as she rested against his chest.

Inside her barn, she repeated her mother's invitation to supper. He declined.

She laid a hand on his arm to forestall his departure. "Don't try and avenge me, Quinn. It'll grow back."

"It goes against my upbringing to allow this type of behavior to go unchecked. They are a danger to you, Nicole. Next time might not be so innocent."

The fury was boiling up again.

"Before you act, think of the store and the possible consequences."

Unable to resist, he stroked her cheek, mesmerized when her lids drifted closed and she wove toward him. When he'd first met Nicole, he couldn't have imagined she'd one day welcome his touch.

"Do not worry about me," he whispered. "Let me handle this my way."

Her expression grew troubled. "Easier said than done."

Chapter Eighteen

He confronted Kenneth first.

Having ridden directly from Nicole's to the jail, he'd told Shane everything and requested his company during the formal visits. The lawman had grimly agreed. Now they stood inside the doorway of the Joneses' home, explaining the evening's events to his dismayed parents.

Kenneth lounged defiantly in the bedroom doorway, arms crossed and a scowl on his face. "That conceited witch deserved it and more," he drawled.

Fists balling, Quinn lunged.

Shane barely caught his arms in time. "Don't. He's not worth it," he growled.

"Go to the barn," Mr. Jones ordered his son.

Clearly unrepentant, he slunk past and slammed the door behind him. Only then did Shane release Quinn.

He plunged a shaky hand in his hair. "I shouldn't have let my emotions get the better of me," he told the couple in a formal tone. "I didn't come here to fight with your son. I came to inform you that he is no longer welcome to do business at my store."

The farmer appeared flustered.

"I understand what the boys did was wrong, but to bar them completely is taking it too far."

"Kenneth and his friends aren't boys," Quinn said "They're grown men who ganged up on a young woman and terrorized her with their actions. What they did wasn't only wrong, Mr. Jones, it was cruel."

"Will he ever be allowed to come back?" the farmer's wife asked.

"Once Nicole has left town, I will reconsider my decision."

The couple didn't attempt to argue the point, but they clearly weren't happy. Shane bid them good night and, no doubt alert to potential problems, stuck close to Quinn as they passed the barn where Kenneth waited.

Mounted on their horses, they headed for Timothy's place.

Though Shane's expression was indiscernible in the lamplight, the warning in his voice came through loud and clear. "You're aware there will be repercussions, right?"

"I refuse to stand by and do nothing."

While Alice had leaned toward asking Shane to bring charges against the trio, Nicole had refused outright. She was convinced Kenneth's bitterness would only grow, perhaps spill over to the twins.

"Look, I understand your motivation. But you're a newcomer. Not everyone has accepted your presence here." Shane bent his head to avoid getting swiped by a low branch. "We still haven't discovered who trashed your springhouse supplies. Barring these young men just might stir up a hornet's nest of trouble."

Gripping the reins with one hand, Quinn lifted the

lamp a little higher. "I knew what the consequences might be going into this." Recalling Nicole's tearstained face, his conviction strengthened further. "She's my assistant, and it's my duty to protect her and provide a safe workplace for her."

The lawman was silent for a minute. "You care about her."

"Yeah." He blew out a breath. "Probably more than I should."

"I did tell you there was more to her than what was on the surface."

Quinn had grown to care for her, deeply. He fervently hoped that's all it was. Caring, as for a friend. Not love.

He came here to find a new life. It'd be the height of foolishness to fall for the one girl set on having the life he'd left behind.

Everyone was staring.

Why wouldn't they? She was the only female in attendance with cropped hair.

Of course, her family's pew would be situated in the front of the church, within spitting distance of the reverend's podium. Throughout the service, her exposed neck burned with unseen stares of parishioners behind her. Quinn was back there somewhere.

Quinn, who'd wiped away her tears and held her until her fear melted away. She'd lain awake for hours after he'd gone, reliving those tender moments and yet too cowardly to examine her heart.

In Nicole's arms Victoria stirred. Gnawing on her chubby fist, her lids struggled to remain open as she fought sleep. During those times when Nicole was too busy to visit Kate during the week, she looked forward to services so she could hold the baby. Seated beside her, Caleb reached out and ran a finger along the baby's cheek, a smile of affection easing the sternness of his features. He shot a look of such wistfulness at Rebecca that Nicole fought the wetness springing to her eyes.

For a long time, she'd wondered if her cousin would ever find peace. And here he was, married to a wonderful woman and about to become a father.

When the closing prayer had been said, she reluctantly returned Victoria to Josh's arms.

"Join us for lunch." He cradled his daughter close to his chest. "You can cuddle with this little girl once she's been fed."

Caleb and Rebecca added that they were going to be there, as well. Rebecca looked hopeful. "It's been weeks. I'm dying to hear more about your young friends."

Nicole's attention shot to the rear of the church, to where Lucian and Megan were introducing the siblings to folks. They'd arrived late and so hadn't seen Nicole's chopped locks. Dread soured her stomach.

She hated to think of poor Lillian's reaction. While she was thrilled about their change in situation, a tiny part of her was reluctant to expose them to her "real" life.

"I'll come," she told Rebecca.

"Well, if it isn't the most stylish lady in Tennessee."

A shiver of awareness whispered down her spine and, spinning, she met Quinn's shining eyes. "Hi."

Caleb and Josh took turns shaking Quinn's hand. "Can't thank you enough for what you did for Nicole," Josh said.

Before he could respond, the other male members of her family surrounded them in order to echo the gratitude. Others joined the circle to offer their pledges of support. Not everyone in attendance agreed with his decision, however. Some chose to take the young men's sides. Out of the corner of her eye, Nicole saw the angry glances and scowls directed his way.

When most everyone had trickled down the aisle, Rebecca invited Quinn to lunch.

"I wish I could," he said, "but Claude Jenkins and his wife asked me first."

"Another time, then," Josh said.

"I would enjoy that very much." Quinn addressed Nicole. "May I have a quick word before you go?"

Nodding, she accepted his proffered arm and allowed him to guide her out into the overcast day. They turned in the direction of the cemetery.

Once they were away from prying ears, he glanced at her. "How are you holding up?"

"I'm fine." Belatedly, embarrassed color suffused her cheeks. Focusing on the horizon instead of him, she said, "I apologize for blubbering all over you. I can't believe I overreacted like that."

Quinn halted, silent until she looked at him. Gone was the easy charm. His brown eyes were intent. "Don't apologize. You had every right to be upset."

His nearness proved too much of a temptation. She'd experienced the wonder of being in those arms and wanted to experience it again. She mustn't want or expect such things from him. More importantly, she would be saying goodbye in the not-so-distant future.

For much of her life, Nicole had relied on no one but herself. Whenever she'd been hurt or lonely, she'd escaped those feelings by losing herself in her work. She couldn't start relying on Quinn.

Pulling free, she walked a few steps away to rest her fingers on the cemetery gate, her attention on the procession of weathered headstones. A thick veil of whitish-gray clouds stretched across the sky. The air carried moisture that hinted of an impending rain shower.

"By defending my honor, you've put yourself in a terrible position. I wish you hadn't done that. I could've put up with their presence in the store a while longer."

He joined her at the gate. "My father taught me to stick to my decisions. He said that second-guessing them would foster distrust in my employees." Angling toward her, he gently tugged on a curl. "I did what I thought was right. I'm trusting God to work out the rest."

Quinn's solid faith was yet another quality she admired. Worrying wasn't going to solve anything. Plus, it surely didn't please God. She offered up a silent prayer for help in remembering to trust Him.

"I should go," he said, his reluctance plain as he gazed over his shoulder at the emptying churchyard.

Nicole had mixed feelings. While she would've liked his company at dinner, it really wasn't wise. His incredible gentleness held immense power over her, scattering her defenses like the wisps of a dandelion on the breeze.

Starting off toward the church, she said, "I'm glad folks are beginning to extend the hand of friendship to you. It's about time."

He fell into step beside her. "Your family has made me feel welcome from the very beginning. They're good people." His focus on his polished shoes travers-

ing the trampled grass trail, he observed, "I have a suspicion you'll miss them more than you realize."

Before Quinn's arrival in Gatlinburg, Nicole
would've refuted that statement with vehemence. Not
now. Her relationship with the special women in her life
had altered because she'd risked opening up to them.
The move would interrupt that progress.

"You're probably right. However, distance from
family and friends didn't stop you from pursuing your
goals, did it? You're surviving."

"I am not trying to dissuade you. Simply warning
you it's not easy, starting over in a new place all alone."

Her own doubts surging, she stopped midstride.
"You don't think I can make it, do you?"

His soft laughter surprised her. "Quite the opposite,
my dear. If anyone can make it in the business world,
it's you. Not only do you have the mental tools—" he
tapped his forehead "—you're passionate and driven. I
have no doubt the ladies of Knoxville and beyond will
be clamoring to model your clothes."

They parted then, and Quinn's words stayed with
her the remainder of the day. As she sat in her living room and added inch-long ruffles to a skirt, she
attempted to pinpoint why those words troubled her.
While she wanted people to admire her creations and
enjoy wearing them, her aim wasn't popularity. She
didn't dream of nationwide renown.

What she wanted was to be a successful boutique
owner, to consult clients and create fashions that would
best suit their coloring and figures, kind of like what
she'd done with Nathan's wife, Sophie. A tomboy growing up, the girl had had no one to guide her in the ways
of feminine dress or grooming. Helping Sophie trans-

form into a stylish young lady had been one of the most fun experiences of Nicole's life.

She would love to repeat it. To help others achieve their fullest potential.

Couldn't you do that here? a tiny voice prompted. *In Gatlinburg?*

Quinn's disturbing questions that night in the springhouse came rushing back.

Are you sure this desperation to leave isn't a simple case of you running from your family? Your reputation?

Lowering the material to her lap, Nicole stared unseeing at her surroundings. Could he be right?

Squeezing her eyes tight, she tried to will away the unease tightening her midsection. This was her lifelong dream. She couldn't allow petty doubts to derail her plans.

Or the memory of strong arms. Sturdy shoulders to cry on. Quinn calling her Duchess in that cultured accent of his.

"I'm going to Knoxville," she announced to the empty room. "I'm going to open my business. Make scores of interesting friends. And I'm going to enjoy every single minute of it!"

Business was slower than usual for a Monday. On edge and self-conscious about her hair, Nicole kept busy dusting shelves and sweeping the floor of debris. Some of the customers who came in were vocal in their support of Quinn and had gone so far as to express encouragement to her. Those opposed to his actions didn't openly voice their feelings, instead conducted their transactions with pinched expressions and obvious disdain. Through it all, Quinn remained pleasant and upbeat. He treated everyone with respect and civility.

She was going to miss him. A crazy thought considering she'd once dreaded the prospect of working with him day in and day out.

That morning, he'd informed her that her wage increase took effect today. And while she'd wrestled with accepting it, in the end she'd set aside her pride. The more time she spent with him, the more entangled her emotions became.

She'd just finished restocking the sewing needles when the bell above the door announced new arrivals. Looking up to offer a greeting, the words died in her mouth.

Her sister Megan and Lillian were coming down the outside aisle toward her, goofy grins on their faces. Gone was Lillian's signature ponytail. Her beautiful blond hair had been cut off to match Nicole's length, and it fell in soft waves about her cheeks.

When the girls reached her, Nicole lifted a hand to gingerly touch the short ends. "What have you done?" she whispered.

Megan proceeded to pull off her bonnet, revealing her own haircut. Not as short as theirs, her curls brushed the tops of her shoulders.

Nicole promptly burst into tears.

Lillian's arms came around her, and Nicole rested her forehead on the slender but sturdy shoulder. Megan patted her back.

Then Quinn's distinctive footsteps neared. "Is she all right?"

The grave concern vibrating in his low voice only

made her cry harder. More than any other time in memory, she felt deeply cared for.

Pulling herself together, she scooted back and found a handkerchief pressed into her hands. Quinn's, of course. Sniffling, she wiped her cheeks and shot the girls a tremulous smile.

"I can't believe you cut your hair for me."

"We love you." Megan's eyes grew misty.

Lillian waved a hand. "This is nothing compared to what you sacrificed for me. Besides, it takes a lot less time to dry."

Quinn stood watching them, the crease in his brow slowly smoothing. He looked impressed. Proud. And happy for her. Happy that she had friends and family who supported her.

"Lucian was okay with this?" she said, disbelieving.

Megan smiled. "When I explained my intentions, he encouraged me to do it." To Quinn, she said, "He would've liked to come with us, but he's taking Patrick to see Doc Owens."

"You'll let us know what he says, right?" Nicole said, worry mingling with hope the doctor could do something to alleviate Patrick's pain, as well as restore the full use of his leg.

Promising she would, Megan invited them to that Friday's story hour. "Lillian's going to read to the children this time."

"I wouldn't miss it for the world," Nicole said. "You'll be wonderful."

Her friend was blossoming in Lucian and Megan's care. Healthy color had been restored to her cheeks, and happy sparkles replaced the disquiet in her eyes. *Thank you, God, for providing for them. I shouldn't*

have tried to shoulder their care alone. Forgive me
for not seeking Your guidance.

Quinn slipped away to help a customer interested
in the china collection.

Megan sidestepped Nicole to observe the row of
fabric bolts on the shelves. "As you know, sis, Lillian
could use new clothes. I'm planning to make most of
them myself since your time is limited. However, I'd
like to hire you to make several Sunday dresses. What
do you say?"

Nicole tucked Quinn's now-damp handkerchief in
her apron pocket and linked arms with Lillian. "I say
that sounds like a fine plan to me."

The younger girl flushed with excitement. "Pink is
my favorite color."

Megan dangled a fat ribbon in that color. Snatching the silky length, Nicole held it up to Lillian's hair.
"Perfect."

"This is going to be such fun," the younger girl
gushed, handling various ribbons.

By the time they'd chosen the necessary articles
for Lillian's wardrobe, two hours had passed. Nicole
couldn't remember feeling so relaxed around her sister.
And she thrilled to see her young friend's excitement.

All those years she'd dreamed of a different life in
Knoxville, she hadn't had connections to anchor her
here. She would've thought strengthening ties to the
people around her would be a positive thing. Only now
did she understand how difficult they'd be to sever.

Chapter Nineteen

Quinn honored his promise to escort Nicole to the children's story hour Friday evening, despite the fact he'd rather be drawing out plans for his house. He was both physically and mentally exhausted. Maintaining an upbeat disposition for Nicole's sake, not to mention the constant effort of keeping his distance, had taken its toll. Craving space, he left her in the parlor with the other guests and found his way onto the back porch.

Deserted. Good.

He sagged against the railing and looked out over the rainbow-hued gardens. The rain clouds that had stuck around much of the day had finally dispersed, and water droplets clinging to the petals and blades of grass winked in the evening sun. The pungent smell of moist earth mixed with the sweet scent of the rose-bushes hugging the porch.

Roses were his mother's favorite flower. More like obsession. Didn't take much to picture her in the es-tate gardens, on her knees in the dirt, babying her pre-cious plants.

He missed his family. His mother's latest letter had

been filled with nonessential tidbits about friends and business associates. Nothing substantial, like how Trevor was getting along and whether or not Tilly had been accepted in the ballet school she'd set her heart on. Frustrated, he'd penned an immediate response posing those questions and more and, on impulse, bragging about his efficient assistant and lamenting her impending departure. Only after he'd posted it did he realize his mother would likely seize on such information and assume there was more to what he'd shared. Like many mothers, his wanted him happily wed and producing grandchildren.

Instantly, the image of Nicole snuggling with baby Victoria filled his head.

He shook it away. *Nope. Can't go down that path.*

The door opened and closed, and Shane sauntered over, dainty china cup out of place in his big hand.

"Been looking for you," he said.

Turning so that his hip supported his weight, he folded his arms. "As a matter of fact, I've been waiting for you to find me. What did you learn about the stepfather?"

"Simmerly claims they stole from him, and that's why he has persisted in the search." Shane's fingers tightened on the cup until Quinn thought it might shatter. "The man's shifty. My gut says there's more to the story than he's telling."

Quinn had figured as much. "Did you question him about the mother's death?"

He shook his head. "Didn't wanna scare him into bolting."

"What's the next step?"

Glancing at the house, the people mingling beyond

the windows, Quinn thought of the vast improvement in Lillian's appearance and overall demeanor in the short time she'd been here. And the doctor had given them hope Patrick's leg could be rehabilitated. Returning them to that monster was not an option.

"I've written to the sheriff and other local leaders near Simmerly's homestead asking for information. I need to put together the entire picture before moving forward."

The door banged open then, and both men jerked.

Nicole's eyes were huge in her face. "Quinn! I need you. Please hurry."

Closing the distance between them, he took her hands. "What's the matter?"

"It's Carl. He's here, and he's demanding Patrick and Lillian go with him." Her grip tightened to an almost painful degree. "Quinn, you have to do something."

Shane was already striding through the door.

"I promise they aren't going anywhere with him," Quinn vowed.

She looked so distraught he couldn't resist pressing a kiss to her forehead. "Go. Stay close to Lillian. She'll need you nearby while we deal with Carl."

"All right."

Nicole trailed him inside. Although foolish sentiment, he couldn't help being pleased she'd come directly to him for help. Not the sheriff, who was the obvious choice to handle matters. *Him.*

Striding down the hall, he caught sight of Megan and her friends, Cole and Rachel Prescott, calmly shepherding the parents and children out the front door. Loud male voices reached him from the library up ahead on his right. He paused in the doorway to give

Nicole a reassuring nod as she continued on to the parlor to where Lillian waited.

Carl's irate voice boomed through the arched opening. "You can't keep them from me. I'm their legal guardian."

Quinn surveyed the room's occupants. Carl stood in the middle, nasty boots dirtying the brilliantly hued rug. Lucian had taken up a post at the window. The New Orleans native looked displeased but surprisingly calm considering his home had been invaded and guests asked to leave. Shane had parked his large form between the older man and Patrick, who was seated on the far end of the sofa.

Although his features lacked color, Patrick's eyes burned pale fire. "We don't belong to you," he cried, surging forward. "You killed our ma!"

Carl's face turned an ugly shade of puce. "That's an out-and-out lie." To Shane, he said, "Don't believe a word this boy says, Sheriff. He's hated me since the day his ma brought me home. He'll say anything to be rid of me."

Shane held up a hand, the other resting on his gun holster. "You've wasted your time coming here, Simmerly. These kids aren't going anywhere until I've completed my investigation."

Carl's hand sliced the air. "What is there to investigate? I told you they stole from me. Did you search their things?"

"The necklace belonged to my ma." Patrick gripped the cane propped across his knees. "She always said it would go to my sister one day."

"You're lying through your teeth," Carl snarled, took

a step toward the boy until he caught himself, seeming to recall there were onlookers.

Quinn had no doubt that if the siblings were ever returned to his custody, they would be in grave danger. Shane obviously agreed. He edged sideways so that he blocked the older man's view of Patrick.

"It's your word against his, I'm afraid. Like I said, I'm sorting through the situation and will let you know what I decide."

"But—"

"In the meantime," he continued, blue eyes flinty, "Lucian Beaumont and his wife have agreed to be Patrick and Lillian's temporary guardians."

"I won't stand for this," he cried. "I'll involve my sheriff—"

"I've saved you the trouble."

Carl's head reared back. "You've contacted Sheriff Davis?"

Quinn's gut was telling him the man wasn't too happy about that bit of information.

"I have. Now, I suggest you start on home before it gets any later."

With a parting glare, Carl made for the exit.

"Oh, and Simmerly?" Shane called out.

"Yeah?"

"Don't attempt to come near these kids again until I've given you permission. Got it?"

He stomped past Quinn, mumbling beneath his breath.

Lucian strode after him. "I'll give him a proper escort off my property."

Shane headed for the door. "I'd better make sure there's no trouble. Lucian's unarmed."

When there were just the two of them, Quinn went and sank into the chair opposite the sofa. "You all right?"

Tension radiated from him. "I won't let my sister go back there. I don't care what I have to do."

Leaning forward, Quinn rested his elbows on his knees. "Did Carl ever hurt your sister?"

"No."

"You're certain?"

"I know her. She swore to me that he'd never laid a hand on her, and I believe her."

"Good." He looked around at the sumptuous furnishings. "You two comfortable here? Are you happy with Nicole's family?"

"They're nice folks."

"Why the hesitation?"

"I'm tired of accepting handouts. Being a burden. First to Nicole. Now Lucian and Megan."

"I'm not an expert, but the way I see it, you and your sister are fulfilling a need in that couple's life."

Patrick's brows crashed together. "What need?"

"They don't have children of their own. They want to share this home and the resources God has given them with others. You two being here has allowed them to do that. So, in a way, you're an answer to prayer."

He could see his words took Patrick by surprise.

Finger tracing the cushion stripes, he said, "I didn't think of it that way."

"Trust me, you're not a burden. Besides, you won't always be on the receiving end. You're still planning on helping me in the store, right?"

His chest puffed out. "Absolutely."

Slapping his knees, Quinn stood to his feet. "See?

You'll soon be earning your own money. And ask Nicole. I'm sure she'll tell you I'm a patient and understanding boss."

"Among other things."

Turning, he saw Nicole beside the bookshelves, hands clasped behind her back.

"How long have you been standing there?"

"Long enough."

Patrick struggled to his feet. "I'm going to speak with Lillian."

Nicole's smile was tinged with compassion. "She's in the kitchen with Mrs. Calhoun, who's plying her with pastries. I'm sure they'll be willing to share."

His uneven gait echoed down the hall as he left.

Of their own accord, Quinn's feet carried him over to her. "Naughty girl." He wagged his finger. "It's not nice to eavesdrop."

She kicked up a shoulder. "Patrick saw me. Besides, you weren't divulging intimate secrets."

He chuckled. "Like you would've left if I had been."

"You're right," she cheekily agreed. "I would've stuck around."

Quinn fisted his hands to keep from reaching for her. He'd once asked himself who the real Nicole O'Malley was, confused by the cool composure she often hid behind. His question had been answered. Deep down, she was generous and brave, with a heart desperate to love and to be loved. He saw in her eyes the desire to be accepted for who and what she was.

You can't be the one to love her, he sternly reminded himself.

When she laid a hand on his bare forearm, he inwardly flinched. Her skin was warm and soft. He felt like a drowning man flailing about for a safety net that wasn't there.

"I heard what you said to him," she said softly. "You couldn't have said anything more perfect."

"I'm right, aren't I?" He strove for an even tone. "Your sister and Lucian needed someone to look after. Now they have two."

"Without your intervention, Patrick and Lillian would still be living in that shack. And I—" She worried her lower lip. "I'd still be an outsider looking in at my own family."

She was regarding him as if he was a hero in a storybook, as if he could fix the whole world's problems, and it was a 180-degree change from how she used to look at him. A heady thing, that.

"Nicole…" Her name was more of a groan than anything.

Her fingertips lightly caressed his arm. His gaze dropped to her mouth.

Quinn lowered his head a fraction. She sighed a sigh of surrender. Tilted her chin up.

The front door slamming at the end of the hallway stopped him cold. Footsteps neared.

He'd just stepped away when Lucian reached them. He took one look at their faces and smiled knowingly. "I don't mean to interrupt, but Megan is requesting your presence in the dining room. Seems everyone left before the refreshments were served, and she doesn't want them going to waste."

"We're right behind you," Quinn rushed to say, gesturing for Nicole to go ahead of him. Cheeks a bright pink hue, she followed her brother-in-law without a word.

Glad for the interruption, Quinn lagged behind. Strange, he'd never before suffered this sort of weakness where a woman was concerned. It shouldn't be this difficult to keep from kissing Nicole.

Lord, give me strength.

He was going to need it.

Two weeks later on a Sunday afternoon, Nicole left Megan's house in a daze.

Her first reaction was to find Quinn. How would he respond to her news?

He wasn't in his quarters. She paused on the stairs and surveyed the river and the woods beyond. There was no sign of him.

Determined to speak with him, she paid the Prescotts a visit. She'd seen his new horse following their wagon after services. Maybe he was still there.

Cole answered the door, his adorable little girl, Abby, in his arms. "You missed him. He left about half an hour ago. Is everything okay?"

"Everything's fine. Did he say where he was going?"

Frowning, he stroked his chin. "He did mention his property and plans for a house. You might look there."

"Thanks, Cole."

Hurrying on her way, she ignored the pinch in her toes. She was wearing her Sunday boots, and they weren't exactly meant for traipsing all over town.

The church's bell tower came into view. To reach Quinn's property, she bypassed the white clapboard building and proceeded along the lane leading away from Main Street. She walked slowly, scanning the woods for a sign of him. Unlike her homestead, there wasn't yet a trail leading to the clearing where he'd put up his home.

There. A flash of white. Rapid movement registered, but no sound.

Lifting her skirts, she wound her way past lichen-encrusted tree trunks, avoiding stepping on mushrooms and watching out for exposed roots. When she reached the edge of the clearing, she froze, taken in by what she was seeing.

Fencing foil in hand, Quinn thrust and whirled in a graceful choreography of movement, his expression focused as he battled an unseen adversary. His white fencer's breeches and jacket outlined his taut physique, muscular legs supporting his weight as he parried and swung his weapon. Perspiration glistened on his forehead. His black hair was mussed, strands falling forward into his eyes.

He was magnificent. If only she could watch him square off against a flesh-and-blood opponent.

She stepped into the clearing, and he faltered, head whipping in her direction as he lowered the foil to his side.

"Nicole." Dark brows crashing together, he didn't look particularly pleased to see her. "What are you doing here?"

Fascinated by this sweaty, messy version of her boss, she came nearer. He was winded. That broad chest heaved as he sucked in air.

She dared to touch the thick, white glove covering his hand. "Will you teach me to do that?"

His throat convulsed as he visibly swallowed. "I don't think that's a good idea."

Spinning on his heel, he crossed to a fallen log

where he'd left his things and seized a towel, mopping his face with it. His hair stuck up at odd angles.

She really, really liked this version of Quinn. She frowned, not moving from her spot. Problem was, she liked the cleaned-up version of him, too. Her news pulsed in the back of her throat, begging to be shared. Once she told him what she'd learned, everything would change. She wasn't sure she was ready.

Watching him remove his gloves and place the foil in its box, she said, "Why won't you teach me? Because I'm a female?"

"No."

Irritation bubbled to the surface. Ever since their exchange in the library, when Lucian had forestalled their embrace, Quinn had treated her differently. Oh, he wasn't harsh or unkind. Yet there was a distance in his honey-colored eyes that hadn't been there before. A reserve in his conversation that cut her to the quick.

The hurt wouldn't be so deep if he acted that way with everyone. But no. It was just her he'd chosen to freeze out.

Stalking over to him, she poked his unyielding back. "I want to know why you're acting this way. Lately, you've hardly spoken a word to me. You act as if you can't stand to be in the same room with me."

Oh, no. Those weren't tears clogging her throat, were they? She couldn't cry in front of him again.

Twisting sideways, his expression was cool. He said tightly, "I've spoken to you. Of course I have."

"About business. That's it." Fists on her hips, she continued, "With everyone else but me, you smile that charming smile of yours and chat about the weather. You're the suave, too-slick Northerner you've always been. So tell me Quinn, *darling*, what exactly have I done to deserve your disdain this time?"

He matched her stare, posture stiff and hands fisted at his sides, clearly unhappy at being questioned. For long, tense moments, he didn't speak. Nicole struggled to maintain eye contact. Bewilderment, hurt and forbidden longing swirled inside her.

Then, in a move so fast she gasped, he grabbed her hand and placed it over his heart.

"Feel that?" he ground out.

Beneath her flattened palm, his heart thundered against muscle-cloaked ribs. "Y-you've been exercising."

"Your presence is the culprit."

Moving away from her touch, he stepped behind her and, close but not touching, brought his arm around and took hold of her hand. His hot breath stirred her short curls, sending shivers of delight along her skin. She never wanted to move from this spot. Shameful, but true.

"In order to teach you, I'd have to hold you like this." His voice was low. "Do you see the problem?"

Problem? There was a problem?

His jaw skimmed her ear. With a sigh, he released her. Nicole's heart fell. She hugged her middle against the yawning loneliness creeping in.

"I'm sorry," he said behind her. "The reason I've been distant is because I'm having an extraordinarily difficult time honoring my promise to you."

She whirled. "What promise?"

A muscle jumped in his jaw. "I gave you my word I'd provide a professional environment for you. You shouldn't have to worry whether or not you're safe from my advances."

Before she could form a coherent reply—and honestly, was begging him to break his word and take her in his arms the right thing to do?—he continued on.

"I'm drawn to you, Nicole. That's no surprise. It would be very wrong of me to kiss you again when we both know we're not meant for each other. My world is here. I'm convinced this is where God wants me." A glimmer of indefinable emotion shimmered in the brown depths. "And you're meant to follow your dream."

His words arrowed through her, sharp and honest and poignant.

He was a good, good man. Ever her protector, even from this invisible force pulling them together.

"I have to sit down."

He followed her to the log, where she sat and stared at his black boot tips amidst a smattering of blue, purple and orange wildflowers. The July air was sweltering, and yet her bones were brittle with cold.

"You won't have to endure my presence very much longer."

He waited, unspeaking, until she lifted her gaze. He'd gone very still.

"Shane dropped by Megan and Lucian's after lunch with some news. It appears the siblings' maternal grandfather has been searching for them. He'd lost contact with their mother in recent years and, when he learned of her passing, hired a detective to find them. The detective paid a visit to Carl's and let slip that they were due a substantial inheritance."

Brows rising, he dropped onto the knobby log next to her. "Their mother had money?"

"She kept it a secret. Patrick and Lillian were dumbfounded when they heard the news."

"That's why Carl was desperate to get them back. He planned to get his hands on the money."

"The grandfather also hired a lawyer, who contacted Carl and demanded to see the siblings before granting him access to it."

Quinn shook his head in disbelief. "Where is he now?"

"The sheriff there has him in custody while he investigates the murder. The grandfather is planning to travel to Gatlinburg. I'm not sure if he'll try and take them east with him or not."

She frowned, recalling Megan's troubled features. Her sister had grown close to the siblings in a short amount of time, as had Lucian. They would be devastated if they left.

"I hope he lets them decide their future. They've been through a lot." He studied her profile. "So what has this to do with your leaving?"

"Patrick and Lillian insisted they repay me for the supplies. They wouldn't be dissuaded, no matter how much I argued." She tilted her head to return his regard. "With that money, I'll have enough to go ahead with my plans."

He shoved his fingers through his unkempt hair, messing it further. "When?"

"Caleb offered to take me next week to scout out potential shop locations. Once I've decided on one, we'll return to pack up my things. I suppose the timing depends on when the shop becomes available."

Quinn's expression growing earnest, he said, "You've worked hard for this, Nicole. You deserve to get what you want. I'm happy for you."

She drummed up a smile. He was encouraging her to go. What did she expect? That he'd beg her to stay? She didn't want that…did she?

No, of course not. This was her much-thought-about future. The future she'd plotted and planned and co-ordinated in her mind for years. The one she'd slaved to be able to afford.

"I'm sorry I can't give you an exact date. If you need for me to go ahead and quit so that you can hire someone else, I will."

"That's not necessary." He casually brushed off her suggestion, standing to his feet and gathering his things. "I'll put the word out that I'll need a new assistant soon, but that the start date hasn't been determined. I've already promised Patrick he could come in on the days he feels up to it. He'll be my part-time help."

His nonchalant attitude stung. Her leaving didn't come as a shock to him. Still, expressing a bit of regret couldn't hurt, could it? Something like, *I'll miss you, Duchess.* Or, *I'm not sure how I'll ever find anyone to replace you.*

Don't be absurd. He's clearly fine with my imminent departure.

She'd promised herself she'd leave town with her whole heart intact. She had a sinking suspicion she'd failed to keep that promise.

Chapter Twenty

Thunder rumbled in the distance, and Alice frowned at the darkening sky outside the kitchen window. "Maybe you should stay home."

Nicole laid the sandwich in her lunch pail and covered it with a cloth. "I can't. Quinn needs me. If I hurry, I'm sure I can reach the mercantile before it starts raining."

"You're going to miss that young man, aren't you?"

"I'm going to miss a lot of people," she said over a lump in her throat, impulsively going and hugging her mother.

Last night, her mother had invited Nicole into her room, where she'd taken out a small wooden box containing tintypes of various family members. Nicole had lingered over the portraits of her father, especially, and his mother. Alice had smiled fondly. "You're the exact likeness of Grandmother O'Malley," she'd said.

The resemblance was undeniable. She'd died when Nicole was very young, so she didn't remember her. Alice had offered to let Nicole keep the tintype.

She eased out of the embrace, but not before she glimpsed her mother's concern.

"You don't seem as excited about this move as I thought you'd be. Is something bothering you?"

"Everything is happening really fast, that's all."

In a few short days, she'd be in Knoxville searching for the perfect spot to open her boutique, as well as a place to live. Once her choices had been made, she'd have to say goodbye to her family and friends. She wouldn't be around to see Patrick's progress or visit with Lillian. No more snuggling with Victoria.

"If you're going, you should scoot along," her mother said, interrupting her musings.

A strong gust buffeted the cabin. "I'll see you tonight."

"Be careful."

With the warning lingering in her ears, Nicole hooked an umbrella over her wrist and hurried to the lane. The air was damp and heavy with impending rain, the forest unnaturally devoid of animal life, birds and squirrels likely in hiding. She walked as quickly as she could and reached the short wooden bridge leading into town just as fat raindrops splattered on the ground.

Opening the umbrella, she picked up her pace. Bad weather meant not many customers would venture out. She wasn't looking forward to being cocooned in an empty mercantile with Quinn all day, not after his utter complacency regarding her news. She'd clearly overestimated her importance to him, both professionally and personally. The revelation stung far more than it should.

A crack of thunder rattled the living room windowpanes, and the ground vibrated with its intensity.

Quinn reluctantly tore his focus from the unfinished house plans spread across the kitchen table. Through the window overlooking the river, he could see entire trees swaying in the wind. That didn't bode well.

Tossing his pencil down, he strode into the hallway and threw open the rear door. The store was due to open in half an hour. The low, churning gray clouds made it appear more like dusk than early morning. As the first smattering of raindrops hit the stair landing, he glimpsed a bobbing pink-and-white umbrella in the vicinity of the bridge.

Nicole.

He almost wished she'd stayed home today. Yesterday's scene in the woods still had the power to make his ears burn. He'd been too blunt with her. While he'd spoken the truth, declaring his inner struggles—*showing* her how she affected him—it wasn't conduct becoming of a gentleman.

The wind whipped his hair in his eyes, flattened his pants against his legs.

Quinn wasn't sure if it was this place or the woman bringing about these changes in behavior. He certainly wouldn't enjoy his current pristine reputation if he'd treated the socialites in his circle in a similar manner.

Rain pinged against the landing and bounced up, splattering his boots.

Caught by the wind, Nicole's rose-colored skirts tangled with her legs. Her bonnet strings whipped about her neck. "Hurry up, Duchess," he murmured as the rain intensified.

She was going to be soaked from head to toe if she didn't.

Directly across from where he stood, the limbs of a

massive maple tree bowed beneath the onslaught. The river pulsed and swirled between its banks. A wall-shaking rumble sounded directly overhead, and he flinched as a jagged lightning bolt split the purple sky.

Nicole stopped in the middle of the lane, tipped her umbrella and lifted her gaze to the tree.

"No." Quinn didn't attempt to raise his voice. She couldn't hear him above the rain and wind and rushing water. "Don't stop. Get inside." He stared hard at her as if he could will her to obey.

Light flickered in the gloom. Another thunderclap reverberated overhead, followed by an earsplitting crack.

Everything happened in slow motion after that.

The trunk groaned. Snapped. Branches twisted.

The centuries-old tree toppled straight for the mercantile. For him.

The last thing he saw was Nicole's face, frozen in abject terror.

It took several seconds to register what had happened.

One minute she was looking up at Quinn, framed in the doorway at the top of the landing, the next she was watching the tree smashing into the mercantile. The roof had given way. Walls buckled.

A large limb with numerous branches filled the hallway where Quinn had been standing. The section housing his quarters had been crushed. She couldn't even make out where the window had been.

The umbrella slipped from her fingers. Horror locked her muscles into place even as the rain pelted her like sharp stones, dripping off her bonnet's brim.

He hadn't had time to get out of the way.

Please, God, no.

Adrenaline dumped into her system. Screaming at the top of her lungs for help, she scrambled down the grassy bank leading to the river, circumventing the damaged tree base and slipping and falling up the incline to reach level ground. The stairs were no more, flattened beneath the barrel-like trunk. No matter. She would get to him, one way or the other.

He can't be dead. He can't be dead. The refrain poked and tore at her, inciting bone-numbing fear. *Stop it, Nicole. That's not helping.*

"Help! Someone help!"

Edging along the narrow ledge of earth along the building's rear wall, she batted away branches and stepped over thinner limbs to reach what had been the doorway. Glass crunched beneath her boots. Several times, her skirts snagged on jutting log fragments, hampering her progress.

"Quinn!" Unmindful of her hands, Nicole snapped off leafy branches one by one and tossed them aside. "Can you hear me? Quinn?"

Half climbing onto the tree, she squinted into the darkness, steeling herself for what she might find. Heart in her throat, she considered going in there.

"Miss Nicole?"

A small cry slipped through her lips. Startled, she twisted and, through the downpour, saw the bent outline of Mr. Walton from the barbershop. He stood near the building's corner, rivulets of water streaming from his hat. Successive lightning strikes lit up the sky.

"Quinn's trapped," she called. "I need help getting to him."

He nodded. "I'll fetch the sheriff!"

Turning back, she pulled herself entirely onto the trunk. Bark bit into her knees as she inched forward. Juts of wood scraped her palms. Frantic prayers tumbled from her trembling lips.

She eyed the remaining beams overhead. Rainwater leaked through the holes. Would they hold? And for how long?

"Quinn?" she tried again.

When there was no response, she pressed a fist to her mouth and blinked away useless tears. He was probably unconscious. Or unable to hear her over the storm.

The long interior walls looked to be intact, for the most part. There were gaps here and there. Through one she could make out his kitchen stove. Through another she glimpsed a flash of red and white. The checkered curtains.

When she had passed under the doorway, she gulped in air and, gathering her courage, scoured what parts of the floor were visible on either side of the tree trunk.

There was no sign of him.

He hadn't been crushed, then. He'd somehow managed to move out of the way.

Why then wasn't he answering her?

Suddenly, a powerful arm twined about her waist and lifted her clear. A muffled scream lodged in her throat as the unidentified male swung her around and set her on her feet.

"Quinn?"

But the hard blue eyes didn't belong to him.

"Shane." Fingers fisting in his shirt, she brought her face close, her bonnet brim slamming into his

Stetson. "You have to find him. He's in there. Maybe hurt. Bleeding." *Dying.* Panic ratcheted up her pulse. "Please."

His hands on her shoulders steadied her. "Breathe, Nicole," he ordered. "Tell me what happened."

In the recesses of her mind, she acknowledged the fact she'd never dared come this close to the intimidating lawman.

"He was standing right here in the doorway when the tree fell. I—I don't see how he could've gotten to a safe spot." Her gaze bounced off the broken logs where his living room had been. "But I didn't see him in the hallway."

No articles of clothing. Nothing.

Shane surveyed the debris. "We need tools, mostly saws and axes. As many as you can get. You'll find what we need at the livery. Walton's already combing the streets for able-bodied men to assist in the search."

"I'm not sure—" She bit her lip. What if she left and they found him? What if they wouldn't let her see him? What if—

Squeezing her eyes tight, shudders racked her as her imagination called forth disturbing images of Quinn's broken body.

Shane's fingers bit into her flesh, not bruising but enough to ground her thoughts. "Listen to me."

She forced her lids open. The lawman's eyes blazed, but his features held unanticipated gentleness.

"I need you to do this for me, Nicole. Without those tools, we can't get to him."

"I understand." *Help me, Father. I'm drowning in possibilities. Horrible, gut-wrenching possibilities.*

"Good." With a firm nod, he assisted her to the corner of the building before turning back.

Her boots squelched in the mud as she made her way through the driving rain to the livery. The clouds had stalled over Main Street. Thunder rolled through the town, sounding like boulders crashing into one another. Beyond the sound, she heard the faint calls of men sprinting to the mercantile.

The balding, built-like-an-ox blacksmith must've heard the news, for he was dumping tools into a wheelbarrow when she stumbled inside. Smells of horse and damp hay washed over her.

"Mr. Latham."

He didn't spare her a glance. "Give me five minutes."

Five minutes didn't sound like much in the grand scheme of things. But for Quinn, who was somewhere in that broken-down wreck of a store, five minutes could mean the difference between life and death.

Chapter Twenty-One

Something heavy and unmovable pinned him face-first to the floor.

His right shoulder ached clear through to the bone. Pain ricocheted against his skull, and he tried to blink away the misty haze marring his eyesight. His living space—what was left of it—was cloaked in watery shadows. Bits of leaves and bark and spilled coffee grounds littered the wet floorboards. Broken mugs and dishes, too.

By the grace of God, he'd managed to get inside this room, out of the way of the larger tree section. All he had to do now was wait and hope the roof didn't give way.

That final image of Nicole shimmered in his mind's eye, intensifying his discomfort. Not knowing where she was, whether or not she was unhurt, was far worse than any physical pain he had to endure. *Please Lord, let her be okay.*

Shifting his lower body, he tried to dislodge the object holding him down. The bad news? It didn't budge an inch. The good news? He didn't seem to have suffered any major injuries in his legs or back.

Stars danced in his vision. His temples throbbing, Quinn rested his cheek once more against the floor and focused on steadying his breathing. The weight made it tough to fully expand his lungs. As he lay there, he began to make out repetitive sounds above the noise of the rain splattering through the ceiling.

He couldn't identify the source for long minutes. The hammering in his head made it difficult to string thoughts together. *That's it. Hammers.*

Or were they saws?

A male voice called out, followed by a series of replies.

People were out there, trying to get to him.

Was Nicole out there? Or was she lying unconscious on a bed at Doc's?

He had to get free. Had to find her. *Now.*

Gritting his teeth, he braced his palms beneath him and pushed upward with all his might. His shoulder screamed in protest. Beads of sweat popped out on his forehead. Frustration swept over him as the futility of his actions registered.

A familiar voice pierced the fog clouding his brain.

"Shane?" he pushed out, wincing at the breathy weakness of his voice. No way was the lawman gonna hear that.

The minutes crawled by. Quinn wasn't certain how much time passed. The rain lessened to a pitter-patter, and the peals of thunder echoed from miles away. He fought against the need to sleep, no matter that it would bring relief.

"I see him." Shane's excited shout dimly registered.

Rest. That's all he craved…a couple of blessed minutes in the encroaching blackness.

There came a shuffling sound. Boots scuffing against the boards.

"We're gonna get you out of here, friend." A hand skimmed his back.

"Where—" He gulped in air. "Nicole?"

"She's fine. Actually, that's not entirely true. She's making my job nigh impossible."

If Nicole was giving the lawman fits, she really was fine.

Quinn let go of the fear and worry he'd been holding on to. Then he slept.

"Something's going on." Slipping her arm free of Jane's, Nicole craned her neck in an effort to see past the dirt-and-sweat-streaked men sorting through the debris. From her position near the side wall, she couldn't make sense of the increase in activity.

The earth was a muddy morass, the skies a gray, undulating cauldron. Word of the accident had spread like wildfire through the town. A large crowd of onlookers—mostly women, children and the elderly, who weren't directly involved with the search—filled the street and the area beside the mercantile, where she and her mother and sisters waited anxiously.

They'd tried to convince her to go home and change out of her torn and sodden clothes, but she'd refused. She'd also refused to seek treatment for her bloodied, splintered hands. She wasn't leaving this spot until Quinn was located.

Rain-scented wind tugged at her damp hair. "I'm going over there."

Jane protested. "Maybe you should wait—"

"I'm done waiting!"

Weaving around the workers, she reached the place where Caleb had been sawing through the logs. He'd moved to the doorway, attention on someone inside.

"What's happening?" she demanded.

His mouth flattened. Neither he nor the lawman were happy with her almost constant requests for updates. That was okay, because she wasn't too happy with them for not letting her help.

Beneath the irritation, sympathy swirled in the brown depths. "Shane found him."

The world tilted, and she shot out a hand to balance herself against the building, oblivious to the stinging sensations crawling up her arm. "How is he?"

"A little banged up, but he's going to be all right. We just have to free him first."

Something in his voice sounded an alarm.

Free him? Nausea roiled. "I want in there."

"Absolutely not."

"If it were Rebecca in there, would you be content to remain an onlooker?" She glared at him.

Surprise flitted across his face. "Are you saying… you and Quinn—"

"N-no," she sputtered, heat climbing into her cheeks. "I didn't intend to make it sound like— Look, he's more than my boss. He's my friend. I care about him." With deliberate, careful steps, she closed the space between them, looking up at him beseechingly. "I know without a doubt that if our positions were reversed, Quinn would do everything in his power to help me."

He'd already put his community standing on the line for her. She'd no doubt he'd risk his very life for her.

"The building isn't stable, Nicki. I understand how you feel—"

"If you don't let me in, I'll simply find another way."

There were men working to clear the broken glass and logs at the front of the store. She could try there.

One black brow arched. "Or I could throw you over my shoulder and take you home this instant."

Desperation burned in her veins. "Caleb, please," she whispered, her voice raw. "If you've ever cared about me, you'll let me do this."

Eyes narrowing, his jaw worked.

Claude Jenkins appeared in the hallway. "Sheriff wants you to fetch Doc right away."

"Got it. He headed up front a few minutes ago." Caleb sighed and balanced his saw against the wall. "Try to stay out of trouble, will you?"

"I promise."

Addressing the banker, he said, "Help her inside."

Claude hesitated for an instant before extending his hand. Her legs suddenly like jelly, she concentrated on where to place her feet.

Nicole wasn't prepared for the sight of Quinn's still, prone form facedown on the floor.

Ignoring Shane, whose frown deepened at the sight of her, she fell to her knees beside him and lightly stroked his cheek. "Quinn?"

Behind her, Claude resumed his attempts to saw through the spot where the limb on top of Quinn connected to the larger, thicker trunk.

"He was awake when I found him," Shane said, gloved hands clamped around the limb and lifting up, trying to relieve the pressure on Quinn's back. "He asked about you."

She blinked away tears. Blood matted his hair. The sight of it, along with his torn shirt and more of the sticky red substance soaking through the material, left her insides numb.

"Should I put a compress on that?" She pointed to his shoulder wound.

Strain tightening his features, Shane jerked a nod. "Go easy. He's having trouble getting enough air in his lungs."

With trembling fingers, she peeled the cotton away. The gash didn't appear too deep.

Scanning the kitchen area, she located a stack of cloths scattered across the work surface. She grabbed the one on top. When she dropped down to place the makeshift compress on his shoulder, she noticed his lids fluttering. A groan escaped.

Gingerly smoothing the hair from his forehead, she leaned close. "We're going to get you out soon."

He blinked. Confusion and discomfort lent his eyes a glassy look. "Duchess?"

"I'm right here."

"You wouldn't happen to have a peppermint in your pocket, would you?"

His question elicited a surprised laugh. "Only you would be thinking about such things right this minute."

He licked his lips. "Dry mouth."

"We'll get you water."

An overhead beam creaked and bits of dirt rained down. Shane, who'd been observing them with open interest, eyed the ceiling with concern.

Quinn speared her with an imperious look that no doubt had had his employees back in Boston scrambling. "You should go."

"I'm not leaving."

"I'm your boss."

She gestured to the ruined quarters. "Not anymore," she said gently.

He closed his eyes. "How bad is it, Shane?"

"The building's a total loss. Should be able to salvage some of the merchandise, though."

"What wasn't damaged in the initial accident was probably ruined by the rain," he said, and sighed, eyes still closed.

Claude paused to swipe his sleeve across his forehead. His cheeks were red from exertion. "I'm about to sever the limb. Be ready."

On his knees facing her, Shane nodded and braced his body. Nicole scrambled to assist. Her hands would pay for this later.

Within moments, they had it rolled off him. Quinn started to push himself up.

"Whoa, there," Shane hurried over. "Maybe you should wait until Doc takes a look at you."

"I'm fine," he panted, easing into a sitting position. "Just light-headed."

His skin was pulled tight across his cheekbones, his lips colorless. Her heart pinched in the face of his pain. *At least he's awake and coherent. His injuries could've been worse. Much worse.*

Offering up a prayer of heartfelt gratitude, she was about to go to him when Caleb appeared in the doorway. He shot Nicole a searching look and, apparently satisfied she was unharmed, sidestepped to allow Doc Owens room to pass.

The cursory examination didn't take long.

"You're a fortunate man, Mr. Darling. I detect no

broken bones." To the other men, he said, "Help him to my office so I can stitch up those gashes."

Caleb and Shane assisted Quinn to his feet. Claude waited by the door.

"Come with us," Caleb told her. "Doc will need to tend your hands."

All heads swiveled to her.

Quinn's features sharpened and his brow creased. "What's wrong with your hands?"

"It's nothing."

"Let me see." Despite his weakened state, the command brooked no argument.

Acutely aware of their intent audience, she held them out, wincing at his quiet gasp.

"How?"

Nicole wasn't about to explain that, in her desperation to reach him, she'd paid no heed to the obstacles, had clawed at the branches and broken boards blocking her way. "Doesn't matter."

"I beg to disagree." He started forward, only to weave slightly and put a hand to his head.

"While I admit I'm fascinated by this conversation," Caleb drawled, a twinkle of amusement in his eyes, "I think we'd best concentrate on getting out of here."

Quinn's jaw went taut. "I'll let it drop. For now."

Progress to Doc's house was slow. The crowd cheered and clapped at the sight of him walking out of the wreckage. Disregarding his physical injuries, folks surged forward to offer a word of encouragement or to tell him not to worry about the store. Nicole lost count how many offers of assistance he received.

He patiently responded to each person, sincere in his appreciation. Was she the only one who noticed his increasing pallor? The deep grooves carved on either side of his mouth?

Just when she was about to stomp her feet in frustration, Shane shooed everyone away.

At Doc's, Nicole waited alone in the parlor while Quinn's injuries were tended. He'd sent the lawman and her cousin on their way. And she'd insisted she didn't need her mother and sisters hovering while she waited.

When the unflappable doctor motioned for her to enter the treatment room, she paused on the threshold. She hadn't expected to find Quinn still awake. His hair had been washed, and he wore a clean shirt that was several sizes too big. No doubt one of Doc's.

"I thought you'd be asleep," she said, going to sit in the chair Doc indicated.

"I don't particularly like taking medicine." He followed the older man's movements as he methodically gathered gauze, a jar of white paste and tweezers.

"Put your hands on the table," Doc ordered, lowering his bulk into the chair opposite.

Nicole did as instructed, averting her eyes to a waterfall painting in order to avoid Quinn's scrutiny. She did her best not to flinch. By the time he was finished, she was tempted to toss those hateful tweezers in the river.

Standing with her back to Quinn, she flexed her stinging, gauze-encased hands and wondered how she was supposed to complete her sewing projects on time. Or pack.

When Doc left them to rejoin the cleanup efforts, she trudged to the bed Quinn occupied. Her uncomfortable clothes were finally getting to her. She longed for a hot, steaming bath and her favorite nightgown.

"How's your shoulder?" Nicole said.

"Bruised."

"And your head?"

"Doc sewed up the gash."

Taking hold of her wrist, he tugged her close until her legs nudged the mattress. Against the crisp white linens and mountain of pillows propping him up, his raven hair gleamed and his brown eyes were shadowed. "I'd like an explanation now, please."

In her mind's eye, she pictured him as he'd looked seconds before that tree collapsed. The exhaustion and jumbled emotions she'd been holding at bay rushed in, buckling her knees. It was either take refuge on the bed or land on the floor. She sat down on the edge, the mattress dipping beneath her weight.

Residual fear muddied her throat. "I wasn't thinking clearly. I…needed to find you."

His fingers traced lazy circles on the skin above the gauze. "You were worried about me, Duchess?"

"Yes."

"I was worried about you, too." His expression darkened. "I don't like that you hurt yourself on account of me."

Her gaze freely roamed his face, his dear and familiar countenance, and she wondered how on earth she was going to function without encountering it on a daily basis. Those eyes full of life and humor, the languid, too-confident smile that did crazy things to her equilibrium.

I can't love him, can I? I don't even know what that feels like.

"My reaction would've been the same no matter who was trapped in the store."

That's not entirely true, though, is it?

His fingers stopped their motion. He folded his hands atop the blanket, and she hid hers behind her back, missing the reassurance of his touch.

"Speaking of the store—" she pushed herself up, relieved when her legs held her weight "—I'm so sorry."

His temporary home, along with his business, had been utterly destroyed.

"I can rebuild. Restock the supplies. What matters is that no one was killed."

"I know you're right. Still…" His dream was in ruins. Her heart ached for his loss. "Tell me something. Have you ever regretted embarking on this crazy adventure of yours?"

"Not once."

She gaped at him. "Not even when we were locked in the springhouse?"

"I don't deny there have been obstacles along the way. This is the biggest one of all. But I'm confident this is where God wants me."

Was she confident Knoxville was where God wanted her? Had she even prayed for His direction?

I can't alter my plans now. What reason could I possibly have for giving up my dream?

"I'll miss you, Quinn Darling," she blurted.

He blinked, dark brows lifting.

Something sorrowful flitted across his face. Surely she'd imagined it.

"Would you like for me to come and visit you? Knoxville isn't that far away, after all."

Quinn visit her? "You would visit an ex-employee?"

"No. But I would visit a friend."

"I would like that very much."

Had he noticed the hitch in her voice? She hoped not. Averting her face, she attempted to gain control of her unruly emotions.

He hadn't said he'd miss her.

He hadn't asked her to stay.

Chapter Twenty-Two

Quinn felt numb inside.

Her admission had rocked him. He'd had to bite his tongue to keep from begging her to stay.

He sternly reminded himself not to be selfish. If his family had tried to talk him out of leaving Boston, he would've been torn, confused and, more likely than not, resentful. He would've left home with mixed feelings and regrets. Thankfully, they hadn't burdened him with that. While they'd expressed their sadness at his leaving, they'd ultimately freed him to pursue his dream.

Asking Nicole to give up her dream wouldn't be fair. And what, exactly, would he be asking? Not only had she made her views on marriage plain, he didn't know how deep her feelings for him went.

She deserved his support and encouragement, and he would give them no matter how much it cost him.

Settling into the pillows, he soaked in her bedraggled appearance, his gaze lingering on her wrapped hands. She must've been terribly upset, and he hated that he'd inadvertently caused her distress. Remaining in this bed while Doc had dug bits of wood out of her tender skin had gone against every instinct. He'd wanted to hold her, comfort her, absorb her pain.

Watching her now, his heart twisted with acute regret. It wasn't difficult to imagine spending the remainder of his days with her, loving her and any children God blessed them with. He disagreed with her summation of her maternal instincts. All a person had to do was watch her interact with her cousins' children to know that she'd be a kind and nurturing mother.

You are not a part of her plan, Darling. And neither is a future in Gatlinburg.

Funny, he'd initially deemed her unsuitable for the role of his wife. He'd had this preconceived notion of a sweet, biddable woman. Someone like his mother, who catered to his father's wishes. Only now did he understand how skewed his thinking had been. He wasn't his father. He wouldn't be content with a relationship like theirs.

Nicole kept him on his toes. He certainly couldn't fathom ever being bored with her. She brought sunlight and joy to his days. Her reaction to his teasing charmed him, and he found himself searching for new and innovative ways to do it. From the beginning, her work ethic had impressed him, and the depth of her generosity was something he hadn't encountered before.

All solid reasons for wanting to marry her, but not the chief one. Plain and simple, he yearned to be the man who poured love into her life, who made her feel special and wanted and needed.

It was a new and unexpected dream, one he hadn't anticipated, one destined to go unfulfilled. Something told him the loss of it would stick with him the rest of his life.

She stopped in her pacing. "I think I should postpone my trip to Knoxville."

"What? Why?"

"You're going to need help rebuilding." At the sight of his expression, she said, "I don't mind waiting a little longer."

Although he hadn't thought it possible, his love for her grew in that moment, making it difficult to speak. "You are not postponing your move. I refuse to be the cause of another delay. It's time you thought about yourself for a change."

The look in Quinn's eyes nearly caused her heart to stop.

No one had ever looked at her with that degree of earnestness before. Having warmth and approval directed her way was a heady thing. Disconcerting, too. Because, as the knowledge of what might've befallen him hit home, she'd accepted how precious he'd become. The idea of him hurting hurt her.

It was a novel experience. For years she'd lived a selfish existence. Afraid of rejection, of not measuring up, she'd closed everyone out and focused on her own wants and desires. For whatever reason, Patrick and Lillian had breached that self-absorbed bubble, and she'd let herself care without reservation. But that was a friendship type of love. Things were different with Quinn.

He'd waltzed into her life, breezing past her barriers and thawing her heart with barely any effort. He'd teased her, pushed her to try new things, comforted her. For the first time ever, she desired someone else's good above her own. She would sacrifice everything if it meant he'd be safe and happy.

Why was she surprised he wouldn't let her?

Quinn Darling was an honorable man. Noble and good.

"That's the thing. I've spent most of my life thinking about myself. It feels good putting others' needs first." She shook her head. "I'm not sure I can leave with your store in ruins."

"Pray tell me, how could you possibly assist me?" He gestured to her injuries. "I appreciate the sentiment, but there's nothing you can do."

He hadn't said it with the intent to wound her. She knew that. "I understand." Sliding errant curls behind her ears, she edged to the door. "I'll let you get some rest."

He lifted a hand. "Nicole, wait—"

"No. I'm hungry and dirty and too tired to think straight. We'll talk later."

Hurrying outside, she took the long way home, skirting Main Street and the lingering crowds. She shouldn't have worried about Quinn. A determined man, he wouldn't let this setback derail his goals. He would rebuild, and the mercantile would be better than before.

He'd be fine.

He didn't need her anymore.

The following evening, bathed and clad in borrowed clothes, Quinn paid Nicole a visit. After her hasty departure, he'd remained in that bed at Doc's, too drained to deal with either well-meaning townspeople or the damages wrought by the storm. He'd half expected her to come back this morning. She hadn't. And when he'd gone to the site, he'd been disappointed over her absence and oddly disgruntled at having been forced to examine his store's demise alone when he'd have given his right arm to have her beside him. What would she say if he admitted that he'd come to value her practical outlook, her unwavering confidence in his abilities?

Rebuilding would take some doing—many hours of hard labor clearing the rubble, assessing what to scrap and what to keep, not to mention compiling inventory and reordering supplies. He thanked God he had the means available to start over. Not every man in his situation would be so fortunate.

He'd been stunned by the outpouring of concern and support from the townspeople. Claude had organized a cleanup crew, and Quinn had arrived to find men of all ages—including some who'd opposed his barring of Kenneth and his friends—clearing logs and sweeping up the debris. Shane had ordered him off the site the instant he spotted him, insistent he rest his shoulder, at which point Lucian had stepped forward and invited him to stay at his and Megan's house. With his quarters buried and his personal items beyond reach, Quinn had gratefully accepted.

He'd spent much of the day assuring Patrick and Lillian that Nicole was fine. Thinking it best they not witness the mercantile's destruction, Megan had assured the siblings they'd be able to visit her the following day after she'd had a chance to rest.

Strolling along the path to her cabin, he'd passed the vegetable garden when he noticed the barn doors standing open and soft light spilling into the night.

He paused to peer inside. His mouth dried at the inviting picture she made. Her hair gleamed, skimming the elegant sweep of her neck. She was dressed more simply than he'd ever seen her in a serviceable black skirt and loose-fitting white blouse. In her arms, she cuddled an adorable rabbit.

Seated on a hay square, she looked up at the sound of his approach, raven brows sweeping upward.

"Quinn. What are you doing here?"

He gestured to the spot beside her. "May I?"

Scooting over to give him room, she eyed the proper sling Doc had bullied him into wearing. "Is your shoulder paining you?"

Constantly, as did the stitched laceration at the back of his head. Aloud, he said, "It's not too troublesome. The sling is Doc's way of insuring I don't use my arm during cleanup." Reaching out, he petted the trembling creature in her arms. "Who's this?"

Head bent, her fingers—the tips that weren't swallowed up in gauze—followed the path his took. "Puffy. Isn't he sweet?"

He chuckled. "What kind of name is that?"

"Considering he's a puffball, an appropriate one." She lifted her head and smiled. The lavender rings around violet irises were more pronounced tonight, her inky lashes thick and lush.

"I wouldn't have guessed you were an animal person when I first met you."

Kicking up a shoulder, she looked at the horses in their stalls. "Animals don't judge as harshly as people do."

Quinn was silent, continuing to pet Puffy as he pondered her telling words. He hated that she'd felt isolated and unwanted growing up and worried she'd experience the same in a new city. Since his arrival, he'd seen Nicole blossom and flourish, growing closer to her family. A small part of him had hoped the new development would change her outlook on Gatlinburg and that she would reassess her reasons for leaving. A foolish hope, it turned out.

He rested his hand on his thigh. "Are you taking him with you?"

"I'll probably be staying in a boardinghouse for a while. He wouldn't be allowed. Besides, he'll be happier here. The twins will take good care of him."

Standing to her feet, she replaced the bunny in his hutch and faced him. "What I said earlier about staying... I—I don't think it's necessary. You're right. There's nothing I can do at this point to help you." Hands linked behind her back, she rubbed the toe of her boot across the straw-strewn floor. "And since you don't need me anymore, I'm leaving the day after tomorrow for my scouting trip."

He desperately wanted to tell her she was wrong, that he did need her. Instead, he stood and nodded in agreement. "You will come and say goodbye first, right?"

"Yes. Of course."

Moving to where she stood, he cupped her cheek, thumb caressing the satiny skin. Her breath caught. Her eyes were wide and luminous, beckoning him closer, tempting him to pour out all his wishes and regrets.

This would have to be their one and only private goodbye. While she'd planned to return for the bulk of her things and to attend a going-away party, he wasn't sure he'd be able to trust himself to keep his true feelings hidden once he'd experienced her absence. He'd have to keep his distance, no matter that it'd kill him to do so.

"It has been a pleasure knowing you, Duchess."

She blinked, and he thought he glimpsed a tear clinging to her lashes.

His throat grew muddy. "I wish you all the best."

Bending his head, he placed a kiss on her cheek. It wasn't the ending he'd envisioned for them. Dissatisfied, what-ifs pounding at his temples, he let her go.

Chapter Twenty-Three

"I know this is going to sound selfish, but I wish you weren't moving." Lillian removed another blouse from the wardrobe, a wistful air shimmering about her. "Couldn't you open a shop here?"

Nicole clumsily placed the folded skirt in the trunk at her feet. Her hands were sore, and the gauze made it difficult to control her movements.

"I don't think Gatlinburg is large enough to support something like that." She reached for another skirt.

"It's just that you are my first real friend."

Nicole stopped midmotion. "Truly?"

Lillian held the blouse against her chest. "Our closest neighbors were three miles away. We were rather secluded. Patrick and I were all each other had besides Ma."

Forgetting the packing, Nicole settled a hand on her shoulder. "You are my first real friend, too."

Lillian enveloped her in a hug. "I'm going to miss you so much!"

"I'd take you with me if I could," she said truthfully.

Pulling back, she inspected the guileless face. "Are you happy at my sister's? You can be honest with me."

Her expression brightened. "Oh, yes! They've made us feel very welcome. I have free run of the place, even Lucian's study. Not that there's anything of interest in there. I spend the majority of my time in the library."

"And Patrick?"

"He's content. I can tell he really likes and respects Lucian. And Lucian treats him like an adult, which Patrick needs right now. He's felt helpless for so long."

As it often had in the past twenty-four hours, emotion welled up and threatened to spill over in an ugly outburst. "I promise to come and visit you as often as I can. And we'll write letters. Lots and lots of them. You'll be sick of seeing my return address."

"I'll hold you to that."

Lillian's smile was tempered with sadness, eyes bright with unshed tears.

Nicole sniffled. "Back to packing." Waving a hand about the room, she said, "I've lots to do between now and tomorrow morning."

"Right. No more whining."

They set to work emptying her wardrobe. Since this was to be a short trip, Nicole would pack only a few changes of clothes and personal items. The rest of her things she'd take with her on her return trip. Jane came in to help them, conversing easily with Lillian and sharing her and Jessica's plans for the going-away party.

She wished she could stretch out these final moments. All too soon, the supper dishes were cleaned and put away and Megan arrived to escort Lillian home. It was impossible to hold back the tears as she bid her older sister goodbye. Silly, really, when this wouldn't be the last.

She slept fitfully that night, thoughts of the upcoming trip plaguing her. And thoughts of Quinn. He'd worn a look of resignation in the barn last night. For a split second, she'd believed he might ask her to reconsider, and when he hadn't, her capricious heart had actually mourned.

I'll feel better once I reach the city and see with my own eyes the endless adventures awaiting me.

The lack of proper rest did nothing to improve her mood the following morning. As Caleb pulled the wagon to a stop in front of what used to be the mercantile, he remarked on her silence.

"Something eating you?" Beneath the hat's brim, his dark eyes probed hers. "I figured I'd be hard put to keep you in your seat at this point."

"I'm simply fatigued from all the packing yesterday." She shrugged, averting her gaze to the rubble.

She was supposed to be excited. Over the moon. Today was the first day of her new life, after all. Gatlinburg would soon be nothing but a memory.

Instead, her heart felt heavy, weighted with sorrow.

Fiddling with her bonnet strings, she prayed. *Lord, I don't understand why I'm feeling this way. Help me to embrace change. Lead me to my new store.*

Caleb tipped his hat up. "Looks like they're making progress." He squinted at two figures working where the sales counter used to be, digging for salvageable items. "Is that Kenneth and his pa?"

"Surely not."

Caleb hopped off the wagon seat and came around to assist her down. He pointed to the spot where the checker game and stove used to be. "That's got to be Timothy. Can't miss the red hair."

She spotted Quinn the same moment he became aware of their presence. With a word to the man beside him, he quickly picked his way through the site, long strides carrying him across the street. He was still wearing the sling, she was glad to note. He'd heal faster that way.

When he'd reached them, he and Caleb shook hands. "You've got a lot of helpers."

Quinn ran his fingers through his windswept hair. His intense gaze locked onto her face, as if loath to look at anything else. "I was not expecting a turnout like this, that's for sure. I'm grateful for the support."

Nicole dragged air into her oxygen-starved lungs. She could hardly think, trying desperately to imprint everything about him into her memory.

"Is that Kenneth and Timothy?" she forced out.

"It is. All three families came to me yesterday. Your tormentors apologized for what they did to you. They wanted to apologize to you in person." He frowned. "I hope you don't mind that I suggested they write letters instead. I knew you were busy and… I wasn't sure how you would feel about conversing with them face-to-face."

Quinn was intent on protecting her to the very end, was he? How would her life suffer without such a man in it?

"That was thoughtful of you. You were right to suggest such a thing."

A little of the tension holding him rigid seemed to ease.

"And I'm glad you allowed them to assist you," she said. "Why hold a grudge, right?"

He didn't smile, but affection broke through the clouds in the honeyed depths of his eyes.

Caleb cleared his throat and pushed off from the wagon. "I'll be over there talking to Shane."

She and Quinn watched as he sauntered across the street. The ensuing silence bordered on awkward, and she hated the uncomfortable tension stretching between them.

Eyeing the sling, she said, "You're taking it easy, I hope?"

"Following doctor's orders to the letter."

Free hand fisted at his side, he was somber and still, nothing like the lighthearted boss she'd come to know. But then, he was injured and dealing with the stress of rebuilding.

"They seem to be making fast progress," she said to fill the silence. "I'm eager to see what all is accomplished while I'm gone. Maybe I'll be around long enough to see your new store take shape. Who are you going to hire in my place?"

His gaze was hooded. "I've been talking to a few young men who've voiced interest in the position."

Nicole's relief that he wasn't hiring a female was short-lived. It didn't matter. Eventually, he'd turn his attention to finding a suitable wife. He'd made his wish for a wife and children plain.

What felt like a physical pain dug into her chest and wouldn't be displaced.

"Quinn," someone called. "We need your advice over here."

He twisted and lifted a hand in acknowledgment.

Turning back, he clipped out, "I have to go. And you should, too. You've a long journey ahead of you."

Why was he being so distant and formal?

Where was the easy smile?

Swallowing the sudden thickness in her throat, she wrung her hands. "You're right. I'll, uh, see you in a few days?"

"Take care of yourself."

He was going to walk away.

On impulse, Nicole threw her arms around his neck and hugged him tight. He stiffened. Then, after a moment's hesitation, his free arm came around her and crushed her to him. Her entire being rejoiced.

Until he let go and, without another glance, spun on his heel and left her alone.

The trip was uneventful.

Nicole tamped down her emotions and concentrated on the changing scenery. Beside her, Caleb was quiet, thoughtful, as if in tune with her wish to remain locked in her own confusing world. They reached Knoxville around suppertime. The downtown area near the Tennessee River was bustling with people—young dock workers, professional gentlemen, well-dressed ladies walking arm in arm and peering into shop windows. Wagons and single riders clogged the dirt streets.

She'd forgotten how noisy the city could be. Covering her nose, she attempted to block out the overpowering scent of manure and animal sweat. Above the rooftops was nothing but endless sky. Already she missed the familiar mountain peaks.

Between the occasional jostle of passersby, Nicole gave herself a stern talking-to. This was the fulfillment of a lifelong dream—she was not going to allow minor irritations to detract from that. Besides, Caleb had taken time away from Rebecca to accompany her here. She owed it to him to at least act overjoyed.

He chose a moderate-size hotel that, while not up-scale, was clean and respectable-looking. After he'd secured two rooms, they shared a hot meal in that establishment's dining room.

She sipped her lemonade, wondered if Quinn was sitting down to supper with Lucian, Megan and the siblings right then.

"For a small hotel, they provide a fine-tasting meal." She indicated the buttery roll and steak that was surprisingly tender.

Caleb washed down his food with a healthy swig of steaming coffee. His assessing gaze touched on the other diners quietly conversing. The clink of silverware against china provided background noise. "We chose well. Centrally located, affordable and safe. Listen, why don't you retire to your room. I'll inquire about a reputable lawyer who can point us to available properties."

She was tired and would love a chance to rid herself of trail grit. Laying aside her napkin, she dredged up a grateful smile. "Thank you, Caleb. I know you'd rather be at home right now. I appreciate your assistance in this matter."

Concern darkened his eyes, the scar fanning across his temple stretching. "If you've changed your mind, we can leave for Gatlinburg first thing in the morning."

She shook her head. "I owe it to myself to give this a shot."

He studied her a long moment, then dipped his head. "All right."

Leaving him to settle the bill, Nicole retreated upstairs to her room. While not spacious, it was tidy, and a colorful quilt covered the bed. The view from the water-spotted window was one of the wide, murky green river. Boats bobbed in the water and workers scurried about the docks.

She watched the activity for a while before seeking out the water pitcher in the corner. While preparing for bed, her mind was consumed with thoughts of home. What were the twins doing? She hoped they'd give Puffy ample attention. He liked to be held and scratched behind his ears. Lillian was likely tucked into the library chair, curled up with a book. And Mrs. Calhoun was no doubt plying Patrick with treats in an effort to fatten him up.

Perhaps the shop space she chose wouldn't be available for some time. She could return home and spend several more weeks with her loved ones. Maybe even a month or two. She'd be able to see Quinn's new store.

She was about to blow out the lamp when a knock sounded. Caleb filled the doorway, hat in hand, expression confident.

"I located a lawyer, a Mr. John Arthur. The hotel manager recommended him, and I have to say he strikes me as an honest sort. He's going to show us several properties tomorrow morning."

"Wonderful."

He tipped his head to indicate the room. "You all settled in? Need anything before I retire?"

"No. I was just about to turn in when you knocked."

"I'm right next door if you need me."

"Sleep well, Caleb."

"You, too, Nicki." With a wink, he continued along the dim hallway.

The next morning, after a sumptuous breakfast of sausage, bacon and eggs and a stack of johnnycakes, she and Caleb walked to the lawyer's office. Once again, the boardwalk was crowded, the street traffic more than she was accustomed to. After introductions, Mr. Arthur took them to the first shop not far from the hotel. Nicole studied the long, narrow room with a critical eye. It had been used as a barbershop, which made her think of Tom Leighton and Jane and home.

"Not this one."

Mr. Arthur graciously bowed his head and swept them off to a quieter location several streets away from the hotel. Nicole liked the space, but the price was higher than she'd planned to pay.

Caleb's expression was disapproving. "This is too far from the activity. You wouldn't get as many customers here."

The lawyer cocked his head. "I have one other location I think will better suit your needs."

Located close to the river yet a fair distance from the dock entrance, the former millenary shop occupied the corner lot. There was even a view of the water from the front window. Diagonal from her was a nice-looking café called Rose's.

Caleb joined her at the window. "The shops on this end appear to be more upscale. And the customers going in there—" he pointed to Rose's "—look like possible future customers of a boutique like yours."

Nicole turned to the older man. "When is this one available?"

"Actually, it's ready for occupation now. You could set up today, if you were so inclined."

"Today." That meant no waiting period.

Instantly, those final, heart-rending moments with Quinn filtered through her consciousness. Could she truly find the wherewithal to say goodbye to him a second time? Going back, knowing she was leaving again would be too much to bear, she realized.

"I'll take it."

"I'll draw up the paperwork."

Nicole grabbed Caleb's arm. "Can I talk to you for a moment?"

His black brows met over his nose. "Of course." To the lawyer, he said, "My cousin and I are going across the street for coffee. We'll meet you at your office in an hour."

While Mr. Arthur locked up, she and Caleb walked to the café, which surpassed her expectations. The interior was both sophisticated and airy, with embossed cream-and-rose wallpaper and crisp white linens on the tables. The wood floors gleamed. Scents of freshly roasted coffee and cinnamon lingered in the air.

When their coffee and sweet buns had been delivered, Caleb leaned back in his chair and crossed his arms. "What's on your mind?"

"Since the shop is available immediately, I'd rather not return with you."

She held her breath, waiting for an explosion that didn't come. He blinked. Confusion furrowed his brow.

"I thought the twins were planning a big to-do in your honor."

"It's just in the planning stages and can be postponed for when I visit next." At this point, she couldn't imagine when that might be. It would destroy her to see Quinn moving on with his life, possibly with another woman.

"Don't you want to say proper goodbyes?"

Tears threatened. She crushed the cloth napkin in her lap. "I need for you to trust me on this."

Silence met her statement. Finally, he spoke. "This is your fresh start, Nicki. We'll do it however you want."

Blinking rapidly, she managed a watery smile, grateful he wasn't choosing to be stubborn and challenge her decision. "Thank you."

He picked up the sweet bun. "So, I wonder where we can find a good boardinghouse around here?"

Chapter Twenty-Four

Nicole had been gone a month.

Thirty-one days of battling misery every waking minute. The selfish part of Quinn clamored for control, demanding he go to Knoxville and beg her to come home. That wasn't the man he aspired to be, however. God's Word instructed him to put others' needs above his own. Authentic love didn't seek one's own good above another's.

While his conscience was clear, living without her was the most difficult thing he'd had to do.

Standing behind the wooden counter, Quinn surveyed his new store. Perhaps recreating the original one hadn't been his smartest idea. Everywhere he looked, he envisioned Nicole.

Nicole dusting shelves. Laughing with the old men in the corner. Wrapping up purchases.

A sigh escaped his downturned lips.

He turned to his new assistant, Donald. "I'll be in the office."

The hardworking twenty-year-old looked up from rearranging the jewelry case. "Okay, boss."

Stalking into the office, he slumped into the chair and extracted the letter from his jacket pocket. The paper was thinning at the creases, a result of his constant handling.

He'd been floored when Caleb had returned without her. Deeply hurt, too. Did he mean so little to her, then? Oh, he knew they'd said their private goodbyes in her barn. And a not-so-private one here on Main Street.

Had she known beforehand? Was that why she'd surprised him with that fierce, almost desperate hug?

As the days had crawled past, he'd come to accept that her decision had saved him. Watching her leave for what he'd thought was a temporary trip had ripped his heart out. He wasn't so sure he'd have been able to retain his dignity if he'd had to do it all over again, knowing it was permanent.

He sniffed the paper. Already her sweetly feminine scent was fading.

At least she'd taken the time to send this letter along with her cousin, explaining her need to seize the opportunities presented.

"Mr. Darling?" Donald hovered in the doorway. "Mr. O'Malley is here to see you."

Hastily returning the letter to his breast pocket, he strode into the front area. Caleb was leaning against the counter.

"Is everything okay with Nicole?" Quinn pushed out. "Has she written to you?"

"Got a letter yesterday, as a matter of fact. She's fine. Business is picking up to the point she's contemplating hiring someone."

His unease evaporated, leaving behind a hollow sensation. "That's good news."

Apparently he didn't sound convincing, because Caleb arched a mocking brow.

"I want her venture to be a success," Quinn said with more starch. "And I'm glad she's happy. That's what counts."

Caleb grinned.

Okay, time to stop talking.

"The thing is—" Caleb leaned over the counter, lowering his voice "—I'm not so sure she is happy."

"What do you mean?"

"She sounds lonely."

Propping an arm along the silver-and-crystal case, Quinn ignored the compassion squeezing his chest. He'd been afraid of this. *She doesn't need me to rescue her. I'm not her protector.*

"I'm speaking from experience when I say it will take time to adjust and make new friends. Has she found a church yet?"

"She's visited a couple but hasn't decided on one in particular."

"And her lodgings? Is she content there?"

Caleb shifted to let another customer view the contents of the jewelry case. "The proprietress is a kind Christian widow. She's a substitute mother figure for Nicole."

Another customer approached the counter needing help with the fabrics, and Donald was busy packaging vanilla extract. "I have to help my assistant."

With a nod, Caleb waved a small paper scrap. "And I have to gather supplies for my wife."

Quinn considered asking the other man to include his regards the next time he wrote Nicole, but decided against it. He didn't want her thinking he was pining

away for her up here in the mountains. Even if that was
exactly what he was doing.

With one final glance in the mirror to inspect her
hair, which had blessedly grown out enough to brush
her shoulders, Nicole went to the door to flip the open
sign. Judging from the still, stagnant air inside her
shop, it was going to be a scorcher. Her gaze snagged
on a man and woman strolling along the boardwalk.
With his jet-black hair and her fair good looks, they
made a handsome couple. Behind them trailed two
young boys, as neatly dressed as their parents, making faces at each other and giggling.

Regret wrapped its tentacles around her and
squeezed every last drop of contentment she'd managed to grasp since her arrival. Not that she'd managed
much. No matter how many self-directed speeches she
made about focusing on her blessings, the distance
from Quinn overshadowed everything.

A cold chill seizing up her insides, she rested her
forehead against the glass.

*I admit it, Lord Jesus. I was wrong. Prideful and
foolish. I thought I had my life all figured out, that I
didn't need Your direction. I got what I wanted, yet
I'm miserable.*

She missed her sisters and mother. She missed Patrick and Lillian. She missed her cousins—she wouldn't
even mind hearing Caleb calling her Nicki. She missed
home.

Oh, her landlady was nice, and she provided tasty
meals. There was a charming flower garden behind the
house where she could sit and sew in peace.

Business was steady. Already she was having trouble keeping up with the orders for new dresses, in addition to the alteration requests she'd received from both men and women.

Nicole had every reason to be happy. The fact that she couldn't escape this melancholy made her feel childish and ungrateful.

Missing Quinn was normal. He'd been an understanding boss, a wonderful, supportive friend, her protector and avenger. But after six weeks of not seeing him, shouldn't this aching hole in her chest have disappeared by now? Shouldn't the sadness, the desperation to be near him, have already faded?

Forgive me, Lord. I'll get over this soon, I hope. I really am grateful for Your provision, despite the fact I don't deserve it.

Frustrated, she retreated behind the counter to where her brand-new sewing machine was set up, along with an assortment of threads and needles and other supplies. She set aside the dress Mrs. Elizabeth Moore had ordered and reached for the pair of men's trousers that needed hemming. She was in the wrong frame of mind to create something out of nothing. Better to stick with mundane tasks.

Nicole had just finished when the door swished open. Hanging the trousers on the rack beside her machine, she ran her hands along her full skirts and turned to greet the customer.

The words died on her lips.

Quinn, *her* Quinn, was standing inside the door, hat in his hands and looking more handsome than she'd ever seen him. Glossy hair slicked off his forehead, cheekbones stark and pronounced, his hard jaw clean shaven and his light eyes steady on her.

Advancing on wooden feet, she almost pinched him to check if he was indeed real and not a figment of her imagination. "Quinn Darling, you are the last person I expected to walk through my door today."

"I did promise to visit you."

Mouth crooking up at the corner, his warm, soothing voice washed over her in waves of true bliss.

"You *are* real." And he was here, in her store, close enough to touch. Somehow, she restrained herself.

The smile didn't quite reach his eyes. "Did you think you were dreaming?"

Clasping her wayward hands behind her back, she laughed softly, unable to hide her joy. "I'm very glad I'm not."

Oh, the sight of his face was so dear. Precious. Her heart vibrated with unbridled happiness, and she nearly bounced on her toes in giddy excitement.

He nodded, assessing the space, inspecting the shelves on either wall and the two table displays in the middle. Walking past her, Quinn leisurely explored, touching a long finger to this fabric and that blouse. Nicole remained in the same spot, blatantly soaking up his every movement.

Finally, he pivoted and smiled that peculiar, not-quite-happy smile again. "You've done well for yourself. Caleb tells me business has been good."

"Yes. I've been blessed."

Nicole didn't wish to discuss business. She wanted… what? For him to whisk her into his arms and kiss her senseless? To fall on his knees and confess his undying love for her?

"Yes," she blurted aloud.

His brow lifted.

A flush worked its way up her neck even as the truth registered, solidified within her soul. Quinn proposing to her was exactly what she wanted. Looking into his eyes, breathing the same air after too many days apart, it all became clear…why she couldn't shake the sorrow, the jealousy over the mere idea of Quinn with someone else, the envy she'd experienced while observing the family on the boardwalk.

She was in love with him.

Marrying Quinn, building a life and raising a family together—that was her true dream.

Another customer chose that moment to enter her shop. Nicole uttered a distracted hello. A muscle in Quinn's jaw twitched as he dipped his head in acknowledgment of the lady, who made a beeline for the ribbon rack.

Striding over to Nicole, he spoke in lowered tones. "I'll let you get back to work."

"You're leaving?" she squeaked, panicked.

He couldn't leave. He'd just arrived. They'd barely spoken.

"Not yet. I've procured a room." He named the same hotel that she and Caleb had lodged in. His hesitation, indeed his entire reserved manner, was at odds with his usual easygoing attitude. "Would you like to have dinner with me?"

"I'd like nothing better." She gave him directions to the boardinghouse.

"I will pick you up at six o'clock."

Emotions in a jumble, Nicole watched his retreating figure until he turned a corner. Today was going to be the longest day of her life.

* * *

Back in her rented room that evening, Nicole chose her favorite outfit, a lilac dress with tiny bows adorning the short sleeves and delicate black lace overlaying the skirt. With it, she paired black lace gloves and a filmy shawl. She wore her curls loose save for a single, sparkly hair clip on one side. Silver earbobs adorned her ears.

Picking up her reticule from the bedside table, she slipped it over her wrist and offered up a silent prayer for calm. The day had dragged. However, she couldn't recall a single exchange. Hopefully she hadn't offended any of her customers with her utter distraction. *Or sewed on the wrong color buttons. Or taken too many inches off Mr. Corelli's trousers.*

Her legs didn't want to support her as she navigated the steep staircase to the lower level. The smell of Mrs. Keene's pot roast permeated the entry hall. Instead of reacting with hunger, her stomach rebelled.

How was she supposed to make it through the meal with Quinn studying her with his enigmatic, too-knowing regard? What if he guessed her feelings?

They'd both wind up embarrassed, that's what. He hadn't asked her to stay in Gatlinburg. Quite the opposite. He'd encouraged her to follow her dream.

He couldn't know her dream had changed. Quinn had affected the change, barreling into her life and challenging her to take risks, to let others see the real Nicole O'Malley.

At the heavy tread of boots to her right, she whipped her head around. The object of her turmoil appeared in the wide parlor archway, elegant and intimidating in his coal-black suit, his dark gaze doing a slow inspection of her.

He let out a soft whistle. "You are…well, words really wouldn't do you justice. Consider me speechless." Closing the distance between them, he lifted her hand and placed a kiss on her knuckles, the heat of his mouth burning through the lace.

At her swift intake, he released his hold and gestured to the wood-paneled door. "Shall we go?"

Passing onto the wide veranda, she chatted nervously about Rose's Café and their mouthwatering beef stew. "Unfortunately they don't have chicken and dumplings on the menu," she said when they reached the boardwalk. "I know that's your favorite."

Quinn held his arm out to her, and she settled her hand in the crook of his elbow, hard put not to edge closer to his side. The enticing scent of peppermint wafted over.

"I get enough of that at Plum's."

Her gaze flashed to his profile. "You're not staying at my sister's?"

"I decided to rebuild the store pretty much the same as before. I moved back into the private quarters until my home is complete. The men I hired from Gatlinburg and Pigeon Forge will start work next week."

Although he continued to stare straight ahead, she glimpsed his slight frown.

"Is something wrong?" she ventured. "Have you changed your mind about the property?"

"It's not that." Guiding her around an elderly man walking his dog, Quinn exhaled. "I'm simply wondering if my plans for a large home aren't excessive. After all, what do I need five bedrooms for?"

Nicole bit her lip. Quinn wasn't acting like himself. He seemed distracted and...sad.

Not about to mention his desire for a wife and children, she said, "You'll need them for when your family visits. Have they indicated when they might come?"

Curious about his family, she wondered if she might arrange a trip home at the same time. His sister, Tilly, sounded sweet, and she was curious whether his younger brother was anything like him.

"They are waiting for me to send word. I plan to see how construction progresses before I do."

"I can hear in your voice how much you miss them."

Quinn angled his head to look at her then, his probing gaze making her feel as if she were missing the key clue to a riddle. "Is that all you've deduced in my voice? That I miss my family?"

Mouth working, she stumbled over an uneven board. His free hand shot out to steady her.

"I'm fine," she insisted, cheeks pinking as a trio of younger girls heading in their direction giggled and gaped at Quinn as if they'd never seen a handsome man before.

Quinn didn't repeat his question, and Nicole couldn't help but feel relieved. She despised the strained energy enveloping them, the uncertainty where camaraderie used to exist. Fortunately, the café's pink awning came into view. Surely the delicious fare and relaxed atmosphere would put them at ease.

The hostess on duty recognized Nicole and, with a friendly greeting, led them to a window table in the corner. Quinn pulled out her chair and waited for her to be seated before taking the one across from her. His lean form dominated her vision.

For the second time that day, she was tempted to pinch him. It was still difficult to believe that Quinn Darling was here, close enough to touch yet off-limits.

Constance inquired if they wanted coffee. Out of habit, Quinn accepted for himself but declined for Nicole.

"Actually, I would love a cup," she inserted, laying her reticle on the chair beside her.

With a dip of her head, Constance set off for the kitchen.

Quinn's jaw sagged. "I thought coffee and tea stained your teeth?"

She grinned. "If the amount of hard candy you consume hasn't affected yours then I feel free to indulge now and again."

He tapped his chin, trademark grin bursting through. "About that, I think your boutique would benefit from penny candy. I'm speaking as your former employer and the owner of an extremely successful country store."

"Oh, do you now?"

"Definitely. Not only would jars of penny candy add a splash of color, it would set your shop apart. When a customer is in need of alterations and is deciding where to go, they'll say, 'Hey, that Nicole O'Malley, she has penny candy. I should go there. I'll indulge my love of lemon drops while I wait.'"

"I will keep your advice under consideration, Mr. Darling."

"You're gone for a month and a half and already you're defaulting to formal address?" He shook his head in mock incredulity. "I wouldn't have thought it of you, Duchess."

The coffee arrived then, and, concentrating on stirring in milk and sugar, she attempted to gather her scattering wits. This charming, teasing Quinn was the man she'd fallen in love with, the one she desperately wanted to keep with her forever.

Nicole made it through the meal by plying him with safe questions, anything to maintain light conversation. There were a few hiccups. Like the moments before their pie arrived and she caught him staring, his honey eyes soft.

"What?"

"Your hair," he said quietly, elegant fingers skimming the fork and knife handles against the pristine tablecloth. "It's grown out."

She touched a finger to the ends self-consciously. "More slowly than I'd like, but I no longer receive odd stares."

"Are you sure they weren't stares of envy? In my opinion, you could make most any hairstyle look stylish. I can't say the same for every female of my acquaintance."

"You are very good for my self-esteem."

The memories of Kenneth's prank crowded in, and she was in that field again, Quinn comforting her, making her feel safe and beautiful despite everything. He was the only person she could envision beside her for the remainder of her days, facing life's trials and sharing in life's blessings together.

Could she...*should she* confess her feelings?

And put Quinn in an awkward position? If he'd returned my feelings, he never would've let me go. No, it was better to keep her secret to herself. That way their future interactions wouldn't be marked with humiliation.

Heart in turmoil, Nicole struggled to project a casual attitude. Aware she was wasting her scant time with Quinn but unable to alter her feelings, she craved the sanctuary of her room where she'd be free to let the pain out.

She left half the pie uneaten on the plate. Subdued once more, Quinn didn't comment on it. He was quiet during their return stroll to the boardinghouse. Dusk cast a yellow haze over the river. A mourning dove cooed above them. With every step, her heart sank a little lower.

Quinn didn't accompany her to the veranda. Instead, he stopped beneath the leafy bower of a dogwood tree, where they had a modicum of privacy.

"I'm leaving first thing in the morning."

Nicole dug her fingers into her skirts, uncaring she was crumpling the delicate lace. "I understand."

"Donald is a trustworthy assistant," he went on, "but he's not…you."

"I see."

"I'm not comfortable leaving him in charge for very long."

"That makes sense." Her throat was closing up. How many more goodbyes could she take?

Stepping close enough that she could see the pulse point on his throat, which at the moment was quite erratic, Quinn's large hand curved around her nape. She tried to sort the emotions in his hooded gaze and failed. His generous mouth lowered to graze the outermost corner of her lips, evoking shivers of pent-up longing.

He abruptly pulled away, disappointment palpable. "I should go."

"Quinn?" Apparently she wasn't done tormenting herself. "Will you stop by the boutique in the morning?"

Jaw working, he jerked a nod. Then he was gone.

She gingerly touched the spot where his lips had been. "I'd give all this up in an instant if only you'd ask."

Chapter Twenty-Five

Coming here had been a huge mistake. Massive. What had he been thinking?

Oh, that's right. He hadn't. He'd acted purely on impulse, anxious to see her after too many weeks apart.

Anger focused inward, Quinn didn't immediately return to the hotel. He kept walking until he found himself on the docks. At this time of night, when darkness crept across the sky and the sliver of the moon was already visible, the riverside was practically empty. Boats of all sizes bobbed in the murky water. A handful of late arrivals tied off their vessels and began unloading supplies.

The cool breeze coming off the river pushed his hair into his eyes. Not bothering to fix it, he walked without seeing or caring where he was going.

Dinner was a disaster. He'd had trouble containing his emotions, had been on the verge of pushing his own wishes on her despite what an untenable position that would've put her in. His own uncomfortable state had made her anxious. He'd seen the distress in her beautiful violet eyes and hated himself for it.

He could not come here a second time.

Whenever she visited Gatlinburg, he'd make a point to avoid her.

All he had to do was get through yet another farewell tomorrow morning. No extended speeches, and absolutely no touching allowed. Quick and to the point.

Turning his feet toward the hotel, he took his time returning to his room. The ticking of the clock, along with the dread weighing in his chest, kept him awake until the wee hours. He skipped breakfast. Settled for several cups of bracing coffee before heading to the boutique.

He parked his wagon directly in front, beneath the branches of a solitary tree. Even at this early hour, the streets bustled with activity, similar to those in Boston only on a smaller scale. Was Nicole truly happy here? Did she long for the slower pace of Gatlinburg?

They hadn't spoken of such substantial matters last night, and he wasn't about to bring them up now.

Leaving his hat on the wagon seat, he hurried inside, intent on keeping this meeting brief. Nicole rounded the counter and met him in the middle of the store, fragile looking in the same demure, snowy-white dress she'd worn the first night they met. While there'd been fire in her cheeks and retribution sparkling in her eyes then, today shadows dulled her vitality. Her skin was nearly translucent. Soft and delicate.

He thrust his hands in his pockets. "I came to say I'm proud of what you've accomplished here. It took an extraordinary amount of courage to do what you've done."

Teeth worrying her bottom lip, she nodded. "Thank

you, Quinn. Your approval means more than you know."

"You don't need my approval. The success you've achieved through your hard work and determination, aided with God's strength and guidance, is what matters."

Worry lines marred her brow. Hands tightly clasped at her waist, she looked everywhere but at him.

Battling the need to soothe away her tension, to say or do something to evoke that sunshine smile of hers, he edged backward. "I'll write to you."

"I'll write back."

The doorknob dug into his hip. "Goodbye, Nicole."

"Take care," she whispered, arms hugging her middle. "Stay safe."

The bell jingled as he pushed outside, humid air closing in on him, choking him. *Don't look back. Put her needs first. Give her the freedom to follow her dreams.*

He'd reached the wagon when he heard her call his name.

Dense branches providing shade from the overbright sun, Quinn stared as Nicole burst through the door. Rushing to join him beneath the tree, she clutched his arms.

"Take me with you," she pleaded, her eyes wide and earnest.

Confusion roughened his voice. "What?"

"Being apart from you has been the worst kind of torture." Her face turned up to his, he noted the trembling of her full lips. "I miss coming to work and seeing you dip into the peppermint jar. I miss watching you slip an extra scoop of sugar into the widow Weber's sack when you think no one is looking. I miss your scowls at the old checker players when they get too rowdy and the way you inhale Mrs. Greene's biscuits and gravy. I daydream about watching you practice your fencing." Pink flooded her cheeks. "I could do that all day without complaint, actually. I miss so many things about you I'd never be able to list them all. Quinn, I'm miserable without you."

"What are you saying exactly?"

"I'm saying I love you."

Her confession rocked him to the core. He hadn't let himself picture her saying such things to him and was unprepared for the elation bubbling through his system, edging out reason and sensibility. Nicole *loved* him? Wanted to be with him? Images flared in his mind, clear and vibrant images of him and Nicole exchanging marriage vows, moving into their new home behind the church, hosting family dinners…welcoming a baby.

Caught up in the prospect of a future together, he couldn't speak for long moments.

But then the gold lettering of her store sign glittered in the light and the images scattered like dandelion wisps on a stiff breeze.

Gently dislodging her hold, Quinn crossed to the shop's entrance and opened the door, turning to look at her expectantly. Her raven brows crashed together. Unease tightening her features, she preceded him inside haltingly.

"What is it, Quinn?" Pivoting toward him, she held out her hands in appeal. "Is it that you don't want me—"

"Look around you," he bit out, anguish and frustration coursing through him. "I cannot be the one responsible for destroying what you've strived to achieve. Why do you think I didn't ask you to stay in the first place?"

Hope flickered in the luminous depths. "So you did want me to stay?"

"Of course I did." Her feelings for him didn't change anything. The situation was impossible.

"Do you love me, Quinn?"

Nicole held her breath. The courage that had spurred her to run after him and admit her feelings was waning.

Quinn stared at her incredulously. "All I can think about is making you my wife. Does that answer your question?"

Tears blurred her vision, and suddenly he was before her, his touch featherlight on her shoulders. "My darling Nicole." Tenderness marked his words. "'I love you' hardly expresses what is truly in my heart. You've captivated me from the moment you hit me with that pan." He hooked a curl behind her ear. "You challenge me to be a better man, to look beyond the surface to the person beneath. You make me laugh. You make me want to pull my hair out sometimes, too."

The side of his mouth lifted in a rueful smile, and she matched it with one of her own.

"In short, you make my life richer, fuller, brighter. If you were to accept my hand in marriage, I'd be the happiest man on earth."

"Oh, Quinn." He was saying all the right things, but there was a guardedness in his eyes she didn't trust.

"What worries me more than anything is the possibility you'd resent me later on."

"That won't happen."

"Maybe not tomorrow or a week from now. But months, perhaps years from now, would you be happy with your choice? You wanted to leave Gatlinburg long before I showed up. I'm not convinced you'd be content."

"You're right. For many years, I dreamed of a different life far from there. I didn't seek God's guidance as you suggested earlier. I decided what I wanted, what I thought would make me happy, and pursued it without consulting Him. I've come to realize how foolish I've been." She gestured to the intricate dress she'd designed and created in the window, the colorful fabric bolts lining the walls, her sewing station behind the counter. "The thing about dreams is this—reality doesn't always measure up to your imagination. You of all people should understand that."

"I do. I also know that it's hardest in the beginning. You're just starting out. Until you feel more at home here…find a church you like and make friends, it's bound to be lonely. That's not a sign that you should give up."

"I don't deny I'm lonely, but that's not what this is about." She had to make him understand. Their future depended on it. "Don't you see? Maybe if I'd never met you, I could be content with this life. But I did, and those weeks with you were the most frustrating, exhilarating, *liberating* weeks of my life. Thanks to you, I felt more at home in Gatlinburg than I did my whole life. I finally felt I fit in. Accepted for the person that I am, not because of my last name or for my sisters' sake." Resting her hand against his cheek, she looked deep into his eyes, letting him see every drop of love and devotion she had for him. "You changed me, Quinn."

The color of his eyes deepened, intensified to dark caramel. Reaching up, he cradled her face with both hands. "I want very much to believe you. To trust in us."

"Then do."

Disquiet flashed. "What about your business? You were born with a needle in your hand, Nicole. You can't waste your God-given talent."

"That's the beauty of what I do. I'm not required to have a building to fill orders. I can sew anywhere." She paused. "Remember that night in the springhouse?"

"Are you referring to the night I used the cold as an excuse to hold you in my arms?"

"What? You didn't even like me then."

He hummed deep in his throat. "You just assumed I didn't."

Heady warmth fizzed in her middle. "I admit I reveled in your closeness. It was a new experience for me, leaning on someone else's strength."

The pad of his thumb grazing her lower lip, his voice grew husky. "Get to the point before my good sense fails and I kiss you like I've been tempted to do since I arrived."

Blinking at his bluntness and wishing he'd do just that, Nicole rushed out, "That night, you questioned my reasons for this move. You asked if I was running from my reputation. My family. Oh, I was madder than a hornet at such an outrageous assumption."

Quinn's lips twitched. "Really? I couldn't tell."

"I've had a lot of time to think in recent weeks. You were absolutely right. All those years of planning… I wasn't running *to* something. I was running *from* something."

Slowly, like clouds drifting across the moon, the doubts in his eyes cleared. "And now there's nothing left to run from?"

"Nothing at all."

"This is a lot to take in," he said in mock seriousness. "I may need some convincing."

At the sight of his glorious, mischievous smile, happiness chased away all the anxiety and fear and sorrow she'd been carrying around the past weeks. Going up on tiptoe, Nicole brushed her lips against his.

A shudder rippled through him. "Greet me like that every morning for the rest of my life?"

She smiled, shyness kicking in.

Quinn winced. "I'm not doing this right, am I?"

Releasing her, he dug in his jacket pocket and fished out something small and yellow. A lemon drop.

"Um, that's not what I was after."

Nicole pressed her lips together to hold back a nervous laugh. This moment was a turning point, one that would alter her life. She literally shook from the high emotions humming through her.

Putting the sweet in his other pocket, he went searching again and extracted a silk handkerchief. "This is for you."

She stared at the neat square he pressed into her palm. "Is it a peppermint stick?"

"No."

"A chocolate-cream drop?"

"Not even close."

Gingerly unwrapping the material, she gasped at the intricate ring in the center.

Quinn's smile lit up her world. "It belonged to my grandmother. I've carried it on my person since the day I discovered you alone and upset in that field. That day, I knew you were the woman I wanted for my wife. I didn't know if I'd ever get the chance to give it to you, but I kept it with me just in case. Hoping against hope…"

Taking her hand, he dropped to one knee. "I love you, Nicole O'Malley. Please make me the happiest of men and say you'll marry me."

With a half laugh, half sob, tears of joy skimming her cheeks, she nodded. "Yes. Yes, I'll marry you."

Quinn quickly slipped the ring on her finger and, standing, pulled her close. Adoration glowed in his eyes. "If my proposal is bringing you to tears, we have a problem."

"Oh, do be quiet and kiss me."

He kissed her until the bell dinged and a customer walked in. Lifting his head, he said, "I apologize, madam, but we're closed."

Nicole laughed at the woman's scandalized expression and held up her hand so that her ring was clearly visible. "We're moving locations."

Epilogue

September 1882

"Seventeen years ago today, I welcomed not one but two precious daughters into the world." Standing behind a table where a scrumptious-looking cake and jars of tea and lemonade had been set up beneath the trees, Alice beamed at the crowd. Close friends and family had come out on this pleasant autumn afternoon to celebrate the twins' birthday. "Some people might assume a man would be disappointed at having two more girls added to our brood. Not your father. He fell in love the instant he set eyes on you. If he were here today, I know he'd be bursting with pride just as I am. Happy birthday, my dears."

Whistles and hearty clapping echoed through the yard. On one side of Alice, Jane blushed. On the other side, Jessica smiled boldly, unfazed by the attention. Nicole studied the white dresses she'd designed for them during her weeks in Knoxville, satisfied with the results. Similar in material and outline, Jane's skirt sported a panel of royal blue beneath white eyelet lace, complemented with a ribbon about her slender waist. For Jessica's dress, she'd used forest green. They looked elegant and beautiful.

"Hard to believe they're seventeen." Taking their seats once the noise quieted and Alice began slicing the cake, her older sister Juliana reached up to readjust the pins holding her heavy flame-colored hair. "They seem older than the last time I saw them. Mature young women."

Nicole glanced around at the guests, noting the number of young men watching the girls with undisguised interest. "I have a feeling Mama won't have them at home for much longer."

Juliana touched her hand, deep green eyes frank and approving. "Jane and Jessica aren't the only ones who've changed. I noticed something different about you as soon as we arrived. You're…"

"Less annoying than usual?" Amusement marked her words. "Not as self-absorbed?"

A wide smile softened Juliana's features. "I was going to say content. At peace with yourself."

Conversation filtered around them as people found their seats at the handful of makeshift tables or on thick logs her cousins had dragged in for the occasion. Near the cake table, Kate comforted a sleepy Victoria while chatting with Rebecca, whose large tummy had seemed to drop in recent days.

"It took a while to get to this point."

Too much of her life, she'd depended on others' opinions and treatment of her to dictate how she viewed herself. Now she knew the truth. What counted was how God, her Creator, saw her. According to the Scriptures, she was wonderfully and fearfully made. She was God's beloved child, with her own unique strengths and shortcomings—His prone-to-weakness vessel to be used for His glory.

"I like Quinn. Evan does, too. He's a perfect match for you."

On the far side of the yard, Caleb, Lucian and Quinn lounged along the barn wall with Evan, Juliana's husband. Their son, James, a mini-version of dark-haired Evan, held tightly to his father's hand and sucked his thumb.

Of course, her attention was all for her fiancé. Watching his animated face, she said, "Quinn balances my serious side. He makes me laugh."

"He makes you happy."

"Yes."

Quinn glanced in her direction and winked, lazy smile and waggling brows promising stolen kisses later. Her heart melted. She could hardly wait until she officially became Mrs. Quinn Darling. Fourteen more days.

"You make him happy, too," Juliana mused, studying their interaction. "That much is obvious."

"I try."

"You don't have to try. You just have to be. Trust me on this. It's plain he adores you, little sis."

"I wish you could move back here."

Longing surged in her eyes even as her ginger brows creased. "Evan and I have discussed the subject. We're praying about it. I've made precious friends in Cades Cove, but it's not the same. I miss my family."

Grateful she'd figured out how important family was before it was too late, Nicole squeezed her sister's hand. "I'll pray about the matter, as well."

"At least we get to stay for your wedding."

"The day can't get here soon enough."

Jessica arrived, balancing three plates, and passed Nicole and Juliana pieces of cake before sitting across the table with her own. "I wish you'd let me at least peek at your wedding dress," she complained before scooping up a bite.

Jane delivered lemonades and headed back for more, stopping briefly to thank well-wishers.

Nicole picked up her fork and repeated the answer she'd given over the past weeks. "You'll see it once I'm finished."

Returning to her seat, Jane sipped her drink. "I've no doubt it will be the loveliest creation you've made to date."

Jessica swept her long ponytail behind her shoulder. Nicole had offered to arrange her hair, but she'd insisted on keeping it simple.

"Well, hurry up. You know I'm not the most patient person in the world."

Juliana laughed outright. "Oh, we know."

Across from her, Jane sighed and scanned the faces as if searching for someone specific. Her shoulders slumped in disappointment.

"What's the matter, Jane?" Nicole had a feeling she knew, but she asked, anyway.

Jessica rolled her eyes. "What do you think? She's pining away for her one true love."

"Who's that?" Juliana swiped a napkin across her mouth.

"Tom Leighton," Nicole said quietly. "He used to own the barbershop."

"Oh. I remember now. Megan mentioned him in her letters."

Silence descended, Tom's proposal to Megan hovering unspoken between them. While Megan had considered him a good friend, she hadn't loved him. Her heart belonged to Lucian. He sold his shop and left town after she turned down his proposal.

Setting aside her fork, Jane gave up all pretense of eating. Nicole's heart broke at the evidence of her sister's misery. Tom had been a friend to the entire family, but he'd had a soft spot for Jane.

"He hasn't written. Not one single letter to let us know he's safe. He knows how I worry!"

Jessica rubbed her twin's back. "I'm sure he's fine, sis."

Jane touched a hand to her elegant, upswept hair. "I thought he'd come home for my birthday. Surprise me, you know? What a fool I've been."

"He's been gone a long time," Jessica said quietly. "Maybe it's time to move on."

Tears glistening, Jane reluctantly nodded. "I think you're right. I've wasted enough time on Tom Leighton. It's time to forget him."

Nicole wondered if Jane truly meant what she said and, if so, how long it would take to get over him.

Nicole's wedding day arrived crisp yet sunny, not a single cloud in the brilliant blue sky. Her cabin had been invaded by every last female in her family. Her mother and Aunt Mary were in the kitchen admiring the two-layer cake, a vanilla-and-cream confection that Jane had topped with chopped peppermints as a nod to the groom's candy obsession. Everyone else was upstairs with her. As if she needed eight people to help her prepare.

Seated at the dressing table, Megan carefully tucked flowers into Nicole's upswept curls, and lighthearted chatter and giggles enveloped her. In the mirror's reflection, Nicole watched Rebecca give her younger sister, Amy, a hug. Sophie and Kate admired the wedding dress hanging in the corner. Jane was trying to convince Jessica to let her fix her hair into something more formal than a ponytail, and Juliana stood quietly by, eyes shiny as she observed all her sisters.

Contentment eclipsed the beginnings of nervous jitters. She was incredibly fortunate to be in this place, in this moment, with people who loved her. And whom she loved in return.

A flurry at the stairs caught everyone's attention. A slender form with bright blond hair emerged from the opening in the floor.

"I'm so sorry I'm late!" Lillian strode across the spacious room, covering her mouth when she saw what Megan was doing to Nicole's hair. "Quinn is going to swallow his tongue when he gets a look at you."

That startled a laugh out of Megan. "I certainly hope not."

Nicole smiled. "You look gorgeous. Did you get that dress in New Orleans?"

Nodding, she twirled. "Megan picked it out."

Patrick and Lillian had accompanied the couple on their yearly summer trip to New Orleans to visit Lucian's father. All these weeks later, Lillian was still talking about everything she'd seen and experienced. While Carl was in jail awaiting trial, their guardianship had been officially transferred to Lucian and Megan. Sheriff Timmons had assured them that they'd never have to go back to Carl. Their grandfather planned to visit around Thanksgiving, and both were eager to meet him.

"Pink *is* your favorite color," Megan said, affection for the young girl sparkling in her eyes. "Good thing it complements your fair complexion."

Nicole listened quietly as the two spoke of the fashionable shops they'd visited. In a different time, she would've been envious of those shop owners. Not now. She didn't equate giving up her shop to giving up a dream. Instead, she saw it as exchanging it for a new and better one.

A life with the man she loved was what she truly desired, a life made rich with relationships. Quinn had surprised her with plans for an addition to the mercantile. Once they got settled in their new home, he was going to transform the store's private quarters into her very own seamstress shop. He'd also offered to help her design an advertisement for surrounding communities so that she could receive and ship orders and not rely solely on the people of Gatlinburg for business. It was the perfect solution.

"Nicole, are you listening?"

"Oh, sorry. My mind was wandering. What did you say?"

Megan's smile was knowing. "We're returning to New Orleans at the end of this week. I'm not sure how long we'll be gone. Would you mind checking in on Patrick? He decided to stay here and continue helping Quinn at the store."

"You were just there. Why so soon?"

Hope burned in her sister's eyes. "Lucian and I plan to revisit some of the orphanages. We prayed about it and feel God is leading us to go back. We'd appreciate your prayers."

Twisting in her seat, Nicole squeezed her hand. "You have them, sis."

Their mother's voice carried up the stairs. "We have to leave in twenty minutes, girls!"

A flurry of excitement engulfed the room. Nicole was urged into her dress, her sisters fussing over the delicate buttons marching up her back.

"Quinn is not going to like this feature," Juliana chuckled.

She wondered what he was doing right that moment, what his thoughts were, if he was nervous.

Her flaring skirts were fluffed and straightened and a wildflower bouquet was pressed into her hands. And then they were making their way to the awaiting wagon.

Caleb's jaw dropped. Coming around to the front steps, he braced his hands on his hips. "This can't be my little Nicki."

Nerves and anticipation zipping through her, she shot him a mock glare. "Don't start with me, Caleb O'Malley. It isn't nice to tease the bride-to-be."

Taking her hand, he helped her down the stairs and

lifted her onto the seat. "You're right. Besides, you don't look like Nicki today." He waved a hand to indicate her dress. "Quinn is going to have trouble speaking his vows."

"Have you seen him this morning?"

He grinned. "I have."

She gripped the flowers. "And?"

"He seemed calm and focused. And eager to hitch himself to you."

Smiling in relief, she closed her eyes and anticipated seeing her groom while Caleb helped the girls into the wagon bed, where hay squares had been set up and covered with quilts for makeshift seating.

Quinn was thrilled to have his parents and siblings in town. Her nervousness over meeting them had proved pointless. While Edward Darling was a tad intimidating, with his booming voice and authoritative manner, he possessed a kind heart, and Edith Darling had treated Nicole with warmth and affection from the moment of their arrival. Quinn had apparently written glowing letters to his mother, and she was thrilled her eldest son had found love at last. Eighteen-year-old Trevor was even more outrageous than Quinn. Jessica had taken one look at the brash, handsome young man and become instantly smitten. And Tilly was a sweetheart, if a tad superior in her outlook. Nicole couldn't really blame her. Not considering her lavish upbringing and well-to-do friends. Having two protective, doting brothers probably hadn't helped matters.

Lucian and Megan had generously allowed the Darlings to stay with them. The past several weeks, Nicole had been given a glimpse into Quinn's previous life. Much to his dismay, Edith had regaled her with all sorts of stories from his childhood. She was looking forward to visiting his Boston home at Christmastime.

The ride to the church passed quickly. Soon she was being ushered up the stairs and through the doors. The interior was packed, but all that mattered was Quinn.

The piano music swelled. Clasping her uncle Sam's outstretched arm, she took her first step toward her future, toward the man God had brought into her life at just the right time. The moment their eyes met, Quinn's went wide and his lips parted. Frank admiration replaced the initial shock. His honeyed eyes warmed with pride and love, and his mouth curved in a smile that made her feel as light as an air balloon.

When she'd reached the front and Sam joined his wife on the pew, Quinn took her hands in his and, in a swift and unexpected move, placed a quick but searing kiss on her lips.

Everyone in attendance laughed, including Reverend Monroe. "Try to have some patience, young man. We haven't gotten to that part yet."

"My apologies." The twinkle in his eyes belied his words.

Happiness bubbling up, Nicole's smile stretched from ear to ear. With her hands tucked safely in her groom's, they exchanged the sacred vows committing themselves to each other for the rest of their lives. When the reverend pronounced them husband and wife, he said, "*Now* you have leave to kiss your bride."

Soft laughter again carried through the lofty space as her husband pulled her close and kissed her with a tenderness that caught her off guard.

The time of congratulating and opening presents and partaking in refreshments passed in a happy blur. Quinn never left her side. The moment came a couple of hours later when the expression on his face warned he was done waiting to have her to himself.

Leaning close, she whispered, "Take me home now?"

"I thought you'd never ask," he whispered back.

Firmly taking her hand in his, he loudly thanked everyone and urged them to stay and enjoy the celebration. Amid much teasing and clapping, they made their getaway. Their new home, a two-story home built in the same Victorian style as Lucian's but painted a deep green instead of yellow, blended in with the surrounding forest. Her favorite feature was the wraparound porch. She was already envisioning relaxing evenings seated on the porch swing with her husband.

Setting the brake, he came around to her side to assist her. Only, he didn't set her down. Instead, he swept her into his arms and started for the door.

Arms going around his neck, she relished the feel of his strong shoulders and chest supporting her. "You don't have to carry me, you know."

"Yes, I do. The first time you enter our home, I want it to be in my arms."

Opening the door took some doing because he kept stopping to kiss her. Finally they made it inside. When he set her on her feet, she didn't release him, instead using her hold on his neck to pull him closer.

"Alone at last," she breathed, fingers playing in his hair.

Quinn's hands tightened on her waist. Smiling, he

dipped his head and explored her mouth in a kiss that branded her as his forever.

"When I saw you today," he murmured, "I couldn't help thinking how fortunate I am. You are the woman of my dreams."

"I know a thing or two about dreams." She cupped his smooth cheek. "And you're it for me. I love you, Quinn Darling."

He brushed another thrilling kiss across her lips. "I love you, Duchess."

* * * * *

Award-winning author **Keli Gwyn**, a native
Californian, transports readers to the early days of
the Golden State. She and her husband live in the
heart of California's Gold Country. Her favorite
places to visit are her fictional worlds, historical
museums and other Gold Rush–era towns.

Books by Keli Gwyn

Love Inspired Historical

Family of Her Dreams
A Home of Her Own
Make-Believe Beau
Her Motherhood Wish
Their Mistletoe Matchmakers

Visit the Author Profile page at Harlequin.com.

FAMILY OF
HER DREAMS

Keli Gwyn

A man's heart deviseth his way:
but the Lord directeth his steps.
—*Proverbs* 16:9

For my mother, Patricia Lannon,
who instilled a love of reading in me at an early age,
introduced me to Harlequin romances when I was a
teen and rejoiced with me when my dream of writing
for their Love Inspired Historical line came true.

Chapter One

July 1866
Shingle Springs, California

"Look out, ma'am!"

Tess Grimsby jumped back to avoid a fellow about fifteen pulling a baggage cart with far too much speed for the bustling rail station. She collided with a mother herding her four youngsters, causing the weary-looking woman to drop her wicker basket. Several children's books slid across the wooden platform.

"My apologies. I didn't mean to bump into you." Tess stooped to pick up the books that had landed at her feet.

The woman made sure her children were all right, dropped to her knees and reached for a copy of *Little Bo-Peep*. "It wasn't your fault." She scowled at the baggage handler. "He needs to watch where he's going."

The young man parked his cart beside the baggage car and sprinted over to them. "Sorry 'bout that. It's my first day on the job, and my boss said to hurry. I've got to make a good impression." He grinned, reminding

Tess of one of the many boys she'd befriended when she lived at the orphanage.

She smiled. "No harm was done."

A man with a voice as rich as Belgian chocolate addressed the teen. "Be more careful next time. Getting the baggage moved quickly is important, but Mr. Flynn wouldn't want you to endanger our passengers, nor would I."

"Right, sir." The lad left.

"Come, children. We need to get home." The mother took the books Tess had gathered, muttered something about troublesome teens and hustled her children across the crowded platform.

Tess slid her satchel back on her shoulder, straightened and found herself face-to-face with a broad-shouldered, golden-haired gentleman. He was younger than any of the men she'd worked for—and far more handsome with his strong chin and arresting sky-blue eyes, currently clouded with sadness. If he was Mr. Abbott—the widower she'd come to see—she could understand.

He held out her journal and said nothing for several seconds as he gazed at her, his expression unreadable. No doubt the tall man wasn't used to looking a woman in the eye.

"Sir?"

The frown he'd worn faded, giving way to a hint of a smile that caused her breath to hitch. "I believe this is yours. It fell out of your bag during the commotion."

"Thank you." She took the diary from him, its pages so full of her hopes and dreams—as well as the mementos she'd tucked between the pages—that she had to grip it tightly to keep items from falling out. She would add her train ticket to the collection of memorabilia, a symbol of the new chapter in her life she was eager to embrace. "You must be Mr. Abbott, the stationmaster."

His forehead furrowed. "I am, but I don't believe we've met."

She shoved the bulging book into her satchel. "Not in person, although we've corresponded. I'm Tess Grimsby, Polly's friend. I've come about the housekeeper position."

"Ah, yes. She told me you'd arrive today." He clutched a notebook with sun-bronzed hands that obviously did more than complete paperwork, and scanned the platform, where several passengers lingered. "I need to see to a few things. Could you come to my office in ten minutes?"

"That would be fine." She could use the time to compose herself.

"Actually, let's make that twenty. I need to see if anyone requires my assistance, and then we can take care of the interview."

He certainly didn't sound eager to meet with her. Not that she could blame him. Hiring someone to care for his motherless children could be difficult. "Very well. I'll see to my trunks and meet you there." She should have time to rent a room at the hotel.

Tess set off for the baggage area, weaving her way through those waiting to board the train for its return trip down the hill. As the end station of the Placerville and Sacramento Valley Railroad, the depot was one of the busiest in the state. While it handled a great deal of freight, a number of travelers passed through Shingle Springs, too. However, few remained there, which she hoped to do.

People watched as she swept past them. Some even craned their heads to follow her progress. As much as she'd like to fade into the bustling throng, she couldn't. Everywhere she went she encountered the thinly veiled surprise and outright stares of strangers. You would think they'd never seen a tall woman before.

Peter Flynn, Polly's russet-haired husband who worked at the station, saw her and hustled over, a smile on his tanned face. They made quick work of their introductions.

"Polly said you were tall, but…" He tilted his head to look at her. "You could dust the ceiling at our place with the feathers on that hat of yours. Just how tall are you?"

Most people didn't come right out and mention her height, although she would prefer that to whispers behind fans. Polly had warned Tess that Peter spoke his mind. Since she tended to do the same, she didn't take offense. "Six foot."

He whistled a note of surprise, drawing the attention of several freight men, who viewed her with curiosity and made some less than flattering remarks. Indignation straightened her spine. She wasn't *that* much taller than other women. Why must everyone make such a fuss about a few inches?

She lifted her chin and gave the workers the impassive look she'd practiced in the mirror until she'd perfected it. Once she had, she'd pasted it on whenever the sharp-tongued orphanage director maligned her, unwilling to let him see her pain. Nearly nine years had passed, but the recollection of Mr. Grimsby's cutting remarks left a bitter taste in her mouth. Thank the Lord she'd been able to leave the orphanage the day she turned sixteen, having secured a position caring for the children of a family heading West.

"At least you and Spencer will see eye to eye." Peter chuckled at his play on words but quickly sobered. "And speaking of him, I'd better get back to work. I'll have one of the boys deliver your trunks to the hotel." He doffed his hat and returned to his duties.

Standing on the platform in front of the depot, Tess surveyed the small town. Shingle Springs sat at the foot of the majestic Sierra Nevada mountain range, which rose up to meet the cloudless sky. The steady stream of wagons headed east had dug deep ruts in the wide main street. Most of the businesses and houses lining it were made of wood, but an impressive stone building on the south side stood out.

She crossed the street and made her way to the Planter's House hotel, a two-story white clapboard building with a balcony that shaded the porch below. With the temperature approaching triple digits, she would welcome getting out of the early afternoon sun.

A glance at the watch pinned to her bodice caused her to move quickly. She'd have just enough time to change and dab on some rosewater to mask the lingering smell of the ashes and soot that had rained on her. Not that a railroad man like Mr. Abbott would notice the smoky scent.

From what Polly had written, he'd become so preoccupied since his wife's passing he could barely get himself to the depot on time. Once there, all he had time for was work—to the exclusion of everything and everyone else. Tess understood. Grief could immobilize a person. How many times had she seen newly orphaned children go through their days as though encased in a fog?

If all went well, she'd soon be caring for Mr. Abbott's two little ones and helping them deal with the loss of their mother. She looked forward to easing their father's burden and helping him cope with his grief, too.

"If you'll step inside, Mr. Drake would be happy to send a telegram for you." Spencer Abbott directed the elderly couple to his ticket agent's cage and resumed his perusal of the platform.

Other than the new baggage handler's mishap, things had gone smoothly that morning. Spencer had been able to eat the meager pickings in his dinner pail in peace while rereading the letters Tess Grimsby had sent.

Although she had glowing recommendations from two of the families she'd served, her most recent employer had dismissed her. From what Spencer could tell, the banker had no complaints about her work but had taken issue with her personality. Such things happened. Spencer knew that from experience. But a trait one employer disliked another might value. He believed in giving a person the opportunity to prove what he— or *she*—could do. Most people showed their true colors fairly quickly.

What troubled him more than Miss Grimsby's employment history was his reaction to her. When she'd stood and he'd looked into her eyes, speech had eluded him. Rarely had he encountered a woman that tall. She must be at least six foot, although with her hat the size of Texas, she appeared even taller.

While her height had come as a surprise, what had captivated him was the compassion in her warm brown eyes. Clearly she was a caring person. Rather than rail about the young man who'd almost barreled into her, she'd defended him and shown him kindness, which spoke well of her character. A woman like her should be able to take Luke's antics in stride.

What had kept Spencer riveted to her had nothing to do with her personality, though. He hated to admit it, but the reason he'd gawked at her like some smitten schoolboy had everything to do with her lovely features, from her delicately arched brows and high cheekbones to her rosy lips lifted in that mesmerizing smile. She was the first woman to capture his attention since he'd lost—

Focus, Abbott. He had no business thinking about another woman. Trudy had only been gone three short months. He was a widower in mourning who'd loved his wife, not a man in search of someone to take her place. Not that anyone could. She'd held a special place in his heart and always would. It must have been loneliness that led his eyes to stray, that's all.

Well, he was master of his emotions. When Tess Grimsby returned, she'd see a man in control of himself. If he chose to hire her as his housekeeper, he would keep things strictly professional.

Tess emerged from the hotel wearing her favorite dress, a cobalt-blue calico that matched the three peacock feathers atop her hat. She tugged on her gloves, crossed the busy street and strolled alongside the tracks until she came to the railway station.

The depot was a hive of activity as men prepared

for a freight train's arrival. Drivers seated on sturdy wagons waited for their cargo in front of three warehouses east of the station. Horses whickered and shook their heads to rid themselves of the ever-present flies.

Although the platform was large, the wooden building at the heart of the action was small. Somewhere inside sat the man who would determine her future. Mr. Abbott must hire her. If he didn't, she'd be forced to return to Sacramento City and pray she found another position before the last of the money in her reticule was gone.

She shook the small handbag dangling from her wrist, the jingle of the few coins inside lacking the reassurance she sought. While Polly had said she and Peter would welcome Tess, she couldn't impose on them, not when they were expecting a second child soon.

Given her recent dismissal, Tess hadn't been able to secure another governess position in the city, despite spending two weeks searching for one. Polly's letter with news of Mr. Abbott's need had been most fortuitous. If he hired her as his housekeeper and her work pleased him, she'd be able to restore her reputation and replenish her depleted savings.

A bell tinkled as she entered the depot. The man in the ticket cage peered at her through the wrought iron grate and smiled. "Good morning, ma'am. May I help you?"

"I'm Tess Grimsby here to see Mr. Abbott. He's expecting me."

The ticket agent nodded. "Welcome, Miss Grimsby. I'm Mr. Drake. I'll let you in."

She waited at the door he'd indicated. It opened, and

he pointed out another on her right. She paused and said a silent prayer.

"Don't be scared. He doesn't bite…often."

She wasn't afraid of Mr. Abbott, but she was concerned about her reaction to the appealing gentleman. Despite his rumpled frock coat and limp collar, it could be all too easy to cast admiring glances his way, and that would never do. She must act like the professional she was and keep her goal of being hired first and foremost. "Me? Scared? He's the one who ought to be. Men have been known to run from me."

Mr. Drake chuckled, the curled ends of his heavily waxed handlebar moustache dancing. "You've got spunk. That's good. You'll need it if you're to work for him. He's a fine boss, but he can be a mite intimidating on his best days. Lately…well, let's just say losing his wife three months back changed him." He inclined his head toward the door to Mr. Abbott's office. "Give it a rap, and he'll invite you in."

Tess peered through the small window inset in the door. Mr. Abbott sat at a desk in a painfully clean office with a ledger spread before him and his head in hands. Like Mr. Drake, who had a shock of wiry gray hair, Mr. Abbott had a full head of hair, as well, although his was the color of ripe rye at sunset. Unlike his ticket clerk, who had a ready smile, Mr. Abbott sported a frown, as he had earlier. Not a promising sign.

She knocked.

"Enter."

She stilled her trembling hand and opened the door. He jumped to his feet.

"Miss Grimsby. Please, have a seat." He held out a hand toward the bentwood chair facing his desk.

"Thank you, sir." She sat, folded her hands in her lap and drew a calming breath. "I trust you received all the documents I sent."

"I did." He remained standing, resting his hands on the windowsill with his back to her. Several seconds passed before he spoke. "You're not what I expected."

Her nervousness fled. She didn't appreciate being challenged at the outset, but she wouldn't let him fluster her. "Neither are you, but I can do the job, I assure you." She'd worked for some prominent families in Sacramento City, the last one having a name anybody in the state would recognize. The wife of the widely respected banker had written her a letter of recommendation, albeit reluctantly. Not that Tess could blame her. The woman's husband had found Tess's direct manner problematic.

Mr. Abbott sat on the corner of his desk with his long legs draped over the side, forcing her to look up. She caught a flicker of feeling in his eyes. Curiosity perhaps? Or was it concern?

"Why would you come to a small town when you're used to living among the elite? I lead a simple life, and I don't want my children exposed to any newfangled notions."

His manner and tone rankled. If she were to work for him, she'd have to show him she wouldn't tolerate his high-handedness. "I'm a simple person myself, eager to leave the bustle of the city behind. I was most recently employed by a family of means, true, but I hail from humble circumstances."

Please, don't let him ask me to explain. She had no intention of educating him about her past. Humble circumstances didn't begin to describe her miserable childhood.

"Your circumstances don't concern me. But your methods do. I contacted your most recent employer. He said you have a tendency to speak your mind. Is that true?"

That was a more tactful description of her supposed failings than the domineering man had used when he dismissed her. "I have opinions, but doesn't everyone?"

His blond brows rose, and he pressed a fist to his mouth. She thought she saw his lips twitch, and it gave her hope, but when he pulled his hand away, the frown was there as before. "Can you cook?"

Mr. Abbott's abrupt change of subject took her aback. "I assume you mean can I cook well, and the answer is yes. I can keep house, do laundry, sew, garden and care for animals, too. But the most important thing is that I'll do all I can to help your children through this difficult time." The Lord had used her to minister to countless youngsters who'd lost their parents, and she could put that experience to good use—provided Mr. Abbott hired her.

He folded his arms and took his time studying her, as though she were a horse or a milk cow. Well, two could play that game. She tilted her chin and let her gaze rove over his fine features, drinking her fill.

At length he nodded. "I'll give you one week."

A week? Her previous employers had offered a one-month trial period. Torn between a desire to laugh or shout, Tess gave an unladylike snort, which she covered with a cough.

In her experience overbearing men like Spencer Abbott responded to a show of force. She couldn't resist the urge to slip in a hint of sarcasm, too. "How generous—but entirely unnecessary. I'll prove my worth to you in a day."

Chapter Two

Spencer wasn't one to refuse a challenge. If Miss Grimsby was bold enough to claim that she could impress him in a day rather than asking for a month as he'd expected, she deserved the opportunity to try. The sooner he found out if her assertion was valid, the sooner he'd know if his search for a housekeeper was over.

As much as he detested the thought of a woman he didn't know helping raise his children, Peter's wife had vouched for Miss Grimsby. Polly had never steered him wrong.

While Spencer was certain Miss Grimsby could fix better meals than those he'd eaten lately, how would she deal with Luke? The poor tyke had taken to misbehaving. Having a different woman watching him every few days didn't help matters.

Miss Grimsby seemed to have the strength of character necessary to tame his spirited offspring. Not that Lila would pose a problem. She'd not even begun to walk. Ever since Trudy's dea— Ever since the service his little girl had been content to play quietly with her blocks.

"You may start now. I'll run you out to the house and return at suppertime. Mrs. Carter, an elderly widow from church, is with the children now. She'll show you around."

She gave a decisive nod. "That would suit me just fine."

Spencer stopped his wagon beside Miss Grimsby a few minutes later and hopped down to help her onto the seat. She climbed aboard before he reached her. Her independent streak didn't surprise him, but her agility did. He wouldn't have expected a woman that tall wearing boots with three-inch heels to move as quickly or gracefully. But there she sat looking as composed as any woman of leisure, the smooth plane of her neck exposed as she peered over her shoulder at the shops across the street from the depot.

"I noticed a general store earlier. Would you mind if I run inside for a moment before we get underway?"

Spencer groaned inwardly. "No, but make it quick. I've got work to do."

"I'll be back in a trice."

He slipped his gold watch out of his waistcoat pocket. He'd give her five minutes. If she wasn't back by then, he'd hitch his team to the post and tend to some paperwork. Waiting on a woman wasn't something he had time for. He closed his eyes to block the bright summer sun and made a mental list of all he had to accomplish that afternoon.

The wagon rocked as Miss Grimsby climbed aboard. "I'm sorry I took so long, but someone was ahead of me."

Three minutes wasn't long. Three minutes was astonishing. Unsure what to say, he grunted an acknowledgment. He pocketed his watch, took the reins and started the one-mile trek to his spread.

With each clop of the horses' hooves, the stabbing pain he experienced every time he saw the place intensified. Memories abounded, as sour as they were sweet. He and Trudy had worked hard to make the house a home. Although she was gone, he could see her everywhere. Why, he fancied he could even smell the rosewater she'd favored.

"What was she like?"

"Huh?"

"Your wife. You looked sad. Were you thinking about her?"

An inquisitive housekeeper was not what he needed. "That's not something I care to talk about, especially with a stranger."

"I'm sorry. I thought—"

"You thought wrong. I need a job done. Nothing more." That had come out harsher than he'd intended. She was only trying to help. Even so, he didn't trust himself to talk about Trudy without choking up. Silence was safer.

"I'll pray for you. I know what it's like to lose a loved one and feel that vacant ache."

He bit back a retort. How could she possibly understand what he was going through? She'd never been married and left with two children to raise alone. "Pray if you like but no more questions please."

She bowed her head.

For some reason her gesture comforted him. He'd reached the point where he no longer knew what to pray and trusted the Spirit to intercede for him "with groanings which could not be uttered," as it said in Romans. If Miss Grimsby's prayers could help, he wouldn't turn them down.

When she opened her eyes, they held unasked questions, but the compassion he'd seen before was there, too. She smiled, and the future didn't seem quite as bleak as it had. Perhaps she was as capable as she'd said and would solve his immediate problems. He'd know soon enough.

Tess remained silent the rest of the way to Mr. Abbott's place. He'd made it clear her attempts to offer sympathy were unwelcome. She could understand. Each child who'd come to the orphanage handled grief differently. Some wept. Some talked about their losses, while others kept their own counsel. Some blamed themselves and suffered guilt, while others lashed out in anger. And there were those like her soon-to-be employer who did their best to go on with their lives despite the near-crippling pain.

As she'd prayed, a sense of peace had descended on her—along with a sense of purpose. She wasn't here to get what she wanted. She was here to give of herself to this hurting family. All those years comforting others had prepared her for this. She would offer the care and comfort Mr. Abbott's motherless children needed, and she would lift some of the burden their grieving father carried.

Above all she would guard her heart. Even though she was drawn to him, she mustn't let herself care too much. This was a job like any other, and she would do well to remember that.

They approached a two-story ranch house painted bright red with white trim. All the windows were open, curtains peeking from beneath the raised frames. A wraparound porch beckoned her to slip into one of the ladder-backed rocking chairs gracing it and spend time sipping lemonade with a friend. She'd often dreamed of having such a house, although the one in her dreams was blue—a lovely slate blue with burgundy trim.

Mr. Abbott parked the wagon, and she was on the ground in a heartbeat. He held out a hand toward the stairs. "After you."

She passed through the open front door and nearly gagged. What was that horrid stench? It smelled worse than the rotten eggs some of the more daring boys at the orphanage had hurled at Mr. Grimsby's carriage once—before he'd meted out the swift punishment he was known for.

"Luke!" Mr. Abbott bellowed and charged inside.

That didn't bode well. Tess followed on his heels. They reached the kitchen where a full-figured woman with white hair attempted to wipe a squirming baby girl's jam-spattered face. Mr. Abbott's four-year-old son ran circles around the dining table in the adjoining room, whooping like an Indian on the warpath.

Everywhere Tess looked, chaos reigned. Soiled shirts had been draped over chair backs, newspapers and toys were strewn about and a path had been worn through the dust coating the floorboards. Although she'd only been there two minutes, she itched to get to work restoring order and a sense of harmony.

Mr. Abbott addressed the older woman, raising his voice to be heard over the din. "What happened?"

"That boy of yours snuck up behind me when I was checkin' the fire and chucked some salve in the stove."

"What next?" He raked a hand through his thick blond hair, causing a swatch of his long locks to stand on end. Tess suppressed the urge to smooth it for him.

The older woman lugged the baby upstairs, and Mr. Abbott strode to the cookstove. Tess tore her gaze from him, entered the dining room and stepped in his son's path. She caught the little fellow's raised arm as he passed. "Whoa there, young man."

He came to an abrupt stop and stared at her with eyes as big and round as washtubs. "Who are you?"

"I'm Tess, and you must be Luke."

"What're you doing here?"

"Your papa is going to see if I'm the right person to look after you and your sister."

He shook his head wildly. "No! I don't want you here. Go away." He flew out of the house.

She took off after him, hitching up her skirts with one hand, holding on to her hat with the other and running as fast as her high boot heels would allow. He dashed into the barn. She found him crouched in the corner of an empty stall, tears flowing over his flushed cheeks, and her heart went out to him. She approached slowly on tiptoes, but she bumped into a shovel leaning against the wall and sent it crashing to the floor.

Luke prepared to bolt, but she caught him by the shoulders and held him tightly as he twisted and turned. She squatted so she wouldn't tower over him. "I'm not going to hurt you, but I won't let go until you settle down. You can't run off like that. A ranch is a big place. You could get hurt."

"No, I couldn't!"

The little fellow showed no signs of giving up his struggle. He flailed his arms as he attempted to break free. "You're coming with me, Master Luke." She planted him on her hip and headed to the house. His fists flew, coming uncomfortably close to her face. Her ears rang from his shrieked protests.

She reached the kitchen, where Mr. Abbott knelt in front of the stove filling two metal pails with glowing embers. He'd shed his coat and rolled up his shirtsleeves, revealing muscular arms. She had little time to take in the unexpected—albeit pleasing—sight because he turned toward her, exasperation etched in every line of his attractive face.

"Quiet down, Luke," he said in a firm voice. "Do something, Miss Grimsby. *Please.*"

The mischievous boy ceased shouting long enough to send her a triumphant smirk.

She'd had enough of his antics. No four-year-old, however unruly, would keep her from securing the position. She'd dealt with his kind before and knew just what to do. "I guess you don't want to see what kind of candy I brought. I won't give it to a boy who's pitching a fit. I'll set you down—if you agree to stay put. Will you do that?"

He crossed his arms over his chest in such an adult manner Tess hid a smile. She rummaged in her reticule with her free hand and withdrew a small package. He followed her every move, his eyes glued to the peppermint stick she unwrapped.

"Here. Why don't you smell it?" She placed the striped sweet under his nose, pulling back when he attempted to snatch it. "You may have it if you'll sit

quietly while your papa cleans up the mess you made."
She indicated a chair at the kitchen table.

The boy's gaze was riveted on the red-and-white
stick. He licked his lips. "I don't like you, and you
can't make me."

"You don't have to like me, and I won't make you.
You just have to do as I ask." She set him down but
kept a firm grip on his shoulder.

His face scrunched in puzzlement. "You're not
mad?"

Tess shook her head. "I understand. You want your
mama, but she's gone now. I know you don't want me
here, but you need someone to cook your food, wash
your clothes and buy you candy, don't you?"

"You'll buy me candy?"

"I will." Provided Mr. Abbott hired her.

Luke studied her with the same intensity his father
had. "Whenever I want?"

"No. Candy is a treat, but you'd get it sometimes."
She released her hold on him.

He sidled over to the chair and stood beside it a moment before sitting down. Tess handed him the sweet,
which he promptly stuck in his mouth.

Mr. Abbott hefted a pail in each hand and headed to
the back door. She beat him there and held it open for
him. His bright blue eyes held a hint of amusement—
and something else. Attraction perhaps? Of course not.
She must be seeing things.

"I didn't expect you to stoop to bribery."

"Oh, I wouldn't classify it as bribery. I prefer to
think of it as a reward for making a good choice."

"Whatever you call it, it worked." She warmed at
his approval and smiled at his retreating form.

When Mr. Abbott and Mrs. Carter returned, he got the story out of her.

"I kept my eyes peeled, Mr. Abbott, but you know how troublesome your young'un can be. Luke got into a scuffle with the baby. Both of 'em wanted to play with that canvas ball you brung 'em last week. Lila wouldn't let him have it, so he smacked her. I told him to stand in the corner, but he don't mind any better than I cook."

Judging by the deplorable state of the kitchen, cleaning wasn't one of Mrs. Carter's strengths, either. Dirty dishes were piled everywhere, chunks of dried food clinging to them. If the house hadn't been filled with the overpowering stench that had greeted her, Tess would have been able to follow her nose to the kitchen.

Mrs. Carter set Lila on a blanket with a pile of blocks. The little girl seemed content to play with them. "Sorry 'bout the trouble with the salve. I opened all the windows, but I don't think it done much good."

Tess wrinkled her nose. "What kind of salve would make it smell like some poor creature died in here?"

Mr. Abbott explained. "My dog has mange. I mixed lard and powdered sulfur, which I've been rubbing on him. It doesn't have much of an odor normally, but it stinks something fierce if it's burned."

She laughed. "I'll say. So, what do we do?"

"I got the stove cleared out. Now we wait for the smell to go away."

"And the dog?" she asked. "What about him?"

"I'm keeping him in the barn until I get the mange under control. Could be a week or more."

Mrs. Carter patted Tess's arm. "I'm awful glad

you're here, young lady. You got a big job ahead of you. The place needs a bit of sprucin' up, but I done my best. Those young'uns need a firm hand. I spent most of my time chasin' after Luke. He's a real handful, that one. Mind you, don't let him out of your sight."

Mr. Abbott washed up and donned his frock coat with its row of shiny brass buttons and a black armband to show he was in mourning. How sad that such a handsome man wore a perpetual frown. Perhaps one day she'd be able to make him smile.

"Might I have a word, Miss Grimsby?"

"Yes, sir." She followed him onto the porch, doing her best to quell the queasiness his request had caused. Had she failed to please him already?

He cleared his throat and ran a finger under his collar. If she didn't know better, she'd say he was as uneasy as she. Surely, in his position, he was practiced in dismissing people.

"I understand you were governess to a number of girls before but only one boy—all of them considerably older than my children. Do you think you're up to dealing with my son? He can be a challenge at times."

Luke couldn't begin to compare with some of the boys at the orphanage. "I am. Does this mean…?"

"What it means is that I'm considering things. Show me what you can accomplish before I get home tonight, and we'll talk." He descended two steps, paused and inclined his head toward the house. "You might want to go back inside before Luke springs a surprise on you."

Tess maintained her composure until she was in the foyer. She lifted her hands to the heavens. *Thank You, Lord.*

She would set the place to rights, prepare a delicious

meal and prove to Mr. Abbott she was the woman for the job. If all went well, she'd have a family to care for at last. It might not be her own, but it was the next best thing.

Chapter Three

A shrill whistle signaled the departure of an outbound freight train, relieved of its load and ready for the return trip to Sacramento City. Spencer checked his pocket watch. Right on time, just the way he liked it.

He crossed the platform and went in search of his freight traffic manager, notebook in hand. The sooner he got the statistics on the latest shipments from Peter, the sooner he could update his records and find out how the station was doing.

Processing the cargo quickly and keeping their customers happy would improve their chances of gaining more business and ensure that he could keep his position as long as possible. He'd known ever since taking the newly created Shingle Springs stationmaster position the summer before that the Transcontinental Route to the north would bring about the end of his company's monopoly, which was why he had a plan that didn't depend on the railroad.

He located Peter talking with one of his workers. He finished the conversation and ambled over. "Come for the numbers, have you?"

"Are they any good?"

Peter consulted a sheaf of papers. "You'll be happy with them. But not as happy as when the Sutro Tunnel Act passes. Should be soon from what I hear."

Handling the many supply shipments needed to construct the six-mile tunnel connecting Nevada's Comstock's silver mines would give them plenty of work—for the time being. "Let's hope we get a fair amount of the business before it's siphoned off by the CP."

"Don't be such a killjoy. They haven't even reached the summit yet. It'll take some doing to blast through all that rock. We got us a few good years before our dreams of being rich railroaders die."

Peter didn't want to accept the bitter truth. Since Congress had granted the Central Pacific the right to lay track east of California, it wouldn't be long before they reached Reno. Word was the CP aimed to make it to Cisco high in the Sierras by year's end and bore tunnels in the mountain passes through the winter. When that happened and the CP met up with the Union Pacific, the Placerville & Sacramento Valley Railroad, now enjoying its heyday, would become a sleepy passenger line.

Unlike his father, who'd counted on selling cattle to the army indefinitely, despite the fact that the war wouldn't last forever, Spencer had a contingency plan. That's why he'd turned down the offer of a company house in town and invested in a place of his own instead. Some thought him crazy, but once his bull arrived and he could begin building a herd of cattle—

"Spence?"

"Yes?" What had he missed?

"I asked if you wanted to take a break and see what kind of pie Miss Minnie fixed today. Based on the mouth-watering smells coming from the café, I'm guessing it's peach."

"As tempting as that sounds, I have too much to do."

"When are you going to relax and have some fun, Cap'n? You can spare ten minutes, can't ya?"

Spencer fought the urge to grimace. He never knew whether the nickname had been bestowed on him out of respect or if his workers were poking fun at him. Sure, he checked up on the various departments, but he trusted his men. He just wanted to assure himself things were running smoothly. His father had spent his time holed up in his office oblivious to his ranch manager's shenanigans, and look where it had gotten him. He'd come close to losing everything.

"Take a whiff. If that hint of cinnamon in the air doesn't win you over, I don't know what will. Then again, perhaps you're saving your appetite for Mrs. Carter's latest culinary catastrophe." Peter gave Spencer a playful punch in the arm.

"She's done her best." The well-intentioned widow had ruined a perfectly good pot roast last night and made chicken as dry and tasteless as paper the night before that.

"Polly tells me Tess knows her way around a kitchen, so your troubles could be over."

"Perhaps." If the food on his table that evening wasn't scorched beyond recognition and he could swallow it without gulping water after each bite, he'd be happy.

"How about joining me, then? That way you know you won't starve."

Peter had a point. The simple dinner of bread and cheese Spencer had eaten at his desk left much to be desired. Supper was hours away, after all. This would give him an opportunity to show his men he wasn't as regimented as they seemed to think. "I'll drop this off—" he held up his notebook "—let Drake know where to find me and meet you there."

Fifteen minutes later Spencer chewed his last bite of pie, savoring the sweetness of the peach filling. "This was a good idea."

"At least you won't waste away if Tess's cooking doesn't pan out." Peter grinned at his pun. "And speaking of Tess, what do you think of her?"

"It's too soon to tell."

"She's tall. At least as tall as you, isn't she?"

Not quite, if his estimate was correct. "It's the hat."

Peter chuckled. "Quite something, isn't it? She could provide shade for half the town under that thing. Although her taste in bonnets might be questionable, she's easy on the eyes. Or didn't you notice?"

He'd noticed all right. Because of her, he'd had a hard time concentrating ever since he returned from running her to the ranch. Memories of her captivating smile kept resurfacing. "My mind was on the interview."

"Do you think you'll hire her?"

"Maybe. Maybe not. I offered to give her a one-week trial period, but she countered, claiming she could convince me of her suitability in a day. I accepted her challenge." Spencer stood, and Peter followed suit.

"Polly said she's got pluck."

She did indeed. Would her plucky ways keep his headstrong son in line? Or would she resort to mollycoddling to get Luke's cooperation, as several of the church women had? One stick of candy to win him over initially couldn't hurt, but a lack of consistent discipline could ruin him.

Since his son was almost guaranteed to act out at supper, he'd have Miss Grimsby handle the situation. If she didn't exert a firm hand, he'd have no choice but to give her a day's wages and put her on a train back to Sacramento City. He hoped it didn't come to that.

Tess surveyed the parlor. Mrs. Abbott had certainly loved red. At least she'd chosen burgundy furnishings rather than the cherry red on the house itself. The plush chairs and settee in the rich color coordinated with the blue flowers sprinkled amid sprays of wine-colored roses on the wallpaper's white background. Some slate-blue accents would bring out the secondary color and add a soothing element. Curtains, pillows and a rug, too.

She could imagine Mr. Abbott in the wingback armchair by the fireplace, a child on each knee. A sewing basket sat on the table beside the settee. His wife's favorite place to sit had likely been the end of it nearest him. The picture of domestic bliss.

A wistful sigh escaped, and Tess chided herself. Giving way to the longing for a family of her own would do no good. She mustn't fuel futile dreams. How many times had Mr. Grimsby told her she'd best prepare for a lifetime of service?

His words uttered on her tenth birthday came back as sharp and piercing as ever. *No man will look twice at you, Tess. You're going to tower over most of them. And those who are tall won't be interested in a woman who can look them in the eye. A man wants to feel superior in all respects. Take my word for it, and apply yourself to your studies, so you can earn a decent living.*

And then came the nickname. Of course Charlie had been the one who'd overheard that dreadful conversation. Charlie, who taunted anyone and everyone, from the youngest children all the way to the orphanage director himself.

Too-Tall Tess.

That's what Charlie had dubbed her, and nothing she could say or do would silence him. So, she'd done the only thing she could—pretended it didn't matter.

From that day on she'd vowed never to let anyone see how much she detested being different. She'd stood tall, proud and unflinching as the other children singsonged the ditty Charlie had coined.

Oh, what a pity! Oh, what a mess!

When God said height, she shoulda asked for less.

She's Too-Tall, Too-Tall, Too-Tall Tess.

It didn't help that Tess wasn't her real name. Mr. Grimsby had given it to her when her father left her at the orphanage, despite the fact that she'd told the domineering director her name was Faith. Although Tess was a fine name, his insistence on using it and offering no reason why had rankled.

After shaking herself from her reverie, Tess smoothed the crisp white cloth covering the pedestal table in the center of the room, repositioned the antimacassar on the back of Spencer's armchair and pronounced the parlor ready for inspection.

Restoring the dining room to rights would take no time at all. The layer of dust coating everything gave evidence no one had eaten there since Mrs. Abbott's passing. Perhaps Mr. Abbott felt her absence in that room more deeply than other places. Replacing old memories with new would help.

Tess gathered the soiled shirts draped over the chairs and picked up the toys. She removed the petrified bouquet serving as the centerpiece. She'd send Mrs. Carter and the children in search of fresh flowers, thus gaining the time needed to scour the kitchen and plan her supper menu.

Discovering the whereabouts of the widow and the little ones was easy. Mrs. Carter must have asked Luke to do something he didn't want to do. His complaints coming from the backyard could be heard throughout the house. That boisterous boy would require a firm hand—and a full measure of compassion. He must miss his mama terribly.

Tess stepped through the back door onto the wrap-around porch. She called to the older woman, who had the baby propped on one hip. They stood beneath a sprawling oak with a rope swing suspended from one of its sturdy branches. "I'd like a fresh bouquet on the table tonight, Mrs. Carter. Might I ask you to pick some flowers? I saw a nice selection in the beds out front."

The widow appeared relieved by the request. Luke even ceased his whining. "The children and me would be happy to do that, wouldn't we, Luke?" She gave him an over-bright smile.

"I don't wanna, and I'm not gonna. I want her to push me on the swing. Right now!" He jabbed a stubby finger at Mrs. Carter.

Tess feigned indifference. "That's all right. I don't want your help, after all."

He eyed her with suspicion. "You don't?"

"No. This is a special job, and you're still quite young. I don't think you could pick flowers without breaking their stems or crushing their petals."

He rammed his fists against his sides and scrunched his face in a sour-pickle expression. "I could, too."

"What do you think, Mrs. Carter? Should we let him try or have him sit with Lila and watch while you pick the flowers?"

Luke snorted. "I'm not a baby. I'm a big boy. Papa says so, and he knows everything."

The snowy-headed woman looked from him to Tess and back again, understanding dawning. "I reckon we could let him try...if he promises to be careful."

"I won't hurt them. I'll show you." He raced around the corner of the house. Lila bounced on Mrs. Carter's ample hip as she hurried after him.

With the children occupied, Tess had the house to herself once again. She donned her apron and plunged her hands into a tub of hot water. Determined to get the mountain of dirty dishes washed quickly, she attacked an encrusted dinner plate with such fervor that soap bubbles formed on the water's surface. Normally she didn't relish the scent of lye soap, but today she welcomed anything strong enough to cut the lingering stench of the sulfur.

What could she prepare for supper that would overpower the horrid smell and fill the air with tantalizing aromas? When she was out back, she'd noticed a garden with a healthy crop of weeds mounting a takeover. Perhaps she could find some ripe vegetables among those that had rotted on the vines. That would be a start.

"Lord, You know how much I need this position,

so please show me what You'd like me to prepare." If He'd led her here, as she believed He had, surely He could provide her with inspiration.

She was eager to impress Mr. Abbott, so he'd hire her. Although he was a bit on the dour side, he struck her as a fair man. Working for the handsome stationmaster could prove to be a distraction, but she was more than willing to deal with that.

Twenty minutes later Tess dried the last bowl, put it in the cupboard and hung the damp dishtowel on its peg. She delivered lemonade to Mrs. Carter and Luke, who'd picked enough flowers to fill two vases.

He leaned back against the porch railing, his ankles and arms crossed, looking adorable despite his dirt-streaked face. "We picked whole bunches of flowers, and I didn't hurt none of them."

Tess smiled. "You did a fine job, Luke. I'll have to tell your papa what a big help you've been."

The little boy beamed, seemed to think better of it and assumed a stoic manner so like his father's it was all she could do not to laugh. She shifted her attention to Mrs. Carter, who sat in a rocking chair with Lila in her lap. "If you're content to enjoy the shade and the cool drink, I'll get to work on the meal."

"We're fine, dearie. Chasin' after these young'uns the past week plumb wore me out, so I'm happy to sit here and keep 'em out from under your petticoats."

Normally Tess would welcome the children's help. She had wonderful memories of working alongside Josette, the cook at the orphanage, when she was a girl. However, since this meal had to be exemplary in order for her to secure the position, she would leave Luke and Lila in Mrs. Carter's care.

Wending her way between the rows of the garden with basket in hand, Tess found what she needed to prepare a light but tasty soup to start the meal.

Luke raced around the house and hollered. "A wagon's coming, and it's not Papa."

She set her bounty by the back door and followed Luke to the front of the house. A wagon rumbled down the rutted road toward them. The young man beside the driver waved. "I wonder who they could be."

The rhythmic creaking of Mrs. Carter's rocking chair ceased. She joined Tess at the porch railing. "Looks like that German man and his son from over yonder." The widow waved her free hand toward the parcel of land to the east. "The young fellow speaks right fine English, but his father ain't learned it so good."

The wagon approached the house with a jangle of harnesses. The driver parked beside the porch. "*Guten Nachmittag. Ve haf Lachs.*" The stocky older man reached in a pail and pulled out a fish large enough to feed Mr. Abbott, his children, Mrs. Carter and Tess with some left over. "Ve haf much. You must some take."

"See what I mean?" Mrs. Carter muttered.

Tess smiled. "I believe he said 'good afternoon.' It appears he's sharing his catch with us." She knew just what to make for supper. The Lord had evidently heard her prayers.

The driver's son, a young man about eighteen, jumped to the ground. He took the fish from his father, wrapped it in a cloth and held it out to her. "We didn't catch them. They came up on the train. When Vati saw them, he got this one for Mr. Abbott. A gift.

Vati knows how difficult it is for a man to lose his wife and be left with children to raise on his own. He wanted to do something to help."

Tess took the fish and nodded at the older man. "That's kind of you, Herr…"

"Mueller," the young man offered. "He's Wolfgang—" he jabbed a thumb at his father "—and I'm Frank."

"Well, thank you both. This is a godsend."

"I've met Mrs. Carter—" Frank nodded in the widow's direction and shifted his attention to Tess "—and you must be Miss Grimsby."

"Yes, I am. I hope to become Mr. Abbott's housekeeper. How did you hear about me?"

"Mr. Flynn over at the railway station told us about you. It seems you stood out. There aren't too many women in Shingle Springs as tall as a *Hopfenpfosten*— a hop pole." He grinned. "I wish you well. I know from helping Vati build the large pen beyond Mr. Abbott's barn that he can be an exacting boss, but he's a fair one."

Mrs. Carter huffed. "If he's to be her boss, she'd best not spend her day yammerin' with the likes of you. She's got a supper to fix."

Tess chuckled. "As much as I've enjoyed meeting you, Mrs. Carter has a point." She bid the Muellers farewell and headed for the kitchen, eager to fillet the fish.

Some time later Mrs. Carter and the children joined Tess.

"That supper of yours is smellin' mighty good, young lady. What're you fixin'?"

"We'll start with julienne soup. Then we'll have the

salmon sprinkled with black butter, served with herbed potatoes and tomato slices. I found fresh peaches in the pantry, so I was able to whip up a pie for dessert."

Lila, who sat on a blanket in the corner, squealed.

Mrs. Carter smiled, proving she had a kind heart beneath her brusque manner. "Sounds like she's happy. Let's hope her papa is, too. I'm more'n ready to leave this place in your hands and get back to mine."

Tess stirred the soup. If Mr. Abbott didn't arrive soon, the vegetables would be mush.

As if on cue, a wagon pulled in.

"Papa!" Luke took off.

Mrs. Carter lifted Lila into her arms. "We'll go meet him, wash up and give you time to get the last of your supper rustled up. You'll find us waitin' in the dinin' room."

The next ten minutes flew by in a blur as Tess grilled the salmon and browned the butter. She removed her apron and said a silent prayer of thanks. Everything had turned out fine, after all. Savoring the sense of accomplishment, she poured the soup into the tureen, grabbed a ladle and headed to the dining room.

Mr. Abbott's deep voice carried, sending a shiver of excitement shimmying up her spine. "It certainly smells better in here. Do you know what we're having, son?"

Luke made a horrid sound like a cat trying to rid itself of a hairball. "I don't want any of it 'cept for the pie. She ruined the soup and burned the fish."

Tess came to an abrupt stop in the doorway, the soup she carried sloshing precariously. Luke's uncomplimentary proclamation was to be expected, but the welcome hint of merriment in Mr. Abbott's eyes had faded all too rapidly, leaving him looking as formidable as ever.

Well, he could frown all he liked. She was an excellent cook and would impress him with her culinary skills, or her name wasn't Tess Grimsby.

She marched into the room with her head held high.

Chapter Four

Spencer didn't know which amused him more, Luke's antics or Miss Grimsby's show of pique. He hid his twitching lips behind his napkin. "Luke, that's unkind. We must be grateful for what we're served."

She set a large bowl of soup on the table, performed an about-face and left the room without a word.

He cast a glance at Mrs. Carter, seated to his left on the other side of Luke with Lila in her lap. The widow appeared to be concealing a smile, too. "You got nothin' to fear, Mr. Abbott. I slurped a spoonful of the soup earlier, and it's delicious."

"I look forward to tasting it myself."

"But she said the soup was ruined, Papa. I heard her."

"I said no such thing." Miss Grimsby placed a platter of fish in front of Spencer that smelled so good his mouth watered. "It's julienne soup. Not *ruined* soup. I gather you've never had it before."

Luke shook his head so soundly his long hair flapped from side to side. "Mama didn't fix things with funny names. She made what Papa likes. Steak and baked potatoes. Not smelly old burned fish."

"I didn't burn the fish, Luke. What makes you think that?" Miss Grimsby gazed at the ceiling for several moments.

All of a sudden she nodded. "I understand. You heard me tell Mrs. Carter I was going to make black butter to drizzle over the fish. The butter's not really black, though. It's just browned, and it tastes good. I'll bring in the rest of the food, and you can see for yourself."

She returned with a dish of small potatoes cut into chunks and sprinkled with herbs, along with a plate of artistically arranged tomato slices. Rather fancy fare for a family supper. Not that Spencer was complaining. Steak and baked potatoes were fine, but a man could do with a change on occasion.

And fresh fish? How had she managed that? This looked to be salmon. His favorite. Trudy couldn't stomach seafood, so he'd not had any in years.

His gut tightened. Trudy. He'd eat steak and potatoes every day for the rest of his life if that would give him one more hour with her. One more opportunity to take her in his arms, pull her to his chest and feel the silkiness of her hair against his chin. One more chance to tell her how sorry he was for—

"Mr. Abbott?"

"Hmm?"

Miss Grimsby sat at the opposite end of the rectangular table with Lila in her lap. "Did you want to say grace?"

"Yes. Of course."

She took Lila's hands in hers, pressed the baby's palms together and covered them with her own.

Spencer swallowed the boulder that lodged in his throat at the site of his little girl in another woman's arms, a capable and caring woman as different from Trudy as California was from Texas. A comely woman who'd filled his thoughts far too often since their track-side meeting. "Thank You, Father, for the meal and for…the h-hands that prepared it."

He cast a furtive glance around the table to see if anyone had noticed his hesitation. Mrs. Carter and Luke's heads were bowed. Miss Grimsby, on the other hand, had something akin to sympathy on her face. When she realized he'd seen her, she blushed a pretty shade of pink and squeezed her eyes shut. He hastened to cover his halting start. "Thank You that we can gather around the table to enjoy this unexpected treat. Be with us as we partake. In Christ's name. Amen."

Miss Grimsby plopped some potatoes on her plate and averted her gaze, for which he was grateful. The only sound was the clink of silverware on porcelain as they filled their plates.

Spencer dipped his spoon into the soup. Despite the strange name, the little strips of vegetables swimming in broth were tastier than he'd expected. Crisp, not mushy—just the way he liked them.

How strange it was to be in the dining room. They hadn't eaten there since Trudy's dea— in months. The shirts he'd slung over the chairs were gone, the tabletop gleamed and his wife's cherished vase overflowed with a massive bouquet. "Those flowers. Where did they come from?"

"We picked them, Papa. Me and her." Luke pointed to Mrs. Carter.

"They're from the beds out front, aren't they?" He hadn't meant for his question to come out with such force, but—

"They are." Miss Grimsby eyed him warily. "I thought they would brighten the table and fill the air with a pleasant aroma. Is there a problem?"

"My wife planted them. They were her pride and joy."

"I'm sorry, sir. I didn't know."

There was no way she could have. The vase was so full of colorful blooms that there couldn't be many left out front. But there would be more. In time. "It's all right."

Miss Grimsby's fine features relaxed, although he detected pity in the glance she sent him. Sympathy was bad enough, but he wanted no part of pity.

Conversation had ceased following his heated question. Not that he could blame the others for being quiet. The same thing often happened at the rail station when his feelings got the better of him, which happened far too often these days. He must regain control.

His normally unobtrusive daughter wriggled and whimpered. His prospective housekeeper had her hands full holding Lila while trying to eat. The baby's flailing fist sent Miss Grimsby's spoon sailing. Then his little girl flung her arms open wide and said "Papa" as clear as you please. Her first word ever, and she'd said it for him.

"It would appear she wants you, sir."

"So it does. Would you mind bringing her to me?"

Miss Grimsby did so and promptly returned to her

seat. He caressed Lila's cheek. She gave him a dimple-producing smile, showing off her first four teeth. It was hard to believe she was already ten months old and had been without a mother three of them.

It soon became clear he wouldn't be able to get much eating done with his squirming daughter in his lap. Trudy had always been the one to hold Lila during meals. A woman seemed to have a knack for juggling a baby while eating that he lacked.

"Would you mind bringing your plate down here, Miss Grimsby, and sitting beside me so you can help with Lila?" He inclined his head toward the chair on his right.

"Certainly." She quickly obliged.

"No!" Luke shrieked. "She can't sit there. That's Mama's chair."

"What do you think you're doing, son? You know better than to yell at the supper table."

"Make her get up."

"She's sitting there, and that's that." Spencer could understand how difficult it must be for Luke to see another woman in Trudy's place, but the sooner he accepted the new order of things, the better. Miss Grimsby had already managed to lift the gloom that had settled in on that dark April day when he'd lost Trudy after her unfortunate accident in the garden. The house wasn't just clean. It felt welcoming for the first time in months.

Lila fussed again, and Spencer turned to comfort her. Something cool and wet hit his cheek and fell to the floor. He hadn't even figured out what it was when another of the sticky projectiles pelted him in the chest, leaving a round, red spot on his white shirt before slid-

ing beneath his waistcoat. Luke must be lobbing tomato slices at him.

Sure enough, a third slab sailed across the table and
landed in his lap. "Lucas Mark Abbott, you stop that
this minute, or I'll—"

"I can handle this, sir. Here." Miss Grimsby handed
Lila to him once again, grabbed Luke by the hand and
forced him to follow her. "You're coming with me,
young man."

Taken unaware, Luke didn't have time to protest.
He shot a pleading look at Spencer, who inclined his
head toward Miss Grimsby. "Go."

Because the attack had taken him by surprise, he'd
forgotten his plan to have Miss Grimsby handle any
needed discipline and had been ready to take his son to
task. She'd taken charge of the situation before Spencer had time to act—a bold but admirable choice. He
was curious to see what she'd do.

As much as he detested the thought of leaving the
care of his children to a virtual stranger, he had no
choice. He'd know soon what type of disciplinarian
she was and if she could be trusted with his children.

Mrs. Carter paused with her fork halfway to her
mouth. "That young woman is just what you been
needin', Mr. Abbott. You'd be a fool to let her get
away." She went right on eating, which suited Spencer, since he couldn't think of a suitable response.

Lila poked his cheek with a pudgy finger. "Papa."
That one word meant more to him than he'd thought
possible. It seemed like only yesterday Luke had said
it for the first time.

"Yes, my sweet. I'm your papa. And you're my little
princess." He kissed her forehead, letting his lips lin-

ger a moment. Trudy used to say nothing was as soft or sweet as a baby's skin, and she was right.

But she was gone, and this precious girl would have no memories of her mother. The all-too-familiar ache squeezed his chest.

Spencer strained to hear what was taking place in the parlor, but other than the murmur of voices, he couldn't make out anything. No screaming. No crying. No spanking. The higher pitch indicated Miss Grimsby was doing most of the talking. He'd like to be privy to that conversation.

A good two minutes went by with Lila gnawing on a potato chunk, Mrs. Carter shoveling in her salmon and Spencer doing his best to clean up the aftermath of Luke's assault while balancing Lila on one knee. If Miss Grimsby and Luke didn't return soon, Spencer would have no choice but to intervene.

Moments later Miss Grimsby and Luke appeared in the dining room doorway. Rather than the defiant stance Spencer expected, Luke's shoulders slumped. He scuffed the toe of his shoe over the wooden floor, his eyes downcast, and mumbled something.

Miss Grimbsy leaned over and spoke softly beside Luke's ear. "Remember what I said. Look at your papa and say it loudly enough for him to hear."

"She said I gotta tell you I'm sorry. So, I'm sorry. I didn't mean to make you sad."

"I'm not sad, son. I'm disappointed. Throwing things is not the way a gentleman deals with his anger. You must be punished for this."

"He will be, sir." Miss Grimsby picked up Luke's plate. "Right now he's going to finish his meal at the kitchen table. Alone. And tomorrow he's going to scrub your shirt until the tomato stain is gone."

With Luke exiled and Lila back in Miss Grimsby's lap, Spencer was free to enjoy the meal, one of the best he'd been served in a long time. The food rivaled that prepared at the restaurants in Sacramento City's finest hotels.

Miss Grimsby chatted with Mrs. Carter about the town, the weather and numerous other topics. Spencer made no effort to join in. He was content to enjoy his supper and the fact that—should his conversation with Miss Grimsby afterward prove satisfactory—he'd be having many more like it in the days to come. The prospect of coming home and finding the good-looking woman in his kitchen lifted his spirits more than it should.

A glance at Luke proved that being forced to eat by himself was an effective punishment. The wistfulness in his eyes made Spencer consider overriding Miss Grimsby and allowing Luke to rejoin them. But only for the briefest moment.

If he did hire her, he couldn't undermine her authority. One didn't treat one's employees that way. She deserved respect, and he'd give it to her. In return she would brighten his world and make his days a bit more bearable.

Tess stood on the porch and watched the wagon grow smaller. With Luke accompanying his father on the trip to take Mrs. Carter home, she could clear the dining table quickly, make short work of the dishes and plan what she'd serve for breakfast.

"If there's time, lovely Lila, I'll give you a bath. It

doesn't look like you've had one in ages." She kissed each of the baby's cheeks and held her close for a minute, savoring the incredible sweetness of having a little one to care for. At ten months, Lila was her youngest charge ever—and so pretty.

The baby had her father's striking eyes—the brilliant blue of an alpine lake—as well as his golden hair. Luke, on the other hand, must take after his mother, although the brown-haired, brown-eyed boy did have Mr. Abbott's broad forehead and strong jaw. If he ended up half as handsome as his father, he'd be a fine-looking man one day.

"What am I doing woolgathering when I have work to do?" She set Lila on a blanket in the corner of the kitchen. The little girl banged her blocks together while making sounds resembling speech. At this rate she'd be adding words to her vocabulary in no time.

Lila held out a block to Tess. "Papa."

"No, sweetheart. I'm not your papa, but he'll be home soon." She left the baby attempting to build a tower and attacked the dishes.

What would Mr. Abbott have to say when he talked with her after his return? Perhaps she'd been hasty in her handling of Luke, but if he was allowed to get away with bad behavior, he could turn out like Charlie. Although the boy from her orphanage days was bright, he'd become a bully and a troublemaker. She wouldn't let that happen to her young charge.

By the time Mr. Abbott and Luke returned, the kitchen was clean, the next day's breakfast was planned, and Lila was bathed and ready for bed. Tess didn't relish the tug-of-war sure to take place if Mr. Abbott expected her to put Luke down for the night.

Something told her the boy would raise a ruckus. After her travel and hard work, along with the pressure to please, her bed at the hotel was calling her name. By the time she walked the mile back to town, she'd have to force herself to stay awake long enough to complete her toilette.

She went out front with Lila resting against her chest. "I'm glad you're back. She's about to nod off."

"He has." Mr. Abbott pointed to Luke, asleep on the wagon seat next to him, his head in his father's lap. "I'll see if I can get him upstairs without waking him."

With slow, steady movements, Mr. Abbott extricated himself, gathered Luke in his arms and mounted the stairs. "Come with me please, Miss Grimsby."

She complied.

Luke didn't stir as his father carried him to his room and put him to bed. Mr. Abbott rummaged under the rumpled bedding, pulled out a crib-size quilt and laid it next to his sleeping son. "Good night, my boy. May God bless your slumber." He placed a kiss on Luke's brow, a gesture so tender that Tess's lips trembled.

She couldn't remember anyone ever tucking her in or praying a blessing over her like that. Mr. Abbott might have a serious mien, but he was a caring father.

"Come to Papa, princess." He took his daughter from Tess and, with a tilt of his head, beckoned her to follow him to Lila's room.

Mr. Abbott repeated the bedtime routine and launched into a lullaby, his beautiful baritone filling the room. Tess, who loved music but was about as melodic as a mule, marveled at the gift given him. If anyone had told her the stoic stationmaster sang to his children, she wouldn't have believed it. What a surprising man. She looked forward to learning more about him.

Lila was asleep before her father reached the last verse. He smoothed the sheet over her and placed a small quilt by her side, as he'd done with Luke.

"Your wife's handiwork I presume?"

"It was the last thing she made. She'd planned to make a quilt for us, too, but…" He released a ragged breath. Tess had a sudden urge to place a comforting hand on his shoulder as he gazed at his daughter but stopped herself just in time.

He cast a lingering look at the sleeping girl and turned to Tess, all business once again. "I'll see to the horses while you're still here to watch the children. Give me ten minutes, and meet me on the porch."

"Yes, sir." He left, and she sank into the cozy rocking chair where Mrs. Abbott had likely nursed the baby. Tess spent a good five minutes listening to the rhythm of the rockers on the wooden floor and drinking in the sight of Lila's cherubic lips parted as she drew in measured breaths. *Lord, if it's Your plan for me to care for these children, I'd be grateful.*

Tess forced herself to leave the nursery. She paused in the doorway of Luke's room. The sheet Mr. Abbott had spread over his son had become tangled in the short time he'd been in bed. Even in slumber the boy was active.

Luke's room was strewn with toys, whereas Lila's was devoid of clutter. Tess would help him clean his, so it would be a pleasant place to play. Not that she could picture him spending much time indoors. He was a boy who needed to get outside and expend some of his abundant energy.

She heaved a wistful sigh, made her way downstairs and busied herself in the kitchen. The parlor clock chimed. A quarter to eight already.

The time had come. She must face Mr. Abbott and find out if her hard work had secured her the position. He'd appreciated the meal. That was clear. But was he willing to welcome another woman into his home and entrust his children to her care—even a competent one such as she?

Tess located him on the porch, his hands resting on the railing, his gaze fixed on some distant point. She'd seen that look on the face of every man she'd worked for, the look of a man surveying his territory, be it his business, his house or his land.

She stood beside him, got a glimpse of his face and fought a wave of nausea. If Mr. Abbott's scowl was an indication of his thoughts, she'd be on her way back to Sacramento City tomorrow. She didn't know which would hurt worse—being denied the opportunity to care for adventurous Luke and his adorable baby sister or saying goodbye to their intriguing father.

Chapter Five

Mr. Abbott spun to face Tess. He caught her staring at his soiled front, where Luke had splatted him with a tomato. "It looks like I'll be hauling out the washtub after you leave."

"You're going to wash your shirt now? Tonight?"

His intention to see to the task himself surprised Tess, but not as much as her desire to tend to it for him. If she did, she'd have another half hour's work before she could leave and would have to arrive early enough the next day to iron the shirt before he headed to the railway station.

He leaned against the porch railing with his arms and ankles crossed, looking quite appealing—aside from the red splotch in the middle of his chest. She couldn't keep from smiling.

"Since this was my last clean shirt, I don't have a choice." He swept a hand toward the unsightly spot and gave a hollow laugh, but his attempt to lighten the mood couldn't mask the embarrassment that had left his neck flushed.

The admission hadn't been an easy one for him.

Somehow she'd have to summon the strength needed, because she wasn't about to let him struggle with a chore sure to be foreign to him. Not when she could make short work of it. "I'll wash one of your shirts, but not that one. Luke's going to help me with it."

Relief flooded his fine features. "I shouldn't accept your offer since it's getting late, but I can't stop myself. The past few weeks have been— Thank you."

Her heart swelled with sympathy. "You are in need of help, aren't you?"

"I've managed."

"Yes, but life would be easier if you had someone to see to such things." Not *someone*. Her.

"My wife…she made sure I had…" He pressed a fist to his mouth. "I never expected to be in this position."

"Things *will* be different, Mr. Abbott. There's no denying that, but I can ease your burden, provided you'll let me. You've seen that I can cook and clean—and that I won't let Luke drive the locomotive."

Her metaphor elicited a smile. A halfhearted one but a smile nonetheless. She'd pushed as hard as she dared. Now to wait for his response.

It came before she had time to take a breath. "You said you could prove your worth in a day, and you've done that. The job's yours—for now. We'll reevaluate in a month after we've had time to see if the situation is agreeable to both of us."

Relief washed over her. It took great restraint not to shout "Hallelujah!" She'd secured the position. Now to make a personal request. "I realize a housekeeper generally goes by her surname, but in the homes where I served as governess, I was called by my Christian name. I'd prefer that."

He raised an eyebrow. "You want me to use your first name?"

"I was thinking of the children. Tess would be easier for them to say." And she wouldn't have to answer to Mr. Grimsby's last name on a daily basis. Every time she heard it she was reminded of the dictatorial orphanage director who'd given it to her when she'd shown up on his doorstep too young and too traumatized to recall hers.

"You make a valid point, so I'll allow it, provided you'll call me Spencer."

She hadn't expected him to agree so readily, but she was glad he had. Spencer was a fine name, and she would enjoy using it. "Really?" She adopted a playful tone. "I thought a man like you who's used to being in charge might prefer *master* or *your eminence*." She fought to keep a straight face but lost the battle and laughed.

His eyebrows shot all the way to the ceiling. Perhaps she'd gone too far. He was a grieving widower, after all.

"You certainly have some spice to you, Tess. I do believe you and Luke will get on just fine." He cast a glance to the west. "It'll be late before you get to town. I can't leave the children alone to drive you. Will you be all right walking by yourself?"

"Yes, sir. I mean Spencer." While she appreciated his concern, she wouldn't be alone. The Lord was always with her. She would spend the time in prayer. After all, she had much to thank Him for. She'd told Him the desire of her heart, and it seemed He'd heard her. She had a family to care for and looked forward to delightful days ahead as she made a difference in their lives.

Spencer bid her farewell and headed inside, slowly shaking his head and sporting an amused smile.

Was the taciturn gentleman actually laughing? *Lord, let it be so. He could use some levity in his life.*

Tess hung the hoe on its pegs in the garden shed and rubbed her lower back. Running a household was harder than she'd thought. Even though she'd been working for Spencer two weeks, she had yet to grow accustomed to the constant juggling required.

The amount of work itself was a challenge, but the isolation made her want to scream. Some adult company would be nice. She saw Spencer at breakfast and again at supper, but their interactions were focused on household matters and the children, which was as it should be. She was his housekeeper, not his friend.

At least she'd get to see Polly while she was in town today. In the meantime she would have to keep Luke from soiling his clothing before she could get the team hitched to the wagon. That boy attracted dirt like a garden attracted critters. The latter problem had been solved by a chicken wire fence. The former seemed a hopeless cause.

She'd had to do some talking before Mr. Abbott agreed to have the fence built. For some reason, he seemed concerned about her working in the garden. She'd had to assure him three times that she would be careful and never leave tools laying on the ground where someone could get hurt. As though she would.

Tess lifted Lila out of the tub she'd set at the side of the garden and headed to the house. Spencer's dog trotted across the yard. The poor creature was bare in spots, but the salve had done its job, arresting the mange. Once his coffee-colored fur grew back, he'd be a fine-looking fellow. He'd proven to be a good watchdog, alerting her when anything was amiss.

"I'm going to leave Luke in your care." She patted the dog's head. "You'll let me know if he starts to wander off again, won't you?" She went inside to get ready for the shopping trip.

An hour later Tess sat on the porch of Polly's small house in downtown Shingle Springs, a glass of lemonade in her hand. Luke darted around the yard in search of insects. Polly's two-year-old daughter, Abby, did her best to keep up. Lila slept on a blanket near Tess.

Polly rubbed her rounded belly. "I've never seen you looking more content. Being a housekeeper agrees with you."

Tess chuckled. "If you'd been privy to my thoughts earlier, you'd disagree. I've gained a whole new respect for mothers with no hired help. How *do* you fit everything into your days?"

"Caring for a house while keeping two little ones out of trouble is much different than supervising the cultured children of Sacramento City's elite as we did before, but it's what you've always wanted."

What she wanted was a family of her own—impossible dream though it might be—not to step into one in the throes of grief, with a woebegone widower and a headstrong four-year-old. But that's exactly what she'd done. Meeting their needs was proving more difficult than she'd anticipated. Despite her desire to help them heal, she'd made little progress. "I have the situation under control."

"So I hear. Peter told me he caught Spencer smiling yesterday. When he asked him why, Spencer said he was looking forward to seeing what you'd fixed for supper. Apparently he's a man who appreciates good food."

"He does tuck in hearty portions of whatever I put in front of him. The only thing I've found that he doesn't care for is cottage cheese. I asked him to let me know if there's anything else he doesn't like, but he just said 'everything's fine.'"

Polly shifted in the rocking chair, causing it to creak. "He's not one for making long speeches, is he?"

Tess laughed. "When I give Spencer a review of the day, I usually get one or two words in reply. If I manage to get five sentences out of him in an evening, I feel like I've achieved quite a feat. I can understand his brooding silence, but he seldom interacts with the children, except when he tucks them in at night. That's so sad. I know fathers have to deal with the demands of their jobs, but their children crave a connection with them." She couldn't keep the wistfulness out of her voice.

Polly patted her arm. "Oh, Tessie, I'm sorry. Whenever I think of your father leaving you at the orphanage, my blood boils. I'll never understand how a parent could walk away from a child like that, especially one as bright and beautiful as you. What *was* he thinking?"

"A man can't raise a child alone." How many times had she told herself that? But her father hadn't even attempted it, giving her up the very day her mother had gone to be with the Lord. She'd never heard from him again.

"I know, but he could have found you a home with a family who would love you. Or gotten help like Spencer has."

Her father didn't want her. No man did. Not that she could blame them. Even if she wasn't taller than most of them, she lacked the beauty or charm that attracted men. It seemed her height was the only thing people noticed. Granted, she had six to ten inches on most women, but she wasn't a circus sideshow freak, although there were days she felt like one.

A sharp cry rang out. Luke had pinned his play-mate's arm behind her.

"Abby!" Polly struggled to stand, but her bulging middle made the task difficult.

Tess leaped to her feet, her long strides carrying her across the yard in no time. "Let go of her this min-ute, Luke."

"It's my ladybug. I saw it first."

She pried his hands from Abby's arm, spun him around and dropped to one knee in front of him. "That may be, but you can't hold her like that. You could hurt her."

"I didn't."

That was true. Abby had flitted away unharmed and was back on the hunt. "You're right, but you could have. Since you're older than she is, you can make good choices—like your papa does."

"What kind of choices does he make?"

"Well, he chose where to live. Where to work. Who to have look after you."

Luke's eyes filled with tears, and he swiped a dirty sleeve across them. "I don't want anyone to look after me. Just my mama. I want her to come back."

"I know, sweetheart. But she's gone. You do have your papa, and he loves you very much." It took all her self-restraint not to pull the brokenhearted boy into her arms. She contented herself by caressing his cheek.

He swatted her hand away. "Don't touch me!"

"It's not polite to hit people. You need to sit on the top step until you calm down."

He sat but bounced right back up and clomped down the stairs.

"Luke," Tess called.

The rebellious boy spun around. "I'm calm. See?" He gave her a toothy grin.

She hid her answering smile behind her hand. "Very well."

Polly waited until he was out of earshot. "He's always been a strong-willed little fellow, but he began acting out after Trudy's death. You're good with him, though."

Tess warmed at the compliment. "I want to show him I care, but he's built a wall. It will take time to bring it down, but I've thought of a way to remove a brick."

She launched into an explanation of her plan, not stopping until she was done, despite the skepticism on Polly's face. "What do you think?"

"I think you're asking for trouble. Spencer isn't one to embrace change on a good day."

"I have a valid argument."

Polly swirled her glass of lemonade. "That may be, but you'd better brace yourself for some resistance."

She could deal with resistance. She'd overcome it a number of times when approaching her previous employers. They'd come to see things her way—eventually. Spencer was a reasonable man, so surely he'd be willing to consider her proposal.

Chapter Six

"Absolutely not." Spencer couldn't believe what Tess had suggested. She'd been here all of two weeks, and yet she had the audacity to barge into his office and stick that aristocratic nose of hers where it didn't belong. He'd come to value her opinions, but she'd gone too far this time.

"If you would allow me to explain…"

He stood behind his desk. She faced him, unflinching. Because of the high heels on her boots, the thick brown braid wound around her crown and that monstrosity of a hat, she had several inches on him. It was too bad he couldn't wear his top hat indoors.

Although he had no intention of changing his mind, he would hear her out. "Kindly take a seat, and we can discuss this."

She sat tall and proud. Spencer remained standing and tapped the toe of his boot. The sooner she got to the point, the sooner he could get back to work.

The forthright woman wasted no time stating her case. "I don't want to leave the children with Polly any longer than necessary, so I'll be direct. Parting with a loved one's possessions can be difficult, but it's a necessary step in the grieving process. I can't begin to imagine how difficult it must be for you to see your late wife's things every time you open your clothes cupboard."

"I'm fine."

"I felt sure you'd say that, but there's another factor to take into consideration—Luke's feelings."

Feelings? Why did women put so much stock in them? He had no desire to discuss his or his son's. "Leave him out of this."

She forged ahead as though she hadn't heard him. "I believe much of his misbehavior stems from the fact that he's grieving the loss of his mother. If you were to allow him to help me pack up her things and face his loss head on, I feel certain you'd see a change."

"I'll have a talk with him and tell him he must regain control of himself."

Tess had the audacity to laugh in his face, a musical sound he usually enjoyed. But not today. "This is Luke we're taking about. A mere boy. He's too young to master his emotions." She sobered at his frown. "Oh, dear. I've angered you."

"You presume to know my feelings now?" She had no idea what he was dealing with. How waking each morning alone in the room he and Trudy had shared brought back the stabbing pain that had pierced his heart when she'd drawn her last breath. How dragging himself to the railway station day after day required Herculean effort.

She persisted. "You're clenching your hands."

He unfurled the fists he hadn't realized he'd

formed. "I'm not angry. I'm…frustrated. You waltz in here with no warning, interrupt my work and expect me to make a decision on the spot." He placed his palms on his desktop and leaned forward. "Let me make myself clear. I want things left as they are. I know what's best for my family, and you will abide by my wishes."

"I would if I could, but I can't keep quiet, not when one of your children is hurting. Luke let it slip that he misses his mother. Please give me permission. If not for your sake, for his." She lifted pleading eyes to him. Warm cocoa-brown eyes with the longest lashes he'd ever seen.

"He told *you* he's missing her? He hasn't said anything to me."

"Boys don't like to admit weakness—even sadness—to their fathers."

She was right. He would never think of telling his father how much he missed his mother. "Fine. You've made your point. You may remove all her things."

"What would you like me to do with them? Store them in the attic? Donate them to the missionary barrels? Or…?"

He spread the next day's train schedules on his desk. "Do whatever you'd like. I don't care. Just don't bring this up again. *Please.*" He had a job to do and didn't have time to think about such matters.

Tess stood. Her every word was clothed with compassion. "I'm sorry this is such a difficult time for you. I wish I could do more to help."

"Do your job. That's all I ask."

Sadness filled her eyes. She quickly blinked it away,

sent him a polite smile and left, giving him the impression he'd disappointed her.

So be it. He didn't need her sympathy. All he wanted was to be left alone.

Red. Every one of Trudy Abbott's tiny dresses boasted a different shade. A petite woman, such as she'd been, could wear the vibrant color and look stunning. Tess preferred her understated blues. People made enough fuss about her height as it was without drawing more attention by looking like a red-hot poker.

The massive wardrobe in Spencer's room held few of his items but brimmed with his late wife's clothing. Tess pulled out a gown and laid the stunning creation on the four-poster bed. Luke sat cross-legged in the middle. He grabbed the dress and plunged his face into the folds. Was the dear boy crying?

He lowered the glossy fabric, his lips downturned in a pronounced pout. "I can't smell her anymore. She used to smell like roses."

"She must have worn rosewater. I do sometimes, but the scent doesn't last long."

He shoved the dress aside, scooted up to the headboard and leaned against it, his arms folded. He narrowed his eyes and shot daggers at Tess. "I don't wanna help."

"Hush now. I don't want you to wake your sister. You can just watch, but I would like your help with one thing. I don't know which of these dresses were your mama's favorites. Do you?"

He shook his head, but the telltale twitch around his mouth was a clear indication he wasn't being truthful. She held up the crimson silk, a gown so exquisite she wondered where the woman would have worn it. "Do you remember her wearing this one?"

Luke's expression didn't change, so Tess set the dress aside. She worked her way through a burgundy brocade, a scarlet satin and a vermillion velvet. Not one of the ornately trimmed garments—none of which showed wear—evoked a response. She reached for a calico the color of cherries generously kissed by the sun that had obviously seen a season or two, and Luke jerked his head. Three more calicos, two lawns and a red-and-white checked gingham elicited similar responses. Tess added the dresses to the growing pile.

Trudy Abbott had owned far more clothing than a small-town housewife needed. If Tess were to venture a guess, she'd say the woman had come from a family of means. If that was the case, how had she ended up married to Spencer and living in a remote community like Shingle Springs? Someone of her tastes generally gravitated to Sacramento City or San Francisco.

Luke inched forward, casting surreptitious glances at Tess. She averted her gaze but kept him in her peripheral vision. When he reached the pile of his mother's everyday dresses, he leaned over and sniffed one as he'd done earlier. He beamed. "I can smell her!"

Tess didn't have the heart to tell the dear boy she'd dabbed herself with rosewater before leaving her room at the boardinghouse and that some of the scent must have come off on the clothing. "How nice."

He clamored off the bed and darted out of the room, making little sound in his stocking-clad state, for which Tess was grateful. Moments later he returned clutching his crib-size quilt. He rubbed a corner of it against his mother's dress, put the fabric to his nose and drew in a deep breath. Seemingly satisfied, he lay on his side, silent but watchful. And still.

By the time Tess had folded the dresses and stowed them in some crates she'd found in the barn, Luke had fallen asleep with the quilt pressed to his cheek. She'd never seen him as relaxed, even in slumber. She leaned over and pressed a kiss to his brow.

An idea struck her. She located the bottle of rose-water that had belonged to Luke's mother and flicked several drops of the floral-scented liquid on Luke's quilt. The fragrance, although strong now, would fade quickly, but perhaps smelling it again would help lock the scent in his memory.

Now to make good use of the unexpected hour while both children slept. She could spare them the pain of witnessing the removal of their mother's things from the house.

Working quickly, Tess stowed the items from the dressing table in a crate. She opened the bureau drawers Spencer's wife had used and removed an impressive selection of nightwear and unmentionables, including several pair of expensive silk stockings.

She picked up a stack of corsets, and a bundle of letters tied with a red ribbon fell at her feet. Letters exchanged between Mr. Spencer Abbott in California and Miss Trudy Endicott of Houston, Texas. Love letters most likely.

Unsure what to do, Tess added them to the crate. Spencer had said he didn't want to talk about his late wife's things, but she had no choice. Surely he'd want to save something so special. He might not be up to reading the letters now, but in time they could serve to bring him comforting reminders of his courtship.

Letters were important. Those she'd taken to writing to her someday fiancé on her birthday each year brought her solace in the midst of her loneliness. She used her real name, Faith, when she penned them. Somehow it seemed fitting that the man she hoped to marry would be the only person to know the name—along with the sensitive side of her that she kept hidden. She certainly wouldn't want to lose those letters.

She carted the crates downstairs and added Trudy's hats and cloak from the foyer, her aprons from the kitchen and her sewing basket from the parlor. Tess didn't have the heart to remove anything more than the most obvious personal items. She stowed the crates in the attic, where they would available should Spencer or the children want to see Trudy's things again someday.

Her task complete, she moved from room to room. Although the changes were subtle, the removal of the ever-present reminders of his late wife might lessen Spencer's pain. Would he notice the difference?

Chapter Seven

Spencer's steps slowed as he neared the house. Trudy used to have their son watch for him each evening and alert her when he approached so she could greet him, but Tess involved Luke in the supper preparations. Spencer missed the warm welcome.

He entered, reached up to set his top hat on the shelf above the coat hooks and froze. Trudy's cloak was gone, as was her profusion of fancy bonnets. His slouch hat and Tess's monstrosity were the only hats remaining. His hat rested on its crown to keep the brim from losing its shape, whereas hers, with its frothy fabric and feathers, sat right side up. It was a wonder the massive thing didn't fall off.

Apparently Tess had wasted no time clearing out Trudy's things. Considering her belief that doing so would help Luke, her haste made sense. Clearly she cared about his son.

Spencer marched upstairs to his room, threw open the wardrobe doors and stared at the empty space. True to her word, Tess had removed every last one of Trudy's dresses. His few items looked lost in the large clothes cupboard. He yanked open the drawers on Trudy's side of the bureau and found gaping caverns. Tess was not only fast. She was thorough.

But why, if she'd whisked away all of Trudy's things, did the room smell so strongly of roses, as though his wife had been there moments before? He had to do something to clear his head. Now.

As quickly as he could, he changed from his work clothes to ranch wear. He shut the doors of the wardrobe with more force than he'd intended and stormed down the stairs, not stopping until he reached the barn. Inhaling deeply of the scents of his childhood—horses, straw and leather—his senses were restored.

Spying his ropes, he knew what to do. He grabbed his favorite one and entered the pen. With the coils of his lariat in his left hand, he spun the loop with his right and let it fly.

Tess wiped her hands on a kitchen towel and stepped out the back door. What was Spencer doing? She'd worked hard to have supper ready when he got home, but he'd raised a ruckus in his room overhead, with doors and drawers slamming, and stomped out of the house a good ten minutes ago. Evidently he was angry about the changes she'd made, even though he'd given her permission.

Regret settled in her stomach like a rock. In her desire to help Luke, she'd neglected to take Spencer's feelings into consideration. What was done was done, but perhaps she could find a way to show that she understood his pain and assure him she was only trying to ease it.

She followed the wraparound porch to the north side

of the house where she could see the barn and stopped, her chin dropping. Never had she seen a man work off his anger by lassoing things. She stood transfixed as Spencer spun his loop and threw it.

He roped fence post after fence post, not missing a single one. His form and prowess were awe-inspiring. She could watch him for hours. If only he hadn't started his roping before supper.

Supper! She dashed inside to rescue her meal, moving pots and pans to the side of the stove where the dishes would stay warm. "Please play with your sister, Luke, while I get your papa."

He grunted a reply.

Tess left the children rolling their canvas ball back and forth. She stepped off the back porch and rounded the corner. To her disappointment, Spencer stood outside the pen with one foot resting on the lowest slat of the fence, gazing into the distance.

Loath to disturb him and yet having no choice, she crossed the yard, her boots making little sound on the hard-packed earth. She reached him and rested a hand on his shoulder.

He started.

"Forgive me. I didn't mean to surprise you, but supper's ready."

His eyes widened, and he shook his head as though clearing it. "The smell. It's you. I wasn't imagining it. I thought…"

"Luke noticed it, too. I didn't know your wife wore rosewater. My intention was to help, not to stir up memories."

"It's fine. The job needed to be done. I was just… surprised."

"I know it's hard. I'm sorry for that, truly I am, but you'll be happy to know that Luke fell asleep on your bed with the quilt his mother made him, breathing in her scent. He rested peacefully. No tossing and turning. When he woke he was more amiable than I've ever seen him. Not that I'm expecting the change to last, but this was a start. He can begin his healing."

Spencer stretched a section of the rope taut and snapped it. She resisted the urge to jump.

"He's a strong boy. He'll be fine."

Eventually yes, but now wasn't the time to delve into the merits of dealing with one's grief instead of acting as though nothing was wrong. She had a more pressing matter to discuss. "I found some letters hidden among your wife's things. I felt sure you'd want to keep them."

Concern creased his brow. "Those are personal. You didn't—"

"Read them? Of course not. I just wanted to know what you'd like me to do with them."

The silence hung heavy until he broke it. "Hide them somewhere. I couldn't bear to see them again."

"I understand. I'll do that." She started for the house but turned when he called her name.

"I'm expecting a shipment soon. A bull. I thought you should know."

"A bull?" She wouldn't have expected Spencer to send for one, although she shouldn't be surprised. He was a rugged, manly man who had quite a way with a rope, so it made sense he knew about raising cattle.

Without realizing it, he'd given her a way to gain a foothold as she attempted to scale the walls the Abbott males had erected—and have fun at the same time. "Would you teach me how to lasso something?"

"You were watching me?" His impassive expression gave no indication of his thoughts.

Heat sped to Tess's cheeks. Since she'd already blurted her request, she might as well make it sound like a reasonable one. "I'd like you to teach me, so I can show Luke how. Or better yet, you could teach us both. He'd love it if you were to spend time with him."

"Would he?"

Although they were talking about Luke, Tess got the distinct impression Spencer was challenging her. Well, she hadn't backed down before, and she wouldn't now. "Your son is much like you. He needs an active outlet for his emo—his energy. I'd love to see him use it for something as impressive as r-roping."

If he'd stop staring at her with that quirked eyebrow, she might be able to complete a sentence without stumbling over her words and saying more than she'd intended. *Impressive* indeed! What would he think of her now? She sounded like a smitten schoolgirl instead of the levelheaded housekeeper she was. "If you'll give it some thought, I'd appreciate it. Now, I must go inside and get supper on the table. I do hope you'll be joining us soon."

She'd taken a total of ten steps when a rope encircled her, tightened around her waist and pinned her arms to her sides. The force jerked her back, causing her to stumble as if she'd run full tilt into a clothesline.

Before she could turn, a tug on the rope spun her to face him. A flash of anger sent a renewed rush of warmth to her face. She struggled to free her hands. "You *lassoed* me?"

The shocked look on his face showed he was as surprised by his out-of-character behavior as she. "I'm sorry. I don't know what came over me. I didn't want you to leave, and then—" he shrugged "—it just happened."

Although the leather rope was smooth and the binding not uncomfortably tight, she didn't cotton to the idea of being bound. "I'm not a cow. I'm a woman."

"You are. And a fine one, too. Here, let me take it off." He rushed to help her. His gaze locked with hers as he gently loosened the rope and slipped it over her head.

The warmth in his eyes melted much of her anger and ignited a different emotion. Her heart was racing so wildly she felt lightheaded. "I could have fallen."

"I wouldn't have let you. I had a solid grip on the rope." He gave her a sheepish smile. "I am sorry. Mostly." Mischief glinted in his brilliant blue eyes, and a corner of his mouth twitched.

"Is this what cattle ranchers do for sport?"

He shook his head, his earnest expression reminding her of Luke when he explained his actions following one of his antics. "I like roping. Always have. I've roped a lot of things, but never a pretty woman—until now."

Pretty? Even if he was teasing, the possibility that he might mean it chased away the remnants of her anger. She smiled. "Thank you for the compliment. I'm flattered."

"You're different from any woman I've ever known. You have a ready laugh, and you don't make a fuss when I—" He averted his gaze and kicked at the ground. "I don't know why I'm rambling. It's not important."

It was to her, but she knew from experience Spencer wouldn't say any more. Once he put the stopper in the bottle, she couldn't get another word out of him.

He turned away and coiled the rope. "Thank you, Tess."

For what? For packing up his late wife's things so he didn't have to? For making inroads with his son? For finding a way for father and son to spend some time together?

Once again he left her guessing what he'd meant. But one thing was clear. He'd reached out to her. Not in an ordinary way, but in his own extraordinary way.

A tingling sensation stole over her, unexpected but not unpleasant. Perhaps she could help this family travel the path from their pain-filled past to a promising future, after all.

Chapter Eight

Tess sat at the tiny dressing table in the room Spencer rented for her at the boardinghouse in town. She had to tuck her feet under the stool to keep from banging her knees into the tabletop. Why must they make furniture so small?

She shook her head, reveling in the feel of her chestnut tresses cascading over her shoulders. She'd loosened her braid just to watch the waves ripple as she swung her head from side to side. Her hair was her one beauty, but she'd best plait it forthwith or risk being late getting to the ranch.

In First Peter, the apostle warned a woman not to take pride in her physical appearance, but Tess appreciated the fact that the Lord had blessed her with nice hair, even if He hadn't seen fit to give her fine features. Good looks could actually prove detrimental to a housekeeper or governess. No mistress wanted a staff member who turned heads and could draw the attention away from her. Tess had never had to worry on that account. Her height was the only thing men noticed.

She wound her braid atop her head, secured it

with hairpins and lifted the plaited hair switch she'd purchase—one of her rare splurges—into place securing the added coil with more pins until the switch was firmly anchored. Surveying the results in the mirror, she smiled. The extra loop added a good inch to her height.

Now for the final touch. She reached for her rosewater, and the scene outside the pen with Spencer the night before came back to her. On second thought, she'd go without.

She had just enough time to add a few words to her journal before departing. Capturing her thoughts and impressions on the page helped her make sense of them. After Spencer's unusual way of getting her attention the night before—and her surprising response to him—she had much to sort out. She'd been certain she'd seen attraction on his part, but perhaps it was only wishful thinking on hers. No matter what it was, she was eager to see him again.

Minutes later she donned her hat and gloves and set out for the ranch, enjoying the coolness of the early morning hours. Nothing cheered her like the start of a new day ripe with promise. And this day would be unlike any other. She and Luke would get their first roping lesson.

She reached the house just as the sun crested the horizon, splashing the sky over the Sierras with vivid yellows and oranges on a brilliant blue canvas, and drank in the Lord's handiwork. A profound sense of peace filled her soul. She felt like singing praises. If she had a pleasing voice, she would. Instead, she lifted her face to the heavens and uttered a silent prayer of thanks.

"Tess? Are you all right?"

She wheeled around to face Spencer. "Very much so. I was thanking the Lord. It's a lovely day, isn't it?"

He brushed some straw from his chambray shirt. "Not much different than yesterday."

"Oh, but it is. I can feel it in the air."

He moistened the tip of his finger and held it up, turning it every which way. "No breeze. Hot and dry. Again."

She chuckled and mounted the stairs with him right behind her. "I cooked bacon and eggs yesterday. Today you're getting a ham and cheese omelet served with peach slices—" the urge to tease him was too strong to resist "—on a bed of cottage cheese. That's different."

"Cottage cheese?"

"Yes. You said it was fine."

"For some people it is, I suppose, but it's not my favorite."

She removed her hat and set it on the shelf in the foyer, turning it just so to keep it from falling to the floor. "So, you do have preferences, after all. If you'll apprise me of them, I'll take them into consideration when I plan my menus."

"I'll make a list."

"Good." She was making progress. First with Luke and now with his father. Small steps, true, but it was a start.

She headed into the kitchen. Rather than going upstairs to change as he normally did, Spencer leaned against the doorjamb watching her. Dressed in his ranch wear, he was quite appealing. She could feast on the sight for hours. "Did you need something?"

He shook his head.

Fine. Let him watch. She appreciated the company—and the view. She donned her apron, pulled out a mixing bowl and set it on the counter.

"It's too low for you, isn't it?"

It was, but she'd grown used to that. Kitchens weren't designed with tall women in mind. "I manage."

"I'll raise the kitchen table, and you can use it instead."

She spun around. "You'd do that for me?"

"How high would you need it?"

"I'm not sure." She started for the table, came to a stop and smiled. Two coils of rope lay on its well-worn surface. He must have planned the gift of her very own lariat as a surprise. The thought warmed her clear through. "Ropes. For Luke and me?"

"Yes. I'll show you how to make the slip noose now, so you can teach him."

Tess watched intently while Spencer formed a loop in one end of her rawhide rope, sneaking peeks at his arresting profile. He handed her the lariat and talked her through the process until she'd produced a loop of her own. She longed to step out back and try to lasso something. "What's next?"

"Breakfast, I hope. That is if you can tear your eyes off me long enough to fix it." He grinned.

"What?"

"You were staring at me."

He was right, but she hadn't meant to be so obvious. Clapping a hand to her chest, she feigned innocence. "What do you mean? I was merely hanging on your every word, so you'd know how eager I am to learn."

"Is that so?" If his wry smile was any indication,

he'd seen right through her ploy. "Well, that bodes well for our lesson, then. I'm looking forward to it."

So was she. That evening couldn't come quickly enough to suit her.

Spencer stood on the platform as the final train of the day prepared for its return trip to Sacramento City. The L. L. Robinson sat poised to devour the track, the shrill whistle warning everyone of the sleek black locomotive's imminent departure.

The freight handlers had made short work of offloading the freight and getting it into the waiting wagons. A steady stream of drivers shouted commands to their teams as they left the station with supplies bound for the Comstock and other points east.

Another day done. A good day.

Peter clapped Spencer on the shoulder. "Is that a smile I see?"

"You and your men did a fine job today."

"A smile *and* a compliment? You feeling all right, Cap'n?"

Spencer chuckled. "Remind me not to be so lavish with my praise next time."

"In all seriousness, Spence, it's good to see you smiling again. I'm thinking Tess and her fine fare may have something to do with that. What's she fixing tonight?"

"I never know what to expect, but it's sure to be tasty."

Peter narrowed his eyes. "I'm thinking you won't be sending her packing when the month's up. That true?"

"I'm happy with her work." The woman herself posed a problem. He couldn't shake the image of her caught in his lasso, her big brown eyes wide. She'd taken her capture well, but he'd have to be careful not to have another lapse of judgment like that. He was a widower in mourning who had no business thinking about a woman, especially his housekeeper with the engaging smile.

"Polly's going to be mighty glad to hear that. She's been looking forward to having Tess nearby again. I'm glad, too. Polly gets chattier and chattier the closer she gets to her time. A feller can only take so much yammering about names, baby clothes and such, but Tess will listen for hours."

"Enjoy it while you can."

Peter smacked his forehead. "Sorry. I didn't mean to make you think about Trudy again."

"It's not a problem. I listened to her, so I don't have regrets." At least not about that.

"Speaking of Polly, I should finish up. She'll be waiting for me." Peter strode toward the main warehouse.

Spencer returned to his office, checked to make sure he had the next day's schedule ready and left the depot, his step lighter than it had been in weeks. For the first time since Trudy's death, he couldn't wait to get home. He might not know what he'd be having for dinner, but he knew what was coming afterward.

Any excuse to do some roping was welcome, and Tess had given him a good one. He'd soon know if her interest in learning to throw a lariat was genuine. It wasn't like her to stumble over her words, but she had last night. Then she'd gawked at him that morning and blushed when he'd pointed it out to her. He wasn't a dandy, but having an attractive woman take notice of him was...nice.

As soon as he reached the ranch, Woof bounded up to Spencer. He scratched his dog behind the ears. "It's good to see you, boy."

A combination of childish and feminine laughter rang out on the north side of the house. "Faster!" Luke shouted.

Spencer rounded the corner and smiled at the spectacle that greeted him. Lila sat on a bale of hay, Luke straddled a stack of two bales and Tess was atop a tower three high. They had saddle blankets beneath them and held ropes that encircled upturned buckets in front of them—makeshift horses from the look of things. He laughed.

Luke spied him first and waved. "Lookee, Papa. I'm winning the race." He used the ends of his rope to flick the side of his so-called steed.

"Oh! Are you home already?" Tess, who'd been "riding" sidesaddle, leaped to the ground and held out the "reins" to him. "That's wonderful. You can take my place. I'm sure you're a much better horse racer than I am."

Did she honestly expect him to engage in a game of make-believe? She might be willing to mount a horse made of hay, but he wasn't about to do something so foolish. He could imagine his father having laughed at his mother if she'd suggested such a thing. *A grown man has better things to do,* he would have said. The man had no patience for childish games, even though Spencer and his brother had begged him to join in the fun.

Truth struck Spencer with the force of a speeding

locomotive. Luke longed to spend time with him just as he had with his father. "That's a great idea, Tess, but Luke had better watch out because I'm fast."

Spencer strode to the stack of bales she'd been sitting on, straddled them and grabbed the rope serving as reins, allowing his hand to brush hers and linger a moment.

Her chin hung to her knees before she snapped her mouth shut. "You're going to do it?"

"You don't have to look so surprised. I used to race my older brother all the time when we were kids—and beat him, too."

"You won't beat me, Papa." Luke kicked the sides of his "horse" and encouraged it to run faster.

Tess pulled her hand away and gazed at it with wonder. She caught him watching her, smiled shyly and hid her hand in the folds of her skirt. "I hope you'll give your son a chance." Her voice was unsteady. "He's not as experienced a rider as you are, although I doubt you've ridden many hay bale horses."

"I'm not as buttoned-up as you might think." Spencer grinned.

"Really?" Disbelief filled those expressive eyes of hers.

"Really." He'd given his mother fits with his adventure-seeking nature—until his father had squashed it with his ironfisted control and cutting remarks. Spencer wouldn't do that to his children. He flicked the rope reins, dug his knees into the hay bales and urged his steed into a gallop.

The broad smile on Tess's face disarmed him. She looked lovely when she beamed like that.

"I'm happy to see there's not as much starch in your collars as I thought." She started for the house.

He couldn't let her have the last word. "What possessed you to do this?" He waved a hand at the hay bales. "And how did you move them? They're heavy."

"I did it because it's fun, and I used that to move the bales." She pointed at the wheelbarrow nearby, her usual self-assurance restored. "I'm more capable than many give me credit for." She shot him an impish grin and disappeared around the back of the house before he could say anything else.

She was capable all right. Capable of surprising him at every turn. What would she come up with next?

Tess flung the dirty dishwater into the yard and put the washtub away. At last she'd get the roping lesson she'd looked forward to all day. Forcing herself not to skip, she crossed the yard to where Spencer and the children waited. Luke held his rope, his slip noose formed like she'd taught him. Lila sat on a blanket in the shade of the barn, with Spencer's loyal watchdog nearby.

Spencer eyed Tess skeptically. "Are you sure you want to do this?"

Surely he wasn't going to change his mind. Luke would be devastated. "Yes."

"Let's get started, then." He demonstrated how to wind the coils and grasp them in the left hand while holding the loop in the right.

Once Tess mastered that, she knelt to help Luke and nearly bumped heads with Spencer, who'd done the same. With both of them on their knees, his eyes were level with hers. A flicker of something indistinguishable filled his before he focused on the rope in his son's hands.

She stood and backed away, startled by the flood of emotion that swept over her—a surge of something she'd never felt before. If she were forced to name the feeling, she'd say attraction.

No. That couldn't be it. Or could it? A man who showed interest in his child was attractive. That's all it was. She turned away and fanned her warm cheeks.

Spencer's dog padded over to her. She stooped to scratch him, and he wagged his tail. "You like that, don't you, Wolf?"

"Did you say Wolf?" Spencer asked.

She straightened. "Yes."

"His name isn't Wolf. It's Woof."

"I beg your pardon?"

Luke chimed in. "I told her it was Woof."

She enunciated carefully. "Woof?"

Spencer nodded. "As in *woof woof*. Luke called him that when he wasn't much older than Lila. Trudy thought it was cute, and the name stuck."

Tess couldn't keep from smiling. "It is cute." What was even cuter was hearing him say it.

Spencer cleared his throat. "Shall we move on?"

Half an hour flew by as he showed her and Luke how to spin a loop and toss it at just the right moment. He continued to work with Luke while Tess practiced by herself.

Despite doing her utmost to follow his directions, she couldn't get the rope to sail more than a few feet, where it fell as quickly as her spirits. She blew out a breath, her lips vibrating as though imitating a horse.

Spencer laughed. Loudly. At her.

She jammed a hand onto her hip. "It's not funny."

"Oh, but it is. My son has more patience than you

do." He inclined his head toward Luke, who coiled the tail end of his rope, spun a wobbly loop and tried unsuccessfully to lasso the bag of oats Spencer had set in front of him.

Luke shrugged and smiled. "I'll get it next time."

Spencer leaned so close to Tess she could smell the sooty scent she'd come to associate with him and spoke softly, his breath warm against her face. "Looks like my boy could teach you a thing or two."

Her breath froze in her throat as she waited to see what he'd do next. She didn't dare move, or his lips would graze her cheek, and she couldn't let that happen. Shouldn't let it happen, even though the possibility was appealing. She was his housekeeper. As such it was her duty to remain professional—although her thoughts at the moment were anything but.

"Some things can't be rushed, Tess." He strode over to Luke, rested a hand on his son's shoulder and offered an encouraging word.

She stood in stunned silence, not trusting her voice to work properly. Had Spencer read her thoughts? Was he letting her know that he found her attractive but could do nothing about it when his loss was so fresh?

The idea was preposterous. She'd let her active imagination get the best of her, which she mustn't do. She would keep things professional and not think about how warm, witty and wonderful her new employer was.

At least she'd try.

Chapter Nine

Spencer stared at the date he'd written in his ledger earlier that day—August 16, 1866. Four months.

It seemed like yesterday he'd held Trudy's slender hand in his, bathed her flushed face and done everything Doc suggested in an effort to bring her some relief—to no avail.

If only he'd gotten Trudy the help she wanted, she wouldn't have been working in the garden that warm spring day, wouldn't have fallen on the rake and wouldn't have developed the raging infection that had robbed him of his wife and the children of their mother. But, no. He'd told her he couldn't afford to hire someone to take over her chores. That he needed to save money to build up the ranch while the rail line was enjoying its soon-to-end period of prosperity.

And yet here he was paying for a housekeeper, after all. A stubborn housekeeper who'd waved away his warnings about the dangers of working in a garden. At least Tess promised to be careful with the tools.

He leaned back and rested his head in his clasped hands. A fly flitted around his office, reminding him of Luke and his boundless energy. Tess channeled it in clever ways.

Spencer had a hard time believing she'd been with them a month already. While the first two weeks had been a rough ride at times, things had settled into a manageable routine the past two. She served delicious meals, saw to it that his clothes were in excellent condition and managed to keep his son under control.

While Luke still tested his limits on a regular basis, he hadn't been as prone to outbursts since Tess removed Trudy's things. Spencer had to admit that his forthright housekeeper knew what she was doing, even if her methods were unorthodox at times. He never would have believed that hay bale horse rides and roping lessons could make such a difference, but Luke couldn't get enough of either.

His son's willingness to practice roping was impressive. He had a real knack for it.

Spencer smiled. That wasn't the case with Tess. While her tenacity was inspiring, her aim was anything but. She had yet to lasso a single thing. If she didn't bristle whenever he offered a suggestion, he could help her, but she'd been pricklier than a pincushion cactus the few times he'd tried.

When she'd first come, he hadn't known what to make of her, but she'd carved a place for herself. He no longer dreaded going home at night because she'd be there, adding spice to his meals as well as his life. Having her beside him at the table each evening filling the chair that had been empty all those months made things not only bearable but pleasant, too.

A knock at the door roused him from his musings. "Enter."

His ticket agent held out a telegram. "For you, sir. From Mr. Walker."

At last some news about his bull. "Thanks, Drake." He left, and Spencer scanned the few lines. Delayed again. He wadded the telegram and hurled it across the room.

How frustrating to be forced to wait three more weeks for the delivery when everything in him cried out to move forward. Trudy was gone, but he didn't have to abandon his plan. He'd take the next step. Now.

He shoved his arms into his frock coat, donned his top hat and found Peter.

"It's no trouble for me to see to things, Spence, but it's not like you to leave early. There's nothing wrong, is there?"

"Everything's fine. I just need to tend to something."

Peter removed his well-worn derby and mopped his brow with a bandanna. "Go on, then."

Spencer covered the mile to the Mueller's place in no time.

"*Hallo*, Herr Abbott. Ve haf you since long time not see. *Wie geht's?*"

Frank had taught Spencer the phrase, so he knew how to answer. "It goes well."

Herr Mueller shook his head. "*Nein, mein Freund.* Your heart is not well. I see in your eyes. You miss your Frau much. *Ja?* Come."

Spencer followed him inside, where Herr Mueller pointed to a painting of a dimple-cheeked woman. "Katrin. She was my *alles*. How you say it?"

"All? Everything?"

"*Ja.* My everything."

Frank burst into the cabin. "Vati, I finished the—

Mr. Abbott. I didn't know you were here. It's good to see you."

Spencer appreciated the interruption. While Herr Mueller was a hard worker, talking to him could be a challenge. Spencer waited while the older man spoke to his son in rapid German.

Frank translated. "Vati wants you to know how sorry he is about the loss of your wife and that he understands how difficult it must be for you now. He wants to know if he can do anything to help."

"As a matter of fact, that's why I've come. I'd like to hire the two of you to build a bunkhouse. If you're available that is." Spencer explained what he had in mind.

Frank filled his father in, and Herr Mueller nodded. "*Ja*. Ve can a bunkhouse build."

"Good. When can you start?"

Frank conferred with his father. "The day after tomorrow. He thinks it will take us about four weeks to complete the job. We'll come before you leave for the station, so you can show us where you'd like it."

Spencer left feeling more optimistic than he had in a long time. One month from now he'd have a bunkhouse and a bull. It was a beginning.

Woof greeted him as he neared the house, his dog's tail wagging wildly. Lila's charming chatter came from the backyard.

"Higher," Luke hollered.

Tess laughed. "I'm going as high as I can."

"You gotta move your legs like I showed you."

Curiosity drove Spencer forward. He skirted the house and stopped, leaning against the porch railing. Tess and Luke didn't notice his arrival.

She was in the swing. It was easy to see why Luke was giving her directions. She was barely moving. From what he knew of her, she was letting his son teach her— or think he was—in order to make him feel important.

"No!" Luke bellowed. "Not like that. You gotta run and jump on the seat to get going like I done. Then you pump."

"I'll try." She did, landing on the plank with a thud and moving her legs forward and back. Because of the proliferation of petticoats Spencer couldn't be sure, but it didn't look like she had the proper rhythm to gather momentum.

"You're not doing it right." Luke threw his hands in the air and stormed off.

"I'm sorry. Come back." He didn't stop. "All right. Fine." She hopped out of the swing and caught up to him.

"Go 'way."

"Not until you listen to me. I want to learn, Luke. Really I do."

"You're dumb."

She recoiled and spoke more sharply than normal. "That's unkind and uncalled for. I didn't have a swi— I didn't get to play much when I was young."

Spencer had heard enough. "She's right, son. That's no way to talk to her."

"Papa!" Luke flew at him full tilt and grabbed him around the waist.

"Whoa there, my boy. You about bowled me over."

Luke tugged on Spencer's arm. "C'mon. I wanna show you something."

Tess stopped at a blanket spread in the shade to pick up Lila, who held her arms out to Spencer and whimpered. "You're home early, but as you can see, your children are delighted. Here's your darling girl." She handed Lila to him, and he had no choice but to take her.

"I have things to tend to." He had plans to draw and a lumber order to calculate.

Tess nodded excitedly. "Yes. Very important things. Wait until you see what Luke can do."

That wasn't what he meant, and he was sure Tess knew it. The sooner he got this over with, the better.

Spencer trooped after her and ended up in front of the barn. Luke held his lariat. He stepped back, got into position, swung and missed. Undaunted, he tried again and dropped his loop over the sack.

Fatherly pride filled Spencer. "Why, look at that. You did it."

"I been practicing. She has, too—" Luke aimed a smug smile at Tess "—but she can't rope nothing."

"Not yet, but I will," Tess countered. "You'll see."

Luke wouldn't give up. "You can't even swing, and anybody can do that."

"What did I tell you about talking to Tess like that, son? Say you're sorry."

He mumbled an apology.

Tess took her time responding. When she did, sadness tinged her reply. "I didn't have a fine family like yours, Luke." She rested a hand on his shoulder, but he shrugged it off. "You're doing a good job roping. Why don't you show your papa how many times you can get the loop over the sack while I see to supper?"

Spencer almost stopped her but thought better of it. Although he was curious about her comment, it wasn't his place to pry into her past. For some reason, though, he wanted to ease her pain. He knew just what to do.

Tess changed Lila into her nightclothes and prepared to cajole Luke into putting on his, as well. He'd been having such a good time doing some more roping with his father after supper that he'd made a fuss when she said it was time to come inside.

She entered his room, but he wasn't there. A quick check under the bed and in his wardrobe and toy chest showed he hadn't hidden from her. When her search of the rest of the house proved fruitless, she laid Lila in her crib and headed outside. The sun hung low on the horizon, preparing to bid the day farewell.

Luke wasn't on their makeshift horses, on the swing or in front of the barn where he practiced his roping. Perhaps he was inside. She slipped though the open door. The scents of animals, straw and leather mingled with the sounds of the horses shifting in their stalls to create an earthy atmosphere that might tempt Luke, since he was enamored of the outdoors.

Tess scoured the barn, even climbing into the loft, and yet she found no sign of the wayward boy. For that matter, Spencer was missing, too. If they were together, he should have told her he was taking his son.

She stepped into the yard, scanned the area, spied Spencer kneeling on the far side of the pen and tromped through the dried bunchgrass. "Have you seen Luke?"

Spencer stood, folded a hastily drawn diagram and stuffed it in his waistcoat pocket. "I thought he was in the house with you."

"He's not there, in the yard or in the barn. I'm getting a little concerned."

A dog barked in the distance, and they turned their heads simultaneously. Luke was far afield trotting after Woof and swinging his rope.

Tess shook her head. "Well, grease my griddle. He's trying to lasso the poor dog."

Spencer chuckled.

He was enjoying this? While the sight was amusing, he didn't have to keep the adventurous lad out of harm's way day after day. "You mustn't laugh. We can't encourage him. We have to be firm."

"So we do." He stuck two fingers in his mouth and produced a loud whistle. Woof bounded over to Spencer with Luke right behind.

Tess opened her mouth to scold the fun-loving boy, but Spencer spoke before she could.

"I'll handle this." He leaned over, placed his hands on his knees and addressed his son in a commanding but controlled manner. "You know better than to run off like that, Luke. You're to do as Tess says, and you're not to try roping Woof again. Do you understand?"

Luke nodded. "Yes, Papa. I'm sorry."

"Good. Now go with Tess. She'll put you to bed."

"But you'll be in to sing, right?"

Tess rested a hand on Luke's shoulder. "Of course he will."

Spencer shook his head. "Not tonight. Since Luke disobeyed, I won't be singing to him."

"But, Papa—"

"You heard me, son. Go on. I've got work to do." He returned his attention to his project.

Tess accompanied the disappointed boy, as was her duty, but what she really wanted was to question Spencer's decision. When someone let a child down, they didn't forget. Ever. She'd have to make that clear to Spencer.

She tucked Luke in and offered to sing in place of his father, but as expected, the sullen boy refused. "I don't want nobody but him. You can go 'way."

The sight of his sorrow-filled eyes and trembling chin, which he attempted to hide by facing the wall, squeezed her chest. She'd spent many nights as a young girl quelling her loneliness as thoughts of her father swirled in her head. She used to lie in the dark making up stories in an attempt to block her persistent longings. Only when she accepted the fact that he wasn't coming back for her had she been able to regain control.

Control was what she needed now, or she was likely to snap at Spencer. How could he hurt this precious, precocious boy? Luke hadn't meant to misbehave. His curiosity had just gotten the best of him.

He yawned. Within minutes he nodded off.

Tess returned to the site where Spencer was working. He'd marked off three sides of a good-size rectangle using stakes and twine. "The children are asleep, and we need to talk. I don't believe I made myself clear earlier. I asked you to be firm, but I didn't mean for you to deny Luke his bedtime ritual."

"He'll be fine." He stooped and stretched twine along the final side of the figure.

She chose her words with care. "A child counts on certain things and has every right to do so. You hurt Luke."

Spencer straightened. "He has to learn that there are consequences for his actions. Sometimes denying him what he wants is an effective deterrent. My housekeeper taught me that." He smiled.

How could he use her words against her? "This isn't the same. Not allowing him to eat at the table is one thing, but not singing to him seems a bit…harsh."

"One night without his song won't hurt him that much, but it might make him think twice about running off next time."

She had to make him understand. "You didn't see his tear-stained cheeks or hear his muffled sobs."

Spencer studied his string-framed figure. "I've witnessed them before and will again, but knowing Luke, he'll greet us with his impish grin at breakfast."

"Perhaps." What he said made sense, but she couldn't drop the matter without a final attempt to make her point. "I feel it's my duty to tell you when your child is…is aching. If you prefer not to be told such things, it's best I know now."

He continued staring at the marked-off plot of land but said nothing.

She counted to ten under her breath, and yet he'd still not spoken. "Fine. The month's trial is up today. I'll get my things and go—as soon as you give me my pay packet."

Spencer spun around. "Go? No! I need you. I mean, I need a housekeeper, and you're doing a fine job. I have no complaints."

Hope planted itself deep inside and grew until she couldn't stop herself from smiling. "You want me to stay? Permanently? But what about my concern?"

"You're right, Tess. It is your job to tell me how my children are doing, but you can trust me to do right by them. I would never let any harm come to Luke or Lila."

His assurances rang true and calmed her fears.

Spencer was a good father, the kind every child deserved.

"Even though their mother is gone, I'll do my utmost to let them know they're loved." He winced at his mention of his late wife.

Tess placed a hand on his arm and pulled it back, aghast. "I'm sorry."

He rubbed his arm where her hand had been and gazed at a lone hill on the back of his property. "Today was a trying day. It's been four months since I lost her. I thought it was supposed to get easier."

She ached to see him in such pain but was certain he wouldn't appreciate her sympathy any more than he had her touch. A matter-of-fact approach seemed a wiser choice. "It does, but it takes time."

He tossed the spool of twine in his toolbox. "You sound like someone who's experienced loss."

More than he could ever imagine. "I have. That's why I want to help. I know what Luke's going through."

"A parent perhaps?"

His perceptiveness surprised her. "How did you know?"

He scuffed the toe of his boot in the dirt, looking so boyish she had the urge to hug him. "I saw you on the swing earlier and heard some of what you told Luke."

"Oh, yes. You did, didn't you? I'm sure I looked anything but ladylike."

"I won't tell anyone." His radiant smile turned her knees to applesauce. Not the response a housekeeper was supposed to have, but no matter how hard she tried not to take notice of her employer, she couldn't help herself. If only he weren't so handsome or so endearing. She stooped and picked up Luke's rope to keep Spencer from seeing the color sure to be staining her cheeks.

"If you'd like to learn how to swing, I can teach you."

She spun around. "Really? I mean, yes, I'd like that." Very much.

He grabbed the pail filled with his supplies, led the way to the backyard and had her sit on the swing. "I'm going to give you a push to get you started. Get a good grip on the ropes."

She did. He grabbed the wooden seat, pulled it back toward him and let her go, sending her soaring. The swing reversed course, returning her to where he stood. He placed his hands on the small of her back, shoving her forward again. The wind whipped her skirts and fluttered the loose tendrils at her temples.

When the swing was out of his reach, he stopped pushing and stood to the side in her line of vision. "Now lean back a little and extend your legs toward the house when you go forward. Lean forward and tuck them under the seat when you go back."

By following his instructions, she got the swing to go higher and higher until she could see the barn over the roof of the house. She ceased pumping her legs and reveled in the sensation of flying through the air as free as a bird.

As much as she'd like to stay longer and enjoy Spencer's company, she let the swing slow. "I can see why Luke likes swinging so much. It's fun. But I should be going. I've stayed later than usual, and it'll be dark soon."

"Allow me." He grabbed the ropes, brought the swing to a stop and helped her to her feet. His gaze roamed over her face. There was no sign of a frown on his.

She said nothing, unwilling to shatter the mood. He'd actually alluded to his grief for the first time. And he'd taught her to swing.

At the moment he was looking at her as though he saw her as a person—not just a domestic fulfilling her duties—and seemed pleased with what he saw. She was certainly aware of him. Decidedly so. She should do something. But she couldn't move if she tried, content to savor the sweetness of the moment.

He released the swing, and it bounced behind her. "I almost forgot to tell you. The Muellers will be over in the morning to start work on a bunkhouse. That's what I was marking. I'll need you to fix enough to feed them while they're here."

So much for the mood. He'd smashed it to smithereens, but that was a good thing. She had no right thinking fanciful thoughts about him anyhow. She'd passed his test, and she would do her best to ensure that he had no reason to regret hiring her.

Chapter Ten

"You may pick out ten gumdrops, Luke." Tess reread her list while the owner of the general store assisted him. Mr. Hawkes had added all the household items on it to the crates. He carried them to the waiting wagon and returned.

Now to see to her special purchase. Since her position with Spencer was secure, she could afford to treat herself. She shifted Lila from one hip to the other. "I'm interested in getting a new fragrance, but I don't want anything smelling remotely like roses. What might you have?"

"Let me see." The kindly proprietor reached into a display case and withdrew three stoppered bottles. He opened the first and invited her to inhale.

She wrinkled her nose at the musky fragrance. "I'm not partial to heavy scents."

"See what you think of these." He held the other bottles for her one by one so she could sniff the contents, but neither scent suited her.

"I'm not after anything woody or spicy, either. I'd like something fresh and light."

Mr. Hawkes smiled. "I have just the thing, but I must warn you. It costs a pretty penny." He withdrew a dome-shaped bottle covered with gold-painted bees and an emblem bearing crossed swords. Placing one hand beneath the stunning creation and the other behind, he presented it with flair. "This is *Eau de Cologne Imperial* by Guerlain, imported directly from France and used by Empress Eugénie as well as Queen Victoria and Queen Isabella—or so the vendor told me."

"It's beautiful." The bottle itself was a work of art, but she wasn't one to be taken in by fancy packaging. "What does it smell like?"

"You can be the judge." He removed the stopper.

Tess took a whiff. She had to have the citrus cologne, one so gloriously sparkling and bright she couldn't resist, no matter the cost. "How much is it?"

Mr. Hawkes lowered his voice and said the price almost apologetically. She did her best not to flinch. Never in her life had she spent the better part of a month's salary on a single luxury item, but this would be her present to herself. A woman deserved something special for her twenty-fifth birthday—especially when she didn't have a husband to buy her fine things. "I'll take it."

The cologne would provide a sharp contrast to the rosewater she'd worn before. Its crisp, clean scent was suitable for a housekeeper and shouldn't raise any eyebrows—as long as no one knew how much she'd paid for it.

Luke tromped over and tugged on Tess's skirt. "I got all black gumdrops. Know why?"

"Because you like the taste of licorice?"

He gave his head a sound shake. "Because they turn my tongue black."

"That they will."

The proprietor completed the sale. Tess took the children—and her precious package—to the wagon.

"Wuke!"

The childish squeal drew her attention. Abby pointed at Luke and tugged on her mother's hand, urging Polly forward. Tess's friend plodded along, looking fatigued. The hot August days would be hard on a woman in her condition.

Polly reached Tess, grasped the side of the wagon and blew out a breath. "While I prefer the dry heat of California to the humid summers back in Baltimore, this is not the time of year to be great with child."

"I'd be happy to carry a child anytime, but I agree with you about the humidity. I don't miss it one bit."

"You don't miss anything from those days, do you? I still remember your excitement on our final Sunday in Maryland when we sat in our favorite pew at church and you told me you'd found a job out west, too. You were so excited. By the time we boarded the ship the following Wednesday you were downright giddy. I dreaded leaving my friends and relatives, but you couldn't wait to get underway."

Tess didn't care to revisit her dismal childhood. "I had an opportunity to make a life for myself, and I embraced it. Things have worked out well for me."

"And for me, too. You're here in Shingle Springs now, and I can wish you a happy birthday in person. I have a little something for you." Polly held out a package.

She removed the tissue paper and smiled when she

saw the embroidered handkerchief bearing the verse from Proverbs she and Polly had chosen as theirs years ago, "A friend loveth at all times." Tess hugged Polly. "It's lovely. Thank you."

"If I weren't as big as a barn and slow as an ox, I'd have done more to make the day special for you. You should have a birthday cake at the very least."

Tess grinned. "I made myself one. Chocolate with chocolate frosting."

"Mmm. Chocolate cake. The best kind."

Luke clamored for Tess's attention. She sat him beside Abby on one of two benches in front of the shop and gave each of them three gumdrops—along with a challenge to see how long they could make the candies last, thus buying her some time with her friend. She had to know what Polly thought of her latest idea.

The women settled on the other bench. Polly didn't give Tess a chance to say a thing before she peppered her with questions. "I know you, Tessie. You've got something on your mind. Does it involve a certain stationmaster? Is Spencer in for another surprise?

"When I cleared out Trudy's things, I found some letters the two of them had exchanged. It appears they were written when he was courting her."

Polly eyed Tess with curiosity. "Does he know?"

"I told him. He said he didn't want to see them ever again and that I could hide them somewhere."

"Did you read them?"

"I was tempted to, but that would be wrong. I didn't know what to do with them—until now."

"Go on." Polly's enthusiasm was encouraging.

"He told me his wife had intended to make a quilt for their bed. But she was taken from him before she'd even begun. Since I love to sew, I can make that quilt for him myself. Not just any quilt. One to honor Trudy. I'll use the Double *T* pattern. I plan to make the *T*s out of red fabric from her dresses and mount them on a white background."

"I'm sure he'd be thrilled to have such a special remembrance, but what's that got to do with the letters?"

"I've heard women sometimes use paper as batting material when fabric's scare. Newspapers, catalogs and…letters. Although I would only have enough sheets of stationery to add two or three to each of the blocks, their words would be preserved this way, but he wouldn't have to see them."

Polly's round face creased in confusion. "But if you put the letters inside the quilt, you'd have to take them out of the envelopes."

"I'd turn the pages over, so I wouldn't see the words." Tess heaved a wistful sigh. Trudy had been blessed to find a man who enjoyed writing. "The letters he wrote to her are nice and thick. He must be a prolific writer."

Polly laughed. "Spencer? The man who won't use two words if one will do?"

Tess recalled the conversation they'd had the evening he taught her to swing. "He does talk when he has something to say, but it seems putting things on paper comes more easily to him. If only I could get him to tell me about his loss…"

Eagerness lit Polly's green eyes. "I have an idea."

"Do tell."

"I learned the hard way when Peter was courting me that a woman can't force a man to discuss his feelings, but I think you could get Spencer talking if you try.

You need to find something he's interested in and start with that. In time he'll feel more comfortable opening up to you."

Tess bounced Lila on her knees and enjoyed the resulting smiles. "Do you think that would work?"

"It did with Peter. Once I wised up, I asked him what it was like to work at the depot in Sacramento City. He loves the railroad and spent hours telling me everything he knew. Although he was only a baggage handler in those days, he got permission to give me a tour of the railway station."

"That must have been exciting."

Polly sighed dreamily. "It was. Peter introduced me to everyone. To hear him talk, you would have thought I was a princess and not a lowly governess. I knew then that if he asked for my hand, I'd say yes. But enough about me. If you were to ask Spencer what it's like to be stationmaster, you might be able get the words flowing."

"Perhaps." Tess couldn't wait to give it a try, although she wouldn't ask him about his job. He didn't seem all that interested in it, but she knew what made him come to life.

Where were they? Tess held her journal over the bed in her room at the boardinghouse that night and shook it. A shower of ticket stubs, theater programs and other memorabilia rained on the coverlet. She rummaged through the pile of papers, but the letters she'd written to her imaginary fiancé weren't there.

That was odd. She distinctly remembered seeing them shortly before boarding the train bound for Shingle Springs. The ribbon around them had slipped off.

She'd tied it again, reached into her satchel and tucked the packet inside the back cover of her journal. At least she thought she had.

Perhaps she'd misjudged and the letters had gotten wedged between her magazines and Bible. Considering how many times she'd swapped her reading material while waiting to board, she might have pulled out the packet by mistake and dropped it. No doubt someone had found the letters and tossed them in the dustbin.

Oh, well. They'd been fanciful musings anyhow. She was better off without them. Penning sentimental missives was for poets and romantics, not levelheaded housekeepers.

Although she couldn't perform her annual ritual of rereading the letters she'd written on her previous birthdays, this birthday had been memorable. She'd enjoyed her visit with Polly, even if it was brief. Sharing her cake with Spencer and the children had been fun, too. Not that she'd told them it was her birthday. It was hard enough reaching her twenty-fifth year and knowing that, unless the Lord decided to answer her prayers for a family of her own, she was destined to spinsterhood.

The best part of the day was the time she'd spent with Spencer after they'd put the children to bed. Due to the long summer days, she could leave later than usual and have plenty of daylight for her walk back to the boardinghouse, so she'd taken advantage of that. By following Polly's advice, Tess had been able to get him talking.

She'd asked him to tell her about his earliest roping lessons. Watching his face light up as he'd leaned against the column at the top of the front steps and recalled a memorable time from his childhood had been an unexpected gift. He'd given her one of his too-rare smiles, the kind that transformed him from attractive to breathtakingly handsome, and launched into a tale of good-natured rivalry as his three-year-old self had attempted to best his older brother. He'd actually laughed—a genuine laugh that really got air into his lungs—as he recounted the day when he, at the tender age of five, had succeeded in roping a calf on his father's cattle ranch before his brother, who had two years on him.

Although Spencer had stopped after ten short but delightful minutes, saying he shouldn't keep her, it was a start. If she bided her time and waited for other such openings, perhaps he would grow more comfortable and move beyond childhood recollections. She could hope.

Yes. She *could* hope. Even though she'd marked another birthday, she didn't have to give up on her dream of having a family of her own to love and care for. Not every woman was wed by the time she was twenty-five. The Lord knew how much love was inside her ready to be poured out, so surely He had someone in mind for her.

Diving into her trunk, she found her writing supplies. She squeezed herself under the tiny dressing table and dipped her pen in the inkwell. The nib scratched across the blue-bordered stationery as she poured her heart on the page.

Monday, August 20, 1866

To the man I look forward to marrying…

Chapter Eleven

Tess left the general store, her shopping complete, and set out for Polly's place.

"Papa." Lila pointed at her father, who was headed straight for them.

Spencer dashed between two wagons rumbling past and doffed his top hat to Tess. "Where's Luke?"

"He's with Polly. She offered to watch him so I could get the grocery order filled more quickly."

"That's good, since the Muellers will be expecting their dinner shortly."

He didn't really think she'd forgotten, did he? Frank and his father had spent the past week working on the new bunkhouse Spencer had staked out, and she'd been feeding the two of them three meals a day right on schedule. "I got everything ready for dinner before I left the house and will return in plenty of time to serve it."

"Of course you will. How are things going? Did they get started on the west wall as expected?"

"Yes. Why? Is there a problem?"

He ran a finger under the stand-up wing collar of his white shirt. "Just keeping tabs on things."

"You seem a bit restless. Is there something you wanted to tell me?"

Leaning toward her, he sniffed. "You're wearing a new perfume. It's lemony. I like it."

He'd noticed. How nice. That eased her regrets regarding her impulsive purchase. "I appreciate the compliment, but surely you didn't leave your job and rush across the street to discuss my choice of fragrance."

"I, um…" He closed his eyes and scrunched his face in a gesture so like Luke's she couldn't keep from chuckling. His eyes flew open, a flash of something akin to hurt in them.

"I'm sorry I laughed. I—"

"How are you at giving haircuts?"

"What? You want *me* to cut your hair?" He could use a trim in the worst way, but why had he asked her?

"I received an unexpected summons to a meeting at the rail station down in Folsom tomorrow, and I can't go looking like a scarecrow. I thought, with all your skills, you might have given a cut or two."

"I have, but…" She'd trimmed more heads of hair at the orphanage than she cared to remember, but they'd belonged to young boys and to Mr. Grimsby, who was old enough to be her father. Not to her golden-haired twenty-eight-year-old employer. How could she perform such an intimate service for Spencer? She'd have to touch him, and she wasn't sure he was ready for that—or if she was.

He held up his hands in the surrender pose and took a step back. "I can see by the shocked look on your face that I've asked too much."

She swallowed and hoped her voice wouldn't come

out of her constricted throat as a squeak. "Couldn't you go to a barber?"

"I suppose so. It's just that Tru— that I always had it cut at home. Forget I asked."

He spun around and left without another word, but not before Tess spotted sadness in his eyes.

"Spencer, wait." She was sure to regret her hasty decision, but she couldn't let him think she didn't care. Not when she did, far more than she should. "I'll do it."

His stop was so abrupt it was a wonder he didn't stumble. He returned and stood before her, relief apparent in every line of his handsome face. "If you're sure."

She was anything but. "Quite sure."

"Will you charge me?"

Was he serious? She tilted her head. Lila mirrored the motion, giving Tess an idea how she could lighten the mood. "Did you hear your papa, Lila? He thinks he has to pay me extra for a haircut, something that will take all of ten minutes—provided he sits still and does what I tell him."

"Papa." Lila twisted in Tess's arms and reached out to him.

He brushed his daughter's cheek with the back of his hand. "I have to go to work, princess, but I'll see you tonight." He shifted his gaze to Tess. "And I'll see you, too, with your shears at the ready. Yes?"

She nodded.

"That's settled, then." The lingering look he gave her, filled with gratitude he couldn't put into words, eased her earlier misgivings. Spencer had given her an opening. While asking her to cut his hair wasn't the same as sharing his feelings with her, he had come to her with his request. That was promising.

* * *

Tess dried the last of the supper dishes and put them away. She hadn't been thinking straight when she'd agreed to this. Caring for Spencer's children and his house was one thing. Cutting his hair was another. If only she didn't have such a soft spot for hurting souls. One look into his sorrow-filled eyes was all it had taken to override her usual good sense.

Luke burst into the room. "Papa's waiting out front for his haircut."

She was all too aware of that fact. "Please tell him I'll be there soon."

The energetic boy raced out of the kitchen. She gave it a final look, making sure everything was ready for the following morning. The bowl, wooden spoon and dry ingredients for the flapjacks she'd planned sat on the table Spencer had raised for her. Satisfied, she hung her apron on its peg and went upstairs.

She collected the shears, comb and hand mirror from Spencer's bureau and a sheet from the cedar chest. With steps slower than a gout-riddled old woman's, she descended the stairs. "You can do this. It's just a haircut like any other."

Who was she fooling? Although Spencer was her employer, he was also a man. A handsome man with a head of beautiful blond hair she'd soon be snipping.

She stopped on the bottom landing, clutched the things she carried in her left arm and held out her right hand. Trembling, as she'd expected.

By flexing and straightening her fingers several times, she brought an end to the shaking. If only she could calm her quaking nerves as easily.

She crossed the foyer and stood in the doorway.

Lila saw her and scampered across the porch. The baby hadn't been crawling long, but she could cover ground. Craning her neck, she looked up at Tess. "Eff."

Tess wanted to believe the darling girl had attempted to say her name, so she pointed at herself and said it. "Eff."

Yes. Lila *was* trying to say *Tess*. How wonderful.

Tess set the items in one of the rocking chairs, hugged Lila to her and kissed each of the baby's cheeks. The little girl patted Tess's face and said her name one more time.

Luke laughed. "*F?* That's not right, Lila. You gotta start with *A, B, C.*"

"She's not old enough to say the alphabet, Luke. She's trying to say my name, but she can't make the *T* or *S* sounds yet, so it sounds like *F.*"

"That's dumb."

Spencer leaned back against the porch railing, his characteristic frown in place. "What did I tell you about using that word, son?"

"Not to say it."

Tess decided to see if she could get Luke to use her name. "You could help your sister by saying my name for her."

The hardheaded boy acted as though he hadn't heard her. He ran down the steps and threw a stick for Woof to chase instead, which was not surprising. Whenever Luke referred to her, he used *she* or *her*. She tried not to let it bother her, but it would be nice if he called her by name on occasion.

"If I can pry my lovely daughter out of your hands, Tess, I'd like you to begin, so you can finish before the sun goes down."

Clearly Spencer wasn't going to echo her suggestion. He probably hadn't even noticed Luke's obstinate refusal to call her by name. Oh, well. She had more important things to deal with. Such as giving Spencer his haircut. "By all means." She handed him his little girl.

Spencer set Lila in a large washtub with her blocks. They would have to put up with her banging them against the side from time to time, but at least the now-mobile toddler wouldn't be in danger of tumbling down the stairs.

"If you'll take a seat, I'll get started." Tess pointed to the dining room chair she'd carried out earlier.

She stood behind him, took a deep breath and prepared to tuck his collar inside his chambray shirt. No sooner had she touched his neck than he shuddered. She jerked her hands back.

"I'm s-s-sorry," he spluttered. "It's all right. Go on."

Evidently he was as jumpy as she, if not more so. Perhaps if she focused on making him comfortable, her uneasiness would lessen. "I just need to get your collar out of the way, and then I'll cover you with the sheet."

Those tasks completed, she braced herself for the next one. "I'm going to, um, run my fingers through your hair to gauge its thickness."

"Do what you need to." He sat as rigid as a broom handle.

Tess lifted her gaze heavenward. *Lord, help me through this.*

The sooner she began, the sooner the ordeal would be over. She dove her hand into his hair and lifted a hank of it between her fingers. Habit took over, and her nervousness eased. "It looks like you need a good two inches taken off if you want it up over your ears."

"Fine."

His blond hair was thick and healthy. The only things she had to watch out for were the cowlick on top and that lovely wave over his right eye. The rest would be easy. She set to work.

Birds joined in a jubilant chorus as the sun sank lower. Luke shouted to Woof, while Lila occupied herself clapping blocks together. Spencer maintained his customary silence.

As the cut progressed, the tension in his neck and shoulders eased, and his breathing grew slow and deep. Something resembling a sigh escaped him. Tess leaned to the side to get a glimpse of his face. His eyes were closed, and his features relaxed. He'd never looked as at peace as he did at that moment.

He turned toward her. "You're not finished already, are you?"

How interesting. He sounded disappointed. She was almost done, but it wouldn't hurt to make sure she hadn't missed anything.

A profound sense of pleasure enveloped her as she lifted one section of his satiny hair after another between her fingers and clipped the few strands that were longer than the others. She'd found a way to minister to him. Surely the Lord wouldn't mind if her act of service brought her enjoyment, would He?

Moving to the front, she prepared to trim the portion at Spencer's temples and urged him to keep his eyes closed. Looking into the brilliant blue depths would be her undoing.

When the cut was nearly complete, she squatted so they were face-to-face and examined the sections over his ears to check for uniformity. Just right. She brushed loose hairs off his forehead with her fingertips.

His eyes flew open, his gaze locking with hers. Pleased with her efforts, she smiled, receiving a subtle lifting of his lips in return.

A flush rushed up his neck and flooded his cheeks with color. Oh, bother. Things had been going so well. How sad to have embarrassed him right at the end.

Doing her utmost to maintain a professional demeanor, she handed him the mirror, not realizing her mistake until it was too late. He wouldn't want to see his face so red. Apparently she was right because he laid the mirror in his lap, reached behind his head and fiddled with the knot she'd tied in the sheet. Rather than rushing to help, she busied herself sweeping up the golden locks littering the porch, allowing time for his blush to subside.

Once he'd freed himself, he gathered the sheet by the corners, flung the contents into the yard and returned to the porch, where he examined the cut in the mirror. "It looks good. Thank you."

Coming from him, that was glowing praise. Tess schooled her features. "If you'd prefer to visit the barber in the future, I understand."

"That won't be necessary. I'm happy with the cut."

"I thought… It seemed you were…" Why was talking to him so difficult? Words didn't usually fail her.

"I like having my hair cut. I was used to Trudy doing it. That's all." He folded the sheet in a perfect square, set it on the chair he'd vacated, lifted Lila into his arms and strode out to where Luke romped with Woof.

Tess bit back a sigh. Evidently Spencer was eager to

get away for her. She gathered the supplies, took a lingering look at the heartwarming scene and went inside.

God knew the desires of her heart. Although it did no good to dwell on hers, she couldn't deny her dream of having a family. If only she had one like Spencer's, she'd be a very happy woman.

Chapter Twelve

As soon as Spencer arrived at his place, he went directly to the bunkhouse. The invigorating scent of freshly cut pine greeted him. Although the Muellers had only been working on the project two weeks, the structure itself was finished and the roof on. The bunks and kitchen area were all that remained. As hard and fast as the father-son team worked, they'd be done in another day or two.

Spencer stooped to pick up a claw hammer and placed it in the Muellers' wooden toolbox beside its twin. He'd better hurry and get washed up for supper. The tantalizing aromas he'd smelled when walking past the house promised that he'd soon be enjoying another of Tess's mouth-watering meals.

She could certainly cook. And she gave a mighty fine haircut. Unlike Trudy, who'd hurried through the task, Tess had taken her time. Having her touch him had been awkward at first, but once he'd gotten used to it, he was able to relax—until the end.

Opening his eyes to find her looking into his had startled him. He'd been so busy thinking about his plans for turning his place into a successful cattle ranch that he'd forgotten Tess was the one cutting his hair.

She had a way of making him forget the past and believe in the future again. Perhaps it was her willingness to listen. She'd encouraged him to tell her stories from the early years he'd spent working on his father's cattle ranch, before his father had become such a strict disciplinarian. Spencer couldn't forget the way she'd chuckled when he told her how determined he'd been to best his brother at roping or the smile she'd sent his way when he'd boasted about his first takedown.

He shouldn't have taken such pleasure in another woman's company, let alone her touch. He'd loved Trudy and missed her something fierce. So much so that the emptiness seemed overwhelming at times. He was lonely, which was understandable, but that didn't excuse his traitorous thoughts.

Spencer passed Elmore Dodge's carriage. His neighbor to the west must have arrived shortly after he had. He doffed his hat to the shifty fellow on the driver's seat and went in the house. Animated voices floated into the foyer from the kitchen, a combination of English and German. He set his hat on the shelf and joined the group.

Tess was the first to see him. "Oh, good. You're home. Frank and his father have been occupying the children while I put the finishing touches on supper. Then Mr. Dodge arrived, so we've got quite a houseful tonight. You needn't worry, though. I've made plenty."

Spencer wasn't worried about that. What did concern him was Dodge's unannounced visit. The ruthless cattle rancher didn't come by unless he wanted something. Spencer extended a hand, which Dodge shook far too enthusiastically. "What can I do for you?"

The lanky man bared his gums in an overly wide smile, his top two gold teeth gleaming. Word was he'd lost his real ones in a barroom brawl some years back, but no one knew for sure. All Spencer knew was that a visit from Dodge wasn't a friendly social call.

"Heard in town you've got a bull on the way, and now the Germans are putting up a bunkhouse for you. That true?"

It was none of his business. "The Muellers have been doing some construction work. And a fine job of it, too."

Frank acknowledged the compliment with a nod and leaned over to translate for his father.

Wolfgang's tanned face bore a smile filled with all the warmth Dodge's had lacked. "*Danke schön*. Ve like for you to work."

His son was quick to reword the sentence so it made sense. "Vati's right. We like working for you. You're a fair boss and pay good wages."

"Better watch it, Abbott, or word will get out that you're an easy mark." Dodge thumped Spencer on the back in an overly familiar gesture so unexpected that he had to tamp down his temper. "You wouldn't want all the sauerkraut set heading your way, now would you?"

Tess caught Lila as she scooted past her, propped the baby on her hip and pulled Luke to her side in a protective gesture that stoked Spencer's ire toward Dodge. Evidently she was uncomfortable around the overbearing man. "I'll not have you speaking ill of my guests. State your business, Dodge, and then you can be on your way."

"My business, as you well know, is cattle ranching. I've been in Shingle Springs building my herd for six years, and no greenhorn is going to cut in on my profits. If you know what's good for you, you'll stick to railroading and leave the raising of beef to those of us who know what we're doing."

Frank chimed in. "But Mr. Abbott does know—"

"I know a threat when I hear one." Spencer regretted having to cut the young man off, but the less Dodge knew, the better. "I don't take kindly to them. There's room for all of us, and I have no intention of stopping."

Hours later Spencer stood on the porch after putting Luke and Lila to bed. He gripped the railing and gazed at his land. Tess's footfalls sounded on the foyer floor. She was at his side in seconds. What would she think of his display earlier? Trudy would have been appalled, reminding him that a gentleman didn't give way to his anger and he certainly didn't openly challenge another.

"Your show of force earlier was impressive."

Tess had surprised him once more. Unsure how best to respond, he said nothing.

"Do you think Mr. Dodge will make good on his threat? I wouldn't want anything to happen to the children."

He looked into her eyes. Apprehension filled their brown depths. "In my experience, those who issue threats rarely follow through on them. It's the ones who don't divulge their evil intentions I watch out for. Dodge is all talk."

"I hope that's the case." She perched on the top rail and leaned back against a support column, with one foot on the floor steadying her, the other swinging like a pendulum. She must not realize she was giving him glimpses of her ankle. He dragged his gaze from the alluring sight.

"He has a surprise coming when he finds out you're not a greenhorn. I'm curious. If you enjoy cattle ranching so much, why did you leave Texas and come to California?"

A desire to put as much distance between himself and his father as possible. "The same things that bring most people I suppose. A chance for a fresh start, the abundant land, the climate."

She laughed. "You left out the opportunity to make one's fortune. Isn't that what the Golden State is known for?"

"Many came expecting to get rich, but a man has to work as hard here as anywhere."

"I know. I was teasing you, although I gather you have grand plans for this place. Frank said the bunkhouse could hold twelve men. But how can you run a ranch if you're working at the station? Will you have a foreman handle things?"

"You're full of questions tonight, aren't you?"

She stood, and he followed suit. "Apparently I've asked too many. It's getting late. I'll get my things and be on my way."

"Wait a minute, please."

She stopped. "Yes?"

He would have to broach his plan in a way that would meet with her approval. "I'll be staying in the bunkhouse once it's finished. After I've cleared out my things, you can have my—the extra bedroom."

Her mouth gaped, but she quickly composed herself. "Are you asking if I want to move out here...or telling me I will?"

"I'm offering you a room so you don't have to walk to and from town once it starts getting dark earlier."

She held herself flagpole straight. It seemed she was trying to appear as tall as possible. "Am I to be on duty all day and all night, too?"

He hadn't thought about that, but if she was living in the house, she would be the one to see to the children if they woke in the night. "I could hang an iron triangle out here, and you could ring it if you needed me."

"Give me a moment, please."

She went inside and returned shortly. Her enormous hat added to her height. Determination radiated from her, almost palpable in its intensity. What an impressive woman she was, not to mention attractive. Peter was right. She would turn any man's head. Spencer didn't like to admit it, but she'd turned his.

"I'll consent to live here if you'll agree to my terms. I will prepare dinner on Saturdays and have the rest of those afternoons and evenings off—in addition to my Sundays—but you will not reduce my pay. In fact, since you will no longer have the expense of my room at the boardinghouse, you will increase my salary by one dollar a week to compensate me for the added duty time."

Her requests were reasonable, but perhaps he could get her to accept some other benefits in lieu of increasing her pay. He needed his funds to build his herd. "That's a tall order. Too tall, Tess. Perhaps we could—"

She inhaled sharply.

"What's wrong?"

"I'm sorry. I know what you meant, but hearing those words again…"

He went back over them. "Oh, you mean…?" Someone must've teased her about being tall. That explained a lot of things.

"I thought I was over it, but I can still hear the other children chanting that awful name."

"There's nothing wrong with being tall."

She toyed with a button on her bodice. "Not for you. You're a man. In your case, height is an advantage. It's different for tall women. We're seen as odd or ungainly or even intimidating."

He started to contradict her but stopped. She was right. He'd thought those very things when he first met her. But that was before he knew her. Despite her height, she was a woman like any other. She could be somewhat formidable at times, but she was remarkably agile—except when it came to throwing a rope. He recalled her awkward attempts and smiled.

"You find it funny?"

"I was thinking about how determined you are. The truth is, you stand head and shoulders over other women in many respects, but that's not necessarily a bad thing. Come with me, and I'll show you what I mean."

She eyed him dubiously but followed him into the foyer. He pointed at his Henry repeating rifle resting on its pegs above the front door. "Not that I expect it to happen, but if anyone were to make trouble, you'd be able to reach the gun without having to drag a chair over. That could make a difference at a time when every second counts."

"You expect me to fire that thing? I don't even know how to load it. And look how long it is."

"I keep it loaded, which is why it's mounted well out of reach of the children. Your height would be another advantage when it came to firing it. Holding on to it would be easier for you than for a shorter woman." Trudy had balked at the idea of using his rifle. When he'd forced her to fire it once, she'd ended up on her backside.

Tess wouldn't have a problem. She'd be the master of the gun, not the other way around. He was tempted to ask her to hold it just to see how she'd look.

He didn't have to. She removed the gun, stepped through the open door and sighted down the lengthy barrel, keeping her finger away from the trigger. What a sight she made, both amusing and admirable. It seemed she would attempt just about anything.

She ran a hand over the gleaming stock before passing the gun to him. "This a beautiful piece of workmanship. I certainly hope I never have cause to fire it, although if the children were in danger, I wouldn't hesitate."

"I'm counting on that." He placed the rifle on its pegs and joined her on the porch. They stood side by side, a chorus of crickets and bullfrogs filling the silence that hung heavy between them.

At length she spoke. "Thank you, Spencer."

"For what?"

"For not laughing about the name. For giving up your room for my sake. Most of all, for entrusting me with your children. Does this mean you accept my terms?"

"I do." He never knew what to expect from Tess,

but this was a welcome change. He wouldn't have to deal with the children alone night after night. Perhaps they'd sleep better knowing she was there for them. He certainly would. "You'll be moving out here, then?"

"I will, so if you'll drive your wagon into town tomorrow, I'll have my trunks packed and ready for you to pick up." She descended the stairs and tossed her parting words over her shoulder. "I'll enjoy that extra afternoon off—and the larger pay packet, too."

So much for negotiating with her. Tess was Tess, and she knew how to get her way. Not that he minded as much as he should.

Chapter Thirteen

A rap on his office door rescued Spencer from his search for the error in his tallies.

Peter poked his head inside. "Got a minute?"

"Sure. What do you need?"

"Help solving a mystery." Peter plopped down on the bentwood chair and slapped a packet of papers on Spencer's desk.

"What are those?"

"Letters that were lost on one of the trains a couple months back and made a reappearance today."

"Why bring them to me? Drake's in charge of the lost and found office. Just have him drop them in the mail."

"Can't do that. There are no envelopes and no address."

Spencer shrugged. "Then I guess you'll have to toss them in the burn barrel."

"Can't do that, either. I gave the woman who turned them in my word. Said we'd do what we can to return them to their rightful owner."

"Why would you do that? We're not detectives."

"See for yourself. I took a quick look. These aren't just any letters, as the woman pointed out." Peter shoved the packet toward Spencer.

Curiosity propelled him to slip the top sheaf of stationery out of the blue ribbon binding three sheaves together. He unfolded the crisp white sheets, read the salutation and met Peter's expectant gaze. "They're love letters."

"Sure enough. I reckon the fellow who lost them would like to get them back."

"I agree, but how are we supposed to get them to him without a name or address?" Spencer pinched the bridge of his nose. "Did the woman who gave them to you say anything that might help us find him?"

Peter leaned back in the chair, raising the front legs off the floor. "Not much. She found the letters inside one of her children's picture books that hadn't been opened since their trip to Shingle Springs in July. Her parents gave her children the copy of *Little Bo Peep* to read on their way up the hill. She figures the letters must have accidentally ended up in her basket en route and gotten lodged between the book's pages."

"Do you know where the mother and her children first boarded the train?"

"Sacramento City."

Spencer groaned. "That means the gentleman could have lost his fiancée's letters anywhere along the line. Finding him would be highly unlikely."

"Maybe, but we can't just throw 'em out. They might be all he has to remember her by."

Peter had a point. Letters were often the only ties a fellow had to his lady back home. The fact that this man had still been carrying a letter his intended had written him three years before showed how important it was to him.

If Spencer had lost the letters Trudy sent him during their long-distance courtship, he would have wanted them back. As it was, he'd asked Tess to hide the letters he and Trudy had exchanged. And he had no regrets. A man couldn't cling to the past. He had to go on. "How do you propose we find him?"

"The way I see it, you'll have to read the letters. There might be some clues in them."

"Why me? You're the one who gave your word."

Peter grinned. "You're the one in charge, Cap'n." He grew serious. "The truth is, I don't have time to do any sleuthing. I oversee freight shipments all day. At night I go home to a pregnant wife who's mighty uncomfortable in this heat and needs my help."

Spencer couldn't argue with Peter's logic. He did have more free time than his friend. "I can't read them. They're private."

"What choice do you have? That's the only way to find out who they belong to. I figure the fellow will be so happy to get them back he won't care that you saw them."

Spencer chuckled. "I didn't know you were such a romantic, Peter." He wasn't. His friend would no sooner write a love letter than he would jump in front of a speeding train.

"I'll have you know, I am too romantic," he said with mock indignation. "Polly's been whirling through our place like a tumbleweed in the wind lately, cleaning every nook and cranny, so I gave her a new feather duster. Might not have been the best choice, though, since she went to smack me with it—after rolling her eyes that is." Peter returned the chair legs to the floor with a thump and grinned. He stood and tilted his head toward the letters. "Let me know what you find out."

The sound of Peter's boot heels thudding down the hallway soon ceased. Spencer set the letters aside and studied the numbers that wouldn't balance. He added the columns again but got the same sums as before. He closed the ledger and stared at the beribboned packet.

Somewhere out there a man could be mourning the loss of those letters. Spencer couldn't do anything to change his own situation, but perhaps he could brighten another man's day.

He took the first of the three letters in hand, unfolded the sheets of fine stationery and admired the elegant handwriting of the woman who'd filled several blue-bordered pages. She must be a lady of refinement.

Spencer began reading.

Thursday, August 20, 1863

To the beloved gentleman I look forward to marrying,

As I think of you on this most glorious of summer days, a delightful sense of anticipation envelops me. I'm eager to gaze into your eyes and see my love for you reflected in their depths. After years of dreaming dreams and lifting prayers, I can only imagine how wonderful it will be to have your arms around me, to feel your lips pressed against mine, to become the wife of the man the Lord handpicked for me.

I hope that wherever you find yourself things

are going well for you. God has given you many gifts and talents, and I trust Him to direct your steps as you go about your business. May He bless your endeavors, help you through the dark days we all face at times and draw you ever closer to Him.

The more Spencer read, the more his admiration for this godly woman grew. Her fiancé—or perhaps he was her husband by now—must thank the Lord repeatedly for having brought her into his life. What a gift it would be for a man to have a supportive wife like her who had such unrelenting faith in him and his abilities.

Trudy had tried her best not to complain, but she'd longed for a life of leisure like the one her cattle baron father had provided, which was understandable. She'd spent countless hours in Sacramento City's most highly respected dressmakers' shops.

Memories of those outings assaulted Spencer. Although he'd given his wife all he could afford—and then some—he hadn't succeeded in sating her appetite for fine things or lightening her workload. His failure to put her desires ahead of his own ambitions had cost him dearly.

He shoved his self-recriminating thoughts aside and read the final paragraph of the letter.

As difficult as the waiting can be at times, I cling to the promise in Psalm 37. The Lord knows the desires of our hearts. Mine is to be the wife you deserve, giving my utmost to the task of loving you and any children He grants us the privilege of parenting. Until that glorious day arrives when I take the long-awaited journey down the aisle and we say our vows, know that you are ever in my thoughts and prayers.

With love from Faith

A sense of awe enveloped Spencer. This woman—Faith—was a woman among women. Her kindness, compassion and loyalty leaped from the page. A man with her at his side could accomplish great things. No matter how slim the chances of finding the recipient of this letter after so much time had elapsed, Spencer had to try.

As tempting as it was to read the remaining letters, he had enough information to begin his search, and that's what he'd do. Reading any further would be dishonorable. If and when he met the man this remarkable woman loved, Spencer wanted to be able to look him in the eye.

Minutes later Spencer stood behind Drake and listened to the clicking of his ticket agent's telegraph key. The carefully composed message Spencer had written was on its way to all the stationmasters from Latrobe to Sacramento City.

Please post the following: Seeking male passenger who lost items given him by woman named Faith. Must describe to claim. Direct inquiries to Spencer Abbott, Stationmaster, Shingle Springs.

Drake's tapping ceased. "Deed's done, boss."

"Thanks. Let me know if I get any replies."

Spencer returned to his office and stowed the let-

ters in the back of his deepest, darkest desk drawer.
Flipping open the ledger, he prepared to find the er-
roneous number that had eluded him. If only he could
find the recipient of the letters as easily...

Tess slipped into the pew next to Polly and leaned
over to whisper to her friend. The prelude covered their
hushed conversation. "How are you feeling?"

Polly shifted on the wooden bench. "Pretty good
considering how big I've gotten. My back's been bothering me a bit, though."

"At least you don't have to wait much longer."

"Two weeks if Doc's estimate is correct."

The minister entered, and a hush descended on
the room. Reverend Josephs opened the service in
prayer. An enthusiastic quartet led the congregation
in the singing of two hymns. Tess stood, reveling in
the wealth of voices lifted in praise.

One in particular stood out—the rich baritone belonging to Spencer, who occupied the pew behind her
with Luke and Lila. Tess closed her eyes and concentrated on Spencer's voice, isolating it, savoring it. What
she'd give to be able to sing like that.

The final chord faded, and Reverend Josephs bid
them be seated. Even though he was a mouse of a man
with round-rimmed spectacles, a transformation took
place when he preached. Emboldened by his passion
for the Word of God, he seemed taller, larger and more
compelling. He was such a dynamic speaker that she
hung on his every word, eager to learn all she could
about how to live out her faith day by day.

"Brothers and sisters, members of the flock, our
great Shepherd has given me a message for you today

from the Twenty-third Psalm. A message of hope and healing. A message sure to fill your hearts with a hunger to know Him more deeply and live more fully for Him."

Tess's skin tingled with anticipation. She loved that psalm. She'd spent time in the valley of the shadow of death craving comfort, and the Lord had been there for her. No matter how difficult life at the orphanage had been, she'd clung to the One who would never leave or forsake her. Ever since she'd first learned about God from the French cook, Josette, at the age of seven, Tess had sought solace in His arms, faithfully visiting His house every Sunday morning.

Those precious times of worship had filled her soul and equipped her to endure the endless toil as she tackled the many chores Mr. Grimsby assigned her. Why he'd required more of her than he had the other children was a question she'd never been able to answer. The one time she asked him about the inequity, he'd merely stated that he had her best interests at heart.

If equipping her for a life of service had been his goal, he'd succeeded. Her abundant skills had enabled her to secure employment. Until now, she'd been unable to put all of them to work. These days she was governess and teacher, housekeeper and cook, stable hand and gardener, laundress and seamstress. A wonderful blend that kept life interesting and fulfilling.

Reverend Josephs raised his voice to make a point, rousing Tess from her musings. So powerful was his message about the care given His flock by a loving Shepherd that she was drawn in deeply, her surroundings fading as she focused on the minister's every word.

All too soon the sermon ended. The leader of the

quartet that led the singing addressed the congregation. "We have a treat for you today. Our pianist, Mrs. Brubaker, received a piece of sheet music from her sister in Boston. It's a new hymn that embodies the spirit of our good reverend's sermon called 'He Leadeth Me.' I think you'll blessed by it. We'll sing the first verse and chorus for you once. Then we'll start again, going through all the verses, and you can join us on the refrain if you'd like."

The moving words soaked into Tess's soul. How she longed to let the Lord lead her. If only His plans included a family of her own with a warmhearted husband and precious children to love and care for, she would thank Him every day for the rest of her life. She wouldn't complain if that husband happened to be handsome, too.

The final verse mentioned "death's cold wave," jerking her back to reality. Spencer's wife had been taken from him. How was he feeling, having been reminded of that, first with the talk about death in the sermon and again in the hymn? She couldn't turn around and gawk at him, but the closing prayer was coming.

The final note of the chorus rang out. She waited for the prayer with bated breath. *Forgive me, Lord, but I must know how he's doing.*

As soon as all heads were bowed, Tess grasped her locket with its filigree front and smooth back. She'd bought it years ago on a whim, dreaming of the day it would hold photographs of her children. Today she hoped it could serve as a mirror. If she angled the shiny back just so—

An elbow jabbed her in the side. Polly cast her a questioning look.

Tess smiled and pretended to polish the locket by rubbing it against her bodice. Polly shook her head and bowed it.

Hoping the minister was as generous with his prayer as he'd been the past seven Sundays, Tess held the locket above her shoulder and tilted it to and fro. A ripple of satisfaction shimmied up her spine when Spencer's face came into view. As she'd suspected, his frown was in full force.

Compassion squeezed her heart. He wasn't morose, as she'd first thought. He was just a man in mourning.

Reverend Josephs followed his closing prayer with an impassioned benediction. The congregation filed out of the stuffy sanctuary. Tess stood in a cluster with Peter, Polly and Spencer, who held Lila in his arms. Luke and Abby searched for ladybugs nearby.

Polly cast a longing look at a bench in the shade. "If you gentlemen will give me a few minutes with Tess now, I'll see that you get an extra slice of pie later. I feel the urge to talk about baby booties coming on."

Peter grinned and backed away. "Take all the time you want. Spence and I will watch the children, so you ladies can gab to your hearts' content."

The men moved out of earshot. Polly gazed at her husband with adoration. "He teases me about what he calls 'baby talk,' but he's as excited as the little one as I am. I hope it's a boy. I'd love to give Peter a son who's a red-haired replica of him."

Tess hoped her smile didn't look as halfhearted as it felt. She loved Polly dearly, but witnessing her friend's happiness gave Tess a twinge of jealousy.

Polly rubbed her swollen abdomen and frowned. "What is it?"

"Peter Junior is usually moving around this time of day. Perhaps he's resting after his antics yesterday. He was so active I was convinced he was turning somersaults."

"How do you sleep with all that going on inside you?"

Polly chuckled. "It's not easy, but sometimes fatigue takes over."

"I've always been curious what a birthing is like. How do you feel when you see your child for the first time?"

"Hmm. How can I describe the indescribable?" Polly gazed at the cloudless sky a moment before returning her attention to Tess. "I won't do you any favors if I glamorize things, so I'll be truthful. A birthing is some of the hardest work a woman ever does, but the rewards are far sweeter than any piece of pie. Somehow the memory of the pain fades the instant you gaze into the face of that beautiful baby the Lord's entrusted to your care, replaced by a love so intense it threatens to steal your breath away."

"It sounds wonderful. Not the pain part, but the rest." Tess fidgeted with the fan hanging from her wrist. "Does it matter if a woman's older when she has her first child? Would that make things more difficult?"

"I've known women who didn't wed until they were thirty, and they went on to have children with no trouble at all."

"I have at least five years, then." Although she'd attempted to sound lighthearted, the sympathy filling Polly's eyes told Tess she'd failed.

"My dear Tessie, the Lord has a plan for you. Your job is to trust Him. As it says in that new hymn we sang, He'll lead you. And who knows? Maybe you'll end up with a family right here in Shingle Springs."

Tess shook her head. "I don't see that happening."

"I saw you peeking at Spencer. You obviously care for him."

"Of course I care *about* him, but that doesn't mean I'm harboring foolish notions." She hadn't intended for her voice to have such a sharp edge and softened her tone to match Polly's. "He's my employer—and a grieving widower."

"That gives you a unique opportunity to minister to him. Did you take my advice about engaging him in conversation?"

"I did."

Polly leaned forward expectantly. "And?"

"We've had some good talks about his childhood back in Texas. I've enjoyed them, but…" Her gaze rested on Spencer, who held his adorable daughter in his arms.

"But you're impatient. I understand. You want him to unlock the door to his feelings and let you in. If you take your time, it will happen. Have faith."

"I do."

Polly shifted and rubbed her back. "Spencer might not give you the key to that door as soon as you'd like, but the way I see it, you've made progress. I never expected him to move you out to the ranch. He must trust you wholeheartedly, and that isn't something he does easily. How are things working out? Do you two sit in the parlor after the children are in bed, or does he head to the bunkhouse?"

Tess smiled. Leave it to inquisitive Polly to pepper

her with questions. "I don't know what he does. As soon as we tuck them in, I go to my room."

"Why? Since you want him to open up to you, I thought you'd welcome the opportunity to be alone with him. Or could it be that you're afraid to spend too much time in his company because you care *about* him?"

"I'm not afraid." Tess toyed with the button on her glove. "Although I would enjoy talking with him, I need time to work on the quilt. I can't when Luke's around. He'd be too apt to tell his papa what I'm doing and spoil my surprise. I want to present the quilt to Spencer on the anniversary of his wife's passing. If I'm to have it ready by then, I mustn't tarry."

"If you continue to slip off the minute the day's work is done, he won't see you as anything but a house-keeper. If you want him to confide in you, I suggest you spend a few minutes together before you head to your room. Show him you're interested in him. You *are* in-terested in him, aren't you? Or at least in helping him?"

"Well, yes, but I—"

Polly gasped and clutched her middle.

"What is it?"

"My water just broke!"

Chapter Fourteen

Concern sent tremors through Tess. "The baby's coming? But it's not time yet."

"Obviously the Lord has other plans." Polly winced and drew in a series of shallow breaths.

Tess leaped to her feet. "I'll get Peter."

"Wait!" Polly grabbed Tess's hand. "I believe this is the Lord's timing. It's your day off, so you can stay with me and witness a birth for yourself."

"I couldn't. It's not my place."

"Please, Tessie. I could use a friend to help me through it. I do my best to appear as strong as you are, but inside I'm a quivering mass of jelly."

Tess couldn't resist the plea in Polly's eyes. "I wouldn't be much help, I'm afraid. I don't know the first thing about birthing babies."

"Doc will see to all that. You could bathe my forehead and give me something to focus on besides the pai— besides the work ahead of me."

Compassion and curiosity combined, making it impossible for Tess to decline. "I'll stay, but right now I'm getting Peter."

Twenty minutes later Tess eased Polly's head onto her pillow following a contraction. "It won't be long, and Peter will be back with the doctor."

"I hope so. Things are happening much faster than they did with Abby."

"That's good. It means the work will be over quickly, and then you can see your baby."

Another contraction overtook Polly a minute later, causing her to groan. Tess offered her hand. "Hold on."

Polly did, squeezing so hard Tess gritted her teeth to keep from protesting. She was grateful when the pressure eased and Polly fell back against the mound of pillows.

"Talk to me, Tessie. Tell me something. Anything. How's the quilt coming along?"

"I've cut out the pieces for the *T*s. I decided to use blue fabric from my rag bag for half of them so there's part of me in the quilt. But before I begin sewing the squares, I'm going to make a gown for your baby."

"That's nice."

Tess dabbed Polly's flushed face with a cool cloth. "I know you're convinced you're having a boy, but what if it's a girl? Do you have a name picked out?"

"Peter likes Elizabeth. It was his sister's name. They called her Beth, so we would use Lizzie. Oh!" Polly breathed her way through another contraction, her mouth open and her rigid body hunched forward. The pain subsided, and she relaxed her hold on Tess's hand. "Doc had better get here soon."

Tess did her best to sound convincing. "I'm sure it won't be much longer." *Please, Lord, let that be true.*

Four more contractions seized Polly, the intensity of each increasing and the time between them decreasing, making conversation difficult. As she rested during the brief interval following the latest one, she patted Tess's arm. "I hope I'm not scaring you. It is worth it. You'll see that when the baby arrives."

"Don't worry about me. I'm fine." Tess needed no convincing. She would do anything to have a child of her own, would endure any amount of pain.

The thundering of hooves out front sent waves of relief rippling through her. Peter shouted something indistinguishable to Spencer, who was on the porch watching the children.

"They're here!" Tess's exclamation was drowned out by Polly's sharp cry as another contraction overtook her.

The doctor entered the room, black bag in hand, an air of competence and calm about him. He greeted them warmly, rolled up his shirtsleeves, rinsed his hands in the basin Tess had filled and took his place at the end of the bed. "Let's see what's happening."

Tess sat with her back to him, her attention focused on Polly, murmuring words of comfort while he completed his initial examination.

"I got here just in time, Mrs. Flynn. This baby's ready to join your family."

Tess tingled from head to foot. She was about to behold a newborn baby, one of God's greatest marvels.

The following five minutes passed in a blur as Polly followed the doctor's instructions, clinging to Tess as though she were a lifeline. Never had Tess felt as needed—or as privileged.

"One more push, Mrs. Flynn, and it will all be over," the doctor assured Polly. "You can do it."

Polly bore down, her cheeks turning the color of

ripe cherries, and let out a keening wail like that of a wounded animal. She fell back into the pillows, spent.

Tess turned in time to see the doctor swat the baby's bottom. The little fellow gave a single lusty cry. She inhaled sharply. "You were right, Polly. It's a boy! A strong, healthy boy."

"I knew it." Polly gave a weak smile. "Can I see him?"

"Momentarily." The doctor cut the cord, held out the tiny baby to Tess and inclined his head toward the blanket nearby.

"Me?" Tess pressed a hand to her chest.

"Yes. I need to see to your friend now. Wrap the little fellow and let her hold him while I finish up."

Tess took the squirming newborn in her hands, exercising the utmost care as she followed the doctor's instructions. A profound sense of awe consumed her. The baby was so much smaller than Lila, but he had plenty of hair that was every bit as red as his father's. Polly would be so happy.

"Here's your son." She placed the bundle of wide-eyed boy in his mother's arms.

Tears of joy streamed down Polly's cheeks. "He does look like Peter. Please, get him for me. He needs to see his namesake."

Tess opened the bedroom door and nearly crashed into Peter. He lifted his ashen face. "I heard the baby cry and then nothing."

"Everything's fine. She's asking to see you."

He flew past her. "Poll, are you all right?"

"Very much so. Come see your son."

The happy couple kissed, and Tess sighed. Oh, to be loved like that.

She closed the door behind her and stepped onto the porch, eager to escape the confines of the small house. Standing at the railing, she watched Luke and Abby ride pretend ponies and reveled in the hint of a breeze.

Spencer crossed the yard with Lila in his arms, his little girl busy exploring his features. He dodged a finger aimed at his eye. "How did it go?"

"Polly and her son are both doing well. She's exhausted, but he's alert, looking at everything."

"And how are you?"

"I'm fine."

He raised a brow. "Just fine? You witnessed the wonder of birth, and that's all you have to say?"

"Everything went so quickly. Polly didn't have to suffer very long."

The color drained from Spencer's face. He sank onto the top step and planted a kiss on top of Lila's head. "I—" His voice came out raspy. He cleared his throat. "I'm happy for them. It doesn't always go as well. Sometimes a delivery takes an eternity—and an enormous toll on the mother."

Tess plunked down beside him and rested a hand on his forearm. "You're thinking about your wife, aren't you?"

He glanced at her hand, his expression unreadable, and she removed it. "Lila's birthing went on forever, but that's not something I like to talk about."

She ached for him. "It must have been difficult for you."

Several seconds passed in silence as Spencer stared at his daughter standing in his lap, her tiny hands grasping his fingers. Tess didn't say a word. Didn't move. Didn't even breathe. *Lord, please help him open up. It's clear he's in pain. Talking about it might make things easier for him.*

When at last they came, his words were halting, as though forcing each one out required considerable effort. "Trudy was a small woman and lacked Polly's strength. She labored long and hard with Luke, but that was nothing compared to what she went through with Lila. She came early, and Doc was out of town. I'd helped birth many animals, but this was different. This was my wife and child. If I made a mistake, I knew I'd never be able to live with myself. But I had no choice."

Spencer pulled his daughter toward him and placed a kiss on each cheek. Tess blinked to clear the sudden moisture in her eyes.

He released an audible breath and continued. "Trudy labored eighteen long hours. There was little I could do for her. I'd never felt as helpless or prayed as earnestly as I did then. When Lila finally made her appearance, I saw a foot. She was breech. Fear had me in a choke-hold, but I couldn't give way to it. Her life depended on me getting her out quickly."

"And you succeeded."

"Yes, but I came so close to losing them both that day. Trudy lost a great deal of blood during the delivery, which left her weak." He swallowed, his Adam's apple bobbing. "At least she was with me seven more months before she fell on the tines of a rake and developed an infection she wasn't strong enough to fight. I'm grateful for that."

His concern about using garden tools finally made sense. She felt his pain, but as much as she longed to wrap an arm around him and offer words of comfort, she restrained herself. A man who fought to keep his feelings in check wouldn't welcome an effusive show of sympathy. She focused on Lila instead, tugging the hem of her dress into place. "You saved this precious girl's life, and look how much she loves you."

"Come here, princess." He cradled her to his chest and nuzzled his face in her golden hair.

Sensing his need to be alone, Tess stood and rested a hand on Spencer's shoulder. Not the wisest choice perhaps, but she couldn't help herself. He tensed. She removed her hand and turned to leave. "I should go inside and see what Polly had planned for her Sunday dinner. I'm sure everyone's getting hungry."

"Wait." Spencer should let Tess go, but he couldn't. Not yet.

She spun around. Uncertainty and curiosity waged a battle on her lovely face.

Lovely? Where had that come from? She was attractive, to be sure, but he was still in mourning. He had no right to be admiring another woman.

"Did you want something?"

He cleared his throat. "Forgive me. I didn't mean to blather."

"You didn't. You just gave me some history that helps me better understand your situation." She returned and sat beside him but didn't press him for a response.

How considerate of her not to shower him with sympathy and platitudes. He'd seen the caring and concern in her chocolate-brown eyes, but she wasn't one to let her emotions get the better of her. He admired her self-control, but there were times he wished she wasn't quite as restrained.

Ever since reading the letter Faith had written to her intended, he'd found himself wondering what it would be like to have such a woman in his life. Her way with words spoke to the brokenness that had him in its clutches. He felt certain someone like her would understand and appreciate him.

At times he thought Tess did, but lately she seemed to be holding back. She'd moved into the house eight days back, but every evening since she'd headed to her room the instant the children were in bed. Sitting alone in the parlor with nothing but his memories for company wasn't how he liked to spend his evenings. Despite her previous attempts to get him talking, it seemed she preferred keeping to herself of late when what he'd really like was for her to unleash her laughter and chase away the shadows that hovered in the corners.

Even though he missed their conversations, keeping things professional was probably wise. It was one thing to imagine life with a woman he'd never met but quite another to entertain thoughts about a woman who could take his thoughts down a track he wasn't ready to travel. Especially the woman living in his house.

He forced himself to come up with a suitable response. "I don't make a habit of talking about such things."

Her matter-of-fact manner gave way to one of the sweetest smiles she'd ever sent his way. It had the power to turn darkness into sunshine. "I understand. It can be difficult to recount painful experiences." Her voice conveyed compassion but not an ounce of pity. "Perhaps you could write about them. I keep a journal, and I've found writing in it beneficial."

Was that what she was doing in her room at night? It would explain why her lamp burned for an hour or two after she'd gone upstairs. Not that he made a point of noticing. "I'll have to give that some thought." His stomach rumbled. "Pardon me."

"That's quite all right." She stood. "I'll get a meal on the table right away."

Three of her lengthy strides carried her across the porch. She paused in the open doorway and studied him for a moment before smiling once more, an understanding smile that eased the dull ache in his chest. "I'll continue to pray for you."

Tess didn't have Faith's way with words, but her simple statement meant a great deal to him nonetheless. It came from a pure heart and a genuine desire to serve others. Look at her now, giving up her day off to care for Polly and her family without a second thought. She'd been there for him, too, when the memories had become too much to bear. And he hadn't even— "Thank you, Tess. I appreciate that."

Surprise at his gratitude parted her lips before she shook herself and entered the kitchen. He had the unexpected urge to chase after her and plant a kiss on those rosy lips.

What had come over him? He'd given way to his feelings, sensed a bond and come far too close to telling her how he'd failed his late wife, that's what. Well, he wouldn't do that again.

Chapter Fifteen

As soon as she'd completed her chores the next morning, Tess hitched the team to the wagon. She'd not been able to get a moment alone with Polly after Petey's earlier-than-expected arrival.

Although Tess was eager to prepare enough food to last a couple of days so her friend could devote herself to her infant son, she would have arranged to pay Polly a visit no matter what. Tess couldn't wait to tell her friend about the conversation she'd had with Spencer after the baby's birth.

When Spencer had stopped her as she'd headed inside to fix dinner after having told her about one of the most difficult days of his life, she hadn't known what to expect. Although entirely unnecessary as far as she was concerned, his apology made sense. He wasn't one to openly address his past or his pain.

While she'd felt a connection to him born of concern, everything had changed when she'd assured him he hadn't "blathered." He'd gazed at her with such admiration that her cheeks had warmed. No man had looked at her that way before.

He'd gone on to thank her for offering to pray for him and given her a smile so disarming the heat had intensified, fueled by her wayward thoughts. Thoughts an upstanding Christian woman had no right thinking—especially about her employer.

What had possessed her to wonder what his lips would feel like on hers? Perhaps the fact that she was twenty-five and had never been kissed. Or perhaps it was witnessing a birth and seeing Peter kiss Polly afterward, dredging up the dream of having a husband and children of her own that she fought to keep at bay. Whatever the reason, she'd forced herself to focus on Spencer's eyes after that, although her gaze had continually strayed to his mouth.

"Why are you smiling?"

Luke's question roused her. "Because we get to see little Petey again. Won't that be fun?"

"No. He didn't look too good. He was all red and wrinkly."

True, but Tess had never seen anything that moved her as deeply as her glimpse of Petey in the first seconds of his life. Arguing with Luke was pointless, though. "Climb on up. We're ready to go."

He scaled the side of the wagon in no time, plopped himself in the driver's seat and grabbed the reins.

"Be careful, Luke. You'd be sorry if the team took off on you." She took control of the reins, set Lila in the crate she'd wedged between the seat and the wagon's front gate and sat beside the overeager boy.

"I wanna drive."

"All right."

He fixed eyes as big as wagon wheels on her. "Are you telling the truth?"

"I am. You may sit next to me and hold the reins."

Luke grinned from ear to ear as the docile horses plodded along. Tess took over when they reached town and parked the wagon in the Flynn's barn. She carried Lila inside, unloaded the crates filled with supplies and saw to the horses. Luke raced off to find Abby.

Tess set to work preparing fried chicken, coleslaw and other easy-to-serve fare for the Flynn's upcoming meals. The older children played in the yard while Polly and her infant son dozed in the bedroom.

When Peter arrived at noon, Tess dished up pork chops, mashed potatoes and green beans. Polly joined them for the meal, which passed quickly.

Peter returned to the depot, and Tess made short work of the dishes. She went outside to sit on the porch with Polly. Luke and Abby piled rocks into a mound, and Lila napped on a blanket nearby.

The creaking of Polly's rocking chair ceased. She adjusted the thin blanket over her infant son, who nursed beneath it. She resumed her rocking. "I know why you came. Something happened with Spencer yesterday."

"I came to see you and do a little cooking so you can get a good rest before you have to resume your duties. I saw how hard you worked bringing that little fellow into the world."

Polly snickered. "That's a fine excuse—and a much appreciated gesture—but I saw the way your face glowed when you came inside after talking with him. No more stalling. Tell me."

Tess ran her hands over the arms of the ladder-backed rocking chair. "I'm probably making more of it than I should, but he talked to me. Really talked."

"Go on."

"He told me about Lila's birthing, how difficult it was for his wife and how close he came to losing them both."

"I didn't know him as well then. We hadn't been here long, but I remember Peter telling me how haggard Spencer looked. Did he say anything else?"

Tess shook her head. "He mentioned how weak Trudy was afterward and how grateful he was to have had a few more months with her before the accident and resulting infection took her from him. It's sad that he's suffered so, but I'm glad he told me. It helps me understand him better."

"I knew he'd open up to you in time. Maybe now you'll feel better about sitting with him in the parlor after the children are in bed. The more he gets to know you, the easier it will be for him to see you as a young, attractive, *unattached* woman instead of a housekeeper."

"Why would he? I'm not young or attractive."

Polly huffed. "Oh, Tessie, how many times must I tell you how beautiful you are before you'll believe it?"

"I'm tall."

"And lithe, and you have striking features many a woman would give her eyeteeth for. Me included."

"You? But you're short and have the prettiest face ever. Peter couldn't keep his eyes off you at dinner." His admiration had been so evident as to be almost embarrassing.

"He's just happy because I've given him a son. If you want to talk about a man whose gaze wanders to a certain woman, look no further than Spencer. He steals glances at you quite often."

Tess stopped rocking and sat bolt upright. "No! That's not true."

"'The lady doth protest too much, methinks.' He's a man, Tessie, and he's bound to be lonely. If he sees a beautiful woman, he's going to take notice. Especially when that woman is capable and caring...and close at hand."

Polly meant well, but Spencer was a widower in mourning, not a man looking to find a wife.

"No, Wuke! Bad boy."

Tess snapped to attention. She expected to find him pestering Abby again, but the little girl had called to him from where she sat at the rock pile. Luke stood inside the picket fence holding a large stone over his head while facing three school-aged boys on the outside.

She approached them, and the older boys took off running. "Put the rock down and come over here, young man." She pointed to the spot in front of her.

Luke threw the stone, narrowly missing her. She had half a mind to take him over her knee and give him a swat, but he sniffed, sending a tear trickling down his dirt-streaked face. Her irritation fled. "What did those boys say to you?"

He stood with his feet apart, his arms crossed and his face scrunched in a fierce scowl. "Nothin'."

"All right. You don't have to tell me. I can just punish you for throwing rocks."

He relaxed his stance. "If tell you, will I still get in trouble?"

"Throwing rocks is wrong. But if I know why you were going to do it, you wouldn't get in as much trouble."

He wiggled his mouth back and forth as he considered his options, looking so cute Tess tamped down a smile. "I'll tell you, but you can't laugh at me like they done."

After hearing his sad tale, she had half a mind to hunt down those boys and give them a tongue-lashing. Why did children have to be so cruel to one another? "I'm sorry they said those mean things, sweetheart. Would a hug help you feel better?"

He swung his head from side to side, his long brown hair slapping against his cheeks.

His resistance came as no surprise, but the plea for help in his watery eyes did.

She needed to make another change—one Spencer might balk at—and the sooner the better.

Spencer checked his watch again, shoved it into his waistcoat pocket and resumed pacing the platform. Only five minutes until his bull arrived. He whistled a few measures of Handel's "Hallelujah Chorus."

Drake approached and fell in step beside him. "I couldn't quite make out your note, boss. Was this how you wanted the telegram to Boston worded?"

Spencer scanned Drake's block letters and returned the slip of paper. "That works." A number of times he'd caught Tess singing that new hymn introduced in church last week, although she stopped as soon as she realized he was there. He'd decided to surprise her by getting a copy of the sheet music from the pianist's sister back east.

"Papa!"

"Luke?" Spencer spun around, spotted his son barreling toward him and braced himself for the impact. Luke flung his arms around Spencer's waist in an exuberant display of childish affection. He tousled his son's hair. "Where's Tess?"

"She's a slowpoke." Luke pointed at the far end of the platform. Tess clutched Lila with both arms and weaved her way between baggage handlers awaiting the arrival of the incoming freight train.

When she reached Spencer and his son, her chest was heaving. "You're faster than a lizard outrunning a cat, Luke. Even with my long legs, I didn't stand a chance of winning our race." She finger-combed his long hair. For once he didn't bat her hand away.

"I am fast, aren't I, Papa? I got to you first."

"That you did, my boy."

Tess handed her fan to a squirming Lila, who quieted and examined it. "Might I have a word with you, Spencer?"

This wasn't the best time for a discussion. "Could we talk tonight? I've got to check with Peter before my bull arrives. I want to be sure he and his crew have everything ready."

"It'll only take a minute. I'd like your answer before the children and I head back to the ranch because I might need to make a stop at the general store."

"All right, but you'll need to make it quick."

"Thank you." She gave him a smile as sweet as the slice of apple pie she'd put in his lunch pail that day. He'd have offered to give her more than a minute if he'd known he would receive such a nice reward.

She shifted her attention to Luke. "I'll let you drive again...*if* you'll sit over there while I'll talk with your papa." She held out her free hand toward a bench in the shade of the depot.

Luke took off without a word and planted himself on the spot she'd indicated.

Spencer couldn't believe what he'd heard. "You let my four-year-old son drive the wagon?"

"Right. Just like I let him play on the barn roof this morning." She smirked and gave her head such a sound shake that the three peacock feathers atop her hat did a dance.

"So he didn't drive?"

"I let him sit beside me and hold the reins, but I kept my hands on them, too. And don't you dare tell him. It'll be our secret." She winked—an action so unexpected that a cross between a cough and a chortle escaped him. My, but Tess was bold. He didn't care. He liked seeing her playful side.

Her gaze roved over his slouch hat, ranch wear and boots, and returned to his face again. The admiration in her beautiful brown eyes surprised him. She'd never looked at him that way before. As though she was seeing him as a man and not just her employer. "While you look nice in your stationmaster attire, the more relaxed look suits you."

A shrill whistle in the distance announced the incoming train—and kept him from having to come up with a response. He studied the sky to the west, looking for the plume of gray smoke that signaled the approach of an inbound train.

She cleared her throat in an obvious attempt to get his attention. "About my request?"

He divided his attention between her and the locomotive barreling toward the station. "What was it you wanted?"

"Since Luke's been growing, he could use a new

wardrobe. I'd like to purchase fabric and trim so I can get to work on some outfits right away."

He pulled out his money clip and withdrew several bills. "Buy whatever you need."

She took the proffered banknotes and stuffed them in her handbag but didn't leave. He'd given her enough to buy an entire bolt of material. What more could she want?

"I want to be sure you understand my intentions. Luke's tall for his age, so rather than wasting your money on more of the loose-fitting little-boy outfits, I'd like to—"

"Put him in short pants? Yes. I understand. Do it."

Tess stared at him, her lips parted, looking entirely too attractive for her own good. He tore his gaze from her and listened to the rhythmic clacking of the wheels on the rails as the train covered the final half mile, a welcome sound any day, but never more so than today.

"I didn't think you'd agree, at least not so readily."

"I'm glad to know I can surprise you." He headed toward the edge of the platform, keeping his face forward so she couldn't see his grin.

She matched his pace stride for stride. "About the outfits. Do you have any preferences?"

The train pulled into the station, coming to a stop with a screech of metal on metal and the hiss of steam. "Do whatever you want, Tess. I trust your judgment."

Spencer jumped off the platform, jogged around the last rail car and disappeared. Tess smiled. He'd not only agreed with her plan to update Luke's wardrobe. He seemed eager for her to do so.

She couldn't wait to get started making Luke's first

tunic and pair of short pants. He'd be so happy when he was found out he'd be wearing big-boy clothes that he might begin to trust her. If she could break down his walls, she'd be better able to help him heal.

He sat on the bench swinging his legs as he watched the flurry of activity on the platform. Tess balanced Lila on her hip and sidestepped a stack of crates on her way to him. "How would you like to watch the men unload your papa's bull, Luke?"

"It's here?" He jumped off the bench, his head swiveling.

"In one of those cars, yes. It looks as if they'll be unloading it on the north side of the tracks. Come on. Let's go."

They rounded the end of the train. Tess kept the children at a safe distance.

Several men strained to push a heavy wooden ramp up to the doors of a boxcar with holes drilled in the sides. The ripe smell of animal leavings caused Tess to wrinkle her nose.

Peter cupped his hands and called to Spencer, who'd mounted his big black horse. "They've got the ramp in place, Cap'n. You ready for us to open the doors?"

Apparently the shouting had upset the bull. The sudden bellowing and stamping from the angry animal inside the car made the hairs at Tess's nape stand on end.

"Yes—" Spencer hollered "—but be on your guard. Sounds like he's madder than a miner facing down a claim jumper."

Peter clambered onto the ramp. "Don't worry," he yelled over the commotion. "The freight traffic manager in Sacramento City telegraphed. Said they've got the big guy tied to the sides of the car. We'll bring him out nice and slow."

Luke hopped from one foot to the other in his excitement, creating a cloud of dust. "Papa said he's real big and I gotta stay away from him."

Spencer had cautioned Tess, as well, but he'd assured her the animal wouldn't pose a threat. "He'll be in his pen. As long as we keep our distance, we'll be safe." She'd walked the perimeter the day before to assure herself of that fact. The Muellers had built a sturdy fence.

Peter beckoned to one of his men, who joined him on the ramp. They each held a handle and slid the doors aside.

"Watch out!" Spencer shouted. "He got loose."

The men jumped back.

The largest animal Tess had ever seen charged down the ramp. She'd heard of longhorns and seen sketches in the newspaper, but she'd never expected to see one for herself.

The behemoth pawed the ground, used his horns to throw up dirt and took off running in the direction of the ranch, trailing broken pieces of rope behind him.

Spencer grabbed his lariat, formed a loop, set it to spinning and gave chase. My, but he sat a horse well. "Be careful!"

"Get 'im, Spence!" Peter yelled.

Luke chased after his father. "Go, Papa! Go."

"No, Luke. Stop," Tess called. "He'll be all right." *Please, God, let it be so.*

Spencer caught up to the bull in no time and let his rope fly.

He missed.

The bull changed directions. He was barreling straight at them.

Tess's mouth went dry.

Chapter Sixteen

The pounding of Tess's heart rivaled the pounding of the bull's hooves as it raced toward the station. What would happen if Spencer couldn't stop the huge animal in time? She'd heard of men who'd been killed by raging bulls.

She grabbed Luke by the hand and rushed the children to safety behind a nearby freight wagon.

Spencer recoiled his rope, formed a larger loop than Tess had ever seen him throw and spun it as he raced after the bull.

Lord, help him stop that brute.

When Spencer was within a few feet of the charging creature, he sent his lasso sailing.

Tess held her breath.

The loop caught not one, but both horns.

Spencer whipped the end of his lariat around his saddle horn, grabbed the rope and, with a series of clever maneuvers, steered the rampaging bull away from town and back toward the ranch. At the speed they were traveling, it would be some time before their pace slowed.

Peter loped over to Tess and the children. "Are you all right?"

She drew in a shaky breath. "We're fine, but thank you for checking on us."

"Spence sure knows his way around a rope, doesn't he? I've never seen anything like it."

Luke chimed in. "Papa's the best roper ever. He's teaching me."

"So I hear. Heard tell he's been teaching you, too, Tess."

"She's no good," Luke scoffed. "She can't get her loop around anything."

Peter quirked an eyebrow. "Hasn't your papa taught you it's not nice to talk about a lady that way?"

"She's not a lady. She's just Te—" Luke slammed his mouth shut and stormed off, kicking a stone.

"Polly said the boy's got it in for you. What do you aim to do about it?"

"Bide my time. And pray."

Peter removed his sweat-stained derby and passed a sleeve over his damp forehead. "I'd best do some praying myself. Don't think Spence is going to take too kindly to having his bull bust out of the car like that after I told him we had things under control. He's counting on the big fellow to launch his cattle-ranching empire. Can't see what the draw is myself. I'd take railroading over ranching any day." One of his men hollered for him, and he returned to his work.

"Come on, Luke," Tess called. "I have an errand to run before we head back to the ranch."

Minutes later she entered the general store. The

friendly owner greeted her. "Afternoon, Miss Grimsby. What can I do for you?"

Tess shifted Lila from one hip to the other. "I'd like some sturdy fabric in colors suitable for an active young boy."

"Master Luke's getting some new togs, is he?"

She glanced at Luke, who was engrossed in the toy display, and lowered her voice. "He doesn't know what I have in mind, and I'd prefer to keep it that way. If he were to find out, he'd pester me endlessly."

Mr. Hawkes chuckled. "I didn't have a whole lot of patience when I was his age, either. Let's see how soon we can get you out of here then, shall we?" The proprietor cut and wrapped her selections quickly.

Since Spencer had been so generous, she had more than enough money to buy everything his son needed. A quick glance revealed that Luke was enraptured by a brightly colored Noah's ark set.

She returned her attention to Mr. Hawkes and kept her voice low. "I'd like to get him a new pair of boots, too."

He rubbed his chin. "I can't help you with that. Since I don't have much of a demand for children's shoes, I don't carry them. The shoemaker in Folsom would be able to help you, though."

"It appears I'll have to plan a trip down the hill. In the meantime, I'd like you to set aside a couple of items for me—some early Christmas shopping. I could get them a week from today." She would receive her second month's pay packet that coming Monday.

"Certainly."

Tess tucked the brown paper package under her free

arm and lured Luke away from the store with an invitation to drive the wagon again. She couldn't wait until that evening when she could start working on his first big-boy outfit.

The wagon lumbered into the yard with Luke driving, assisted by Tess. He jumped to the ground as soon as they came to a stop and ran toward Spencer. He caught his son in a hug.

"Oh, Papa, you were so brave. You chased after that big ol' bull and caught him. I wanna see him." He slipped out of the embrace and raced toward the pen.

"Hold up there, son. We need to go slow and easy." Spencer was comfortable around cattle, but Tess would have his hide if he didn't impress upon Luke the need to exercise caution.

The bull's escape had probably confirmed her fears. Although the longhorn had given up the fight well before reaching the ranch, she'd seen him fresh out of the rail car, some sixteen hundred pounds of angry, ornery, seemingly out-of-control animal. Now that the big fellow no longer felt threatened, he stood contentedly munching hay in the pen.

If things went according to plan, this bull would be as calm as the sires Spencer had helped raise on his father's ranch and would do his job as well as they had. The future of the ranch rested on this fellow. Two ranchers eager to incorporate the admirable characteristics of a longhorn into their herds had agreed to give Spencer a heifer in exchange for every four calves his stud sired.

Tess held Lila out to Spencer. "Would you please hold her so I can get these crates inside?"

"I'll carry them for you." He completed the task, took Lila and strode toward the pen.

Tess fell in step beside him. "I thought you'd want to care for the team right away since that's what you've asked me to do each time I drive them."

He had, but a man could change his mind once in a while. "The horses won't care if they have to wait a few more minutes. I want you to—"

"Take a look at your new addition?" She sent him a smile so bright it rivaled the September sun slanting from the west. "Oh, Spencer, I can't begin to tell you how scared I was when that bull burst from the rail car. And when you charged after him, my heart was pounding something fierce. But then you roped the beast by both horns. I've never seen anything quite as—" she spun her hands in small circles as though willing the words to come "—awe-inspiring."

He'd never seen Tess as animated—or as full of compliments. She was gushing like a schoolgirl. Not that he minded. He hadn't set out to impress her, merely to capture the bull before it harmed someone, but he liked having his skills admired.

"Well, grease my griddle. What am I doing carrying on like that when you want me to see your latest acquisition? Let's go, so you can introduce us to the king of the pen." She took Luke by the hand before he had a chance to protest. "Let's skip, shall we, like I taught you this morning?"

Spencer followed with Lila. Tess was acting strangely. While she'd ridden a hay bale horse and spent many an evening practicing her roping, she hadn't dropped her guard to this extent before. Something must have happened while she was in town.

Of course. She'd seen Polly and little Petey. That had to be it. Nothing caused a normally controlled woman to turn to mush quite like a baby. Even his stiff-as-a-starched-shirt grandmother had gone misty-eyed whenever she saw a newborn.

Tess neared the pen, ground to a halt and released Luke's hand. "I could tell your bull was huge, but he's even bigger than I thought. How close can we get and still be safe?"

Spencer stood beside them. "As you can, see he's settled down. He let me go right up to the fence."

Her eyes widened. She inclined her head toward Luke, who stood slack-jawed. "Surely you don't want *us* to get that close?"

"It's best to stand back a ways, since we don't know him yet."

"What's his name, Papa?"

"I haven't picked one yet. Do you have any ideas, son?"

Luke tilted his head from side to side, studying the bull.

Before he could answer, Tess did, merriment dancing in her dark brown eyes. "Moo." She dragged out the vowel sound.

Spencer laughed. "I'm not about to call him that."

She feigned surprise. "This, coming from a man who calls his dog *Woof*?"

Luke crossed his arms and scowled. "*I* called him Woof."

Tess managed to look genuinely apologetic, a feat Spencer admired. She rested a hand on Luke's shoulder, removing it when he shrugged. "Yes, you did, and it's a fine name. But I think your Papa's prized pet needs a different kind of name. Something that sounds big and powerful."

Prized pet? This bull was a working animal. Spencer would have to set Tess straight. But wait. Her lips twitched. She was teasing him, and he'd almost taken the bait. "Since he is king of the pen, what about King?"

"Yes, Papa. King David. Like they talked about in church. He was big and powerful."

Tess nodded. "That's a good idea, Luke. But who was even bigger than David?"

His face lit when he remembered. "The giant man, Goliath. We could call him that."

Spencer nodded. "That's a fine choice. Goliath it is."

The bull looked up from the mound of hay he was munching and grunted. Lila let out with a good imitation, causing the rest of them to laugh.

Spencer's gaze met Tess's. Something flickered in her eyes before she broke the connection. Perhaps it was attraction. No. She wasn't interested in him. Sure, she'd admired his rope work, but that was as far as it went. His loneliness was fueling his imagination.

"Papa!" Luke tugged on Spencer's sleeve, dragging him back to the present. "Tell her I can rope Goliath if I want." He jabbed a finger at Tess.

"Not until you're older, son."

Tess beckoned to Luke. "Let's go meet Goliath. I'm sure your Papa will be happy to introduce us."

Spencer followed them to the slat fence surrounding the pen. Tess stood back a good three feet as she watched the bull enjoy his meal. She kept hold of Luke, although he was none too happy about that.

She studied the bull intently. "Just how big are those horns?"

"I haven't been able to measure them yet. My guess is they're over four feet from tip to tip, but he's only three years old. They'll continue to grow as he ages. My father had one old fellow whose tip-to-tip measurement was a hair over six feet."

She turned to Spencer, her mouth agape. "Amazing. That means his horns were as wide as I am tall."

He resisted the urge to smile at her unbridled surprise. "Would you like to touch him?"

Luke broke free of Tess and rushed to Spencer's side. "I would, Papa."

"Um, Spencer. Do you think that's a good idea? I'm not so sure we should encourage him. I don't want him to think he can approach Goliath on his own."

"He won't go near him, will you, son? Not without one of us close by?"

Luke shook his head.

"Then if you'll hold this little lady, Tess, I'll let Luke have a closer look."

She took Lila from him. He hefted Luke onto the fence, planted his son's feet on the middle slat and stood beside him. The bull lifted his head. Luke stroked Goliath's muzzle. The longhorn studied the curious boy. Without warning, the bull stuck out his tongue and swiped Luke's hand.

"Lookee, Papa. He likes being petted. He licked me. Like Woof does."

"Seems that way, doesn't it? I'm going to put you down so I can take Lila and let Tess have a turn."

She shied away. "Oh, no. I'm fine."

"I can understand your hesitation, but he's settled down now. You two should make friends."

Luke laughed. "She's scared."

"It's not polite to laugh at people, son."

She lifted her chin. "I'm not scared. I'm…cautious."

Spencer dipped his chin behind Lila's head so Tess couldn't see his smile. He could understand her fear, but when she assumed her "I've been affronted" pose, she looked cute.

Cute? Tess was many things, but cute wasn't one of them. Striking, perhaps. Even beautiful. But not cute. "Caution can be a good thing, but you're usually more adventurous. Perhaps you'd feel more comfortable if I were to help you the way I did Luke."

She caught her lower lip between her teeth and looked from him to the pen and back again. "I don't think that would be wise."

"You're right. It's probably a bad idea. It takes a brave woman to contend with a massive longhorn and a rugged cattle rancher at the same time." He grinned and turned to leave. If he knew Tess, she wouldn't back down.

"Please, don't go. I'll do it—if you'll stay right beside me."

Gladly. "If you're sure. I wouldn't want to rush you."

She nodded and handed Lila to him. Tess held herself poker straight and approached the fence with halting steps. Spencer stood beside her, so close he could hear her rapid breathing as she mustered her courage.

"Now what?" She faced him.

Her eyes held such warmth he could do nothing but gaze into them, his resolve to remain impassive melt-

ing. Seeing Tess's uncertainty had brought out an unexpected desire to protect her.

"I suppose—" Her voice broke, and a becoming
flush spread over her cheeks. "I suppose I should get on
with it." She clutched the top slat with her left hand and
held out her right. Several tense moments passed before the bull raised his head. She grimaced but stroked
him—once—and jerked her arm back. "H-how was
that?"

"It's a start. It'll be easier next time."

"I'm not so sure there will be a next time. I plan to
give Goliath a wide berth." She took two steps away
from Spencer, sending the message that she'd be keeping her distance from him, as well. Not that he could
blame her after the way he'd stared at her.

Luke bounded up to them. "Someone's coming,
Papa."

Sure enough, a rider approached from the east.
Frank Mueller. He'd recognize the young man's pinto
anywhere.

Frank reined in his mount and doffed his hat to Tess.
"Afternoon, Miss Grimsby. Mr. Abbott. I came to see if
either of you found— What is *that*?" He stared at Goliath. "I know it's a bull, but I've never seen one like it.
Look at the size of those horns. When did he get here?"

"Today," Luke announced. "He ran off the train, and
Papa had to throw his rope and catch him. He done it,
too, and it only took him two throws. He's real good.
I got to pet Goliath. That's his name."

Spencer warmed at his son's praise. "Thanks to the
work you and your father did on the fence, I've got
a sturdy pen to hold him. What brings you out here
today?"

Frank dragged his gaze from the bull and shifted in his saddle, the leather creaking. "Vati was wondering if you'd seen his hammer. The last time he remembers seeing it was when we were working on the bunkhouse. I thought maybe he'd left it here."

"I haven't seen it," Tess volunteered.

Spencer handed Lila to her. "I found one a couple of days before you finished the job and put in your tool-box next to the other."

"I figure he's misplaced it in our shop, but if you see it, would you give us a holler?"

"Will do."

Frank left. Luke darted off to play with Woof, and Spencer started for the barn.

"Spencer." Tess caught up to him. "May I take the children to Folsom?"

"What for?"

"Luke's outgrown his shoes. I'd like to get him a pair of boots, but Mr. Hawkes doesn't carry his size. He suggested I see the shoemaker down the hill."

Woof barked and raced after the stick Luke had thrown. The familiar pain gripped Spencer, squeezing his chest so hard that drawing a breath was an effort. "Luke's growing up so fast, and his mother's not here to see it."

"I'm sorry it's so difficult. I wish I could ease your burden." Compassion filled her eyes.

"I'm fine."

"Papa." Lila reached out to him.

He took her from Tess, kissed each of his daughter's round cheeks and inhaled her fresh, clean fragrance. No. That hint of citrus wasn't Lila's scent. It was Tess's.

Tess. The woman who cared for his children, fed

him delicious meals and continued to offer solace even though he'd done precious little to thank her. He must do something to show her how much he appreciated her. "I'll take you."

"I beg your pardon?" Confusion creased Tess's brow.

"You said you want to go to Folsom. I'll take you there. Luke's only ridden the train once. He'd be delighted to do so again. I could arrange for him to ride in the locomotive. We could do the shopping and have a picnic down at the river."

"A picnic on the riverbank would be wonderful. I love being near the water. When shall we go?"

"A week from today. I'll ask Peter and Drake to see to things at the station while I'm gone."

She gave him one of her radiant smiles, the kind that made him feel like a king. "I look forward to it."

So did he. More than he would have expected.

Chapter Seventeen

Like Luke, Tess was enjoying her second train ride immensely. She sat beside the open window as the scenery raced past. Sprawling oak trees. Sun-bleached bunchgrass. An occasional glimpse of the rock fences being built by the Chinese. She inhaled deeply, breathing in the sooty scent that would always remind her of Spencer.

Stealing glances at him on the seat opposite her, she was pleased to see him with his head bent over Luke's, answering his son's incessant questions while he bounced his daughter on one knee. What made her even happier was the smile on his face. He still wore his customary frown much of the time, but this morning he was enjoying himself. She tore her gaze from him, lest he catch her staring, and let it rove over the rail car's paneled walls and plush seats.

Had it really been just two months ago that she'd taken her first train ride? She'd hoped to have Luke's first outfit ready for their outing, but she hadn't been able to spend much time sewing. Lila had been miserable due to teething pain. Tess had lost count of the hours she'd spent rocking the poor girl and rubbing her inflamed gums with a fingertip.

When Lila's teeth had finally broken through the previous afternoon, she'd returned to her contented self. Tess had gotten her first good night's sleep in a week and awakened that morning eager for their adventure.

"But she said you were gonna get me a ride in the engine, Papa." Luke jabbed an accusatory finger at Tess.

Spencer pushed Luke's arm down and mouthed the word *sorry* to Tess. "You'll have to be patient, son. The engineer on this train won't let anyone but his fireman ride in the cab, but the one on our way home will. He likes showing little boys what he does."

Luke scowled. "I'm not a little boy. I'm a big boy. You said so."

"You are. That's why you're getting a pair of big-boy boots today."

Tess smiled behind her fan. Wait until Luke saw the outfit she was working on—navy short pants and a matching tunic trimmed with gold braid. She hadn't expected to be so excited about making the clothes, but this was her first time to transition a boy into short pants.

The train pulled into the Folsom station. Tess grabbed the wicker picnic basket. Luke disembarked, followed by Spencer, who held his daughter in his arms.

Tess grabbed the handrail, placed her right foot on the top stop and prepared to put her left on the second. Her boot skimmed the slick surface. She fell forward, came down hard on her heel and crashed into Spencer.

"Lila!" she cried.

He grasped her by the elbow. "She's all right. How are you?"

A bit dazed and thoroughly mortified. "Fine... I think."

She took a tentative step. Her ankle wasn't sprained, but her boot didn't feel right. She stepped aside, out of the flow of traffic. As inconspicuously as possible she lifted her skirts to survey the damage. "Oh, no."

Luke squatted and examined her boot. "The heel's coming off," he announced at an embarrassing volume.

While he was right, that was the least of her troubles. The heel could be reattached, but the jagged tear in the leather side where it had scraped against the corner of the step was another matter. At least they were in Folsom where there was a shoemaker. He ought to be able to repair the boot.

"Son, please lower your voice. Tess doesn't want everyone to know her business."

How kind of Spencer to show her such consideration. She flashed him a smile. "If you don't mind, I'd like to visit the shoemaker first."

"A wonderful idea."

After peeking in the basket and assuring herself their lunch was all right, she headed up to the main street. She'd taken a total of two steps when she stopped.

Spencer followed suit. "Is something wrong?"

Her heel flapped every time she lifted her foot. If she set her foot down wrong, she could end up with a twisted ankle, after all. "I'll have to walk slowly, so you might want to go on without me."

"Why don't you sit over there and let me have a look?" He inclined his head toward a bench.

She managed to reach it without injuring herself, but with her unsteady gait, it must have looked as though she'd spent the morning in a saloon.

"Would you take Lila for a minute please?" He handed his daughter to Tess, lifted her foot and examined the boot.

She did her best to ignore the shocked looks on the faces of several ladies passing by.

"I see the problem. The heel's hanging by a single nail. I could remove it if you'd like."

Without the heel she would walk with a list, but that would be better than staggering. "Please do."

He tugged, and the heel broke free. He handed it to her, took Lila and propped her on his hip. "You'll be lopsided now. Why don't you take my arm?"

Take his arm? The idea sent a delicious shiver up her spine. *Control yourself, Tess.* "Thank you." She tucked her hand around his elbow and hoped he didn't look her way because she couldn't keep from grinning. They reached Sutter Street, and she reluctantly let go.

Luke raced up the stairs onto the raised boardwalk. Spencer held out his free hand to help Tess. She stared at it. Few men had shown her such courtesies. Granted, he was just doing his duty as a gentleman. Even so, she couldn't keep from imagining what it would be like to have him—to have a man care for her on a regular basis.

"Tess?"

"Hmm?"

"Don't worry. I won't let you fall."

She slipped her gloved hand into his strong, masculine one. When she was a girl at the orphanage, Charlie had teased her about having "giant paws." Compared to Spencer's hand, hers looked small and ladylike.

Luke led the way down the wooden walkway. He stopped in front of a plate glass window filled with shoes, boots and fancy slippers suitable for a ballroom. "Is this it, Papa?"

"Yes, son, but you'll have to wait for Tess to—"

"Please. Let him go first. He's been looking forward to this." Although Spencer was clearly torn, he agreed.

The shop smelled of leather, neat's-foot oil and stitching wax. Father and son conferred with the shoemaker, who set to work taking Luke's measurements. Tess sat on one of the varnished benches watching Lila as she held on to it and sidestepped her way up and down the entire length on wobbly legs. At this rate it wouldn't be long before she attempted to stand on her own.

Luke bounded up to Tess a few minutes later. "I don't get my boots now. I gotta wait two whole weeks before the package comes on the train. How many days is that?"

"Can you show me how old you are?"

He held up four fingers, and Tess held up all of hers. "It's that many. Fourteen."

His chin quivered. She resisted the urge to pull him into her arms. If only she'd thought to prepare Luke for the wait, but she did have a way to cheer him up. She could complete his first outfit in half that time. "You only have to wait this many days for a different surprise. How many is that?" She held up seven fingers and waited while he counted them.

"What's the surprise?"

"I can't tell you what it is, or it won't be a surprise."

"Can I guess?"

"You may try." No doubt he'd spend the entire week peppering her with guesses, but that would help keep his mind off the boots.

Spencer finished his talk with the shoemaker and joined them. "I'll take the children to the mercantile, so you can see about your boot—alone."

"Are you sure? I'd be happy to watch Lila for you."

He took his daughter in his arms. "You deserve a break after the challenging week you've had caring for this little one."

"Thank you, Spencer. Where shall we meet, and when?"

"How about the bench at the rail station at noon?"

Luke tugged on Spencer's sleeve. "C'mon, Papa. Let's go. I wanna see if the store has toys."

They left, with Luke skipping alongside his father and Lila clapping as though she was equally excited.

The shoemaker crossed the small shop and eased himself to a kneeling position in front of Tess. "I hear you lost a heel. Shall I have a look?"

"I'm afraid there's more to it than that." She held out her foot.

The stoop-shouldered older man studied her boot, making a series of discouraging grunts. "This pair of boots has served you well, but there's not much life left in them."

"I know they're old and not the best workmanship, but they're all I have." For years what little she'd earned over and above her room and board had gone into her wardrobe. Because she'd escorted the children of Sacramento's elite to a variety of functions, she was expected to represent the families well and had amassed a trunk full of fine dresses. Since her boots didn't show, she'd made do with an inexpensive pair. "Can you fix the damaged one?"

"I can put the heel back on, but the other…" He rubbed his chin. "If you'd ripped out the side welt, I could stitch it back up, but that tear in the back quarter poses a problem. I could sew a piece of leather under it, but it wouldn't be pretty."

Pretty didn't matter at this point. She just needed something to wear. "That sounds fine."

"I have an idea. Would you mind taking off your boots?"

She did and tucked her stocking-clad feet under the bench. The shoemaker took her boots and disappeared behind a curtain at the rear of his shop.

He reappeared shortly carrying a dust-covered pasteboard box. "I didn't want to say anything until I was sure, but I have a pair of boots that might be your size."

"My size? How can that be?" Her feet were larger than most women's, so it was unlikely he would have made a pair of boots that big just to have on hand.

"I got an order for them a few years back, but the woman who placed it never returned. Let's try them on, shall we?" He hitched up his floor-length apron and knelt before her once again.

The boots were beautiful—high quality black leather with side button closures. Each jet-black button winked at her from the center of a scallop. The scallops didn't stop there. They continued all the way around the opening. There was even fancy stitching across the instep.

But they had low heels. Very low heels. She'd be surprised if they were half an inch.

He eased her feet into the boots, pulled out his buttonhook and fastened each of the two dozen buttons. "Would you please stand? I need to check the fit."

She obliged, lifting her skirts so he could complete his inspection.

"Seems like you have plenty of room. Why don't you walk around and see how they feel?"

Across the shop she went, taking tentative steps for fear of catching her dragging skirts with a heel. Another lap around the room boosted her confidence. By the third her feet were so happy she practically skipped back to the shoemaker.

"Are they comfortable?"

"Quite." Comfortable didn't begin to describe the cocoon of soft, supple leather caressing her feet. She wanted the boots in the worst way. *Oh, Lord, what am I to do?*

She'd received her pay packet the day before, but when she visited Mr. Hawke's shop to pay for the items he'd set aside for her, she would have to give him half her month's wages. She might have enough left to pay for the repairs her boot needed, but she certainly couldn't afford a new pair like these.

The talented shoemaker crossed his arms. "You're frowning. Don't you want them?"

"Very much, but…" Sometimes being a housekeeper whose handbag held far too few coins had its disadvantages. "The truth, is I'm not even sure I have enough to pay for the repairs."

"I assumed your husband would see to that."

"My husband? No. Spencer—I mean Mr. Abbott—

isn't my husband. I'm his housekeeper. I've only been working for him two months and have yet to amass any savings. As difficult as it is for me to say this, I'm afraid I must leave these exquisite boots here and ask you to do what you can for my damaged one."

He stood slowly, grimacing as though in pain, and rubbed his back. "Age isn't for the fainthearted." He chuckled and then sobered. "Those boots you're wearing were ordered by a woman almost as tall as you. A saloon girl who insisted on having lower heels, even though her kind usually ask me to make them as high as I can. She said she'd spent too many years looking down on everyone. I got the feeling she wasn't talking about her height."

The shoemaker paused.

Tess had to know more. "What happened?"

"Even though she'd given me a hefty deposit, she moved on before I'd finished the boots. Since you're the first woman in three years to show an interest in them, I'm willing to entertain just about any offer. I could use the shelf space."

Hope welled up inside Tess. If she asked Mr. Hawkes to hold the items she wanted from his general store for another month… She loosened the drawstrings of her reticule, reached inside to locate every last coin in the silky recesses and laid them on the counter. "This is all I have."

"You've got yourself a deal, young lady." He smiled. "I can take your old boots off your hands if you'd like. I could make use of the leather for patches and such."

She had the distinct impression the kindly shoemaker would have accepted less than she'd given him, but she didn't care. The boots she now wore, abandoned years before, had found a home.

Her transaction compete, she left the shoemaker's shop. A glance at the watch pinned to her bodice showed she had an hour before she was to meet Spencer and the children. She'd entertained the idea of having a glass of lemonade in one of the cafés, but that possibly had evaporated due to her purchase. She might as well acquaint herself with Folsom's shops, so she'd know what was available should she get another opportunity to visit the bustling town.

She meandered through a hardware store, dry goods shop and millinery. Passing by a bakery, she inhaled the inviting aromas of cinnamon, nutmeg and freshly baked bread. The mercantile, with its windows boasting a host of interesting items, beckoned. The bell on the door sent out a melodious chime as she slipped inside.

Stooping to study a display of antimacassars like the one on the back of Spencer's wingback armchair, she was reminded of Polly's suggestion to spend a few minutes with him in the evening. Perhaps she was right. Perhaps Spencer would welcome some company. Even though Tess was eager to work on her sewing projects, taking time to ask him about his day before she headed upstairs might be a way to get him to open up to her again, as he had the day little Petey was born.

"Tess."

She'd recognize that rich voice anywhere. She stood and found herself eye to eye with Spencer. Well not quite eye to eye. He was about an inch taller than she. Due to the lower heels, she'd lost her advantage.

The realization was as startling as an earthquake,

shaking her to the core. Had she, like the saloon girl who'd commissioned the boots, enjoyed looking down on people, too?

Chapter Eighteen

Spencer stared at Tess, who stared back at him. Something about her was different. She seemed softer, more vulnerable than ever before. He blinked to break the intense eye contact and shifted his daughter to a more comfortable position. "How did things go at the shoemaker's? Was he able to repair your boot?"

Tess shook her head, causing the peacock feathers on her huge hat to flutter. "I left them with him."

That was it. She was shorter. He glanced at the hem of her skirt, puddled at her feet. "You're not *barefoot*, are you?"

A couple of matrons at a neighboring display case gasped.

"Of course not," she shot back loudly enough for the women to hear.

He'd definitely ruffled Tess's feathers. "I'm sorry, but since your dress is dragging the floor and you said he has your boots, I thought you might not be wearing any."

She lifted that determined chin of hers. "I am wearing boots. Brand-new boots. He had a pair just my size. See?" She hefted her skirts so high he could see a pair of pretty black button-up boots—along with a fair amount of ankle.

"Well, I never…" One of the busybodies cast a withering look at Tess and turned to her companion. "What has come over young people today? Have they no respect for society's conventions?"

Tess let go of her skirts, sending them swishing around her feet. She jammed a fist against her side and glared at the backs of the retreating women. "Some people…"

"Don't worry about them."

She scanned the mercantile. "Where's Luke?"

"At the toy case. He has his eye on a wooden boat. I tried to interest him in the train, but he wouldn't be swayed."

Tess joined Luke, who sat cross-legged with his nose pressed against the display case. Spencer followed her.

She dropped to her knees beside Luke. "Your papa said you like the boat."

"It's not a boat. It's an ark." He jabbed a finger at a set with lots of pieces. "It comes with all kinds of animals—lions and tigers and elephants—and lotsa birds. I like the elephants best because they're the biggest."

"Do you know something, Luke? They're my favorite, too."

His son eyed Tess warily and returned his attention to the toy. How long would Luke continue to push her away? He even refused to use her name. Not that his lack of acceptance stopped her. She kept right on loving him.

Beneath her sometimes-saucy exterior, she had a

kind heart. Spencer had no doubt that in time she would overcome Luke's resistance.

She stood. "Which one's your favorite, Spencer?"

"The giraffe...because it's so tall."

The smile she sent his way radiated warmth and light. With Tess around life didn't seem nearly as dark and depressing as before. She could chase away the clouds faster than a delta breeze. He had a sudden urge to spend more time with her. "Do you have any more purchases to make?"

"No. Why?"

"Neither do I, so what do you say we start our picnic early?"

Luke folded his arms and scowled. "I don't wanna go. I want you to buy me the ark."

Tess answered before Spencer could. "He doesn't have to. We can make one ourselves."

Surprise overcame Luke's irritation. "We can?"

"Yes. We'll draw an ark on pasteboard and cut it out. We can make animals, too. Our set won't be as fancy as this wooden one or have as many pieces, but we can still have fun with it. I'll need your help, though. I can't remember all the animals this one has, but I'm sure you can."

Luke nodded. "Yep. I been looking at them a whole long time."

"That's great. I have another idea. Let's see if we can beat your papa and Lila to the river." She grabbed Luke by the hand, hitched up her skirts and took off, with the picnic basket on her arm bouncing and his son scrambling to keep up with her.

Spencer reached the bank of the American River and found Luke sitting on a blanket beneath a massive oak tree crunching a dill pickle. Spencer adjusted Lila's bonnet so her face was shielded from the sun's harsh rays and joined Tess at the water's edge.

She tossed a rock into the murky depths. It landed with a plop. "No matter how many times I try, I can't get it to skim the surface. A boy I supervised tried to teach me, but he declared me a hopeless case in a matter of minutes." She cast a glance at Spencer. "Would you show me how?"

"I would if I could, but unlike my brother, I never mastered the art of skipping stones. I preferred to spend my time throwing a rope."

"What?" She pressed a hand to her throat and dropped her jaw in an exaggerated look of surprise. "You mean there's something you *can't* do? I heard you could do just about anything."

He chuckled. "Who have you been listening to?"

"Your son. According to Luke you're the smartest, most talented man who ever lived. I tried to set him straight, but he'd have no part of it." She laughed. No. That couldn't be called a laugh. That was a giggle. A girlish sound he'd never expected to come out of her.

He couldn't resist the urge to play along and adopted a wounded tone. "And here I thought you were a loyal housekeeper who would uphold my image, not convince my trusting son that I'm actually human."

"But you are a rather nice human." She smirked.

"You're quite nice yourself."

"Why, Spencer, it almost sounds like you mean that."

"I do."

All signs of her playfulness faded. "You do? I— I'm sorry. I didn't mean to question you. It's just that I'm not used to being paid compliments. At least not often. And only by my friends. Polly mostly."

Interesting. Tess didn't consider him a friend. For some reason that didn't sit well. "Then we'll have to remedy that. I'm sure I could come up with at least three more compliments before the day's out."

"Please don't misunderstand. I wasn't asking you to—"

He pressed a finger to her mouth, and her eyes widened. "I'm aware of that. I'm taking it on as a challenge, so you'll just have to accept them when offered. Can you do that?"

She nodded.

"Good." His gesture had rendered her speechless. It had been a long time since he'd had such a marked effect on a woman. But then, Tess wasn't like other women. She appreciated the simplest of gifts. A single compliment could make her lovely face light up. He was eager to see what three in a row would do.

He removed his finger and resisted the almost overwhelming urge to trace her lips with the tip. She surprised him by trailing a finger over the place where his had rested, as though she wanted to imprint the memory of his touch.

She realized he was watching her, blushed bright red and resumed her earlier lighthearted manner. "I thought it would be fun to play some games after our picnic when this little lady takes her nap." She reached out and caressed Lila's cheek. "I know Luke would enjoy that. If you'll agree, I might consider letting you have the biggest piece of Lila's birthday cake. It's chocolate."

His baby girl had turned one three days ago, but

they'd agreed to put off celebrating until her teething pain eased, "You drive a hard bargain, Tess, but how can I refuse?"

"You can't. That's the beauty of my plan."

He chuckled. "Your plan, eh? And what comes next? I know it's early, but please tell me it's time to eat. The scents coming from that basket have had my mouth watering all morning."

"A picnic luncheon it is. And then our fun." She headed for the blanket and shot him a playful smile over her shoulder. "Just wait until you see the games I have in mind."

They were sure to be child's play, but he didn't care. He would skip rope or jump through a game of hopscotch if it meant seeing her perky smile or hearing her musical laugh.

Pleasantly full after their picnic lunch, Tess sat on the blanket she'd spread beneath an aged oak and leaned back on her palms. Luke roamed nearby looking for insects while Lila napped in the shade. Spencer lay on his back with his feet crossed, the sleeves of his white shirt rolled up and his slouch hat covering his face. He looked entirely too appealing in the relaxed pose.

Tess closed her eyes, tilted her head and let the sun kiss her cheeks. She'd expected the day to be unbearably hot, but the temperature had dropped from the high nineties they'd seen the past two weeks to the low eighties, proving a blistering Sierra Foothills' summer didn't last forever.

The heat she was experiencing now was nothing compared to the liquid fire that had coursed through her veins when Spencer had touched her mouth earlier, as intense as it was intriguing. If a brush of his finger across her lips felt that good, a kiss must be beautiful beyond description. His would be, she was sure of it.

"You have a lovely smile."

Her eyes flew open. Spencer was propped on one elbow watching her. "I didn't realize you were awake. Thank you for the compliment." Apparently he was serious about paying her three of them.

"You're welcome. You have two more coming." He flashed her a grin that made maintaining a professional demeanor difficult. If only he weren't so handsome, charming and—

"What were you thinking? It must have been something pleasant."

Very pleasant. And entirely inappropriate. Flights of fancy might be enjoyable, but she had no business engaging in them. "I think it's time we play those games."

"We could, but I think you'll want to remove this first, won't you?" He tapped the brim of her hat. "I don't see how you could play games with it on. It's rather good-size. Have you ever thought about getting a smaller one?"

"Why would I do that? I like my hat."

"I thought since you got boots with low heels you might want a hat that isn't so—" he swept a hand toward the peacock feathers gracing hers "—lofty."

"Huh! I'll have you know that I didn't set out to get lower heels, but now that I have them I can see the benefits. I could never have raced all the way here in my old boots."

"It's nice to see that you no longer have your head in the clouds." He grinned.

While his words were said in jest, they reminded her of the shoemaker's comment. Why had she worn such high heels? After all, she was already taller than most women.

An image of her sixteen-year-old self facing Mr. Grimsby for the last time came to mind. For years she'd had to look up to him, but that day, wearing the new boots he'd given her as an entirely unexpected parting gift, she'd been on his level.

She could still hear his final words to her. *Keep your head high, Tess, and don't let anyone get the best of you. Remember everything I taught you, and you'll be fine.* And then he'd enveloped her in a brief but awkward hug.

He'd never hugged anyone before, not even the little ones who ached for a loving touch. She'd been with him longer than anyone except Charlie, but the orphanage director's gesture was so unexpected that the scathing farewell speech she'd planned had lodged in her throat. Before she regained the use of her vocal chords, he'd spun on his heel and walked away without looking back.

After all the years under his rule, she'd vowed never to let anyone hold such power over her again. She'd kept that promise—and her hopes and dreams—to herself. Polly was the only one out west who knew about her days in the orphanage and her strong desire to have a family of her own.

Spencer's voice pulled her back to the present. "I'm afraid I might have offended you. I'm sorry."

"It's all right. I was just remembering something. That's all."

"Something unpleasant this time, I'd say. Wouldn't have to do with being tall, would it?"

Her mouth gaped, and she snapped it shut. "How did you know?"

"It makes sense. I was talking about your height. The last time that subject came up, you told me about a painful memory from your childhood. I gather it wasn't easy."

A bitter laugh escaped before she could stop it. "Far from it. I lost both my parents when I was young. The person who became responsible for me was…unkind, but he did equip me to make a living. I had plenty of opportunities to hone my skills."

"A euphemism for hard work, is it not? He must have been happy with yours. I've rarely seen anyone work as hard as you or do as good a job."

"Thank you. That's two compliments in one. You've already fulfilled your quota." She managed a half-hearted smile.

"That wasn't why I said— Never mind. What's important is that you know how much I appreciate you. You do very well with Luke and Lila. Now I know why. You understand what it's like to lose a parent."

She should never have told him about her past, but his perceptiveness had taken her aback. "Please don't feel sorry for me. I love what I do. If there were a way for me to bring joy into more children's lives, I'd welcome it."

Luke dashed over to them, his hands cupped. He couldn't have chosen a better time to interrupt. Her conversation with Spencer had taken her places she didn't like to go.

"Lookee! I found a butterfly." The excited boy pulled his thumbs apart to reveal his find.

Tess didn't have the heart to tell him he held a moth. "That's nice. Don't you agree, Spencer?"

He did, readily, and ruffled his son's hair. "If you'll let it go, we can play some games."

Luke opened his hands to release the insect, and it flitted off. Tess's gaze followed the moth's zigzagging path until it disappeared from sight, once again able to fly freely. What would it be like not to have all the constraints she'd lived with her whole life? To be herself with no thought of ridicule or reprimand? To experience the wild abandon of a child?

She jumped up. "Come on, Luke. We'll start with a game of tag. Your papa can be *it*. Run! Don't let him catch you."

Luke darted away.

Spencer was off the ground in an instant and caught up to Luke. "I've got you, son." He grabbed Luke under the arms and swung him in a circle. The dear boy's joyful shouts were so loud Tess was afraid he'd wake his sister. Thankfully the little girl was a sound sleeper.

Tag led to blindman's bluff followed by Simon Says. Then Tess thought of a way to have some fun herself. What would Spencer think of it? "Have you ever played Barley-Bridge, Luke?"

He shook his head. "What is it?"

"Two people form a double arch. That will be your papa and me, since we're the tallest. You'll run around me, go under the arch, run around your papa and go through the arch again. Keep on going. When I finish the song your papa and I will—" She froze. She'd have to sing, and if Spencer didn't know the words, she'd have to sing alone. How she wished she had a fine voice like his. Even though she didn't, she had no choice but to attempt the tune for Luke's sake and hope Spencer's ears survived the assault.

"Will what?" Luke asked.

"We'll lower our arms to try and catch you between them." She held her raised arms out in front of Spencer. "Take my hands, please."

He laced his fingers through hers without hesitation. Clearly she had no effect on him, whereas the mere thought of touching him had sent tingles racing from her fingertips all the way to her elbows.

Hopefully he wouldn't find her hands revolting. The constant exposure to lye soap, soil and other such things left them rough and chapped.

He gave her hands a squeeze and dazzled her with one of his brilliant smiles so filled with warmth that her concerns dissolved as quickly as butter on a biscuit. Since he didn't seem at all ill at ease—quite the contrary, in fact—she would enjoy herself, too. If anyone saw the two of them holding hands, they would assume she was his wife—the mother of his children. If only that were true...

Where had that thought come from? She loved the children, but she didn't love their father. She did care about him, as she'd told Polly. But love? That was absurd.

They stood face-to-face. Hers was sure to be awash with color, so she avoided looking at Spencer and focused on Luke instead. "Ready to start?"

"Ready."

She launched into the verse slowing the last line so she completed it just as Luke passed beneath the arch.

She and Spencer lowered their arms and captured Luke between them. "We got you!"

Luke's laughter rang out. He begged to play the game another time. Tess started the tune another time, feeling more confident now that Spencer was singing along with her.

Again and again Luke raced figure eights around Spencer and Tess while she did her best to keep her mind on the game and not on the handsome man whose hands she was holding and holding and holding...

She ventured a glance at Spencer, and her breath caught. He was gazing at her with what looked a lot like attraction. Most likely her overactive imagination was at work, but it wouldn't hurt to pretend he was interested—just this once.

"There are advantages to being tall, Tess. We make a good team." He inclined his head toward their linked arms.

Although he was only talking about the arch they'd formed, she wondered what it would be like it they really were a team. A couple. Husband and wife.

Control yourself, Tess. She had no business spinning such tales, even if Spencer was a loving father and would be a wonderful husband.

Lila's chatter drew their attention and brought the game to an abrupt halt.

"Where do you think you're going, princess?" Spencer intercepted his daughter just in time to keep her from crawling off the blanket into the dirt. He tossed her into the air and caught her, eliciting a squeal Tess wasn't sure was caused by fear or delight.

"Mo, Papa. Mo," the little girl cried. Definitely delight.

A short time later they sat on the blanket enjoying generous slices of Lila's birthday cake.

Luke stuffed the last bite into his mouth and licked his fingers. "Is the surprise a cake?"

"What surprise?" Spencer asked.

"The one she said I get in this many days." Luke held up seven fingers.

Tess jogged Spencer's memory. "I told you about it at the depot right before Goliath arrived."

"Ah, yes. I remember now. It's not a cake, son, even though any cake Tess makes would be a right tasty surprise. She's an excellent cook."

Spencer glanced at her, and she acknowledged the compliment with a smile.

"Gumdrops?"

"No. It's even better than that." Tess gathered their picnic items and returned them to the basket.

"You're not the only one getting a surprise, Luke. I have one for Tess, but she doesn't have to wait for hers." Spencer unrolled his shirtsleeves, shoved his arms into his frock coat and pulled something out of the inside breast pocket. He handed her the brown paper package.

"What is it?"

"Open it, and you'll see."

Chapter Nineteen

A frisson of excitement surged through Tess. She'd never received a present from a gentleman. She wouldn't have expected one from Spencer. He tended to be practical and didn't spend money on frivolities, as he called them.

No. He didn't, so why would he now? Her bubble of joy burst. What a ninny she was to think he'd bought her a gift. This must be something for the house. The package was the right size and shape for a saltshaker to replace the one Luke had accidentally broken the week before.

Doing her best to hide her disappointment behind a smile, she untied the string and pulled back the paper. It wasn't a saltshaker, after all. "Oh, Spencer, it's beautiful."

Luke tugged on her sleeve. "Let me see."

"Here." She held out the cylindrical item to him. Clearly unimpressed, he shrugged, plopped down on the picnic blanket and snatched the last slice of cake.

She studied the piece of porcelain from every angle. Sprays of delicate forget-me-nots had been hand painted on the snowy white background. Several holes had been drilled in the top, all of them good-size, with an even larger one in the middle. "I expected a salt-shaker, but that's not what it is."

Lila crawled over to Spencer, and he scooped her into his lap. "It's a hatpin holder. When I saw the blue flowers on it, I thought of you. I figured that since you were up much of the night taking care of this little gal while she battled her teething pain this past week and didn't even take your time off, giving you a small token of my appreciation was the least I could do."

Tess's excitement returned with such force she felt lightheaded. It was a gift, after all. "Thank you. It's lovely."

"I'm glad you like it."

"Like it? I love it. I've never been given anything that pleased me more." Perhaps it was a sign that he was developing feelings for her, as Polly had said.

He rubbed the back of his neck. "I was afraid you might not since I've teased about your hat and all."

Eager to dispel any lingering doubts he might have, Tess grabbed her hat, pulled the pins from it and placed them in the holder. "You've done me a favor. Were it not for you, I might have lost my hatpins since I had no special place to store them."

She couldn't resist the urge to tease him. "Without the pins, I would be forced to wear a smaller hat. Although that might please a certain gentleman I know, it would be a *big* disappointment to me." She grinned. "As it is, thanks to that same gentleman I'll be able to wear my *large* hat, knowing it's not going anywhere." She patted her beloved bonnet, knocking it askew.

He reached out to right her hat, lowered his hand

and let it hover next to her cheek as though he was contemplating caressing it. If only he would. She held her breath.

"Papa, why are you staring at her like that?"

"Was I? I'm sorry, Tess. That was rude of me." Spencer pulled his hand away so quickly she was certain she felt a breeze. "We should be going. If you'll hold Lila, I'll fold the blanket." He practically shoved his daughter into Tess's arms and jumped to his feet.

Clearly she'd misread his intentions. The gift was a token of his gratitude and nothing more. She'd be wise to curb her vivid imagination and do the job he paid her to do.

A glance out Lila's bedroom window reassured Tess that Luke was engrossed in his play. Woof lay not far away, his muzzle resting on his paws. The watchful dog gave her a sense of peace. Anytime Luke went outside, Woof was with him. If the fearless boy got into trouble, Woof's bark would alert her.

Tess leaned over the side of the crib and kissed Lila's cheek as she slept. Learning how difficult her birthing had been and how close Spencer had come to losing his daughter intensified the love Tess felt for the precious little girl.

She would never understand how a father could walk away from a child the way hers had. The memory of being aban— left at the orphanage refused to dim, even though she shoved it to the most remote recesses of her mind. Recalling it never failed to send searing pain through her, which is why she rarely ever mentioned that agonizing day.

Thankfully, when Spencer had asked her about her

past at their picnic, she'd had the presence of mind not to give him anything but the barest of details. She'd been careful to keep their conversations focused on lighter topics ever since. It wouldn't do for him to know her background. He might pity her, and she wanted no part of that. She must focus on doing her best to care for his family.

Luke had been waiting a week for his surprise. The time had come to unveil it. She carried the garments downstairs and had him come inside.

His response exceeded Tess's expectations. He took one look at the outfit and did so much whooping and hollering it was a wonder he didn't wake Lila.

Tess helped him change into the tunic and short pants, gently instructing him in how the fasteners worked. "Was this worth waiting for?"

He nodded enthusiastically. "I'm a big boy with big-boy clothes."

"You are. Now I'm going to give you a big-boy haircut out on the porch, but you'll have to sit still. Can you do that?"

"Yep."

Luke was true to his word, holding a statue-like pose throughout the cut. She ran the comb through his hair one last time and held a hand mirror so he could see himself. "What do you think?"

"It's short." He turned his head from side to side. "I don't look like a little boy anymore."

"You look very handsome." He was adorable. Her work the past week had been worth the sore back and late nights spent sewing by lantern light.

Because she'd chosen to spend half an hour each evening sitting in the parlor with Spencer before going to her room—just the two of them—her free time had dwindled. Not that she minded. Even though he'd said little, often sitting in silence as he oiled a rope or completed some other chore while she raised the hems of her dresses to accommodate her lower boot heels, the homey atmosphere had filled her with a pleasant sense of belonging.

She wouldn't press him to talk, trusting that in time he'd grow more comfortable. One couldn't expect to bring about a significant change in the space of a week.

Satisfied with the haircut, Tess pulled the sheet off Luke and grabbed the broom. "I'm all done, so you may get down."

"I can't wait until Papa sees me."

Neither could she.

Dust swirled at Spencer's ankles as he neared the house. Woof bounded up to him, his tail wagging so fast it was a blur.

Anytime the Lord saw fit to send rain, Spencer would be grateful. California summers could get mighty tiresome after a while. What he'd give to feel the hairs on his nape rise at the first flash of lightening or hear the rumble of thunder. Surely with October right around the corner, a storm couldn't be far off.

He gazed at the house. A figure stood on the porch. A tall figure. It appeared Tess was watching for him. The thought put a spring in his step.

Something had changed at the picnic a week ago. He couldn't say what for sure, but she seemed more approachable. She'd taken to spending a few minutes with him each evening before retreating to her room. While she said little, he appreciated the companionship. He wished she'd tell him more about her past. She alluded to it briefly that day but had been close-mouthed ever since.

Memories of the outing flashed through his mind. Luke's laughter. Lila's delight at being tossed into the air. Tess's hands in his. She had the hands of someone accustomed to work, and yet those work-roughened hands could caress a child's cheek with tenderness—and had many times.

He hadn't intended to enjoy holding her hands as much as he did. What would she think if she knew how much pleasure it had brought him? Most likely she'd feel sorry for him, a pathetic widower so starved for the touch of another person that he'd allowed the game to go on and on in order to hold his housekeeper's hands longer. He missed the contact with another person. With a woman.

While he hadn't expected to feel any attraction to Tess, he couldn't help but notice her. Although she wasn't a dainty woman by any means, when she gave him one of her playful smiles, she was attractive in her own way.

If only she were more like that woman, Faith, who'd written those introspective letters to her intended. She had no trouble sharing her thoughts and feelings. Should the Lord choose to bless him with another wife someday, he'd want someone like that. Such a woman would be easy to talk with and would make a wonderful partner.

"Papa!" Luke charged down the steps and sped down the drive.

Spencer stopped in his tracks and gaped. His son

looked so different. So mature. Tess had taken him from babyhood to boyhood.

Luke reached Spencer and beamed. "The surprise was new clothes. Big-boy clothes. See?" Luke turned in a complete circle. "She cut my hair, too. It doesn't swing around anymore." He shook his head to demonstrate.

A vise-like pain gripped Spencer, squeezing his heart until it ached. He shoved aside the onslaught of memories, both bitter and sweet, and forced himself to share in Luke's excitement. "You look all grown up, son, with your haircut and the new outfit. I like the color, and I like this." He indicated the gold braid decorating the tunic's cuffs and hem.

"And look here." Luke lifted the long top to reveal the short pants beneath. "They got buttons on the front. She made me practice using them lotsa times so I won't have to ask for help when I go to the privy. She said big boys can do it all by themselves. And I can. But she told me not to wait too long 'cause I gotta open the buttons before I can—"

"Take care of business. That's true." He needed to thank Tess, but he wanted her to himself. "Can you run all right in your new clothes, son?"

"Yep. Watch me." Luke took off with Woof right behind him.

Tess balanced Lila on her hip and met Spencer at the bottom of the steps. She watched Luke race around the yard and smiled. "I'm pleased with the way the outfit turned out. He was an absolute darling while I cut his hair. Doesn't he look handsome? Almost as handsome as—" she inhaled sharply and continued in a business-like manner "—as I expected him to."

Spencer tamped down a smile. If he didn't know better, he'd say she'd been about to compare Luke to him. "He looks great. I just wish…" His chest tightened, and his throat grew thick. He cleared it.

Compassion flooded Tess's dark eyes. "I understand. As happy as it made me to sew his big-boy clothes, I couldn't help but think how much joy this would have brought his mother. I'm sure she was looking forward to this day."

"We both were." He couldn't think about that. Life went on despite death and disappointments.

"I'm sorry it's so hard." She patted his arm before removing her hand. It was the first time she'd touched him since the picnic, but this was different—a housekeeper comforting her employer rather than one friend reaching out to another.

Something had caused her to draw back, but for the life of him he couldn't figure out what—or why it mattered so much. "You did a fine job on the clothes. I appreciate your hard work."

"Thank you. I need to go inside and see to supper. Would you take Lila please?" She handed him his daughter, turned and let out with a loud, shrill scream.

"Luke!"

Tess took off running toward the bull's pen.

Luke stood *inside* the fence at the far end, twirling his rope over his head and walking slowly toward Goliath at the opposite end.

Spencer watched in horror as his snorting bull pawed the ground, spied Luke and headed toward him.

Lord, help us! He's going to charge.

Chapter Twenty

Just as Tess reached the pen, Goliath lowered his head, horns forward, and charged.

"Get out, Luke!"

He spun around and pumped his little legs as fast as they could go.

Clutching huge handfuls of her skirt, she raced along the side of the pen.

Goliath picked up speed and gained on Luke.

In the space of a heartbeat, Tess was over the fence. She flew across the hard-packed earth, putting herself between Luke and the bull.

Her petticoats bunched as she ran, and she stumbled. Righting herself, she looked for Luke, jerking her head from side to side.

In a flash of blue, he scrambled between the fence slats.

He was safe, but she was in the middle of the enormous pen.

The pounding of Goliath's hooves, growing ever closer, echoed the frenzied beating of her heart.

There was no way she could outrun the bull.

She yanked off her hat and tossed it over her shoulder in hopes it might distract the angry animal and buy her precious seconds.

The bull's hooves pounded the ground right behind her, putting wings to her feet.

"Help me, Lord!"

Never in her life had she run so fast.

A thundering crash took place.

She didn't look back as she covered the final feet, scaled the fence and kept on running.

Not until she was several yards away did she stop and turn around. Goliath lay on his side. Spencer leaned over the fence at the far end of the pen by the barn clutching the end of his taut lariat that stretched between him and the bull's right foreleg.

She couldn't believe Spencer had stopped the beast so quickly, saving her from a possible goring—or worse. The man was amazing.

Ignoring the stitch in her side, she dashed over to Luke and held him close as she caught her breath.

"Lemme go." He broke free and stuck a leg through the fence.

"No, Luke! You stay out of there."

"I gotta get my rope."

"Your papa will get it for you. Right now you have some explaining to do, young man." She grabbed his hand and marched toward the corner of the pen nearest the house, where Spencer stood. "Here's your son. I have to get Lila. Where did you leave her?"

"Right where we were standing. Woof's watching her. I'll see to Goliath. You stay put, Luke. I'll deal with you later."

Tess's heart had finally ceased its frenzied beating.

She found Lila and the faithful watchdog engaged in what the little girl perceived as a game. Every time she attempted to crawl in one direction, Woof would block the way, so she'd strike out in another, laughing all the while.

"Good job, Woofie. You'll get an extra bone tonight." She patted the dog, gathered the dust-covered girl in her arms and returned to the pen. Luke stood outside the fence watching his father release the rope binding Goliath's leg.

How Spencer could go in the pen after that bull had charged his own son was beyond her. What a courageous man he was coming to their rescue like that. He waited as the enormous longhorn got to its feet and lumbered off.

"Look out, Papa! There's a snake." Luke pointed to a three-foot-long reptile in the center of the pen not far from Luke's rope. A lumpy-looking reptile that wasn't moving.

No! It couldn't be. She patted her head.

Spencer picked up the supposed snake, as well as Luke's rope and her hat. He jogged to the fence and hopped over it.

"Let me see, Papa."

He held Tess's hair switch behind his back, set her dusty but unharmed hat on a nearby hay bale and handed Luke his lariat. "Here."

"I wanna see the other thing. The snake."

Spencer shrugged. "There was no snake."

Luke's face scrunched with puzzlement. "But I saw one. Maybe that's what made Goliath run. Did it get away?"

Tess took pity on the confused boy and held out a hand to Spencer. "May I have it please?"

He hesitated.

"Luke deserves to know the truth."

"If you're sure."

She nodded, and he handed her the hank of braided hair, which she held out to Luke. "It's not a snake. It's a hairpiece."

He looked up at her, his eyes wide. "Your hair broke off?"

"No. It's called a hair switch. It was attached to my head with hairpins. A lady wears one to look…" She searched in vain for a word, but Luke supplied one.

"Pretty?"

Although he was a bright boy, his perceptiveness surprised her. "I suppose that's part of it. But I wore mine to look—" she didn't like admitting it, even to herself "—taller."

Luke glanced from her head to her feet and back again. "But you're already tall. Real tall. Why do you wanna be taller?"

"I don't. Not anymore."

"So you're not gonna wear it now?"

"I'm not." She'd be content with the hair the Lord had given her. "It'll be lighter and cooler without it."

"Can I have it?"

Spencer shot her an apologetic smile. "Son, I don't think—"

"It's all right." While she appreciated his compassion, the loss of her switch was a relief on several counts. She wouldn't have to fuss with her hair as long each morning or worry about the hairpiece coming loose when she practiced roping. "Luke's welcome to it. I would, however, like my hairpins. I appear to have lost several of them in my race to reach him."

Spencer's gaze rested on her disheveled hair. "How many did you lose?"

She patted her head and found two. "Six hairpins—" she glanced at her hat "—and I'm missing two hatpins, as well."

He leaped over the fence in one fluid motion and scoured the ground. He didn't return until he had every last one of her sterling silver pins. "Here you are."

"Thank you. It was kind of you to get my things for me." And brave. She wouldn't get inside that pen again for anything.

"It's the least I could do after you risked your li—"

"I'm fine." She didn't like cutting Spencer off, but there was no need to frighten Luke more than he already had been. If the terror-stricken look on his face when he'd realized the danger was any indication, he'd learned a valuable lesson. Sometimes experience was the best teacher.

Spencer's narrow-eyed gaze coupled with a subtle shake of his head told her he knew what she was up to but wouldn't be letting Luke off easy. He folded his arms, dipped his chin and faced his son. "What were you doing in Goliath's pen?"

Luke looked up at his father, the picture of innocence. "I was gonna rope him like you did."

Spencer pressed his lips into a straight line. Tess could almost see the steam rising off him. "I told you not to go in there, and yet you deliberately disobeyed me."

Luke tilted his head, a quizzical look on his face.

"But you said I could try when I was older, and you told me I looked all grown up."

"When did I say that?"

"When I showed you my new clothes."

Spencer dragged in a deep breath, clearly fighting for control. His frustration was understandable. She couldn't begin to count the number of times the clever boy had tried her patience with his literal interpretations.

"You know now that Goliath didn't see a snake, son. What he saw was you spinning your rope over your head. He was charging at you, and he could have hurt you and Tess if I hadn't been here to help. You have to mind us, young man."

"I'm sorry, Papa." Luke hung his head.

If Tess had read things correctly, the dear boy was genuinely remorseful. He'd only been acting on the impetuousness of youth and hadn't meant to endanger anyone. "We love you, Luke, and don't want anything bad happen to you. That's why—"

"No!" He stomped his foot. "You're not my mama. You can't love me."

She hadn't meant to say that aloud. While she couldn't help but love her charges, letting a child know how she felt was foolhardy. Her best option was to change the subject as quickly as possible and hope Luke would forget what she'd said—and that Spencer had been too preoccupied to notice.

He spoke before she could get a word out. "You're not to yell at Tess. She's right. We don't want you to get hurt. You're a big boy, but you're not big enough to rope a longhorn bull on your own yet. You have to be at least, um…twelve."

"Twelve?" Luke huffed. "That's *old*. Do I really gotta wait that long?"

"Yes, son. Now go to your room and sit on your bed until Tess calls you for supper. I'll let you know then what your punishment will be."

Luke scowled. Tess expected him to protest, but he turned and trudged toward the house.

As soon as he was out of earshot, Spencer let loose. "What was that boy thinking? He could have gotten the both of you killed. I can't lose anyone else." He grasped the fence with a white-knuckle grip.

She was eager to ease his suffering. If only she could.

"Go Papa." Lila squirmed and reached for her father, almost as though she sensed his need for comfort.

"Come here, my girl." He took her and gave her a peck on the cheek. "At least I have one child who won't make me gray before my time. I don't know what I'm going to do with Luke. He's more trouble than a burr under a saddle blanket."

"If it's any help, I don't think he sets out to get in trouble. What we're dealing with is a bright boy who reasons things out differently than we're used to. I have to be very clear in my explanations. I think he could make a fine lawyer one day." She smiled.

"You're quick to defend him."

"He's special to me."

Spencer grabbed Tess's hat from the hay bale and used it in a game of peek-a-boo with Lila, bringing forth round after round of giggles. "You didn't intend to love him, did you?"

Tess shook her head, causing the braid now hanging down her back to swing from side to side. "It's not wise. I do my best not to give way to my feelings, but despite my best efforts, I can't help myself. And then when I have to leave—"

"You're not thinking of leaving, are you?" He pinned her with a gaze so intense it could bore a hole in a cast iron skillet. "I thought you liked it here."

"I do, but I'm realistic. One day you'll meet someone and won't need a housekeeper. I like to think that when that day comes you'll provide me with a solid recommendation."

"You're doing a fine job. Look at Lila. She was withdrawn when you came, and now she's starting to talk. You've worked wonders with Luke. He's a handful, but you have a knack for knowing what he needs. And your cooking… Well, I've rarely eaten meals as tasty as those you fix. I'm happy with things as they are and have no plans to write such a letter for a long time."

His earnestness touched her, but she knew the truth. She'd seen him with his children and witnessed his grief over the loss of his wife. Spencer Abbott had a great capacity for love. He would find someone, remarry and—Tess could hardly bear to form the thought—send her on her way. When that day came and she was forced to take her leave, she would leave a large part of her heart behind.

Rain drummed on the roof of the main warehouse. A decent storm at long last. Spencer brushed off his frock coat and waited as Peter and his crew transferred freight to a wagon. Their job complete, the baggage handlers dashed off to see to a shipment in another of the warehouses. Peter helped the driver cover his load with tarpaulins, and the fellow set out. Even in his India rubber raincoat, his journey over the Sierras would be a miserable one.

"Sorry to keep you waiting, Spence." Peter led the way to his office and held his hands in front of the stove. "I love my job, but on days like today…" He gave an exaggerated shudder. "I've got hot coffee if you'd like some."

"No thanks. I won't be here long."

"Didn't reckon you would since you don't have your notebook. You're frowning. Something troublin' ya?"

Spencer rested a hand on the window frame and watched rivulets trail down the glass. "I finally got a reply from the gentleman in Sacramento City who'd responded to my inquiry about the letters. Turns out he's misplaced a Bible his great aunt Faith inscribed to him and thought he might have left it on a train."

"What're you going to do?"

"I don't know." Spencer leaned back against the windowsill. "I suppose I could wait a little longer."

Peter plopped into his ancient desk chair, the rickety thing creaking under his weight. "You've waited nearly two months. I say it's time to read the rest of the letters. That's the only way you stand a chance of figuring out whose they are."

"You're right." The trouble was, he had a hard time thinking of reading something so personal. The writer of the letters had poured her heart and soul on the page. How would she feel if she knew a stranger was reading her words? "I'd best get back to work."

Spencer sprinted across the platform. He ducked into the depot and hung his soggy coat on a hook in his office.

A full minute passed as he sat and stared at his bottom desk drawer while a battle waged within. Memories of Faith's words had wound their way into his thoughts for weeks. It was wrong of him to think of another man's fiancée, but he hadn't been able to curb his curiosity.

Her betrothed had been given ample time to send word, provided he'd seen the notice. Apparently he hadn't, or perhaps he didn't realize he'd lost the letters on board a train. Either way, Spencer had no choice but to read the next letter if he wanted to find clues to the man's identity.

He opened the drawer and located the bundle in the back corner. Doing his best to ignore a renewed attack of doubt, he slipped the second letter out of the blue ribbon binding the three of them together. He unfolded the pages and began to read.

Saturday, August 20, 1864

To the man I look forward to marrying,

On that special someday when we first meet, I feel certain I'll know you're the one I've been waiting for all my life. Although the Lord has yet to bring you into my life, I continue to lift you in prayer, asking Him to bless you.

Shock, sudden and overwhelming, gripped Spencer. His hands shook so badly he dropped the letter on the desk.

Faith *wasn't* engaged.

At least she hadn't been as of two years ago. Her supposed fiancé was a figment of her fertile imagination. *She* must have lost the letters.

Surely a woman like her with a romantic bent would want them back. Even Trudy, who'd been more practical than sentimental, had saved the letters he'd sent her during their courtship.

Spencer was filled with a sense of purpose as he picked up the pages that had fallen from his fingers. He would learn all he could about Faith, so he could find her and see that she got her letters back. It was the least he could do. He resumed reading, hoping she'd chosen to include information that would make locating her easier.

Several paragraphs into the letter, he'd learned little about her, since she focused on the husband and family she hoped to have and how eager she was to serve them. While her generous nature appealed to him, he needed facts.

The next section caught his eye and gave him hope.

I realized I've told you little about myself and thought I'd remedy that. My mother died when I was three, and my father left me at the local orphanage, never to return. From that day on, I dreamed of being part of a family again, but the Lord never saw fit to place me in one. He upheld me, though, and showed me a way I could make a difference in the lives of others who'd experienced loss. I spent much of my childhood helping care for the precious little ones who came and went with heartbreaking regularity.

What was heartbreaking was thinking of Faith as a young girl, abandoned by her father and longing to be taken into someone's home. How could a man walk away from his own child? Spencer had heard of others who'd done so, citing financial hardship or other valid reasons, but the mere thought sickened him. Not once, even in the darkest days after Trudy's death when the simple act of drawing his next breath seemed an impossible feat, had he considered giving up Luke and Lila.

He corralled his thoughts and continued reading.

An employment opportunity arose when I was sixteen. Since it allowed me to work with children such as those I'd known and loved, I embraced it. I've been blessed to care for youngsters ever since, and I'm grateful. The work can be challenging at times, especially when I must say goodbye, which happens more often than I like, but the rewards are many.

I hope this glimpse into my past has helped you understand why my dream is to marry and have a family. I've known women with lofty ambitions. While I admire them, my greatest pleasure would be creating a home that's warm and inviting, a place you'd be eager to return to after a hard day's work. If that home happened to be filled to the brim with children, laughter and cherished memories in the making, I'd be the happiest of women.

A profound sense of satisfaction filled Spencer. The more he learned about Faith, the deeper his admiration grew. She was proving to be the kind of woman he'd first thought. She'd experienced hardships that could have soured a person, and yet she exuded sweetness.

He could almost picture her standing on his porch

with a child on her hip, greeting him at the end of a long day with a smile as warm and inviting as the meal awaiting him. Afterward, when the children were in bed, they'd sit in the parlor where they'd discuss the day and make plans for a bright future together.

An image of Tess seated on the settee next to his wingback armchair came to him, and the contrast made him smile. While she was wonderful with the children and knew how to have fun, she lacked Faith's gentle spirit and openness.

He'd witnessed Tess's compassion numerous times, but she tended to be a private person. Their evenings were companionable, but he craved a deeper connection.

Even though he'd only read two of Faith's letters, he felt certain there would be no walls to scale with her. She'd be the kind of woman who understood him, accepted him and held nothing back. He was sure of it.

However, the question of how to find her remained. He could read the third and last letter, but he doubted it would reveal anything specific, since she hadn't done so in either of the others. Not only that, but once he read it, he'd have no more of Faith's uplifting words to look forward to.

He'd learned enough to help in his search. He would start by having Drake send a telegram with an updated notice to the other stationmasters right away. And he would pray that Faith would see it, contact him and turn out to be everything he'd imagined her to be.

Chapter Twenty-One

"I can't believe Thanksgiving will be here in ten days, can you?" Polly patted Petey's back.

Tess divided her attention between Polly and Lila. Ever since the darling girl had learned to walk two weeks before, she fussed if she was held. She toddled over to one of Mr. Hawke's display cases and peered inside, her hands splayed on the glass front. While Luke had gravitated to the toys as always, with Abby his shadow, Lila was content to peer at soap flakes and scrub brushes.

"You certainly have a great deal to give thanks for this year, don't you?" Tess patted the wide-eyed boy in Polly's arms.

"Indeed I do. Petey's such a good baby. Abby fought sleep and caused me to lose plenty of mine, but this little fellow goes down with no trouble and only wakes for a feeding once a night."

The door to the general store opened, letting in a gust of cool air—along with Mrs. Carter. She adjusted her shawl. "Brr. I reckon we're in for another storm. Them clouds off to the west are coming on quick." She cast a glance at the crates Mr. Hawkes was busy filling. "Looks like someone's goin' to have a nice Thanksgiving. Too bad my girl can't come, but at least I'll see her at Christmas."

Tess's heart went out the lonely widow. "I can't abide the thought of you spending Thanksgiving by yourself. How would you like to join us?"

Polly's round face registered shock. "Um, Tessie, have you asked Spencer about this?"

"I'm sure he won't mind, not after all Mrs. Carter has done for him."

The older woman smiled. "Aw, Miss Grimsby, you're too kind. I didn't do all that much, 'cept keep Luke out of trouble. And I didn't do a very good job of that. You saw the state of the place when you first come here, and I know you won't never forget the stink."

Tess laughed. "It's not likely. But the smell didn't last all that long."

"Not after you scoured the place and rustled up them tasty vittles. If you're sure Mr. Abbott won't have no problem with it, I'd be mighty grateful to join you."

"She could find out now." Polly inclined her head toward the front window. "The gentleman himself approacheth."

A quick assessment gave Tess a moment's pause. Spencer wore the frown she'd seen far too many times during her first months in Shingle Springs. He'd been much happier in recent weeks, smiling most days and even laughing on occasion. Something must have happened to dampen his mood.

He entered and strode to the counter, determination dogging his every step. "Ladies." He doffed his hat to them. "Where's Mr. Hawkes?"

"In the back," Tess said. "He's looking for the oranges he ordered. I wanted some for—"

"He won't find them. I've kept Drake busy the past hour sending telegrams in order to figure out what happened to a shipment that was due Saturday. Turns out a freight handler in Folsom put several orders on the wrong train and sent them back to Sacramento City."

Mr. Hawkes emerged from his backroom. "So that's what happened. Thought I'd misplaced some crates. I've been known to do that." He chuckled. "When can I expect them?"

Mr. Hawke's obvious lack of concern eased the tightness in Spencer's fine features. "Tomorrow morning."

"Very good. Here's the allspice you wanted, Miss Grimsby. That completes your order—less the oranges, of course. Looks like you're going to be busy. Anyone around your table on Thanksgiving is in for a treat."

Tess detected a note of wistfulness in Mr. Hawkes's comment. If she wasn't mistaken, the longtime bachelor would spend the holiday by himself. Unless...

She needed to talk to Spencer. Alone. "Polly, would you please keep an eye on the children for a minute while Spencer and I talk?"

Having received Polly's assurances, Tess headed for the door. To her relief, Spencer followed her. A quick glance over her shoulder revealed curiosity swirling in his bright blue eyes.

His neighbor, that obnoxious Mr. Dodge, entered the shop and barked an order for chewing tobacco at Mr. Hawkes as Spencer and Tess exited. A gust caught her hat, threatening to send it sailing. She held on to the brim.

Spencer chuckled. "You know, if you wore a smaller hat, you'd be less likely to have the wind carry it away."

Not that again. She'd seen the hat in a milliner's shop two years before and been taken in by the frothy sea of teal tulle on an indigo base topped with three gorgeous peacock feathers. Few women, the hat maker had told her, could do justice to such a tremendous creation. "I like my hat. Why do you care about it anyhow?"

He assumed an affronted tone so overdone she couldn't help but smile. "Dear lady, do you doubt my motives? I simply want to make your life easier. I figure if you had a smaller one, you wouldn't have to perform a balancing act to get it to rest on the shelf back home."

She replied with a hefty pinch of spice. "The way I see it, *I* don't need a smaller hat. *You* just need a wider shelf."

His broad grin was disarming. "You got me there, Tess. I'll see to that. So, tell me. What was it you wanted?"

How delightful to have found a way to elevate his mood. Now to secure his permission so she could get back inside where warmth awaited her. "I've been making plans for Thanksgiving dinner. It's going to be quite a feast. I thought it would be nice to share the meal with some who don't have relatives in the area, such as Mr. Hawkes and Mrs. Carter. I'd like to invite Peter, Polly and their children, too, along with the Muellers. I thought you might enjoy seeing so many people around the table for a change."

"No." The single word hung in the chilly air, firm and final, a stark contrast to his jovial mood moments ago.

She wouldn't give up that easily. "Might I ask why?"

"I don't want anyone else there, and I don't want a fancy meal."

Understanding dawned. "You don't want to face Thanksgiving without her."

"What do I have to be thankful for?"

Tess ticked off the items on her fingers. "You have two wonderful children, a lovely home, a job that brings you a great deal of satisfaction, a promising future as a cattle rancher…and a bullheaded housekeeper who refuses to let you hide away and wallow in your grief."

"Are you done?"

"Not quite." She softened her tone. "The day will be difficult no matter what you do. To my way of thinking, the best way to get through it would be to do something for others so you aren't focused on yourself and your pain."

"You're done now."

Tess knew better than to push any harder. Spencer had to wage this battle on his own. She reached out to offer a comforting touch. "I'm sorry it's so hard."

The longing in his eyes as he stared at her hand resting on his was unmistakable. She would have to find creative ways to reach out to him because everything in her told her she was just the woman to meet his needs and fill his life with light and laughter. "We should be getting back inside, but let me adjust your cravat first. It appears to be askew." It wasn't, but he didn't need to know that.

He stood still as she fluffed the silk, rewarding her with the barest hint of a smile. "I've changed my mind. You may invite whomever you'd like."

Mr. Dodge burst out the door. He paused, tossed a

bag of pungent-smelling tobacco in the air and caught it in his bony hand. "Apparently you don't listen, Abbott, since I see that rangy excuse of a bull is still in your pen—for now. If you care about your future, I suggest you think twice about your plans to raise cattle, or you'll be sorry."

Spencer glared at the gold-toothed bully. "I told you what I think of your threats."

"It's no threat. It's a promise." The lanky man left without another word, passing the wagon that would soon be filled with crates containing everything Tess needed to make this year's Thanksgiving dinner one Spencer would never forget.

All her life Tess had dreamed of sitting down to Thanksgiving dinner surrounded by family and friends. Although this wasn't her family, the people with whom she'd be sharing the meal in a few short minutes were her friends.

She peeked in the oven and peered in pots and pans. The air was thick with the delicious scents of a feast in the making.

Polly reached for a wooden spoon. "Quick. Go change. Mrs. Carter and I will see to things until you get back. And don't tarry. These potatoes will be ready for mashing soon."

Tess made short work of slipping into her sapphire silk, a dress she hadn't worn since her days accompanying her charges to events in Sacramento City. With nimble fingers, she transformed the high bun she'd worn earlier—which she'd kept hidden under her hat during the Thanksgiving service—into a chignon at her nape. Spencer had never seen her without her customary braid that, for the sake of ease, she'd taken to wearing down her back when she was at home.

At home? What was she thinking? The festive atmosphere must be getting to her. This wasn't her home. It was his. And he was downstairs with his guests, awaiting the meal that required her finishing touches.

She peered in the looking glass one last time. Thanks to her hours in the kitchen, she had nice color in her cheeks. It intensified at the thought.

A bubble of laughter burst from her. What a silly goose she was. No one cared what she looked like. They just wanted to savor the food she'd prepared.

The final minutes were a flurry of activity as she mashed the potatoes while Polly and Mrs. Carter filled the serving dishes. At last everything was ready, with the rest of the party having taken their places at the table.

Tess picked up the bowl of sage stuffing.

"Oh, no you don't." Polly took it from her. "Mrs. Carter and I will carry in everything except the turkey. Once we're seated, you can bring it in."

"Fine." Tess surrendered the stuffing. Arguing with Polly did no good. Once she put her mind to something, she clung to her plan tenaciously.

The two women worked swiftly. Before long Polly returned for the last item. She grabbed the basket of rolls. "Give Mrs. Carter and me a minute to get settled, and then come on in."

When the rustle of fabric and scraping of chairs ceased, Tess hefted the turkey platter and entered the dining room. A chorus of oohs and aahs greeted her. She paused a moment to savor the scene before her.

She'd never experienced a Thanksgiving like this.

Her early ones had been spent around long tables in the orphanage's dilapidated dining hall where the children were grateful to get a sliver of turkey. In recent years she'd sat at tables in the servants' quarters of fine homes, unable to eat until the waitstaff had removed the final dishes following the families' feasts.

The look of gratitude Spencer gave her as she set the browned-to-perfection bird in front of him made her days preparing for this moment worthwhile. Although he would likely say little, he appreciated her efforts on his behalf. She took her seat, her heart overflowing with gratitude.

Tess had outdone herself. Spencer could almost hear his dining table groaning under the weight of the many dishes filled with the tantalizing fare. He'd have to show her how much he appreciated her efforts.

She set the turkey in front of him, took her seat and sent a smile his way before turning to her other side to check on Lila, who sat in her high chair watching all the activity with interest. His daughter had never seen so many people around the table.

Due to her weakened state after Lila's delivery, Trudy hadn't felt up to entertaining. He hadn't realized how much he'd missed having guests. The buzz of conversations chased away the memories of quiet dinners that hovered in the corners of this very room.

Tess had been right—again. Although she lacked the gentleness Faith exhibited, Tess's bold request and refusal to accept his initial reluctance had forced him to overcome his objections.

Faith. How often she entered his thoughts these days. Ever since he'd read her second letter and learned she wasn't engaged, after all, he'd found himself imagining where she was or what she was doing. Was she still pining for a family, or had she found someone deserving of her?

Spencer had the impression there was something holding her back. Some reason she had yet to receive a proposal. There must be, because a woman as kind, caring and warm-spirited as she would surely have received numerous offers.

Perhaps she was plain, walked with a limp or had some other shortcoming that kept men from seeing her inner beauty. Such things might matter to others, but he wouldn't care. He'd gotten a glimpse of her heart, and it was filled with love just waiting to be showered on a husband and children. Some wise man would see beneath the surface and be the richer for it. Or perhaps he would find her and—

"Spencer." Tess rested a hand on his arm, leaned close and whispered. "Are you all right?"

"Hmm?" He gazed into her beautiful brown eyes. A man could drown in their depths. Even in her everyday dresses, Tess could turn heads, but she was a vision in the deep blue gown. Gone was the dutiful housekeeper. In her place sat a beautiful lady with all the charm and poise of Sacramento City's elite.

She smiled, merriment dancing in those captivating eyes, and Tess reemerged. But not the Tess he knew. This striking woman stirred feelings in him he'd not experienced in months. There was more to her than he'd realized. Much more.

"We're waiting for you to say grace."

"So I see." He would pray over the meal now, and

later he'd ask the Lord to help make sense of the jumble of emotions tumbling around inside him.

Tess carried the last dirty dish to the kitchen and sighed with contentment. The meal couldn't have gone any better. The sounds of laughter in the parlor tempted her, but she had dishes to wash. She reached for her largest apron, a full-length one big enough to protect her fancy silk dress, and set to work.

"Leave them, Tessie. They can soak." Polly grabbed the stack of plates, set the entire thing in the soapy water and dried her hands. "It's a holiday, and you deserve to enjoy yourself."

"But Spencer expects me to do my job."

"Nonsense. He's the one who sent me to get you."

The spoon Tess had been holding clattered against the side of the metal washtub. "He did? I didn't think he would notice my absence, what with all the people here."

Polly laughed. "He noticed all right. Your appearance in that gorgeous dress captured his attention. He spent the entire meal stealing glances at you."

"Surely you jest. I never once saw him—" That wasn't true. She had caught his eye when he'd put a slice of turkey on her plate. The warmth in the smile he'd given her had sent such a surge of heat into her cheeks she'd wished for a fan to hide behind. "All right. I did see him look my way once. But only once. That doesn't mean anything."

"It could. He's a lonely man. You're a beautiful woman. He's attracted to you, and you obviously care for him. I'd like nothing better than to see the two of you to end up together."

Tess shook her head a bit too forcefully. She pushed a loose hairpin back into her chignon. "It does no good to harbor such dreams. He's a grieving widower who thinks he's responsible for his wife's death."

She gasped and clapped a hand to her mouth. How could she have said that aloud? "Forgive me. It was wrong of me to betray a confidence."

Polly's face registered the same disbelief Tess had felt when Spencer made the surprising confession one rainy October evening. "How could he think that? It's preposterous! Trudy tripped over a rake and fell, was impaled by the tines and died from the resulting infection. It's not like Spencer left the rake in her path on purpose or shoved her so she'd fall on it."

"All I can figure is that in his grieved state of mind he's twisted the facts to support his false belief. Those who've lost loved ones often do. I did my best to get him to tell me more, to no avail."

Polly grabbed the last sweet pickle from the bowl and crunched into it. "Patience, my friend. Patience."

The next two hours were some of the most enjoyable Tess had ever spent. She joined in a lively game of charades, helped Luke search in Hunt the Thimble and watched with rapt attention as Spencer challenged Peter in a fierce arm wrestling competition—and won.

The last guest left, and she went upstairs to change out of her silk dress into one of her more comfortable calicoes. What a glorious day it had been. She couldn't remember the last time she'd felt as carefree.

She returned to the kitchen. Luke sat in the corner with the pasteboard Noah's ark set they'd made, endeavoring to teach Lila the sound for each animal. Her babyish attempts to imitate her brother were adorable.

Water sloshed as Spencer filled a pail from the stove's reservoir and poured it in the rinse tub.

"It's nice of you to help, but I'd be happy to take care of that."

"It's the least I can do after all the work you put into the dinner. Everything was delicious, especially the pies." He rubbed his stomach.

She shot him a smile. "I noticed you sampled all six." She removed the dishes that had been soaking, stacked them on the counter and threw out the cold, greasy water. She refilled the washtub, added soap flakes and set to work scrubbing the plates, carefully sliding them into the steaming rinse water one by one.

To her surprise, Spencer grabbed a dishtowel and began drying them. "I know you appreciated the meal, but I don't expect you to do my work."

"I used to help Trudy. She didn't feel as at home in the kitchen as you do. She said she got lonely, so I took to keeping her company. But if you'd rather I didn't help you…"

"It's all right. I like your company, too."

He deepened his voice. "Do you now?"

The admiration in his eyes stirred feelings she ought not to have. While she enjoyed the surge of warmth coursing through her, she shouldn't encourage him. He was simply a man swept up in memories. Likely he wasn't even seeing her but saw an image of his late wife instead.

"A woman spends hours in the kitchen, so I can relate to your wife's desire to have someone around." Botheration. Desire probably wasn't the best word.

"You looked lovely in that dress today. I liked your hair in that knot thing you wore, but I like it this way, too." He grasped the braid hanging to the middle of her back and ran his hand down the entire length.

"Spencer." She struggled to draw a breath. "The children."

He dropped the braid as though he'd been burned and spoke in hushed tones. "I don't know what came over me. I didn't mean— Please forgive me."

"There's nothing to forgive. You miss your wife. I understand."

"I do, but I wasn't thinking about her, Tess."

He wasn't? Her heart slammed against her corset.

"You worked hard to make this day special for me— for all of us. I haven't had that much fun since—" he took a deep breath and let it out slowly "—since Trudy died. And I have you to thank for it. You helped me through a difficult day, so I'm going to dry every last one of these dishes for you." He shook a finger at her as he did when disciplining Luke, but his grin belied his stern appearance. "And not another word of protest from you, young lady. Understand?"

She couldn't resist playing along, dipping into a deep curtsey and giving a wide sweep of her hand. "Yes, your eminence. Your humble servant hears and obeys."

Never had washing dishes been as enjoyable as it was with him at her side. The task became a game. He pointed out a nonexistent speck of food she'd supposedly missed. She held out the freshly scrubbed gravy boat and pulled it back before he could take it from her. He flicked rinse water at her, and she retaliated, lifting a handful of soapsuds and blowing it at him.

Luke squeezed in between them. "What'cha laughing at?"

Spencer responded before she could. "Tess is being a pest."

She gaped at him. "Me? You started it."

"I wanna have fun, too. Can I help?"

"Certainly." She handed Luke a towel. "You may dry all the spoons."

Lila tugged on Tess's skirt. "Eff."

"You want to join in, as well, don't you, sweetheart? Let me see." Tess scanned the kitchen. "I know. You may stack the soiled napkins."

Luke scoffed. "She'll just play with them."

Tess leaned over and whispered. "You're good at make-believe, aren't you, Luke? Could you pretend your sister's helping?"

He nodded.

Tess cast her gaze from one of the Abbotts to the next. Although pretending was for children, she couldn't help but imagine what it would be like if the four of them were a family. Based on what had just transpired between her and Spencer, she had her first taste of hope.

And it was far sweeter than any pie she'd ever baked.

Chapter Twenty-Two

The small pine gracing the parlor was nothing like the lavish Christmas trees Tess had helped her previous charges decorate with expensive glass ornaments from the East. She preferred this simple tree. She and the children had draped it with handmade paper chains and popcorn strings before the Christmas Eve service the night before. What she liked best were the pasteboard animals Luke had wedged between the branches, pretending they were hiding in the forest. It was a good thing he wouldn't need them any longer, because they'd become quite tattered.

Tess basked in the warmth of the blazing fire and breathed in the invigorating scent of the freshly cut evergreen. She'd awakened an hour earlier than usual on this frosty Christmas morning. Normally, she hoped the children wouldn't wake until she'd seen Spencer off to work, but she couldn't wait to hear Luke padding down the stairs or Lila calling for her.

Since Spencer had assured Tess he wanted her to be part of their celebration, she'd placed her gifts under the tree. Hopefully he and the children would like what she'd selected.

The front door opened, letting in a blast of cold air. Tess rushed into the foyer to help him out of his overcoat. "Merry Christmas."

He blew into his cupped hands. "The same to you. Are the children up yet?"

"Not yet, but I'm hoping the smell of hot cocoa in the air will wake Luke. That boy certainly has a fondness for it. I have some ready for you."

No sooner had she set the steaming mug at Spencer's place than Luke popped into the dining room, still clad in his flannel nightshirt. "Is it morning yet?"

"Yes, son. And a very special morning it is. Merry Christmas!"

Lila woke soon after, and they sat down to a quick but hearty breakfast of porridge and canned peaches. Luke wolfed his portion and waited impatiently for the others to finish. Tess understood. She was every bit as eager to gather around the tree, listen to Spencer read the Christmas story in that rich voice of his and watch as the others opened their gifts afterward.

Twenty minutes later, Spencer closed his Bible and laid it on the side table next to his armchair.

"Can we open our packages now, Papa?"

"Yes, son, but we'll start with the ladies first."

The disappointment in Luke's eyes was more than Tess could bear. "I'd be happy to wait until the children have opened theirs."

"So be it. Here's one for you, Luke, and one for Lila. They must be from Tess."

She nodded.

Spencer pulled his daughter onto his lap and helped

her remove the paper and string. Lila grabbed the rub-
ber-headed doll the moment she saw it and gave it a
kiss. "Baby."

Tess's heart melted.

Luke opened his package and let out a whoop that
reminded her of the first time she'd met him. "It's the
Noah's ark I wanted! This one isn't paper like the one
we made. It's wood."

He examined each and every animal. When he
hugged the wooden boat to his chest, it took every
ounce of restraint she possessed to keep from hugging
him. He turned to her without any prompting from his
father. "Thank you."

"You're welcome." She lifted her gaze to the ceiling. *Thank You, Lord, for that most precious of gifts.*

The children opened their presents from Spencer,
resulting in more cries of delight.

"Your turn, Tess." Spencer passed her a small package.

She opened it, revealing a bottle of citrus-scented
hand cream. He must've noticed how rough her hands
were when he'd held them after their picnic in Folsom.

"I hope you don't take offense at such a practical
item, but those hands of yours serve me and my children in so many ways. They deserve special treatment."

"Thank you. It's such a thoughtful gift." It was, but
his kind words were what she would treasure.

"I have one more for you."

He handed her an envelope addressed to him from
someone in Boston. She shot him a quizzical look.

"Go ahead. It's all right."

She pulled out the papers inside. This wasn't a letter at all. It was sheet music. "Oh! It's that new hymn

we've been learning at church, 'He Leadeth Me.' How did you know I liked it?"

"I've heard you sing it while you're working. I thought we could try singing it together sometime, the way we did the song at our picnic down in Folsom."

"Are you sure *you*, who have one of the best voices I've ever heard, want to sing with *me*? I make a crow sound good by comparison."

"What do you mean? You sound fine."

"Really?" She found that hard to believe.

He nodded. "I enjoy listening to you, but you've always stopped when you saw me. I was hoping that might change."

Why, he sounded sincere. She'd love to sing with him. Perhaps he'd be willing to give her a few pointers. "I'd like that."

He unwrapped the leather journal she'd given him and gave her a warm smile. "This is a fine gift. I look forward to using it."

"I thought you might find it helpful to write down your thoughts. I do. As the words flow onto the page, things that were unclear come into better focus. It also helps me see how the Lord has been directing my paths and working out things for my good."

The Lord had led her to this family. To Spencer. She was certain of that. But what would the New Year bring? In April, his mourning period would come to an end. How she prayed he'd be open to new possibilities—and a new woman in his life.

Rain she could handle, but Tess could do without the wind. Its plaintive cry as it swept past the house and rattled the windowpanes filled her with foreboding. She stood at the kitchen window that blustery March afternoon and rubbed her arms. Days like this reminded her of the one on which her father had left her at the orphanage. A gust of wind had sent his hat sailing. He'd run after it—and away from her.

Once this storm arrived and the dark clouds unleashed their burden, she'd be fine. Well, as fine as a person could be during the worst winter on record. They'd had well over thirty storms this season, with more predicted. The latest one had added six feet of snow to the Sierras, bringing the accumulation to over twenty feet in places.

Spencer's concern was that the Central Pacific had kept their crews working to bore tunnels through the mountain passes to the north in spite of the snow pack. He'd hoped for a respite, but the CP's race to lay track faster and further than the Union Pacific continued around the clock. Since his line's monopoly would soon end, he was forging ahead with his plans to establish a herd and had begun to schedule appointments with the ranchers ready to make use of Goliath's services.

Her primary concern was how to occupy an active boy tired of being cooped up. If it wasn't for the wraparound porch, she didn't know what she'd do. It gave Luke a place to work off some of his abundant energy. He'd declared the area a race track and went round and round, straddling the stick horse Spencer had fashioned out of an old shovel handle, a short section of rope and a pasteboard box he'd painted to look like a horse's head.

A door banged in the distance, and Tess jumped. She was sure she'd slid the latch into place when she'd let Woof out of the barn earlier.

She rushed to the foyer and peered out the window. Someone slinked from the barn, hunched over to avoid the buffeting winds. It couldn't be Spencer. He wasn't due for another hour.

Woof raced across the yard and barked at the figure beneath the hooded rain cloak. A trouser-clad leg kicked at the loyal watchdog. The man appeared to be clutching something to his chest. Had he taken something from the barn?

Uneasiness dug in its claws.

The intruder stood just outside Goliath's pen.

Oh, no! She wasn't about to let him near the bull. Spencer's hopes for the future hinged on that longhorn. She reached for the rifle over the front door.

Luke looked up from the settee in the parlor where he and Lila were playing with their Christmas toys. "Why did you get that down?"

She forced herself to remain calm. "I'm going to see what Woof's barking at. You stay here with your sister. Don't go anywhere near the fireplace, and don't go outside. Do you understand?"

Luke nodded and returned his attention to his ark.

"I'll be right back." *Please, Lord, let that be true.*

Hefting the rifle into place, she stalked toward the pen, her skirts whipping about her ankles. The man slipped a foot through the fence slats and crouched.

When she was close enough for him to hear her over the howling wind, she shouted. "What do you think you're doing, mister?"

He turned, saw the gun pointed at him and took off limping across the field with surprising speed for one with such an affliction.

She called Woof over to her and fired a single shot in the air to send the prowler a warning.

The man stumbled. He straightened and resumed his flight with his limp more pronounced than before.

Raindrops pelted Tess. The storm had arrived at last. She lowered the rifle and moved away from the pen.

Goliath was snorting and butting the fence. She'd learned that loud noises caused the otherwise docile animal to become agitated, as was the case the day she'd seen Luke in the pen and shrieked. She wasn't overly concerned. The bull would soon settle down now that things were back to normal.

A quick perusal of the barn helped slow her racing heart. The animals were fine, and nothing appeared to be missing, although a trail of oats led toward the doors. That must have been what the trespasser had taken. It made sense, considering he'd headed straight from the barn to the bull's pen.

She returned to the house, rested the rifle on its pegs and had Luke and Lila join her in the kitchen. Luke insisted on taking his ark with him, so Tess gathered all the animals on the settee into her apron and hustled the children to their play corner by the pantry where she could keep watch over them. She did her best to remain outwardly calm as she continued her supper preparations, but inside she quaked.

Spencer couldn't get home soon enough to suit her. She stirred the potato soup and sang the hymn she now thought of as their special song, hoping the words would ease her fears.

She'd just started the final chorus when he arrived and added his glorious voice to her shaky one. She ceased singing and spun around. "You're here! I'm so glad."

Before she could tell him about the trespasser, Luke blurted the news. "She shot the gun."

Spencer crossed the room in three strides and faced her. "What happened? Are you all right?"

"We're fine." Speaking in hushed tones so she didn't alarm Luke, she filled Spencer in.

Concern creased his brow. "Do you have any idea who he was?"

"I can't be sure, but the intruder walked with a limp. When Mr. Dodge dropped by the house last fall, I noticed that one of his driver's boot heels was twice the size of the other. I didn't see him walk, but I would imagine he limps. You don't suppose…?"

"That's the logical conclusion, given Dodge's threats."

A chill swept over her, and she shivered. The thought of Mr. Dodge's henchman prowling about the ranch made her mad enough to…to spit. On his boots. At least she'd run the scoundrel off before he did whatever it was he'd come to do. "What if the children had been outside? What if he comes back?"

Spencer placed his hands on her shoulders. "I won't let any harm come to them—or to you. Keep supper warm. I have a message to deliver to Dodge."

Half an hour later hoofbeats signaled Spencer's return. She met him in the foyer. "How did it go?"

"Dodge denied having anything to do with the incident, but I gave him fair warning. If he or any of his men are caught skulking around the ranch, he knows the guns aimed their way won't be pointed at the sky. I'll ask Frank to check on the place regularly and to come right away if he hears any shots fired over here. I'm also going to teach you how to hit your target when you fire my rifle. I'll give you a lesson this weekend."

"Good." She gave a firm nod. "No one's going to hurt the children when I'm in charge—not if I can help it."

"You have no idea how much peace of mind it gives me knowing Luke and Lila have such a fierce defender."

His compliment warmed her clear through. She hastened to put the postponed meal on the table, and everyone took their seats.

They bowed their heads, and Spencer said grace. "And, Lord, I'd ask you to place a hedge of protection around my family and keep us from harm. In your Son's precious name. Amen."

Tess marveled at his use of the word family. Did he consider her part of it now? The possibility fanned the flames of her lifelong dream. She couldn't let herself get too excited, though. As much as she'd like to believe his word choice had been intentional, habit was a more likely explanation. Even so, she couldn't help but hope that someday, the good Lord willing, she'd have a family as wonderful as this one.

Where had that boy gotten off to now? Tess stood in the foyer and shook her head in exasperation. She'd asked Luke to stay indoors until it warmed up outside. Although the rain had let up the day before, the air that sunny mid-March morning had a bite to it. Not only that, but an abundance of muddy brown puddles dappled the saturated ground. No doubt the adventurous boy had found them irresistible. She dreaded seeing the state of his boots.

"He's not out front, so let's look in the backyard." She shifted Lila higher on her hip, stepped onto the porch and paused. "Do you hear that?"

Woof was far afield, barking continuously.

Luke!

Tess rushed into the kitchen, dragged the large bathing tub from the pantry and lined the bottom of the high-sided metal container with the blanket from the children's play area nearby. "In you go." She placed Lila inside and flew out the door.

Grabbing her skirts, Tess hefted them all the way to her knees. She raced across the soggy field toward Woof. He ran back and forth near the spot where Dodge's man had stumbled. The memory of that terrifying ordeal sickened her.

The vigilant watchdog saw her, ceased his frenzied pacing and stood in one spot, his tail wagging wildly. The tone of his bark changed, no longer a cry for help but one of encouragement, urging her forward.

As she drew near, she heard someone call her name. She spun in a circle, scanning the clumps of weather-beaten bunchgrass, but saw no one. Only when she reached Woof and he ceased his barking could she make out Luke's muffled voice coming from beneath a wooden covering. Two of the weathered slats had given way, leaving a hole large enough for—

Her stomach lurched. Was that a well shaft?

"Luke! Is that you?"

"Yep. I fell in a great big hole."

"I'm going to help you." She peered through the opening into an inky black pit. "Are you hurt?"

"I hit my bottom real hard, and I'm all wet. Get me outta here!"

It was definitely a well. "How high's the water?"

"It comes to my belly button, and it smells real bad. My b-b-boots are gonna be ruined." He let loose a heart-wrenching sob.

"Don't you worry about that, sweetheart. If they are, I'll buy you a brand-new pair." She had to see him and assure herself he was all right. "I'm going to move these boards, so you'll hear some noise."

With a series of kicks, she broke off the stakes holding the cover in place. She stooped, grabbed one side of the pallet-like structure, stood and flipped it over, nearly losing her footing on the rain-soaked earth. The mass of dry-rotted boards landed with a thud. Sunlight flooded the shaft, but her angle of vision made it difficult to see inside.

Her first thought was to get Spencer's lariat and pull Luke out herself, but as slippery as the ground was, she risked sliding into the hole, too. "I have to get someone to help, but I'll be back as fast as I can. You'll hear the gun go off, but it will just be me sending a signal to Frank."

"No! Don't leave me here all by myself."

"You're not alone. Woof's here." At the sound of his name, the helpful dog gave a reassuring yelp. "See if you can sing the alphabet song five times before I get back. Will you do that?"

Luke hesitated briefly but launched into the song, his voice wavering.

Tess sped to the house, peeked in the kitchen to make sure Lila was all right and grabbed Spencer's repeating rifle. She stepped outside and fired three shots into the sky in rapid succession. The noise left her ears ringing, and the smoke made her cough, but she didn't care. All that mattered was getting Luke out of that horrid hole as soon as possible.

She hung the rifle back on its pegs, grabbed Spencer's lariat from the barn and raced back to Luke. Desperate to reassure the frightened child, she flattened herself on the muddy ground and shimmied forward until she could see into the well shaft. Although fear had her in a chokehold, she did her best to sound unconcerned. "How many times did you sing the song all the way through?"

"Three."

"I told you I'd be fast, didn't I?" She kept him talking as she kept up a silent prayer, asking the Lord to send someone. Soon.

One minute turned into two, three and four. At last she heard a sound that changed her pleas to praise. Hoofbeats were coming her way. A quick glance revealed Frank's pinto bearing down on her location. She scrambled to her feet and waved her arms.

Luke whimpered. "Don't leave me again."

"I'm not going anywhere. Frank's coming to help."

Their young neighbor reached her in no time. "Am I ever glad to see you." She pointed at the hole. "Luke's down there. Get him out. *Please*."

"Don't you worry. We'll haul him up in no time. I just need to go for a rope."

"I've got one. Here." She shoved Spencer's lariat at him.

"You're prepared." Frank jumped to the ground. He formed a slip noose in one end of the rope and tied the other around his saddle horn.

"Are you having your horse pull him out? Is that safe?"

"I'll do it. This is just a precaution in case I slip. Would you hold him so he doesn't go anywhere?"

"Certainly." Tess gripped the bridle.

Frank stood at the side of the shaft, dug in his boot heels and lowered the loop. "All right, Luke. Let's pretend you're a miner and I'm pulling you out of a mineshaft. I'm sending your papa's rope down. When you have it, tell me."

"I got it."

"Good. Put the loop over your head, and then stick one arm through it at a time. Tell me when you're ready, and I'll pull you out."

A few tense moments later Luke hollered. "Ready."

"All right. Up you go." Grasping the rope, Frank used steady hand-over-hand movements to raise the brave boy.

The minute Luke cleared the gaping hole, Tess rushed to him, dropped to her knees and crushed him to her in a fierce hug. "My dear boy. You're safe now."

"I was calling you and calling you, Tess. I knew you'd come." He burst into tears and buried his face in her shoulder, trembling violently.

"Of course I did. I'd do anything to help you, Luke. I love you." As much as she wanted to relish the feel of his arms around her, she had to get him out of the cold and into dry clothes right away.

"Poor little tyke." Frank shook his head.

Tess stood and snuggled the dear boy to her. "Thank

you so much for coming. You've already done so much, but would you be willing to ride to the station and—"

"Get Mr. Abbott? By all means." He handed her the lariat, mounted his horse and took off.

Chapter Twenty-Three

Luke had fallen asleep clutching his mother's quilt in one hand and an elephant from his Noah's ark set in the other. Tess planted a kiss on his cheek and sank into the rocking chair by his bedside. She'd left him just long enough to change out of her soggy, mud-encrusted dress.

Lila padded over and placed a wooden bear by her brother. "Wuke?"

Tess pulled the precious girl onto her lap and rocked her, the rhythmic creaking of the chair lending much-needed comfort. "He'll be all right, sweetheart."

If only that were true. He'd been in that putrid water for who knew how long and gotten a chill.

The front door opened and closed. Spencer was home at last. Tess breathed a prayer of thanks.

He thundered up the stairs and burst into Luke's room. "How is he?"

"Sh." She pointed at Luke. "He's fine, for the most part, thanks to Frank's quick response."

"My poor boy." Spencer sat on the edge of Luke's bed and caressed his son's face with such tenderness

Tess had to blink back tears. For Spencer's sake, she must remain strong.

He plunked himself in the extra rocking chair she'd dragged in from Lila's room and gripped the armrests so hard his knuckles turned white. "I don't understand how this could have happened. The cover was intact the last time I checked it."

"That question's been plaguing me, too. I think Mr. Dodge's man—or whoever was snooping around that day—ran across it after I fired my warning shot. Apparently the boards broke under his weight, creating the opening Luke fell through."

Spencer said nothing for the longest time. He just held Luke's hand and gazed at his son.

At length he spoke. "Being a parent is the most challenging job I've ever had. It's as though part of your heart is walking around outside your body. If any harm comes to your child, you feel it as intensely as if it were you."

When she'd first arrived, Tess would have been surprised to hear Spencer say such a thing, but it hadn't taken long to see what a loving father he was. "I'm not a parent, but I have a great deal of empathy for those who are."

"Do you think he has any broken bones or sprains?"

"I doubt it. He was moving normally and didn't complain about anything—other than his…backside. I gather he landed on it. He might have a bruise or two that hadn't developed yet, but the only things I saw when I bathed him were the few scrapes he got when he fell through the covering. My concern is that he might have swallowed some of that stagnant water."

"He cut himself?" Spencer's curt question startled

her. He threw back Luke's blankets. "Where? How badly?"

"On his legs mostly, although there are a couple of scratches on his arm. I wouldn't worry too much. I don't think they'll get— I don't think they're serious."

She'd caught herself just in time. She didn't want to mention the possibility of infection and trigger painful memories.

He ran his hands over Luke's limbs, exploring the abrasions with his fingertips, and faced his fear without hesitation. "Infection isn't something to be taken lightly."

Infection of Luke's wounds didn't worry her nearly as much as infection of his intestines. She'd heard about people succumbing to cholera after ingesting contaminated water. But based upon Spencer's experience, his concerns were understandable.

"I'll stay by his side and see that his wounds are cleaned regularly and the air in his room kept fresh. One of my former employers—a doctor—believed cleanliness could help prevent infection." She would ensure Luke got plenty to drink, as well. From what little she remembered about cholera, the resulting dehydration could lead to death.

Spencer returned to the rocker. "I'm in awe of your ability to keep a level head, Tess. I know Luke's in the best of hands with you, but I'm staying here until I'm certain he's out of danger."

"I would have expected no less. That's why I asked Frank to get you."

All day and into the night they sat by Luke's bedside as he slept, exchanging whispered words on occasion. They only left one at a time to eat the simple meals Tess prepared or to tend to Lila.

Around two in the morning, Spencer shifted his position. "I need to rest my eyes a minute. Please wake me if there's any change."

He quickly dozed off. Tess spread a blanket over him, brushed a lock of golden hair off his forehead and fought the urge to plant a kiss on it.

She kept vigil. Although silence was her only companion, she found Spencer's presence comforting. He was there if she needed him. Should the situation worsen, she'd welcome his quiet strength.

He woke as the mantel clock in the parlor chimed six times and rubbed the stubble on his jaw. "How is he?"

"Doing well so far. He roused an hour ago, asked for a drink and guzzled a full glass of water." She endeavored to sound encouraging, but Luke's thirst troubled her.

"That's good."

"I fried some ham and diced potatoes. Would you like me to get you some?"

"I'm going to see to the animals, so I'll grab myself a plate."

She leaned her head on the rocking chair and prayed.

In no time, Spencer returned, clean-shaven once again, and checked on Luke. The flush-faced boy coughed, and she gasped.

Spencer pinned her with a penetrating gaze. "What is it? You're as white as my shirt."

She felt fuzzy headed after her sleepless night. Her thoughts tumbled over one another like leaves in the wind, but one stood out. "I didn't want to tell you, but I think he might have a case of cholera coming on."

"He doesn't."

His certainty surprised her. "How can you be sure?"

"I've seen the disease. He hasn't complained of any stomach pain or vomited, and he doesn't have, um… intestinal issues."

"I'm relieved it's not cholera, but what could it be? Influenza? Pneumonia?"

"Time will tell."

They sat in silence for several minutes. Her head lolled to the side. She jerked herself awake and cast a glance at Spencer, who was watching her intently.

"You need some sleep. I'll sit with him while you rest."

She should protest, but he was right. Keeping her eyes open required tremendous effort. She staggered to her room, removed her boots and climbed beneath her blankets fully clothed. Sleep claimed her the moment her head hit the pillow.

A knock on her door hours later roused her. "Just a minute." The afternoon sun slanted into the room. She threw back the covers and opened the door.

Spencer flashed her a blinding smile. "Someone wants to see you."

Luke slipped past his father. "Papa fixed stew, Tess. Can you smell it?"

"My dear boy." She gave him a hug but released him before he could protest. "You're up and dressed. You must be feeling better."

"Yep. Papa said I could go out and play, but I gotta be careful 'cause I got scabs on my scratches. See?" He pulled up the legs of his short pants, revealing dark red patches covering his abrasions.

She gave him ample attention for his injuries. They

left, and she took a few minutes to freshen up. She checked on Lila, who was napping, and joined Spencer in the kitchen.

Tess looked out the window and watched Luke throw a stick for Woof. "It's wonderful to see him doing so well, isn't it?"

"Thanks in large part to you." Spencer's rich voice came from right behind her.

Guilt ate at her. She took a deep breath, faced him and launched into her confession. "It's my fault Luke fell in that well. I'd told him to stay inside and didn't hear him go out. If it weren't for me, he—"

Spencer held up a hand. "You did nothing wrong."

As much as she wanted to believe that, she couldn't. "I didn't watch him like I should have, and then I couldn't even get him out on my own." Her voice broke. "What kind of housekeeper am I?"

"You do an excellent job caring for the children. If anyone's to blame, it's my son. Luke should have obeyed you. Perhaps he's learned his lesson and won't be so quick to go running off in the future."

"He *was* terribly frightened. I'll never forget the look on his little face when Frank pulled him out. He wept in my arms. And he—" she drew in a steadying breath "—he called me Tess."

"It's about time. You've showered him with loving care. I couldn't ask for more. Thank you."

A ragged sigh rushed from her. She blinked to keep tears from spilling over. "I'm sorry. It's just that when I saw him in the bottom of that horrible pit…"

"Come here." He eased her into his embrace. "Everything's going to be fine."

She rested her head on his shoulder, grateful for

his strength, and savored his scent—part smoky, part earthy and all male.

Far too soon, he released her. They remained toe-to-toe, his hands resting on her upper arms. He was so close she could feel his breath on her cheek. His gaze roved over her face and lingered on her mouth. Her heart beat erratically.

With no warning, his entire demeanor changed. He blew out a long breath, dragged a hand through his hair and turned away. "The stew's on the stove." He flew through the house, letting the front door slam shut behind him.

Disappointment engulfed her. One minute she was sure he'd wanted to kiss her, and the next he looked as though he found the idea revolting.

No matter what he was thinking, she knew exactly what she'd wanted—to feel Spencer's lips on hers.

Try as he might, Spencer couldn't deny it. He'd been about to kiss Tess.

He saddled his horse and rode toward the high point at the edge of his property where he'd taken Trudy the day she arrived at the ranch. He crested the hill, slipped from his saddle and plopped down on a large slab of granite. They'd sat in that very spot, and he droned on and on about his plans. She'd given him that indulgent smile of hers, the one that let him know she didn't mind listening to his dreams. The one that made him forget all else but her. How he missed her.

He was lonely. That's why he'd hugged his house-keeper and come dangerously close to kissing her. Or perhaps he was simply relieved. After all, he and Tess had spent hours at Luke's bedside, afraid he was in grave danger. People had been known to act impulsively at times like that.

It was no use. He had to face the facts. He'd wanted to kiss Tess because she was Tess, the strong, hard-working woman who loved his children as if they were her own. The self-assured woman who wore that ridiculous hat and didn't care what anyone thought about it. The outspoken woman who had an uncanny ability to shift his focus from the past and help him experience the joy to be found in the present.

Tess was right. He had to move on. It's what Trudy would have wanted. She'd said so herself when it became clear the infection was going to take her from him. *Don't spend the rest of your life alone, Spencer. The children will need someone to care for them, and you'll need a partner.*

When Trudy had said those words eleven months ago, it didn't seem possible he could ever care for anyone else, and yet he'd developed feelings for his housekeeper. If that wasn't bad enough, a woman he'd never met had been occupying his thoughts with unsettling frequency. He'd insisted the other stationmasters keep his latest notice on their boards—to no avail. Five months had passed without a single inquiry. Faith was out there somewhere, but despite his efforts and his prayers, he'd been unable to locate her.

He slapped his riding gloves against his leg, his decision made. If he wanted to find Faith—and he most definitely did—he had no choice but to read the last of her letters. He would, first thing tomorrow.

Chapter Twenty-Four

"What can I get for you, Mr. Abbott? A piece of pie, perhaps?"

Spencer set the packet of letters on the table. Miss Minnie's baked goods couldn't compare to those Tess served, but he needed a few minutes to himself before heading home. "I'd like a slice of peach."

"I'll have it for you in two shakes."

His duties at the station had kept him busy all morning, and he hadn't had a moment to himself. He'd have to be quick, though, because Tess was probably eager to enjoy her afternoon off after the ordeal with Luke.

He could finally read Faith's last letter, but he dreaded doing so. While he hoped for information that would lead him to her, there was a strong possibility she'd provided no more clues to her identity or whereabouts than she had in her first two letters.

If that was true, he'd have no choice but to abandon his search and give up the idea of meeting the warmhearted woman who'd captivated him. That's exactly what he would do if this letter revealed nothing that would help him find her.

He reached for the packet of letters and slipped the bottom one from it. With one quick motion, he unfolded the letter and braced himself for whatever it contained.

Sunday, August 20, 1865

To the man I look forward to marrying,

I'm relishing the freedom of my day off. While the temperature has soared as it always does this time of year, I'm sitting on my favorite bench by the river, grateful for the shade provided by one of the many trees stretching its limbs toward the water's edge. The riverboat Confidence, visible in the distance, is enjoying her day of rest, as well.

Hope flowed through Spencer. Faith was in Sacramento City. She had to be. The paddle-wheeler she'd mentioned traveled from the San Francisco Bay, up the Sacramento River and back again. His rail line often received passengers who'd arrived in the capitol city via one of the river steamers.

Since he knew where she was, he could renew his search in earnest. He would place advertisements in all the Sacramento City newspapers seeking a woman named Faith who worked with children and had lost important documents aboard an eastbound train. Even if she wasn't a subscriber, someone she knew might see one of the notices and contact her.

"You're looking mighty happy. Wouldn't be the anticipation of sampling my delectable dessert, now would it?" Miss Minnie grinned and set the piece of pie before him.

"I'm sure it's every bit as tasty as usual."

"That's right nice of you, but I know flattery when I hear it. Enjoy your letter, er, pie." The jovial woman winked and hustled to another table.

He read while he ate, tasting nothing as he savored Faith's words. Unlike her previous letters, this one had a lighter feel, almost as though she sensed the Lord at work in her life and trusted Him to bring her dreams to fruition.

> I've spent far too many years bemoaning my lot in life, but no more. The Lord has showered blessings on me, and I can choose to embrace them with a grateful heart. If you're out there—and I firmly believe you are—I trust He will cause our paths to cross. When He does, I shall rejoice.
>
> Until that glorious day when my wait is over and you ask for my hand, I'm hoping all is well with you and praying you feel the Lord's presence in a mighty way.

> With love from Faith

He was here all right, and he would find her. He had to. Faith embodied all the traits he wanted in a wife. Kindness. Goodness. Faithfulness. And a heart so full of love it overflowed. A woman like her would make the world a brighter place.

Reaching for the packet of letters, he spied the ribbon. Blue. Tess's favorite color. An image of her in the dark blue silk she'd worn on Thanksgiving flashed through his mind. She'd never looked as beautiful as she did that day.

He held the ribbon in one hand and Faith's letter in the other. Guilt gnawed at him. He didn't want to think about what God would have to say to a grieving widower who had feelings for not one, but two women.

The sooner he found Faith, the better. Perhaps she was nothing like he envisioned. If that was the case, he could silence his persistent thoughts, focus on what was right in front of him and begin a new chapter of his life free of doubts and unrest.

"No! Goliath can't be gone." Tess stood beside the empty pen shivering in the cold night air. The past two hours had crawled as Spencer searched for his missing bull. She buttoned the cloak she'd thrown on when she heard him ride into the yard moments before.

"I didn't want to believe it, either, but I've been over my place twice, and he's nowhere to be found."

"What do you think could have happened to him?"

His reply was clipped. "I can answer that in one word. Dodge." He removed his hat and raked a hand though his hair. "I didn't tell you before, but when I noticed Goliath was gone, the gate to his pen was closed. My longhorn didn't let himself out. He had help."

Icy fingers of dread gripped her. "I'm afraid you might be right. Mr. Dodge has made it clear he doesn't want you to raise cattle. What can you do about it?"

He slammed his hat back on. "Nothing at this point. He would deny having anything to do with Goliath's disappearance. I have no proof—just suspicions. I'll have to wait and see if the big fellow shows up, but I'll be watching Dodge like a cougar ready to pounce."

The sadness in Spencer's voice tore at her heart. He'd hung all his hopes for starting a cattle ranch on his prized longhorn. "I'll pray that if Goliath's out there somewhere, he'll find his way back."

Spencer urged her to get in out of the cold, and he led his horse to the barn.

Minutes later Tess bent over the quilting hoop in her room. She had less than a month to finish the quilt. She kept her needle sharp so it would pierce the pages of the letters she'd added to each square.

She was still at it when the parlor clock chimed twelve times. Her restless thoughts had kept her awake. If she couldn't get to sleep soon, she'd be bleary-eyed in the morning. She had to make sense of the turmoil within and knew of only two things that helped.

Since she'd already prayed, she reached for her journal. She opened the leather bound book, dipped her pen in the inkwell and began writing.

My heart aches for Spencer. Losing his wife was hard enough, but having his dream threatened by that conniving neighbor of his has to be a tremendous blow. If only I could do something to ease his pain. I know the Lord will uphold him, but I long to find a way to comfort the man I love.

She stared at the words she'd written. The truth was there in India ink. She'd fallen in love with Spencer Abbott.

Spencer passed the hand mirror to Tess, rose and stood at the porch railing, his back to her. "Thank you for the cut."

"You're welcome." She flung the sheet over the porch railing, snapped it to remove the hairs and did her best to silence the doubts gnawing at her.

Ever since the near-kiss after their night spent at Luke's bedside, Spencer had been withdrawn. He'd spoken to her only when necessary. The long, searching glances he'd been sending her way puzzled her.

She joined him at the railing. "I'm sorry you haven't found Goliath yet, but I trust you will. Things have a way of showing up when we least expect them."

He moved two steps to the side, adding literal distance between them. "That's true. Some things can be hard to find. But I won't stop looking."

She had the feeling he was no longer talking about his bull, but it was clear he wasn't going to confide in her. "I'd like your help with something this afternoon."

"You're not going to hole up in the kitchen creating new recipes?"

That was how she generally spent her Saturday afternoons off, but Lila wouldn't be asleep long. "Not just yet. Luke's still having those nightmares. I thought they would have stopped by now, but he's had one every night this week. I want to see if we can help him."

"I assume you have a plan."

She faced him, but he wouldn't look her way. "I'd like you to let him help you build the new well cover. Perhaps seeing the process for himself would ease his fear of falling down the shaft again."

He nodded his approval. "That's a good idea. Frank will be here with the supplies soon, and we'll get started." He strode toward the barn without another word.

Minutes later Tess accompanied Luke to the worksite. Spencer had removed the hastily patched cover from the abandoned well. The traumatized boy stayed well away from the dark, dank hole.

Spencer's wagon lumbered across the field. Frank reached them and brought it to a stop.

Tess pointed at the load. "Do you know what those big pieces of wood are, Luke?"

"Yep. Railroad ties."

Spencer pulled on his leather work gloves and grabbed the end of one of the massive ties. Frank took the other.

"That's right, son. They'll make a strong cover. Nothing—not even an elephant—could fall through the one we're making."

The two men soon had the ties in place. They wired them together into a square and drilled a hole in each of the cover's corners.

"It's time for you to help." Spencer gave Luke the task of inserting a metal spike in every hole.

Tess sighed. Spencer was as patient with his son as ever and was laughing at Frank's jokes. It seemed she was the only one getting a chilly reception.

His job complete, Luke quickly lost interest in the project and wandered through the knee-length clumps of greening bunchgrass nearby in search of dragonflies. How nice it was to see him acting like his carefree self again.

She watched with admiration as Spencer wielded the sledgehammer and drove the first spike deep into the ground until it was flush with the cover. What a strong, handsome man he was. How sad that he'd reverted to wearing a frown much of the time.

Luke stooped to pick up something and darted over

to her. "Look what I found." He handed her a strangely shaped piece of wood and dashed off again.

She clapped a hand to her chest. "Well, grease my griddle!"

Spencer completed his swing and stopped. "What is it?"

"A boot heel. A very high man's boot heel. This is where the trespasser stumbled when I fired the warning shot that day. It had to be Mr. Dodge's driver, and this—" she held out the heel to Spencer "—would explain why his limp was so much worse than it had been before."

He grabbed the incriminating evidence. "I've got my proof now." He shoved the boot heel in his coat pocket. "I'm going to pay my scheming neighbor a visit. And it won't be a friendly one." He took off running toward the barn.

Luke rushed over to her. "Where's Papa going?"

"To look for Goliath."

Spencer appeared minutes later astride his big black horse and came to a stop beside Frank. "I forgot to ask. Would you finish up here?"

The young man smiled. "Sure thing."

Tess wished him well.

He worked his fingers over the reins and avoided looking at her. "Don't wait supper for me." He tore off toward the east without a backward glance.

She'd keep his meal warm and keep him company while he ate it, no matter how late he returned. And then they would have a talk.

Chapter Twenty-Five

Elmore Dodge stepped onto his porch with his driver and spat a stream of foul-smelling tobacco juice, which narrowly missed Spencer's feet. "What do you want?"

Spencer forced himself not to plant a fist in Dodge's gut. "I have reason to believe you're harboring my bull. The deputy and I are here to take a look around." He'd known better than to go alone, so he'd dropped by the sheriff's office with his evidence and found a ready ear. Turned out others had lodged complaints against Dodge, too.

The seasoned lawman standing beside Spencer spoke with authority—and an impressive show of cordiality. "You don't have a problem with that, do you, sir?" He tossed the boot heel in the air and caught it.

Dodge's driver followed the journey of the mud-encrusted chunk of wood with a telling lift of his chin. His face drained of color. So, the heel lost near the abandoned well must be his, as Tess had suspected.

Dodge sent them a too-wide smile. His gold teeth flashed in the sunlight. "I don't know why you think this is necessary, gentlemen, but feel free to search my barn."

The barn was the last place Dodge would hide the bull because it was the first place anyone would look. Even so, the deputy had advised Spencer to accept the anticipated offer and give Dodge time to make a telling mistake, which guilty parties often unwittingly did.

Spencer and the sheriff waited while Dodge's driver opened the barn's double doors. The weasel of a man limped inside and stood half hidden behind a bale of hay, but Spencer had seen the uneven boot heels. He had no doubt he'd found the person Dodge had ordered to carry out the crime. Now to find his bull.

Their investigation complete, Spencer and the deputy followed Dodge and his driver out of the barn. Dodge linked his thumbs behind his suspenders and jutted his jaw forward. "I told you I didn't have your bull. Are you satisfied?"

Spencer bit back an unsavory retort. "For the time being, but you don't mind if we take a short ride around your property, do you?"

The scoundrel gave a dry laugh. "You're a persistent one, aren't you, Abbott? I have nothing to hide, but unless you've come bearing a note signed by a judge, I reckon you've seen enough for one day."

Dodge's driver cast a furtive glance at a ramshackle outbuilding in the distance, caught himself and flinched. That was the sign Spencer had been waiting for. He looked at the deputy and received an answering nod.

As planned, the lawman didn't argue with Dodge. "I don't think a visit to the judge will be necessary.

We've seen enough." He mounted his horse, and Spencer followed suit.

Counting on the fact that Goliath would react to a loud noise as he had before and that the rundown shack would be no match his bull, Spencer enacted the final step in the plan. He tipped his head back, opened his mouth wide and let out with the longest, loudest, shrillest scream of his life.

The answering bellow and unmistakable sound of splintering wood did his heart good. Goliath burst out of the shed, horns down, heading straight at Dodge and his driver.

The terror on their faces was priceless. They took off running in opposite directions like the spineless chickens they were.

"I'll take his henchman," the deputy hollered to Spencer. "You get Dodge."

"Gladly." Spencer coiled his rope, urged his horse into action and raced after his wily neighbor.

One toss of Spencer's lariat was all it took. He caught Dodge around the ankle, brought him down and dragged him a few feet over the soggy ground before his horse came to a standstill.

Spencer dismounted, bound Dodge's hands behind him and flipped him over. "I have half a mind to let my bull have some fun with you."

Dodge spat once again, but this time he spewed muddy water. Served the slimy snake right. "You haven't seen the last of me, Abbott. I've got money. I'll get the best lawyer money can buy."

Spencer removed his lariat from Dodge's ankle. "No lawyer can help you when you're caught red-handed."

The lanky man lying in the puddle glared at Spencer but said nothing more.

The deputy shoved Dodge's driver forward. "I'll haul these two in, Spencer. You go get your longhorn." He inclined his head toward the north, where Goliath was a speck on the horizon. "I'll stop by your place tomorrow to take care of the paperwork."

"Sounds good."

Spencer coiled his lariat and hung it over his saddle horn. He couldn't wait to see Tess's smiling face when he returned with his bull.

"Welcome home, big fellow." Spencer slipped from the saddle and led his bull into the pen.

The five days his bull had been missing were some of the longest Spencer had ever lived. Had he lost Goliath, his plan to build a herd by receiving calves in exchange for providing his bull's services would have been stopped in its tracks. But he'd found his longhorn well cared for and unharmed.

An idea struck Spencer and lifted his spirits. If he'd found Goliath when he thought all hope was lost, surely he could find Faith. Perhaps it was time to do more than rely on notices and advertisements. He patted Goliath one more time and led his horse toward the barn.

Tess hurried across the yard. "You got here in time for supper, after all. How did everything go?"

He tilted his head toward the pen. "Goliath's back."

"Oh, Spencer! You found him. That's wonderful." She threw her arms around him.

He tensed. As much as he'd like to crush her to him and inhale her citrusy scent, he couldn't. Until he put the matter of finding Faith to rest, he wasn't free to act on his feelings for Tess. She deserved more than a man torn between two women.

She released him and stepped back. "I'm sorry. I don't know what came over me." She clasped her hands, and her shoulders curled forward. "Wh-what happened? Over at Mr. Dodge's place?"

"I got the deputy, and we went there together and presented my evidence. Dodge denied everything and refused to let us search anywhere but his barn, but we didn't need to." He recounted the encounter, ending with Dodge eating dirt. "I knocked that smug smile off his face."

"I wish I could have seen that." She glanced at the bull and back at Spencer. "I'm glad Goliath's all right. What will happen to Mr. Dodge and his driver?"

"They're in jail awaiting trial and are sure to be convicted. The sheriff will be out tomorrow to take your statement. Dodge no longer poses a threat to you, my children or my bull."

"That's a relief." Her smile held little warmth. "I should get inside and put supper on the table."

"Not yet. I owe you an apology." He held the reins in both hands. Keeping them busy would keep him out of trouble. He wanted to caress Tess's cheek in the worst way and show her how sorry he was for shutting her out, but he wasn't about to mislead her.

"I know I've been a bear the past few days. Can you forgive me?"

She nodded. "I know you've had a lot on your mind, what with Luke's accident, Goliath going missing and…" She picked up a piece of straw and rolled it between her fingers.

"And what?"

"It's getting close to April. I thought perhaps—Never mind. You don't need me to remind you about what's coming up."

"I appreciate the thought, but I'll be fine."

"I know. It's not my place. I'll see to supper." She broke the straw in half, threw the pieces down and set out for the house.

Her slumped shoulders spoke volumes. His preoccupation and need to keep his distance had hurt her, and that knowledge stole his appetite.

The time had come for him to take a more active role in the search for Faith. As soon as possible, he would travel to Sacramento City and start knocking on doors.

The Flynns filed into their customary pew and took their seats. Tess joined them.

Polly handed Petey to Tess, who was delighted to hold the good-natured baby. She leaned close to Polly and whispered. "He's gotten so big. I can't believe he's six months old already. Then again, I can't believe Luke will turn five the day after tomorrow."

"Are you planning anything special?"

"I'll bake him a chocolate cake, and Spencer's giving him a wooden train."

"That's nice." Polly reached for the hymnal and flipped to the opening hymn. "And speaking of Spencer, how are things progressing?"

"Not well. He seems to be avoiding me. Ever since he got Goliath back, he's gone straight to the bunkhouse after we tuck the children in."

"He's had a lot to deal with lately. Perhaps he's just tired."

There was more to it than that. There had to be. "He

didn't come home this past Thursday. He said he had business down the hill, but he didn't tell me what it was. I can't help him if he pushes me away."

Polly smiled. "You've fallen pretty hard for him, haven't you?"

"No. Yes. I didn't mean for it to happen. I don't know what to do."

"Pray, Tessie. Pray. Long and hard and often."

Reverend Josephs entered. The room quieted, and he delivered the opening prayer. The quartet led the congregation in singing "Guide Me, O Thou Great Jehovah." As she did each Sunday, Tess listened for Spencer's voice behind her, reveling it in as she sang.

The final note faded, and Reverend Josephs rose. "Brothers and sisters, do you worry and fret, wondering what the future will hold? That's understandable. The world is changing before our eyes. Before we know it, our country will be connected by a ribbon of rails. One can't help but be amazed, but at the same time uncertainty can gain a foothold."

How true. She'd certainly been feeling lost and confused.

Everything had changed after the vigil at Luke's bedside when Spencer had held her in his arms. She'd seen the attraction in his eyes. He must regret his momentary lack of control.

She understood. She'd berated herself numerous times for throwing herself at him the night he'd returned to the ranch with Goliath. He'd been downright rigid. She might as well have hugged a broom handle. While she could understand his surprise, he didn't have to take such drastic measures as leaving town to avoid being around her.

She leaned forward eager to hear more of the minister's message.

"Take heart, dear ones. God has a plan for our nation—and for each of us. Listen to His words in Proverbs 16:9, 'A man's heart deviseth his way: but the Lord directeth his steps.'"

Truth pierced her willful heart. She wasn't in charge. God was. She wanted a family in the worst way, but that might not be His plan for her. Who was she to tell Him what was best for her?

She drank in the rest of the sermon, filling her parched soul. God knew. He cared. And He wanted good things for her. They might not be the things she thought would bring her happiness, but she could trust Him. All she had to do was let Him lead the way.

Spencer was an extraordinary man with more depth than most people knew, and he was an excellent father. While she'd imagined herself at his side more often than she cared to admit, that wasn't her place. She was his housekeeper and the woman privileged to care for his children for as long as the Lord saw fit. And she would do so with a grateful heart.

Tess had left the general store and was on her way to Miss Minnie's café when the postmaster dashed out of his office and called her name. "Yes?"

"You received a letter."

"I did?" She couldn't think of anyone who would write to her.

"Looks to be from your father or brother."

"I beg your pardon." The last time she'd seen her father was that dark day when he left her at the orphanage.

"It's from Charles Grimsby."

Charlie wasn't her brother, but the orphanage director had given his surname to the pesky boy when he was left on the orphanage doorstep as a baby, just as he'd given it to her when she'd been left there four years later.

"Thank you." She took the letter, and the postmaster returned to his office.

She plunked herself on one of the benches in front of Mr. Hawke's store. Memories assailed her, none of them pleasant. Not only had Charlie coined that detestable nickname. He'd made it his mission to torment her on a regular basis. No doubt he'd gotten into some kind of trouble and wanted her help, her money or both.

Using a hatpin, she slit the envelope, which bore a Sacramento City postmark. Apparently Charlie had come west. She scanned the few lines written in an elegant hand quite unlike the scrawl he'd used when they were young.

April 4, 1867

Dear Tess,

I'm sure you're surprised to hear from me. I've spent months tracking you down and am glad I finally located you. It's urgent that you come to Sacramento City to meet with me at your earliest convenience. I have an important financial matter to discuss with you.

He concluded by asking her to contact him at the office of a prominent lawyer with an office in the heart of the city. It would appear Charlie had tangled with the law, as many of the orphanage staff had predicted.

She shook her head in disbelief. As if she would hop on a train at his request. If he wanted to see her, he would have to make the trip up the hill. She shoved the note in her reticule and snapped it shut. Once she reached the ranch, Charlie's plea would serve as fuel for the fire. Right now she'd enjoy a rare afternoon off spent in town—and a piece of pie someone else had made.

Tess reached Miss Minnie's café minutes later. The outgoing owner hustled to her table.

"Good afternoon, Miss Grimsby. I haven't seen you in a month of Sundays, but Mr. Abbott was here a couple weeks back. I caught him reading letters from his sweetheart and wearing a big ol' grin. His head's clearly been turned. I'm guessing it won't be long before you'll be serving a new mistress. That's exciting, isn't it?"

She fought a wave of nausea. Somehow she had to squeeze a response out of her throat even though it had gone dry. "I'd like nothing more than for him to be happy and his children to have a new mother." Apparently it wouldn't be her.

Her shocking news delivered, Miss Minnie took Tess's order and bustled off, leaving her shaken. Despite the roiling in her stomach, she must press on. Just last Sunday she'd decided to let the Lord direct her path. She could trust Him, and she could hope. Miss Minnie might not have her facts straight. Perhaps the letters weren't from a sweetheart at all. Spencer had mentioned an aunt. Maybe he'd been rejoicing to receive news about his relatives back in Texas.

Tess left the café a short time later, set out for the ranch and ambled along the rutted road singing "He Leadeth Me" while tears streamed down her cheeks.

Chapter Twenty-Six

"I'm sorry, son, but we've never had anyone with that name work for us." The white-haired merchant's wife gave Spencer a sympathetic smile.

He resisted the urge to pound a fist into the door-jamb and excused himself with the cordiality of a gentleman. Despite having visited every hospital, orphanage and school in Sacramento City on his two previous trips looking for women who worked with children, he was no closer to locating Faith. He'd taken to calling on individual homeowners, thinking she might work as a governess, as Tess had.

If anyone had told him a year ago when he'd laid Trudy to rest that he would come to care for two women before his official mourning period was over, he would have scoffed at the idea. And yet here he was, the very day he'd removed his black armband, searching for Faith while Tess was back home awaiting his return. How could he be so fickle?

Weary from knocking on doors all afternoon, he plunked himself on a bench by the river, leaned back and listened to the medley of birdsong. The lilting notes of a lark sparrow reminded him of Tess. How she loved to sing. He'd lost count of how many times they'd sung her favorite hymn, her alto and his baritone blending well.

And then there was the day she'd finally let him give her tips on roping, allowing him to stand behind her and guide her arm as she swung her loop. The braid hanging down her back had tickled his chin as it bounced from side to side, and that citrusy cologne she wore had teased his senses. She'd finally lassoed her first fence post and done the cutest little jig afterward.

Tess was quite a character. Not only was her hat as big as Texas. So was her heart. She loved Luke and Lila deeply and without reservation. But did she love him? He'd thought she might, but then he'd tried to kiss her and made a mess of things. He couldn't forget the shocked look on her face. Ever since then, he'd kept his distance, biding his time until he met Faith.

A church bell chimed nearby, sending out an invitation to anyone seeking the Lord. Spencer answered the call. He could use some guidance, and there was no better place to find it.

He entered the redbrick building, sat on a back pew and bowed his head. Instead of praying, he listened. The Lord had led him here, so surely He had a message to deliver.

For several minutes all Spencer heard was the rumble of wagons as they passed by. Then came muted footfalls and a rustle of skirts. Someone else had come to spend time with the Lord. A woman.

She sneezed, and Spencer looked up. She was tall and wore a huge hat that rivaled Tess's in size. It was unlikely to be her, but...

The woman sank onto a pew and rummaged in her sleeve as though searching for a handkerchief but found none. He reached her in a few strides and held out his crisp, clean one. "You may have mine if you'd like."

"Thank you, young man." The woman with many years etched in her friendly face took it and wiped her nose daintily. She tucked the soiled square in her drawstring bag and smiled. "Was there something you wanted?"

"What? No. I'm sorry. I didn't mean to stare. I thought you were someone else. Forgive me."

"I know that look. It's the one my dearly departed Abner wore when we first met. The look of a man in love."

He hadn't realized his feelings were so obvious.

"Who is she?"

"Tess. My housekeeper. She came after my wife died and helped us learn to live again."

"A recent loss?"

He heaved an audible sigh. "One year ago today."

"So your mourning period is over, and you're torn."

She didn't know the half of it.

"You didn't ask, but I'll give you a bit of advice. If you've found the woman of your dreams, tell her how you feel. You'll regret it if you don't. I speak from experience. I held on to my grief far too long and missed out on the love of a fine man who came into my life several years after I lost Abner."

"I have found her." Although he'd been infatuated with Faith, Tess was the one he loved.

A glance at his pocket watch showed he had just enough time to visit a jewelry store before the shops closed. He'd return to his hotel, get up early tomorrow morning and take the first train up the hill.

If all went according to plan, he'd arrive in Shingle Springs before noon, make sure everything had gone all right at the station in his absence and head home. After dinner he would invite Tess into the parlor, ask her to marry him and hold his breath.

Polly went to the window to check on Luke and Abby. They were out on the porch that sunny April morning playing with his new train, adding the sounds of hissing steam, wailing whistles and clacking wheels. She repositioned the crocheted antimacassar straddling the back of Spencer's armchair. "I have something to tell you, Tessie, and it's not something you'll want to hear."

Tess focused on Petey. He sat on the rug in the middle of Spencer's parlor watching Lila build a block tower. The little fellow shot out a hand and knocked it over. Tess had a sinking feeling her dreams were about to come crashing down around her, as well. "Don't keep me in suspense. Just say it."

Polly plopped on the settee next to Tess. "Peter received a telegram from Spencer right before quitting time last night." She pulled a slip of paper from her reticule.

Tess's vision blurred as she read the ten words. Found woman of my dreams. Back tomorrow. Wish me well.

"Oh, Polly, I thought I was prepared for this, but…" Two tears escaped, and Tess flicked them away.

Lila toddled over, climbed into Tess's lap and patted her damp cheeks. "Ess no cry."

Tess blinked to prevent the torrent that threatened from spilling over. "It's all right, sweetheart." She pressed her lips to Lila's golden hair.

Polly rested a hand on Tess's arm. "What will you do when he gets here? Tell him, or act as though nothing's changed?"

"I can't face him. I love him." She drew in a shaky breath and continued. "I tried so hard not to, but I do. He'll see it my eyes, so I can't be here when he gets back. I must go. Now. I'm sorry to have to ask, but could you watch the children until he can find someone else?"

"Of course. But do you really have to leave? I like having you here."

"I like being here and will miss everyone terribly, but I can't stay. Not when he loves another."

"I understand. I'm so sorry it turned out this way. I was certain he cared for you."

As quickly as possible, Tess packed. She took a lingering look around the room that had been hers the past seven months but would soon belong to Spencer and his new bride.

The quilt had turned out well and looked lovely on his bed. Tess took comfort in the fact that she was leaving a part of herself behind, but she would love to have seen Spencer's reaction when he saw the results of her handiwork. If only he hadn't chosen to leave when he did. She'd been eager to give him her gift the day before as a memorial to his late wife, but perhaps he'd preferred to mark the anniversary of Trudy's passing at a place that wasn't filled with reminders.

Most likely he'd been spending time with his intended. That was a good thing. It meant he was embracing life.

A shuddering sigh escaped Tess. That's what she'd wanted, so she ought to be happy for him. Maybe in time she could be, but her pain was too fresh. "Goodbye, Spencer. I'll miss you more than you know."

She went downstairs, lifted her hat from the shelf for the last time and closed the door on the happiest days of her life.

The ride to the station passed in silence. Tess held Lila. Luke sat beside them, his face pinched and his arms crossed, looking like the sullen boy she'd met that memorable July day. Leaving Luke, Lila and their wonderful father was the hardest thing she'd ever had to do.

The Lord had led her here for a reason, but her work in Shingle Springs was done. Another woman would come and take her place. *Lord, please let her be a good mother to the children and the doting wife Spencer deserves.*

Polly parked her wagon alongside the platform.

Peter met them. "I'm sorry, Tess. I didn't expect him to find her."

She took a steadying breath. "I'm glad he did. He deserves to be happy."

Polly patted Peter's arm. "Would you please help Tess with her luggage and buy her ticket? She has a train to catch."

"Sure, but I think you should stay until he gets back, Tess. I don't think Spence would want you to leave. He speaks so highly of you."

She produced a weak smile. "Thank you for that, but I don't want to be in the way."

Peter took her money and headed for the ticket window. She led Luke aside and knelt before him.

His lower lip trembled. The dear boy was trying not to cry but failing miserably. "Why do you have to go, Tess? I love you. I know I been a bad boy sometimes, but I'll be better. I promise."

She placed her hands on Luke's arms and gazed into his watery eyes, her own just as full of unshed tears. "I love you, too, Luke. I wish I didn't have to go, but your papa's found a new mama for you. She'll be taking care of you now."

"I don't want a new mama. I want you." He threw himself into her arms and sobbed.

The shrill whistle of the train pierced the air, and the conductor hollered "All aboard."

"Come, Luke." Polly placed a hand on his back. "It's time for Tess to go. Let's stand here so we can wave goodbye."

"No!" He took off running.

Peter handed Tess her ticket, wished her well and set out after the heartbroken boy.

Polly stood by her wagon fighting tears as she balanced Petey on one hip and held Abby to her side. "The children will miss you greatly, but so will Spencer. I hope he knows what he's doing, because he's losing someone very special."

Tess reached into the wagon to pick up Lila and plastered the little girl's cherubic face with kisses. "Goodbye, my sweet." She set Lila down, gave Polly a fierce hug and boarded the train.

With a clatter of steel wheels on iron rails Tess was on her way, leaving Shingle Springs and the family she'd longed to call her own behind. She watched the depot grow smaller and smaller through a sheen of salty tears.

Chapter Twenty-Seven

Something was wrong. Spencer knew it. Polly rarely came out to the ranch without Peter, but the Flynn's wagon was in the yard. Since the horses had been un-hitched, she must have been there for some time.

He ran up the steps, burst inside and raced to the kitchen. "Tess!"

Polly stood at the stove stirring something. She spun around, a wooden spoon in her hand. Her face was red and puffy, as though she'd been crying.

Nothing had happened to Peter. Spencer had seen him at the station deep in conversation with a baggage handler. He made a quick count of the children. Two babies in the corner, and the two older ones out back. They were fine.

"Where's Tess?"

Polly's chin trembled. "She left."

He struggled to make sense of the shocking news. "When? Why?"

"First thing this morning. I showed her the telegram you sent Peter, and she said she had to go."

"I don't understand. I was coming home to her."

The wooden spoon clattered on the floor. "You mean…?" Polly stared at him. "*Tess* is the woman of your dreams, isn't she? But she's gone. This is terrible."

Spencer staggered backward and clutched the edge of the kitchen table. "No. Tess wouldn't walk out like that. She loves the children, and they love her. She wouldn't do anything to hurt them."

"She thought…we all thought that you'd found the woman in the letters."

"Peter told you about them?"

Polly shook her head. "Miss Minnie mentioned to Tess that she'd seen you reading letters from your sweetheart in her café. I asked Peter about it, and he said it was true—that you were smitten with the woman who'd written them and were searching for her. And then we got the telegram. It said you found her."

"But I didn't. I realized Tess is the woman for me."

She jabbed a fist against her side and scowled. "Well, you certainly didn't make that clear."

He gripped her by the shoulders. "I've got to find her. Where is she?"

"I don't know. She rode the train to Sacramento City, but she didn't have any idea where she'd be staying. I made her promise to write as soon as she gets settled."

He released his hold and dragged in a breath. "I'll go look for her."

"I know you want to find her, but she'll be roaming the city in search of a job. You won't even know where to look. She said she might be forced to explore options elsewhere, as well. It would be best if you wait for her letter to arrive."

"I can't." He paced. "I have to do something."

"Oh, Spencer, you do have it bad, don't you?" Polly gave him a weak smile. "I must say, I'm relieved. When I thought you'd chosen someone else over Tess…" She growled playfully.

He ceased his restless wandering. "I was blind. I read those letters and imagined the woman who'd written them. After a while she became almost real to me, and I had to find her."

"What made you stop looking?"

"A very large hat and the advice of the wise woman wearing it. She told me not to lose the woman of my dreams. But I've gone and done just that, haven't I?"

Polly rested a hand on his arm. "Don't you dare give up that easily, Spencer Abbott. Tess *will* write, and you *will* go get her and bring her home."

The back door flew open, and Luke rushed in. "Papa, something real bad happened. Tess got on the train and went away. She said you found a new mama for us, but I don't want one. I want Tess."

Spencer ruffled Luke's hair. "I want her back, too, but it might take me a while to find her. You'll have to be patient, son." So would he, although everything in him revolted at the idea.

It took some talking to get Luke to understand the situation. Once he did, he trudged back outside.

Polly stood at the stove again and glanced over her shoulder. "Tess left you something. It's upstairs in your room. Dinner won't be ready for a few minutes yet so why don't you go take a look."

He stood in the doorway to his bedroom moments later. Tess had made him a beautiful quilt with red-and-blue Ts. The red ones must be for Trudy and the blue for Tess. He traced the brightly colored letters with a fingertip and smiled. Now he knew why Tess's light had burned so late at night. She'd spent countless hours making this just for him. What a thoughtful, generous, talented woman she was.

Grabbing a corner of the quilt, he squeezed it. Something inside crinkled. What was it? He bunched the quilt again and heard a rustle that could only be paper. Tess must have hidden the letters he and Trudy had exchanged inside after he'd told her never wanted to see them again. How clever.

If only he were clever enough to find her, but he had no choice. He had to wait for Polly to hear from Tess.

She'd better write soon, or he'd go mad.

Lifting her face to the April sky laced with a few wispy clouds, Tess sent a prayer heavenward. "Lord, please help me find work."

Without a recommendation from Spencer, her chances of finding a position in Sacramento City were slim. She had nothing to show for her work the past nine months, and her previous employer's recommendation was not very flattering.

She strolled down the street, turned the corner and found herself on the block housing the office of the lawyer Charlie had asked her to contact. Thankfully she'd heard no more from her childhood tormentor. Since he was likely long gone by now—or behind bars—she might as well pay the lawyer a visit and ask if he knew of anyone seeking a governess. If he happened to recognize her name and give her some indication of the trouble that had led Charlie to contact her, so be it. Not that she was curious. Well, not overly much.

The rich scent of wood polish greeted her when she stepped into the paneled interior. A young clerk seated at a gleaming walnut desk rose. "May I help you?"

Tess assumed her most businesslike manner, grateful that her silk gown disguised her perilous financial position. After paying her train fare, she had precious little money left. "I wondered if I might have a word with Mr. Livingston."

"I'm sorry, but he's in court. I'll get his partner for you. Please, take a seat." He indicated a waiting area heavily populated with plush chairs and disappeared through a door with a frosted glass center.

The end table beside the chairs bore a display of newspapers from around the state. If the lawyer had no leads for her, perhaps he'd let her peruse the advertisements placed by those in need of hired help. Although she had no desire to relocate, she couldn't be choosey. She had to find a job right away.

The door opened, and an impeccably dressed gentleman with glittering green eyes entered the reception area. She shook her head in disbelief. He looked a lot like— "Charlie? Is that you?"

"Tess." He beamed. "You haven't changed a bit."

"You're a lawyer? I thought…" She waved a hand dismissively. "Never mind."

He laughed. "You probably thought I was on the other side of the law, but I'm no longer the rapscallion I once was."

"So I see."

The clerk joined them, and Charlie clapped a hand on his shoulder. "This is the woman I crossed the country to find, Jones. Meet Miss Tess Grimsby."

"Oh." The color drained from the young man's face. "I'm sorry I didn't think ask her name, sir."

"It's fine. Please see to it we're not interrupted." Charlie turned to Tess and held out a hand. "If you'll come with me, I have good news for you."

Tess preceded Charlie into his office, took a seat in front of his massive desk and folded her hands in her lap. He offered her a cup of tea, which she declined. All she wanted was to find out what he'd meant by "good news." She could use some.

He sat in his oversize leather desk chair, rummaged through a stack of files on his credenza and pulled out a thick folder. "I've been helping Mr. Livingston prepare for his court case. Otherwise I would have headed up the hill to pay you a visit. I've decided to stay here and had looked forward to seeing more of my new state."

She was in no mood for small talk. "Why were you looking for me?"

Charlie smiled. "Direct as always. I like that. I won't mince words, then. Mr. Grimsby named you as a beneficiary in his will. He entrusted me to see that you receive your inheritance."

"Inheritance? Are you saying he's no longer with us?" The news saddened her more than she would have expected.

"His heart gave out a year ago. I was with him at the end. He went peacefully."

"I'm sorry to hear he's passed on."

"I know you remember him as a gruff man, but he changed soon after you left. He missed you greatly. He began attending that church you did and gave his life to the Lord, as did I. His transformation was as remarkable as that of Ebenezer Scrooge."

"He missed *me*?" The idea was inconceivable.

"He loved you, Tess. You were like a daughter to him, and I was the son he never had. Six years back his wife's parents died and left their fortune to him. He adopted me and put me through law school. Said I'd make fine lawyer, since I knew how to argue." Charlie chuckled.

"He was married? I had no idea."

"It's a tragic tale. He was a poor boy deeply in love with the daughter of a wealthy man. Her dream was to open an orphanage and better the lives of children like you and me, but she took ill on their honeymoon trip abroad and died soon after. Although Mr. Grimsby was heartbroken, he forged ahead with their plan. The man you knew was an embittered widower." Wistfulness filled Charlie's eyes. "I wish you could have seen him as the loving father figure he became."

"I can't believe it. I mean, I'm glad he changed, but he made my life so difficult."

"Yes. And he regretted that. He wished he could've adopted you, too, but he did the next best thing. He left you a third of his estate, as he did me." Charlie reached for the folder, pulled out a sheet of paper and handed it to her. "You're a wealthy woman."

She stared at a page titled Tess Grimsby: Portfolio. A list of investments was tallied, the sum staggering. Despite the warm spring day, a chill washed over her. "This can't be. You're teasing me, aren't you?"

"Not this time. When your father walked away that day, Mr. Grimsby's heart ached for you. He didn't know how to show his love back then, but he was determined to see that you'd be able to make your way in the world. That's why he pushed you so hard. You were special to him. Bright, caring and determined, like his beloved bride… Tess."

Her mouth fell open. "He gave *me* her name? Then it's true? He really did care about me?"

"Very much. You reminded him of her. She was tall, like you. Your height is what first endeared you to him. You weren't too tall, Tess. Not in his eyes—or mine. It was wrong of me to pester you the way I did." Charlie leaned forward, sincerity clearly evident in the face of this man who was almost a brother. "Can you forgive me?"

"Yes. I do. We're not who were, Charlie, are we?"

"We're not. The Lord's been at work." He resumed his businesslike manner. "Now, let's discuss your inheritance, shall we?"

"What about the orphanage?" She held up the list of investments. "I can't accept this if it means those poor children—"

"They're fine. Mr. Grimsby had me set up a trust with the remaining funds. There's enough to cover the orphanage's expenses for a good twenty years. Maybe more. He wanted you to have the money and enjoy it."

"I'm curious. If you received a share like mine, why are you working?"

Charlie took a sudden interest in his inkstand. "I felt the Lord leading me to help those less fortunate, so I do a good deal of pro bono work." He returned his attention to her. "But enough about me. Let me go over things with you so you understand your financial picture."

They spent the next hour discussing her holdings. As they talked, a sense of purpose enveloped her. Like

Charlie, she could use her wealth to better the world. The thought lifted her spirits.

She bid Charlie farewell. "Thank you for everything. I'll contact you once I've decided what I want to do." She gave him a sisterly hug and left the office.

When the train had pulled out of Shingle Springs the day before, she'd had no idea where the Lord would lead her or how He would provide. Never in her wildest dreams could she have imagined the blessings He'd showered on her. Her future was secure. Not only that, but she would be able to enrich the lives of many others.

In time the gaping hole in her heart would heal, but she would never forget Spencer Abbott and his children.

Spencer stared at the ledger lying open on his desk. Normally he enjoyed completing the tallies, but he couldn't concentrate that morning. All he could think about was Tess. The three days she'd been gone seemed like an eternity.

Perhaps a slice of Miss Minnie's pie would ease his edginess. It would definitely give him a respite from Mrs. Carter's cooking. The widow was doing her best, but her culinary skills were no better than before. He donned his hat and coat and strode to the café.

"Afternoon, Mr. Abbott." The affable owner smiled. "What can I get for you today? Pie? Or would you care to try my special. It's chocolate cake."

"Cake please."

She set a piece before him in no time and flitted off to wait on another customer.

He took a bite. While the cake was good, Miss Minnie wasn't half the baker Tess was. She'd made chocolate cakes for his children's birthdays. Hers were so moist and tasty he always ate two large slices. Luke had begged her to make another one just last week, but she said chocolate cake was a special treat and that she wouldn't make one again until the next birthday. That would be Spencer's, which was the thirteenth of May. He hoped Tess would be back well before then.

Wait. She'd baked a chocolate cake a few weeks after she'd arrived. Could it be...? He tossed some coins on the table, apologized to Miss Minnie for his hasty departure and sprinted across the street to the Flynn's place.

Polly looked up from where she was hanging clothes on the line. "What's the matter, Spencer? I've never seen you run before. Peter's all right, isn't he?"

"He's fine. Everything's fine. When was Tess born?"

"In '41. That makes her twenty-five, if you have to know."

He waved a hand. "Not the year. The month and day."

"August twentieth. Why?"

Excitement surged through him. He pulled Faith's letters from his frock coat pocket, unfolded all three and fanned them so the dates showed. "Look."

Polly trailed a fingertip across the pages. "Are these the letters?"

Spencer nodded. "They're from Faith. She was raised in an orphanage. Was Tess?"

"Yes."

"I think she and Faith are the same person."

Compassion filled Polly's eyes. "I know how much

you want to find Tess, but I'm sure there are many orphaned women born on that day."

"But how many of them rode the train to Shingle Springs? It could be her. If it is, I know where to find her." Both women liked to spend time at the same place. "I have to go back to Sacramento City right away."

"She might not even be there, though. She was afraid her poor recommendation from the banker she'd worked for prior to coming to Shingle Springs would prevent her from finding a position. I got the impression she was only going to spend a few days looking for work there before she moved on."

He refused to lose hope. "It hasn't been that long. Will you help Mrs. Carter if she needs anything?"

"Yes. And I'll pray the Lord leads you right to Tess."

"Thanks. I'll tell Peter what's happening, and then I'll be off."

If all went well, he'd hold the woman he loved in his arms before nightfall.

Chapter Twenty-Eight

A stiff breeze off the Sacramento River riffled the sheaf of papers in Tess's hands and sent several of them sailing. She jumped to her feet and made a grab for the pages, catching all but two. They flitted toward the riverbank.

Footfalls raced toward her from behind. A tall man in a short black frock coat and top hat dashed to the water's edge, catching the sheets before they met a soggy end. She'd recognize him anywhere.

Spencer.

He scaled the bank and held out her sketches. "Here you are, Tess."

"Thank you, sir." She snatched the drawings from him.

"It's about time you showed up. I've spent the past four days looking for you. I started by visiting every hotel and boardinghouse in the city, but apparently you aren't staying in one."

"No." She hadn't had the money for that when she'd returned to the city, so she'd been sharing a room with a girlfriend who'd taken pity on her.

"I took to strolling along the river. I figured a woman who likes to sit at the water's edge would have to make an appearance sooner or later."

Memories of their picnic in Folsom rushed in, bringing with them a flood of feelings she'd tried so hard to keep at bay. "I'm sorry you were inconvenienced, but I didn't expect you to follow me."

"I had no choice. The woman of my dreams is here."

Her lashes grew damp, and she blinked to keep the tears from escaping. "So I've heard."

He cupped her chin, forcing her to meet his gaze. Never had she seen such joy in his brilliant blue eyes. All those months she'd longed for Spencer to look at her that way, and yet another woman had captured his heart, shattering hers. She'd tried her best not to think about him and to immerse herself in her plans, but her thoughts strayed to him by day and her dreams revolved around him by night.

Not trusting her wobbly knees to support her, she sank onto the bench and stuffed the drawings in her satchel. He sat beside her and gave her one of his most dazzling smiles. While she was happy for him, saying goodbye would be easier if he wasn't so charming—and totally disarming. She drew in a shaky breath, willing herself to remain strong.

"Polly told me I'd made a mess of things, so let me make things clear. You're the woman of my dreams, Tess." He dropped to one knee, pulled a small box from his pocket and opened it to reveal a ring with a deep blue sapphire. "I'd like you to be my wife."

"Me? What about the telegram and the letters Miss Minnie saw you reading? I thought the woman who wrote them was the one you—"

"I can explain." He shoved the jewelry box in his pocket, returned to the bench and took her hand in his, rubbing the pad of his thumb over the back of it and sending tingles racing up her arm. "Last fall Peter brought me a packet of letters that had been left on a train. There were no envelopes or identifying information, so I had to read them to see if I could find the owner. But they weren't just any letters. They were written by a kind, loving, sensitive woman to the man she looked forward to marrying. Her name is Faith."

Tess gasped and began trembling. "You... They... It can't be. Do you have them?"

He slipped his free hand inside his coat and produced the packet of letters she'd thought were long gone. She took one look at them and squealed. "I can't believe it."

"Polly was afraid I might be mistaken, but I see I was right. You and Faith are one and the same, aren't you?"

She nodded. "Faith was the name my parents gave me. Mr. Grimsby changed it."

"I see. Well, here's the best part. You wrote these letters to me. I'm the man you've been waiting for, Tess. At least I want to be. Will you marry me? Please, say you will."

All the love she'd held inside for months broke free. "Yes, Spencer. Yes. A thousand times yes. You're everything I dreamed of and so much more."

She threw her arms around him. This time he hugged her back, holding her tightly and whispering "Tess" over and over with such feeling that she couldn't stop the tears from flowing.

All too soon he ended the embrace. He reached in

his pocket once again and produced one of the snowy-white handkerchiefs she'd washed, ironed and folded while praying for the wonderful man who would use them. He wiped her cheeks with such tenderness that another wave of tears threatened.

"If I hadn't read your letters, your reaction would have surprised me. I've seen the bold, confident Tess who speaks her mind, but there's more to you than that. You're every bit as tenderhearted as I thought. You've kept it hidden, but you don't have to any longer. I love you, Tess—both sides of you." He took her hand and slid the ring on her finger.

His declaration left her so lightheaded she feared she might swoon. She took a series of calming breaths as she stared at the ring. Once she'd regained control, she gazed into the eyes of her beloved.

"I love you, too, Spencer. So very much. I have for the longest time. I didn't mean to. A housekeeper isn't supposed to fall in love with her employer, but I couldn't stop myself. You don't say much, which can be a bit challenging at times, but the few times I did get you talking, it was wonderful. You're good and kind and loyal and…" She paused. "Why are you smiling?"

"Because you love me, and because you understand me like no one ever has." He studied her, his forehead furrowed. "There's something I need to know. Do you really like it here—in California?"

"I've come to love the wide-open spaces and the ruggedness of it. Why?"

"Trudy tried, but she wasn't happy here. She came expecting life to be easy and money plentiful. What she didn't know was that when I left Texas, my father disinherited me. I wasn't the wealthy man she expected, but she agreed to marry me anyhow. I gave her all I could, but it wasn't enough. I denied her the one thing that could have saved her. It's my fault she died."

The anguish in Spencer's eyes tore at Tess's heart. She took his hands, gave them a reassuring squeeze and received a grateful smile in return. "You said that once, but you never told me what you meant. Please. I'd like to know."

"She wanted me to hire a housekeeper, but I wanted to use the money to build a herd. I put my dream ahead of her. She never regained her strength after Lila's birth, which made seeing to her chores taxing. If I'd gotten her help…"

Tess tugged a hand free and, emboldened by his earlier response to her touch, caressed his cheek. "You can't blame yourself. She fell. She could have done that anytime, anyplace. It was an unfortunate accident and nothing more."

"I've tried to tell myself that, but hearing you say it makes it easier to believe."

"It's true. Trudy was blessed to have a man who loved her the way you did. And now that blessing is to be mine. I'll do my best to be the wife you deserve."

"You'll be a wonderful wife and mother, my darling." He captured her hand and pressed a kiss to the back of it, the warmth penetrating the thin cotton glove and setting her senses spinning.

His gaze rested on her mouth, and he leaned toward her. She waited with baited breath. And then he gave her a fleeting kiss, feather-light and far too short.

He pulled back and studied her. "What is it? You look…disappointed."

"I liked it. I just thought it would be different some-how."

He smiled. "You've never been kissed before, have you?"

"Not until now."

"Well, then, let me give you a proper kiss. I'll start by getting rid of the obstacles." He took off his hat and removed hers, too. "Close you eyes, tilt your head and trust me."

She did as he asked. He cradled her head in his hands. His lips met hers—warm, soft and oh, so wonderful. Just when she thought the kiss couldn't get any better, it did. As many times as she'd dreamed of this moment, her imaginings had failed to do it justice.

Long before she was ready, he brought the kiss to an end.

"Was that more to your liking?"

"It was incredible. You're very good at it."

He grinned and glanced at the path behind them, where others were coming their way. "Now that I've gotten a taste of you, I don't want to stop, but this isn't exactly the time or place. Here's what I propose—we get a license and go straight to a church right here in the city. Today. Then tomorrow I'll take you home where you belong. If you're certain you want to marry me, that is. I'm not a rich man, but I'm a hard worker who intends to make a good living as a cattle rancher."

She smiled. "I can help with that. An old friend contacted me a few weeks ago, and I paid him a visit when I reached the city. His name is Charlie. He grew up in the same orphanage I did. He's a lawyer now. He told me that Mr. Grimsby, the director, left us both a sizeable inheritance. That's why I was sitting here making plans to open an orphanage of my own."

Spencer's face fell. "That changes things."

"No. It just means we have more options. I could buy you another bull if you'd like so you can build the herd faster." She chuckled. "What am I saying? I could buy you an entire herd. I'm what Charlie referred to as 'a woman of substance.'"

"I don't want your money, Tess. I just want you."

He couldn't have said anything that pleased her more. "I'm afraid you can't have one without the other. I could use your help managing my portfolio. I've never had more than a few dollars to my name, so the thought of handling my investments is a bit overwhelming."

"In that case, I'd be happy to help, but you'd have to tell me what you want."

"What I want? That's easy. What I want more than anything is to have a family—your family. I want to be your wife and fill your life with as much joy as possible. I want to have lots of children who know they're loved. I want pictures of Luke and Lila to put in my locket. And I hope this won't offend you, but I'd like the house to be painted blue."

"That's all you want?" He deepened his voice and caressed her with his gaze, giving her a delicious case of the tingles. "Nothing more?"

"There is one more thing. Since I want a whole lot more of your kisses, I'd like to get married right away."

His face lit up. "I was hoping you'd say that."

The following afternoon Tess rested her hand on the crook of Spencer's arm as they strolled from the railroad station to the ranch. *Their* ranch. Very soon she would hug *their* children.

"I've been thinking."

"Yes?" Spencer drawled.

"I'd still like to open an orphanage."

"I'm glad to hear that, Mrs. Abbott."

How she loved hearing him use her new surname. Not that she minded the name Grimsby as much as she used to. "Good. Then I can contact Charlie and ask him to scout out possible locations."

"You don't need to do that. We can open it here—" he gestured down the road "—at the ranch. I could teach the boys all I know about raising cattle, and you could teach the girls to cook and sew and garden."

She squeezed his arm. "Oh, Spencer, that's a terrific idea. And when their lessons were over, the children could play, the way children should."

"Exactly."

"Are you sure you wouldn't mind having a dormitory full of children to care for? Orphans can be quite needy. They often arrive with wounded hearts and require a lot of love and attention."

He placed his hands on her shoulders and gazed at her with such love and admiration she felt dizzy with delight. She'd left Shingle Springs expecting never to return, but the Lord had brought her back to serve this special family—her family.

"I've never met a woman with a heart as big as yours, Tess. I watched you reach out to Luke day after day. You never stopped loving him, no matter how cantankerous he was. I don't have your way with children, but I'll do my best to be a father to the fatherless.

Above all, I'll teach them that they have a heavenly Father who loves them and will never leave them."

Tess smiled. "A father to the fatherless. That's what God's been for me. No matter how difficult things were, I always knew He was there. And now He's led me home."

They ambled along talking and talking. She marveled at how much Spencer had to say. Ever since he'd found out she was the one who'd written the letters that had captivated him, he'd opened up to her the way she'd always hoped he would.

"I have a surprise for you. Look." He held out a hand to the arch at the ranch's border. A freshly painted sign bore the words *The Double T*.

"I love it. That's the name of the quilt pattern I used."

"About that quilt. It's beautiful. I can't thank you enough for your months of hard work. I appreciate the way you honored Trudy. I'm not surprised, though. You've always been selfless."

She snickered. "Me? Selfless? I'll have you know I'm a very demanding woman, Spencer Abbott. For instance, right now I'm going to demand a kiss." She tugged on the lapels of his jacket.

"So, you want a kiss, do you, my lovely wife? Well, then, I'll give you a kiss you won't soon forget."

He pulled her to him and, true to his word, gave her a kiss she would remember for a very long time. When he finally released her, she heaved a contented sigh.

"Satisfied?"

"Very much so." She gave him a coquettish smile. "For now anyhow."

"That's what I like to hear. I plan to spend the rest

of my days making sure you're a happy woman. Now, let's go see our children."

They neared the house, and Luke flew out the door. "You're home!" He raced toward Tess with his arms open wide.

She caught him in an embrace. He hugged her back. Then, to her surprise and delight, he kissed her cheek.

Spencer inclined his head toward the house. "Someone else wants to see you."

Polly stood on the porch with her children. Lila bumped down the stairs on her bottom the way Tess had taught her and took off running the minute she reached the ground. Tess met Lila halfway and scooped the little girl in her arms.

She patted Tess's cheeks. "Tess."

"No, Lila." Luke tapped Tess's arm. "She's Mama."

Spencer smiled. "Yes, son. She is."

Tess wanted to respond, but her throat was too thick. God had given her the desire of her heart. She was a wife and mother with a family of her own. A wonderful family that would expand to include many more children through the years. And she would shower each and every one of them with love.

* * * * *

WE HOPE YOU ENJOYED
THIS BOOK FROM

LOVE INSPIRED
INSPIRATIONAL ROMANCE

Uplifting stories of faith, forgiveness and hope.

Fall in love with stories where faith helps
guide you through life's challenges, and discover
the promise of a new beginning.

6 NEW BOOKS AVAILABLE EVERY MONTH!

LIHALO2021

LOVE INSPIRED

Stories to uplift and inspire

Fall in love with Love Inspired—
inspirational and uplifting stories of faith
and hope. Find strength and comfort in
the bonds of friendship and community.
Revel in the warmth of possibility and the
promise of new beginnings.

Sign up for the Love Inspired newsletter
at **LoveInspired.com** to be the first
to find out about upcoming titles,
special promotions and exclusive content.

CONNECT WITH US AT:

Facebook.com/LoveInspiredBooks

Twitter.com/LoveInspiredBks

LISOCIAL2021

Get 4 FREE REWARDS!

We'll send you 2 FREE Books plus 2 FREE Mystery Gifts.

The Sheriff's Promise
RENEE RYAN

To Protect His Children
LINDA GOODNIGHT

Love Inspired books feature uplifting stories where faith helps guide you through life's challenges and discover the promise of a new beginning.

FREE Value Over **$20**

YES! Please send me 2 FREE Love Inspired Romance novels and my 2 FREE mystery gifts (gifts are worth about $10 retail). After receiving them, if I don't wish to receive any more books, I can return the shipping statement marked "cancel." If I don't cancel, I will receive 6 brand-new novels every month and be billed just $5.24 each for the regular-print edition or $5.99 each for the larger-print edition in the U.S., or $5.74 each for the regular-print edition or $6.24 each for the larger-print edition in Canada. That's a savings of at least 13% off the cover price. It's quite a bargain! Shipping and handling is just 50¢ per book in the U.S. and $1.25 per book in Canada.* I understand that accepting the 2 free books and gifts places me under no obligation to buy anything. I can always return a shipment and cancel at any time. The free books and gifts are mine to keep no matter what I decide.

Choose one: ☐ **Love Inspired Romance Regular-Print** (105/305 IDN GNWC) ☐ **Love Inspired Romance Larger-Print** (122/322 IDN GNWC)

Name (please print)

Address   Apt. #

City   State/Province   Zip/Postal Code

Email: Please check this box ☐ if you would like to receive newsletters and promotional emails from Harlequin Enterprises ULC and its affiliates. You can unsubscribe anytime.

Mail to the Harlequin Reader Service:
IN U.S.A.: P.O. Box 1341, Buffalo, NY 14240-8531
IN CANADA: P.O. Box 603, Fort Erie, Ontario L2A 5X3

Want to try 2 free books from another series? Call 1-800-873-8635 or visit www.ReaderService.com.

*Terms and prices subject to change without notice. Prices do not include sales taxes, which will be charged (if applicable) based on your state or country of residence. Canadian residents will be charged applicable taxes. Offer not valid in Quebec. This offer is limited to one order per household. Books received may not be as shown. Not valid for current subscribers to Love Inspired Romance books. All orders subject to approval. Credit or debit balances in a customer's account(s) may be offset by any other outstanding balance owed by or to the customer. Please allow 4 to 6 weeks for delivery. Offer available while quantities last.

Your Privacy—Your information is being collected by Harlequin Enterprises ULC, operating as Harlequin Reader Service. For a complete summary of the information we collect, how we use this information and to whom it is disclosed, please visit our privacy notice located at corporate.harlequin.com/privacy-notice. From time to time we may also exchange your personal information with reputable third parties. If you wish to opt out of this sharing of your personal information, please visit readerservice.com/consumerschoice or call 1-800-873-8635. **Notice to California Residents**—Under California law, you have specific rights to control and access your data. For more information on these rights and how to exercise them, visit corporate.harlequin.com/california-privacy.

LIR21R2